THE PROTECTOR'S RECKONING

BOOK FIVE OF THE TALES OF CALEDONIA

PETER WACHT

Kestrel
Media Group, LLC

ALSO BY PETER WACHT

THE REALMS OF THE TALENT AND THE CURSE

THE TALES OF CALEDONIA

*Blood on the White Sand (short story)**

*The Diamond Thief (short story)**

The Protector

The Protector's Quest

The Protector's Vengeance

The Protector's Sacrifice

The Protector's Reckoning

The Protector's Resolve (Forthcoming 2023)

The Protector's Victory (Forthcoming 2023)

THE TALES OF THE TERRITORIES

Death on the Burnt Ocean (Forthcoming 2023)

Monsters in the Mist (Forthcoming 2023)

THE SYLVAN CHRONICLES

(Complete 9-Book Series available at Amazon)

The Legend of the Kestrel

The Call of the Sylvana

The Raptor of the Highlands

The Makings of a Warrior

The Lord of the Highlands

The Lost Kestrel Found

The Claiming of the Highlands

The Fight Against the Dark

The Defender of the Light

THE RISE OF THE SYLVAN WARRIORS

*Through the Knife's Edge (short story)**

* Free short stories can be downloaded from my author website at
www.kestrelmg.com

SETTING THE STAGE

The Protector's Reckoning, Book 5 of *The Tales of Caledonia*, is set more than one thousand years before the events that occur in *The Sylvan Chronicles* and takes place in a separate land of *The Realms of the Talent and the Curse*. Caledonia, though a monarchy, functions more like a loose confederation of Duchies, even more so now that the King of Caledonia, Marden Beleron, has met his end in the Pit at the hands of the Volkun.

During this time some of the more adventurous and grasping members of the Caledonian nobility accepted King Corinthus Beleron's territorial grants and begin to colonize the Territories far to the west on the other side of the Burnt Ocean. These Territories will eventually become the Kingdoms of *The Sylvan Chronicles*.

In Caledonia, as in the other realms, the ability to use the Talent sets apart the person gifted with this unique skill. But being able to use the Talent is only part of the dynamic. For if a Magus chooses to follow a darker path, the Talent becomes the Curse.

PROLOGUE

Their speckled grey and black skin blended perfectly into the surrounding gloom. The only visible signs of the monsters lurking in the Dark Forest were the blood-red eyes that burned through the murk, devoid of any emotion but one.

A desire to kill.

They were made for a singular purpose.

They had no choice but to obey the Dark Magic from which they were created. To obey their Master.

When the Slayers emerged from the Shattered Peaks and then stalked across the Breakwater Plateau, they had entered the massive wood hopeful that they would have the chance to fill their aching need.

To find their quarry.

To satiate their hunger.

Within a day the beasts had stumbled upon a small village that served as a waypoint between the mines in the mountains and the foundries in Ironhill. It had been a fortuitous discovery for the Slayers, though not for the people living in the village.

The monsters had been starving then, ravenously so, just as they were starving now. They were always hungry, rarely able to recall a time when they weren't a victim of the unrelenting compulsion that they feed. An urge that they could not ignore, the pain of attempting to do so too much even for them.

It was a pain that they hated. A pain that was all too familiar. A pain that they could rarely escape.

It could only be alleviated by obeying their Master. By obeying the Curse that flowed within them, that gave them life. That gave them reason.

For these monsters to live, there had to be death. So much death.

The villagers had filled a need, satisfying their yearning briefly, assuaging their affliction so that it was more tolerable.

But only for a time. Much too short a time.

For them to soothe the pain that was so much a part of their existence, for them to gain the temporary peace that they so desired, they had to kill their prey.

Once the monsters had slaughtered and eaten their fill of the villagers, they had gone west, moving deeper within the Dark Forest, searching for the one so important to their Master that for the first time in centuries he had released them from beneath the Temple of the Ghoules to hunt.

Within hours, however, the Slayers began looking for another small village along the way, needing to satiate their rapacious craving once again. They had found little sustenance.

The soft humans and their succulent flesh that placated the gnawing need within them were nothing but taunting memories, the grim, silent wood empty. Even the few large animals they sensed within the Dark Forest eluded them, staying well clear.

With few other options, the monsters had no choice but to make do with the quarry they did locate. It wasn't what they wanted, though it would do.

This meat, stringy and tough though it was, would sustain them for a day. Maybe two. No more.

That was all right.

The Ghoule Overlord's creations believed that they would be feeding again on something more succulent by then. That they would catch the prey their Master had sent them after. Once they did, they could gorge on the tasty meat of the humans.

The largest of the Slayers, the beast well above nine feet tall, crouched in the darkness, leaning his spiked spine against the trunk of a heart tree. The monster took his time. Despite the remarkably bitter taste, he savored what they had come across hidden within the wood, using his split tongue to noisily slurp the marrow from the bones that he had arranged into a small pile in front of him.

Having sucked the fluid from the vertebrae of the spine, the Slayer picked up a femur, strings of mottled green flesh still hanging from it in several places. Not as delectable as the humans. Still, it satisfied his need. For now.

With little effort and a quick twist of his massive claws, the Slayer cracked the bone in half, then tilted one side toward his gaping maw. His long, snakelike tongue shot out to dig the marrow free from the bone. Finishing one half of its treat in just seconds, the Slayer turned his attention to the other half of the femur, engaging in the same process to extricate the fatty tissue.

That done, the Slayer lifted the skull that lay just off to the side of the pile in one large, razor-sharp claw, the head already scraped clean of flesh thanks to his sharp teeth. He had been saving this delicacy for last. With just a touch of pressure, the top of the head cracked and then split in two, a grey mass appearing beneath the thick bone. The Slayer dug his claw into the skull, picking out the brain and then chewing on the delectable morsel for quite some time before allowing it to slide down his gullet. A tasty treat to complete his meal.

The two other Slayers on the other side of the small

clearing growled at one another, just as they had been doing since they had settled down to eat, tugging on the remains of the last of their kill. One of the Slayers gripped tightly to an arm, the other to a leg, neither willing to let go as they pulled with all their might, both wanting as much of what was left of the corpse as they could take for themselves.

With a sickening snap and crunch, the monsters ripped apart the body at the hip, one of the Slayers dragging the upper torso deeper among the heart trees, the other Slayer pleased to have the two meaty legs to feast on. What had once been a Ghoule was devoured quickly. The two Slayers bit into the flesh with their sharp, serrated teeth, four fangs, two on the upper jaw, two on the lower, helping to rake the meat clean from the bone.

The Slayers were fortunate to have come across the Ghoule pack as they headed toward the northeastern corner of the wood. The Ghoules had been sleeping, unafraid of any predators that might be in the Dark Forest, believing that they had little to fear in the land of the humans.

Until the Slayers fell upon them.

Just like the Slayers, the Ghoules were touched by the Curse. They obeyed the same Master.

The Slayers didn't care. The monsters viewed anything living as food, even another Slayer if they were desperate enough.

If the Slayers had discovered an Elder with this Ghoule pack, they probably would have avoided the beasts as they rested within the wood. Because there were no Elders to be found, because their hunger felt like a burning hole in their stomachs, they gave in to their craving.

Ghoules feared nothing, except for the Slayers, and although these Ghoules had fought bravely -- at least the ones who even realized they were under attack, more than half of their number killed before there had been a cry of warning --

they had not lasted long against their formidable foes. The blackened steel of the Ghoules scraped harmlessly off their armored flesh. Slayers could only be killed with the Talent or Dark Magic.

The Slayer who had been eating on his own, after finishing with the brain, rose from where he crouched in the darkness, kicking through the pile of bones in front of him to see if he could find anything else worth consuming. Nothing piqued his interest, having picked clean the flesh, so he sniffed the air, searching for a particular scent. A magical scent that had been inscribed within him by the Ghoule Overlord.

The other two Slayers soon joined him, having eaten the last of their bounty. Mimicking his action, they sniffed the air, seeking the scent that thanks to their Master they could find even from several hundred leagues away.

The minutes dragged on, and during that time the Slayers remained perfectly still. Perfectly silent. Perfectly focused as they sought their prey. Finally, they growled in unison.

The largest one, the leader, raised his maw to the sky. He couldn't see the light of the moon because of the branches that intertwined above him. Still, in the deepening dusk he howled with pleasure.

The Slayers had located their prey. They were certain of it. They could sense the huge quantity of Dark Magic that was being used in the northeast section of the Dark Forest no more than a few dozen leagues away. They could sense the Talent as well. More important, they could sense the artifact. The Seventh Stone, the scent their Master had given them.

They were closer than they expected, which was a good thing. Because their hunger already was beginning to gnaw at them despite their recent kill. They would be ravenous again soon.

Yet they would have to wait, at least a little while longer.

They would feast when they caught their Master's quarry.

And when they did, they would take the Seventh Stone, just as the Ghoule Overlord required.

Once they attained the desired prize, their Master would set them loose in this land and allow them to feed on the humans until they had finally eaten their fill of soft, tasty flesh. Until they had finally met the demands of their voracious hunger.

1

A LITTLE HELP

Jurgen Klines watched the long grass of the veld sway back and forth, dancing to the music of the winds that swirled off the snow-capped peaks just a league or so to his front. It was a sight to be remembered, he thought, as the last of his troops rode through the greenish brown stalks that brushed against the deep chests of the soldiers' destriers.

So better to savor and value the vision while he could, because who knew what the next day, the next hour, or even the next few minutes might hold for them. Although he did have his suspicions as to what the future might bring. And it wasn't a pleasant thought.

The Blademaster and his troops had reached one of the more remote regions of Caledonia, the eastern edge of the Breakwater Plateau where the open grasslands butted up against the Northern Spine, the mountain range leading to the north and eventually connecting to the Shattered Peaks and the Winter Pass. He had been worried when they started crossing the plain and was thankful now that their passage was coming to an uneventful end.

The beasts who had invaded the Kingdom were an obvious

concern and always on his mind. Yet even more alarming in this part of Caledonia was the weather.

The massive steppe was known for its potent, almost freakish storms. Tornados that could be as vast as a mile and run for leagues, plowing through the tall grass and leaving nothing but dirt and rock in their wake. Hail the size of a man's head striking with such force that the icy onslaught could shatter a man's arm while he was trying to protect himself with his shield. Thunderstorms turning the sky blacker than the night creating a dark abyss with no hope of escape. Driving rain blowing sideways with such power that it scraped flesh raw.

Lightning smashing into the ground with such violence that huge geysers of soil and rock exploded hundreds of feet into the sky, the charge often setting the long grass ablaze. Wildfires expanding in all directions courtesy of the gusts that swept down from the Shattered Peaks to the north crashing into the winds that broke off the Northern Spine to the east, those unstoppable flames leaving behind massive fields of black ash that tarnished the grassland for leagues in all directions.

These storms came on with barely any warning. Klines had seen firsthand the destruction possible when caught up in one, lucky to survive the tempest, so he had sought to cross the Breakwater Plateau while the weather was calm. With that desire driving the companies of Royal Guard forward with an added sense of exigency, they had made good progress.

Almost too good, Klines thought. Because even though he wasn't superstitious, he believed that his luck was about to change. It was probably because of the soldier galloping toward him from the west, urging his horse on as he caught up to the long column that just now was leaving the Breakwater Plateau.

"You have bad news for me, Sergeant," said Klines.

Benin halted his horse with a gentle pull on his reins, the large man's grimace telling Klines all that he needed to know. Even with Benin's surly, concerned expression, Klines did take a second to admire his Sergeant's long beard. The reddish whiskers that could trail below the man's belt had taken on the appearance of a war hammer, which resembled the one tied to the Sergeant's saddle. Klines' believed that design was certainly appropriate considering what he assumed was coming their way.

"My apologies, Blademaster, I do," replied the Sergeant of the Royal Guard. "Our western patrols screening us on the grassland just reported in with some troubling though not unanticipated news."

"How many?"

"Three packs, Blademaster."

"We can handle that many," Klines replied confidently, feeling a little bit better. He had six companies of the Royal Guard with him, slightly more than six hundred soldiers in all. When he took a closer look at Benin, whose face was scrunched up into a discouraging frown, Klines realized that he had spoken too soon. "You have more bad news for me."

"I do, Blademaster. I'm sorry. Three packs coming toward us from the west, behind us. Another three packs coming at us from the south. Three more packs of those cursed beasts from the north."

Klines nodded, trying to keep his countenance calm and poised, as he took in the information. Those numbers were a bit more concerning. Twelve Ghoules to a pack. So more than one hundred Ghoules in all. Still, that many Ghoules, although a tad more worrisome, usually would not trouble him. The number of soldiers under his command would make even nine packs of Ghoules think twice before attacking them.

"What about the scouts we sent into the lower reaches of the Spine?"

"No word from them, Blademaster."

Benin left the rest of his thoughts unsaid. They both knew what that discovery meant. The scouts sent to the east should have returned by now. Their failure to do so only increased Klines' worry.

"Do you believe that the Ghoules have set a trap for us, Benin? Because I certainly do."

"Yes, Blademaster. A rather neat one at that."

Klines nodded his head in agreement. In his mind, he visualized the terrain around them, having traveled this way several times before on the Crown's business. In this part of the Kingdom, his options for finding a defensible position were in short supply.

"And Elders, Benin? Any Ghoules with those blasted black staffs?"

"Yes, Blademaster," sighed Benin, his frown deepening. "Our scouts report at least one Elder with each pack. Maybe a few more than that. They couldn't get an accurate count. For obvious reasons, the soldiers feared getting too close to the beasts."

Klines nodded his head once again. Yes, better for the scouts to be cautious. He was glad that they listened to him about not taking any unnecessary risks.

Having so many Elders with the packs changed things, limiting their options even more. Elders were a different matter entirely. More dangerous even than the Ghoules.

His soldiers could fight the Ghoules. Even with the challenges presented by those beasts, his troops could still kill the creatures if they were smart, maintained their discipline, and employed the tactics they had been perfecting during the last few weeks. Against the Elders, however, they had no way to defend against the Dark Magic that would be used against them. His soldiers would be nothing more than sitting ducks.

For just a few seconds, and not for the first time, Klines wished that he had a few Magii with him. He clamped down on that useless thought quickly. There was no point in hoping for something that he couldn't have. There were no Magii available to help. Duchess Stelekel was a day or two behind him with the Caledonian Army. Lady Winborne and the others were all far to the west on a more critical mission.

So what to do?

Obviously, the Ghoules were herding him. The beasts wanted to push him toward whatever waited for them in the east. Probably even more Ghoules and Elders.

Klines had no control over a great many things at the moment. Even so, a plan did come to mind that might make things a bit more challenging for the Elders.

"I'm assuming that the scouts have not rejoined us, correct?"

"Yes, Blademaster," replied Benin. "Only one rider from each scouting party returned to report. The remainder of the scouts are still several leagues away from us and staying well clear of the Ghoules."

Which meant that soon the pursuing Ghoules would be closer to him than his scouts would be. His scouts would be outside the noose settling around his larger force. That was something that he could work with. Perhaps it would even give them a chance to slip the trap, slim though the odds of that happening might be.

"Benin, this is what I want you to do."

THE TOWERING beasts glided through the long grass at a speed that matched the fastest horse, their passage leaving wakes behind them that resembled a shark's fin cutting through the ocean that swiftly disappeared as the strong gusts of wind regained mastery over the plain. They had been chasing the humans since the night before, the Ghoules' long, fast strides eating up the distance between them and their prey at a frightening rate.

A silent command from the Elder leading them, the creature raising his twisted staff of black ash into the air for all the beasts to see, finally brought them to a stop less than a mile from where the grass ended and the low hills of the Northern Spine began. For several minutes the Ghoules remained where they were, scanning the territory around them. Finding nothing that would give them cause for concern, they settled in to wait.

It wasn't long before dark shapes appeared from the north, gliding through the grass, those shadows quickly materializing into more than three dozen Ghoules. And then from the south. Three more Ghoule packs appeared, a handful of Elders with them.

"The humans have changed their direction," said one of the Elders.

"They know that we are here," said another.

"They do," a third replied. "We saw their scouts. Once we slaughter the larger group of humans, we can return for the scouts. We can take our time with them. Enjoy the hunt. Enjoy the feast."

"Just so," agreed Nezgul, the Elder leading the Ghoule packs given the assignment of eliminating the humans' advance guard. Nibli, second only to the Ghoule Overlord, had been quite specific. Not a single human coming from the west and heading toward the Winter Pass was to survive long enough to set foot in the Shattered Peaks. Nezgul meant to make that so. He would not disappoint Nibli. He would not disappoint his Master. "The main group of humans first, then the scouts. After that, we turn our attention toward the army about to cross the steppe. We will catch them in the open."

"What of the packs to the east?" asked the Elder who had arrived first at the Ghoules' current location.

Nezgul didn't respond immediately, instead taking hold of the Dark Magic gifted to him by the Ghoule Overlord, a dark mist beginning to spin around the top of his staff as he closed his black eyes and turned his focus toward the mountains rising above them. For almost a minute he was somewhere else, his essence flying across the long grass then up into the hills to the east before he found what he was looking for. His remorseless eyes popped open when his spirit returned to his body.

"The Elders to the east of us have their packs in position. They have forced the humans onto a small butte with a large bluff at their back."

"They are trapped?" asked another of the Elders, surprise rippling through the gathered beasts.

"They are," Nezgul nodded. "They have nowhere to run. They have made it much easier for us."

All the Elders nodded now, several licking their lips or running their tongues across their serrated teeth in anticipation. They could taste the humans' flesh already.

"Then we must be fast," said another Elder.

"We will be," confirmed Nezgul, who then issued a series of commands, the Ghoule packs spreading out into a broad semicircle and sprinting off toward the lower hills of the Northern Spine.

Nezgul, following along behind them, watched the Ghoules implement his instructions with a great deal of satisfaction. The humans had made his task that much simpler by picking a place in the hills that limited their options for escape.

He thought very little of the humans to begin with. This decision only confirmed that they were fools, and they would pay for their stupidity with their lives.

～

"Sergeant Akiles, tighten our lines," commanded the Blademaster.

Klines had ridden across the front of his soldiers' formation before returning to his place in the middle of the long column, a second column of soldiers nervously sitting on their horses no more than a dozen yards behind it. He wanted as little space as possible between his men so that it would be that much more difficult for any of the Ghoules to slip between them. He had spoken in great detail with Captain Tentillin and the Volkun about the tactics that had worked so well for them when they fought the Ghoules in the open, and Klines meant to make use of those same tactics now.

Space was the key. Restrict the space and you restricted some of the Ghoules' key advantages. Their agility and speed. That would give his soldiers a chance, perhaps even against the Elders if the approaching clash played out as he wanted.

"Yes, Blademaster. At once."

Sergeant Akiles nudged his horse in the direction from which Klines had just come, spouting a few curses to get the soldiers in order. It didn't take long for the adjustments to be made. All of the men in the advance guard had trained with the Blademaster for hours upon hours in the practice yard. They understood that any command he issued was always done with one primary goal in mind. To keep them alive. So they never hesitated to obey.

Klines watched as the soldiers shifted their positioning according to Sergeant Akiles' instructions, though truth be told he was asking them to close up no more than a foot or two between each of them. He understood that his need to issue that command likely was more a result of Klines having to release some of the tension that he was feeling rather than any failings on the part of his fighters. His men were excellent soldiers, and they had spent a great deal of time practicing the maneuver that he had in mind for the Ghoules once they arrived.

As if his last thought was an invitation, the Ghoules picked that very moment to step up onto the small plateau. The beasts first appeared in a single line that stretched across the length of the mesa, their long, black spears held firmly in their sharp claws.

There were more of the beasts than Klines had anticipated. So many, in fact, that as the creatures continued to show themselves, these new arrivals forced those beasts already on the narrow plain to bunch up into a large mass rather than staying in the skirmish line in which they had first appeared.

On the one hand, the larger than expected number of Ghoules placed his soldiers in greater danger. On the other hand, the even more compact space for the Ghoules created by these additional packs could work to Klines' advantage. If his troops did exactly as instructed.

Only time would tell. Sooner than he would like, he imagined, now that the first Elders appeared behind the Ghoules.

Klines pushed those thoughts from his mind. None of that mattered now. The battle lines had been drawn.

They were the Royal Guard. They would fight until they couldn't fight anymore. Regardless of the odds. Regardless of what was looking to be a potentially dire outcome.

For some strange reason, even as his gaze remained fixed on the Elders holding onto their staffs of black ash, Klines searched his memory for one of Declan's sayings, struggling to recall the aphorism he wanted, his friend having so many and always willing to share them. Then he had it. The Master of the Gladiators had used it when the Blood Company was defending the Colosseum against Marden Beleron slightly more than a week before.

"Stand, fight, die," he whispered to himself.

Yes, that certainly sounded appropriate to Klines right then.

He preferred to live. Although the odds of that happening decreased steadily as the number of Elders stalking arrogantly onto the plateau increased until there were more than a dozen milling about behind the Ghoules.

Stand. Fight. Die.

The soldiers of the Royal Guard would make their stand. They would fight. The cliffs would protect their backs, and if they could get in among the Ghoules, they might be able to limit the danger presented by the Elders' Dark Magic. Even so, there were no guarantees other than the fact that some of them would die, as Klines didn't doubt that some of those corrupted beasts skilled in the use of the Curse probably were more than willing to kill some of their own if it meant killing his soldiers as well.

That thought darkening his mood, Klines pulled his sword from the scabbard across his back, the steel shining brightly when it caught the sun.

"We are the Royal Guard!" the Blademaster shouted in a voice that he reserved for just such moments, his words echoing off the cliffs at his back. "If we are to die this day, let it be with our swords streaked with the blood of the Ghoules!"

With just a gentle nudge to his horse's ribs, Klines' destrier, already chomping at the bit, sensing the anticipation within its rider and the men and other horses around it, dug its hooves into the rocky soil and launched itself forward. Klines was at a gallop in seconds, and with the short distance to be covered between him and the greatly surprised Ghoules, who had not expected to be attacked, he immediately lowered his sword and aimed for one of the beasts who had inadvertently stepped right into his path.

Out of the corner of his eye, he saw the streaks of color staying with him, his soldiers charging toward their enemies.

Charging to their deaths, most likely.

So be it.

They would take as many of the beasts with them as they could.

THE ROYAL GUARD smashed into the Ghoules, catching the disorganized and unprepared beasts at the best possible time. Just as they had been taught, the soldiers used their mounts as their primary weapons.

More than half the Ghoules were knocked to the ground and trampled by the massive war horses during that first charge, the second line of soldiers either riding over the beasts to ensure that they wouldn't rise again or stabbing them with their steel to eliminate the handful of Ghoules who attempted to stagger back to their clawed feet.

Although that initial rush proved successful, it only removed fifty or so of the Ghoules from the battlefield. The other half hurled themselves at the soldiers with an unrestrained savagery, many jumping well above and over the huge destriers to pull the mounted soldiers to the ground from behind.

What had begun with so much promise for Klines quickly devolved into an undisciplined free-for-all as his soldiers desperately tried to bring their larger numbers to bear against the badly reduced Ghoules.

It was no easy task. The Ghoules were faster and more agile than the soldiers, the beasts cutting into and out of the action in a blur, their spears and claws slicing through armor and flesh to leave dozens of men badly wounded or dying on the rocky ground.

The fighters who enjoyed the most success were the ones who tried to put into play another aspect of their training. Rather than attempting to take on a Ghoule by themselves, many of the soldiers banded together into small groups, seeking to isolate a Ghoule and then surround it. If they succeeded in doing that, they greatly improved their odds of killing the beast and avoiding death or injury to themselves and their comrades.

Unfortunately for the Caledonians, it didn't take the

cunning beasts long to adjust to the tactic. In response, the Ghoules formed into small groups themselves that would in turn try to slice a soldier or two away from their squads, killing the isolated men with ease and then going after the others in the now weakened squads at their leisure.

Recognizing the danger presented by the Ghoules' new approach, Klines and his Sergeants began to pull the soldiers free from the beasts, hoping to gain a little breathing room so that they could reform their lines and perhaps use their horses again as they had done with such great effect during the initial charge.

A good thought, perhaps. But, it would go no further than that. Klines realized that the Elders were waiting for just such an opportunity. As soon as his soldiers began to separate from the Ghoules, the servants of the Ghoule Overlord called on their Dark Magic, a black mist spinning across the knobs of more than a dozen twisted staffs.

Nezgul coordinated the assault, directing shards of the Curse toward the first line of soldiers who had begun to reform for a second charge. The Dark Magic, against which the soldiers had no protection, ripped into the Royal Guard, who with the cliffs at their backs had nowhere to go.

They had stood.

They had fought.

And now many were dying.

～

"STEADY, LADS," said Benin in a quiet voice. "On my command."

Benin had followed the Blademaster's orders to the letter. That was to be expected, because that's who he was. When something needed to be done, he did it. Exactly how he was told to do it. And the Blademaster had given him very specific instructions.

The Sergeant had taken several squads of soldiers with him on a wide loop around the rapidly approaching Ghoules who sought to trap the Blademaster and his troops, linking up with the scouts situated at the various points of the compass along the way. Once he had his smaller detachment behind him, Benin trailed the Ghoules to where the Blademaster and the rest of the Royal Guard had positioned themselves.

They had hidden just below the fringe of the plateau and out of sight of the Ghoules, pleased to see their friends and comrades enjoy so much early success against the beasts during their first charge, less so when the Ghoules found their footing and closed with the Royal Guard. Benin and his squads very much wanted to help their friends when the Ghoules started to pull them from their saddles. They didn't give in to that desire even though they were desperate to do so.

Instead, they remained in place. Waiting impatiently. Getting frustrated. Angry.

Although watching the shifting fight gnawed at his gut, Benin did his best to ignore it. He refused to allow his troops to enter the fray. Not yet. Not until the time was right.

The Blademaster had been very clear. They were to join the battle at a very specific moment. Much to the scouts' relief, Benin judged that moment to be now.

"Remember your targets," said Benin, although there was no need for the reminder. The soldiers, having nudged their horses up onto the plateau in silence, arrows fixed to the strings of their bows, were well aware which of the beasts needed to be removed from the clash first.

"Release!"

More than three dozen arrows streaked through the sky.

"Release!" Another flight followed the first just a few seconds later.

"Release!" And then a third, the well-trained soldiers each able to send two more long shafts of steel-tipped death into the air before the first struck home.

And strike home the bolts did, several of the Elders crumpling to the ground with three or four arrows piercing their backs, the beasts completely unaware of the attack coming at them from behind until it was too late.

"Fire at will!" ordered Benin.

Before he had left the larger column on the Blademaster's orders, the Sergeant had picked the best archers to go with him. Those men now were making their presence felt on the battlefield in a huge way.

More than half of the Elders were already dead with multiple arrows sprouting from their flesh, a dozen or more Ghoules as well who had gotten in the way of the targeted assault.

But not all of the Elders, unfortunately. Those surviving beasts were quick to turn their attention toward Benin and his scouts.

One archer fell, a shard of darkness streaking through the air and striking him in the chest, turning his body to ash in seconds. And then another archer, burned to a crisp just as swiftly. Followed by a third. And a fourth.

Through it all, the archers stayed true to their purpose, maintaining their attack, shooting arrow after arrow toward the Elders, even though their effectiveness was diminishing with every quarrel they released now that the Elders had identified the threat they presented. As a result, the scouts were coming to the sickening realization that they had little chance of success against these beasts when they didn't have the element of surprise.

Benin, just like the other soldiers with him, was resigned to his fate. He knew what was going to happen, and he knew that there was little that he could do to prevent it. He would follow the Blademaster's command just as he promised that he would. To his own demise if necessary. He grimaced when he realized that his death would be coming sooner than he had anticipated when he saw the streak of black coming right toward him.

Having no time to get out of the way, he sat on his horse stoically, hoping that the end would be quick. To his amazement, rather than being struck by the needle of darkness that sped toward him, at the very last second a shield of white energy formed right in front of him, blocking the Dark Magic an instant before it pierced his heart.

BENIN and his archers had done well. They had killed more than half of the Elders in just a few minutes.

Klines knew that despite that success it still wasn't enough.

Their efforts had gained Klines and his soldiers the few precious minutes they needed to restore their battle lines. Yet even with so many Ghoules killed and seriously wounded, he and his soldiers stood little chance with another charge against the Elders. Their insipid Dark Magic would tear them apart.

Even so, there was nothing to do for it now. Better to die attacking than to allow the Ghoules to do as they wished.

Klines was about to order his cavalry to charge a final time when he and the men with him were forced to turn away from the skirmish, momentarily blinded as blazing streams of white-hot energy shot across the plateau from the north, burning through more than half of the Elders still standing and leaving behind charred remains that gave off the sickly sweet smell of overcooked meat.

The last few Elders tried to fight back, shifting their attention away from the archers to deal with this new, unexpected, and extremely dangerous threat. These servants of the Ghoule Overlord proved to be too slow. As soon as the beasts spun toward the north, two streams of energy blasted across the battlefield from the south and tore through Nezgul and the remaining Elders, the beasts collapsing to the ground with smoking holes in their chests.

With the Elders removed from the field, the streaks of flaring energy now shot across the plateau from both the north and the south, burning through the Ghoules and often leaving behind little to suggest that the beasts had actually ever existed.

Not one to question his good luck, Klines wasted little time.

"Charge!"

The soldiers of the Royal Guard, though having lost more than a third of their number, were more than enough to eliminate the remainder of the disheartened Ghoules. The first line of cavalry did as it had done before, riding right over the beasts, killing most of the Ghoules with the steel-shod hooves of their mounts, those creatures not dispatched in the first charge left for the second column.

In just a few minutes, it was done.

The Royal Guard swept the Ghoules from the mesa, thanks in large part to the three figures who strode purposefully across the battlefield to stand before Klines. The three looked like schoolteachers. Klines would not have believed in the power that these three wielded if he had not seen it for himself. Then again, most of the Magii appeared to be no different than anyone else.

"My thanks to you," said the Captain of the Royal Guard. "If not for you, we would be dead."

"Probably so," said a woman wearing mismatched robes, her eyes as sharp as a hawk's. "If you don't mind, I'm going to skip the chit-chat and see to the wounded."

"I'll join her," said a tall, gangly man who began pulling what looked like small bags and bottles from a very large rucksack he carried over one shoulder.

"My apologies for my friends," said a woman with a severe expression, her long hair tied tightly in a bun.

"No apology needed. I appreciate their willingness to help my men."

"They are healers," replied the woman, motioning to them as they walked among the blood and gore. "The woman is Maria, the somewhat awkward man Telly. I am Irelda."

"My thanks again to you, Magus Irelda. My name is Jurgen Klines."

"I know who you are, Blademaster. I recognize your sword. You did well against these Ghoules, but it was a tall task to begin with."

"You're right about that, Magus Irelda. We still had to try."

"That we do, Blademaster. That we do." For just a few heartbeats, Irelda stared at Klines, making him feel as if she had taken his measure and stolen his deepest, darkest secrets with just a glance. Then she gave him a surprisingly bright smile.

"I take it, Blademaster, that you are heading toward the Winter Pass."

"We are."

"Good," said Irelda. "We will be joining you. This was a good fight, but this was nothing compared to what we will face once we reach the Shattered Peaks."

2

SHIFTING STRATEGY

"Well done, Corporal. Well done, indeed."

Duke Kevan Winborne sat on his horse a little more than a mile in front of the Caledonian Army, which advanced across the Breakwater Plateau at a trot. The Royal Guard and the soldiers of four Duchies formed a column several hundred yards wide and more than a league long, leaving a trail of crushed grass in their wake. Kevan had no doubt, however, that within days the path would disappear, the long grass springing back into place and the wind whipping it about as if thousands of soldiers had never passed this way.

"It was nothing, Duke Winborne. I was just doing as you ordered."

Kevan stared at the soldier for almost a minute, impressed by what he saw. The Corporal sat ramrod straight in her saddle, the tip of her spear bloodied from the encounter, the dozen soldiers with her waiting patiently just behind her.

Clearly, every member of the squad respected the Corporal. It was obvious. He could see it in their eyes. In their postures. Not only respect. Trust as well. A belief in her abilities. And he knew from experience that was a hard thing to achieve.

He had been a soldier all his life. In fact, he saw himself more as a soldier than as a Duke, which was probably the reason why he chafed so often at some of what was required of him as the ruler of the Southern Marches. Yet that was a reality that he could not escape, no matter how much he wanted to or how hard he tried.

So there really was no point in thinking about that regular and unavoidable frustration with more important matters at hand. Besides, right now he wasn't in his office in Battersea, dealing with piles of paper. He was where he wanted to be. With his soldiers. Out in the wilderness. With a threat to negate.

"How did you know these beasts were hiding here?"

Kevan stared down at the remains of four Ghoules, the beasts who were each at least seven feet tall looking a bit smaller in death. Each one displayed multiple puncture wounds from the spears the Battersea Guard favored, as well as a few sword slashes, these cuts placed expertly along a hamstring or calf, the precise slices clearly meant to disable and force the creatures to the ground so that they could be finished off more easily.

Clean and efficient kills. Just the way he liked them. Just the way these soldiers had been taught by the Protector and the Captain of his Guard.

"I didn't," replied Dani, looking Kevan squarely in the eye. "Markus did. He caught a glint of light off one of their spear-points. We investigated, then saw a flash of movement. Once we pinned them down, we made quick work of them."

"That you did," Kevan replied.

He then nodded in respect to the tall soldier who sat his horse just behind Dani, giving him a visible demonstration of praise for being the one to locate these Ghoule scouts. The soldier's smile told Kevan that Markus was pleased to have been recognized, less so by him, more so by the fact that his

Corporal shared the glory of their very brief skirmish with him and the other soldiers.

Obviously, another of Captain Tentillin's traits washing off onto the Corporal. Giving credit where credit was due. It helped to build camaraderie and respect among the troops. Besides, you never knew when one of your comrades might be required to save your life. What could be a difficult decision would be made that much easier when you liked and respected your fellow soldiers.

"Have you discovered any other scouts besides these?" asked Kevan. "If we located these beasts, there are sure to be more."

"None to the east," replied Dani Langstin. "Some of our scouts to the north and south have reported contact with the Ghoules. However, no lengthy clashes with them yet."

"Thank you for the update, Corporal," Kevan nodded. "And, again, excellent work by you and your squad. Keep it up."

"You can count on it, Duke Winborne."

Tarin had recommended Dani to temporary second in command of the Battersea Guard when he and Jerad had gone west with Aislinn and the others in search of the Sanctuary. Obviously, Tarin knew what he was about because Dani clearly knew what she was about. That pleased Kevan to no end.

The Duke of the Southern Marches turned his horse back toward the main column, which was rapidly approaching at a steady gait. The Caledonian Army was almost across the southern section of the Breakwater Plateau. So far, they had avoided the storms so common to the plain that could form in just minutes.

He still wanted to get off the grasslands as quickly as possible. No one could predict when or where a storm would erupt, although he did see one beginning to brew not too far off to the west, maybe two or three leagues distant.

He was thankful that they were far enough away to not have

to worry about it, because if they were caught in the open a tempest like the one starting to take shape could cause them more damage in just a few minutes than a half dozen Ghoule Legions hungry for blood. Thus, his desire to get the troops into the rolling hills that led into the Northern Spine so that they could focus their full attention on an adversary that they had a better chance of defeating.

This first engagement with their enemy and reports of more and more of the Ghoule scouts tracking them were beginning to worry him. He had expected such activity on the part of their adversaries. He would have done the same if he were in their position. Still, he didn't like it, and he felt the need to do something about it, because he hated the idea of fighting from the back foot.

"You seem lost in thought, Kevan."

Noorsin Stelekel, followed by her personal guard of Murcian soldiers, rode up to him. With a light pull on the reins and a gentle nudge, Kevan's horse was soon trotting right next to that of the General of the Caledonian Army. They continued across the grasslands toward the mountains rising in the east, which were growing bigger by the second.

Kevan gave Noorsin a quick update on what Dani had discovered and how she had addressed the threat. Noorsin then revealed what she had learned from a scout who had arrived from the Northern Spine just minutes before.

"Word from the Blademaster," Noorsin explained. "Just yesterday the advance guard met and eliminated nine or ten Ghoule packs and a dozen or so Elders."

"An ambush?"

"Correct," Noorsin confirmed with a nod. "The Blademaster sniffed it out. The advance guard suffered heavy casualties. Despite that, they still eliminated all of the Ghoules."

"With the Ghoules hounding us, this is what I expected that it would be like," murmured Kevan. "The longer it takes us to reach the Shattered Peaks, the better it is for the Ghoules. The better their chances of breaking free from the Winter Pass."

"I expect you're right," said Noorsin, although a stray thought suggested to her that perhaps there was more going on here than just that. Perhaps they were only observing the obvious and missing what the Ghoule Overlord didn't want them to see. But what could that be?

"That's excellent news," said Kevan, breaking Noorsin's concentration, that stray thought slipping from her grasp, though she hoped that it would return. "How did he do it? I don't by any means want to belittle the Blademaster's abilities, but how did he overcome a dozen Elders? Besides you, we have no one who we can call upon to defend against their Dark Magic."

"He had a little unexpected but fortuitous help. The Blademaster reports that three Magii appeared out of the blue to assist against the Elders. Thanks to them, he was able to focus his attention on eliminating the Ghoules."

"Your work?" asked Kevan.

"Mine or that of Sirius," she replied.

"I should have guessed as much," said Kevan. "You always have a trick up your sleeve."

"That's very kind of you to say, Kevan," Noorsin replied with a smile. "Thank you."

"Any idea how many Magii we can expect to join us? Without them, we'll have a very difficult time taking on the Elders that the Ghoule Overlord can bring to bear."

"Less than a hundred. Keep in mind as well that we have no way of knowing how many will reach us in time."

"That's not very many and not very comforting."

"No, but we will do what we can with what we have."

Kevan grumbled his agreement. The Magii were in Noorsin's bailiwick, and there was nothing that he could do about the Elders, so he concentrated on an issue that he could do something about.

"Based on what Dani discovered and the reports from the scouts, it doesn't appear that the Ghoules have massed into a larger force yet, other than the packs that the Blademaster removed from the gameboard."

"You find that surprising?"

"I do," he replied. "I thought that by now we would face the same challenge that the Blademaster did. The Breakwater Plateau plays to the Ghoules' strengths. I would have thought that they would use our coming across the grasslands to their advantage by attacking us in the open."

"Perhaps you're right and the Ghoules were planning to take us on the plains," said Noorsin. "Perhaps the Ghoules and Elders that the Blademaster defeated were to come for us next."

"Likely so," agreed Kevan. "We are too large an army for them to defeat us."

"True, but what if their objective wasn't to defeat us?"

"To slow us down, you mean," said Kevan, nodding his head as he considered Noorsin's suggestion. "Whittle away at us until a larger force of Ghoules caught up to us?"

"That, yes," agreed Noorsin. "Maybe to distract us as well."

"From what?" Kevan asked.

"I don't know, though I hope to find out," said Noorsin. "In the meantime, we are at a disadvantage when fighting the Ghoules. They are faster and stronger than we are. The only way to improve our chances is to bring more soldiers to bear before they can form into groups larger than just a few packs. If we can do that, perhaps at the same time we can disrupt the Ghoules' plans. Anything we can do in that regard works to our advantage and will prevent them from slowing us down."

"What did you have in mind?" asked Kevan.

"We have yet to see the Ghoules outnumber our scouts."

"True, yet even if our scouts are evenly matched to the

Ghoules, they fight from a position of weakness because of the beasts' inherent abilities."

"That's true, and I certainly don't disagree. That's why I'd suggest that we strengthen the size of our scouting parties once we get off the Breakwater Plateau. We create several companies of skirmishers charged not only with scouting our way forward but also with removing any Ghoules who get in the way. And perhaps offering a few surprises of their own to the beasts. That way the larger host can advance unimpeded."

"You want us to do the hunting for a change," said Kevan with a devilish grin, clearly liking the idea.

"We move faster, and we can bring greater numbers to bear," nodded Noorsin. "That's the idea."

"Who do you want to put in charge of the skirmishers?" asked Kevan, although he believed he already knew the answer and he wasn't sure what he thought about it.

"You, Kevan. This plays to one of your many strengths."

"That's kind of you to say, Noorsin. Are you certain you want me to do this?"

Noorsin caught Kevan with her eyes. Now she looked every inch the Duchess of Murcia, as she hadn't expected him to balk at her suggestion.

"Why the hesitation, Kevan?"

At first, Kevan thought to hedge, then suppressed that initial response. There was no point in doing so. It wouldn't take Noorsin long to sniff out the truth.

"I'm worried that something will happen to you if I'm not around."

For just a heartbeat, Kevan's concern pleased Noorsin. It meant a great deal to her as a person. As the General of the Caledonian Army, it had no relevance as she had to think about so much more than just her own interests.

"If you won't do it, then I will," Noorsin said.

"Noorsin, that's not ..."

"Besides, if you recall, Kevan, I was more than a match for the Elders who appeared right before we set off across the grasslands. I have no doubt that I can handle any dangers that come our way. I suggest you adopt the same perspective."

Kevan stared into Noorsin's blazing eyes. Clearly, she was not a woman to be challenged. He should have known that already. He did know that.

Still, he feared for her, especially after what happened with Tetric in the Broken Citadel. Nevertheless, Noorsin was right. He needed to adjust how he looked at her.

She was more than capable of protecting herself. In fact, she could protect herself better than he could protect himself as had been demonstrated by his enforced stay in Tintagel.

"That won't be necessary, Noorsin. I'll get started on it so that we're ready to go once we're off the Plateau."

Noorsin nodded, pleased that it hadn't taken much to convince Kevan to assume what she viewed as a critical responsibility. He was a fighter at heart, and whether or not he admitted it to himself, he needed to fight.

As she and Kevan continued on in silence for a time, the Shattered Peaks gaining greater definition, she felt good that they were shifting their approach, if only a little bit. Because Noorsin was getting the sense that they were doing exactly what the Ghoule Overlord wanted them to do. She didn't know why she thought that. It was just a feeling, after all. There was nothing of substance to it, though she found it hard to ignore her instincts.

When she was younger following her instincts had proven difficult for her. Noorsin's desire to think through every problem or challenge, over and over, identifying and considering every little related issue and consequence, though useful at times, became an impediment to making any decision at all. She would freeze, unwilling to take a risk, no matter how small.

Her mother had explained that making no decision at all

often was worse than making the wrong decision. You were giving up your agency. You were allowing your decisions to be made for you.

Her mother's favorite saying floated to the surface: "Thinking never hurt until you thought too much." That was excellent advice, and she was glad that it came to mind frequently, but she wasn't doing that now. Thinking too much. Noorsin was certain of that.

She was also certain that she didn't like this feeling. Yet there was little that she could do about it. She could only hope that Bryen, Aislinn, Sirius, Rafia, and the Blood Company reached the Sanctuary and the Protector somehow learned how to repair the Weir.

In the meantime, she would think about what she could do to upset the Ghoule Overlord's plans and make him work just a little bit harder for the victory that he craved. Just because it felt as if she was being guided by her worst enemy didn't mean that had to continue to be the case. She would throw a few twists and turns in the Ghoules' way and see what came of it.

Perhaps something. Perhaps nothing. But there was no good reason not to take a few chances.

3

BATTLE IN THE GLOOM

"It's unnerving how they can sense the Seventh Stone," said Sirius. "There are thirty or more Ghoules and Elders about to walk right into us."

"They won't walk right into us," growled Rafia. "They'll walk right by us."

"Quiet," whispered Bryen, who stood next to Rafia and Sirius at the head of the Blood Company. "They're almost upon us."

This was one of the reasons Bryen had balked at asking the gladiators to join them on this mission. The Elders could sense the Seventh Stone because of the Dark Magic that it stored. That meant that the Elders could sense him. Vaguely, at best, though well enough for the beasts to narrow their search to less than a league.

The fact that the beasts were so close made him worry even more. Having spent so much time with Declan, Bryen didn't give much credence to coincidence. Either the Elders had improved their ability to sense the Dark Magic within him or there was so much of the Curse locked away within the Seventh

Stone that they couldn't help but narrow their search to a few dozen yards.

That last sent a bolt of fear through him, but that was a concern for later. For when they escaped these beasts, assuming that they could.

Bryen had thought that perhaps he could try for the Sanctuary on his own because of his desire to put as few people at risk as possible. He realized after several long discussions with the two Magii that he'd never make it by himself. He wouldn't get there even if he took just the two Magii with him.

He wasn't just squaring off against the Ghoule Overlord, although that was certainly a distinct possibility. He was going to have to fight his way through whatever obstacles the Ghoule Overlord erected in front of him. Because the Magii were certain that the Master of the Lost Land would do all that he could to prevent Bryen from reaching the Sanctuary.

So no matter how much he disliked it, he needed to take with him people whom he could trust to help him, and that meant putting their lives at risk. Just as they were doing for him now. Even though he understood the necessity of it all, he hated being in this position.

Bryen and the Blood Company were close to the northeastern boundary of the Dark Forest, not too far from the Breakwater Plateau. They had covered a good bit of ground that day, halting a few hours earlier than usual because Aislinn detected several Ghoule packs coming in their general direction across the long grass from the Shattered Peaks.

They had hoped that the Ghoules would pass them by a few miles to their west. No such luck. The beasts had adjusted their course and were coming right toward them.

No one doubted that the Ghoules were searching for the Seventh Stone. Searching for him.

With the Ghoules so near, the Company had no chance of escape, so they had done the only thing that they could. Rafia and Sirius employed the Talent to blend the warriors into the Dark Forest, using the wood's natural pall to aid the deception so that any of the beasts who walked by saw nothing but what they were supposed to see.

Heart trees soaring into the sky. Roots thicker than a man was tall worming their way along the forest floor. Shadows and gloom everywhere else because the sun couldn't break through the latticework of branches that had become intertwined into a haphazard web as the centuries passed.

The Company of Blood had lost their disciplined order to a certain degree because of the width of the heart trees and the many roots, their preferred marching column unavoidably breaking down into smaller groups and individuals as they maneuvered through the obstacle course that was the Dark Forest.

Even though they were somewhat separated from one another, the gladiators weren't concerned. All of them remained silent. All of them stayed still. All of them barely breathed. They knew what was required of them for the illusion to work. They had gone through this same exercise several times upon entering the wood just a week past.

Within just a few heartbeats of Bryen shushing Sirius, the Ghoules appeared to their front. At first, there was no way to tell what was approaching. Just a few flits of movement that altered the gloom of the grove. Then, as they came closer, the Ghoules took shape, their mottled green skin and brown leather armor merging into their surroundings with frightening ease.

As the beasts drew parallel on their western side, striding by in a single file, the fighters of the Blood Company watched nervously, only their eyes tracking the creatures, none of the soldiers willing to move their heads for fear that such a motion would untangle the magical deception.

So far, so good, thought Tarin Tentillin. The Captain of the

Battersea Guard stood in the back of the scattered column, Jerad right next to him. They both gripped the hilts of their drawn swords loosely, the steel a familiar extension of their arms.

They trusted in the power of the two Magii positioned at the head of the column. Still, they wanted to be ready. You never knew what might happen. And they found it quite unnerving and a bit disappointing to be standing so close to their enemies, even catching the faint, rank odor of the beasts, yet unable to press the advantage the Magii had given them.

The Ghoules glided past the concealed soldiers, calling to one another in barks and hisses. The beasts saw nothing other than the forest around them, even though they were no more than a few feet from men and women who stared at them with undisguised hatred mixed with a healthy dose of respect.

The Blood Company had fought the Ghoules several times now. They appreciated what the creatures could do with their blades and their claws. Yet they saw them as no more than another enemy to be defeated. All of the gladiators had spent too much time in the Pit to allow the Ghoules to frighten them in any way.

From their time on the white sand, they also had learned to approach every combat with the beasts by acknowledging their abilities -- their own and their adversaries -- understanding that if they failed to do so, that if they demonstrated any over-confidence whatsoever, they were the ones most likely to color the white sand red rather than the Ghoules.

Tarin believed that they just might have dodged what would have been a difficult fight, the several dozen Ghoules and Elders likely testing the gladiators to their limits if they crossed blades. He was about to take a real breath for the first time in the last ten minutes when the unexpected happened, just as it always did.

One of the Ghoules in the middle of the column stumbled

on a root, falling to the side and through the illusion that Rafia and Sirius had created so painstakingly. The Ghoule landed on his back, his chest disappearing, his legs remaining outside the boundary of the illusion, leaving only his lower body exposed to the other Ghoules.

The silence of the Dark Forest reigned for just a second more before the Ghoule behind the one who had fallen reached through the deception to pull his comrade up, still trying to comprehend how a part of him had disappeared entirely in the gloom.

The Ghoule's eyes widened in surprise when he gripped his comrade's leather armor. The fallen Ghoule was a deadweight, his throat a bloody mess from the spearpoint the soldier standing above him had driven through with such force that the tip had dug into the soft ground beneath the beast.

Before the Ghoule who had tried to aid his comrade could screech a warning, Dorlan, the large gladiator who was slow to anger but fought with a terrifying ferocity, lunged with his spear, driving the sharp point through the Ghoule's eye. Kollea, who had killed the first beast, patted his arm in approval. Two quick kills. A good start to the battle that was just moments away from exploding.

When the second Ghoule collapsed, he fell entirely through the illusion, making the magic shimmer for no more than a flash. Still, that was just long enough for the Ghoules to see what was hiding from them just a few feet away. With growls and roars, the Ghoules leapt past the mirage, destroying the illusion entirely to reveal the Company of Blood standing ready to meet them.

In seconds, the soldiers were engulfed by the Ghoules, the bloody skirmish erupting up and down the column. The gladiators knew how to fight the Ghoules. They knew how to kill them. They also knew that they needed to kill them all, because if just one Ghoule escaped, the Company would never make it out of the Dark Forest.

All the other Ghoule packs would learn where they were. Then the beasts would come for them with a renewed vengeance, and their critical expedition would come to an end before it even really began.

DECLAN PARRIED the Ghoule's slash, catching the beast's steel with his own, before spinning away and leaping backward. One foot hit the bark solidly, the other skidded off, and for a very tense few seconds Declan fought to maintain his balance, knowing that if he fell he was dead. Finally, with the help of his windmilling arms, he got both of his feet back under him, coming to stand on top of a large root that rose five feet above the forest floor.

Now he could meet the Ghoule eye to eye. The Master of the Gladiators kept his footing as he twisted his core to the left, and then just as fast to the right, avoiding by no more than a hair the two thrusts the Ghoule attempted, the creature trying to stick him like a pig with his blackened spear.

Frustrated, the Ghoule jumped up onto the root with him, forcing Declan to take a few steps back. It wasn't in Declan's nature to give ground willingly, so he launched himself toward the Ghoule, his blade a grey blur as he cut, slashed, and sliced. So fast, in fact, that the beast failed to parry all of his attacks, the evidence of Declan's success demonstrated by the thick black blood that oozed from several deep slices across the Ghoule's forearms, hip, and thigh.

The Ghoule was an excellent fighter even with the many wounds he received. Nevertheless, Declan wasn't worried. He had fought many warriors who were more skilled than he was.

The difference was that he was still standing, and those others were buried six feet under the ground.

Despite the skill of his opponent, Declan felt good. He was in his element, and it was so much better to be fighting for a reason other than the amusement of the rich and privileged. It was so much better to be fighting somewhere else, anywhere else, than the Pit.

Live or die, he was just glad to be free of the white sand.

Declan took a quick look around him when the Ghoule stepped back a few feet, putting some distance between them so that the beast could examine his many wounds. He was pleased to see that his gladiators were performing well ... his soldiers actually. He needed to remind himself of that daily.

They were no longer gladiators, although he doubted that any of them would ever be able to look at themselves in any other way. They were all free now, fighting because they chose to. Fighting because they believed in the Volkun and the mission that he had set for them.

His gaze returned to the Ghoule when the beast charged at him again. The Ghoule clearly wasn't happy that he had gotten the worst of the combat so far, his expression murderous.

Declan smiled maliciously, pleased that the beast allowed his anger to drive him forward, furious that Declan was able to score his flesh so frequently. Declan was more than happy to make the beast question his assumption that humans were soft and that he should already be dead. It only made the combat more pleasurable for Declan, and it improved his chances of winning.

The Ghoule growled louder as he swung down with his blade, irritated even more when Declan parried the blow aimed for his neck and then twisted the handle of his weapon so that as he curled away his sword slid off the Ghoule's spear and sliced across his ribs. The beast hissed in both pain and rage, doing his best to ignore the burning of this new wound, blood now seeping down his left side as well.

Grateful for his success, Declan continued his attack, noting how the beast's eyes changed when he cut across the creature's left side. The Ghoule's anger had transformed into a fiery rage. That was what he was hoping for. That was something that Declan could work with. He had seen it thousands of times before in the Pit.

Once you gave in to your anger, you gave control over to your opponent. Your decisions were no longer driven by cold reason and a phlegmatic calculation of risk, but rather by your emotions. Declan meant to use that change within the Ghoule against the beast.

And he did with a devastating finality.

Enraged by his latest wound, the Ghoule rushed toward Declan, caring less about protecting himself and more about killing his opponent.

Declan backtracked along the root, giving ground. Each time the Ghoule swung his blade, Declan parried it, and then when he neared the trunk of the heart tree he added an unanticipated twist, pulling the dagger from his belt and striking faster than a cobra.

Now, every time the Ghoule swung his spear, fixated on driving the steel into Declan's flesh, Declan blocked the blow with his sword and punched his foot-long dagger into the Ghoule's flesh. The beast was so enraged that at first he barely noticed the new wounds, the Ghoule's attention so focused on Declan, his eyes never leaving his, that the beast didn't even register the additional damage that Declan was inflicting upon him.

One stab, then a second. A third. A fourth followed just as fast. The Ghoule's movements were slowing, although the beast's strategy hadn't changed. A fifth jab with Declan's dagger, this time straight into the beast's gut. Then a sixth into his groin.

The Ghoule was becoming sluggish now, the beast's agility disappearing, replaced by a disjointed stumble that reminded Declan of watching the marionettes in the marketplace shows when he was a child. It appeared that he had cut almost all the Ghoule's strings. Then came the seventh strike, Declan's dagger sliding straight into the beast's heart.

The Ghoule stood there for a few seconds, Declan's dagger keeping him in place, the creature holding his spear across his chest. After just a few heartbeats, the spear slipped from the Ghoule's claws, the light leaving his eyes as the beast fell back onto the root and then tumbled off and dropped to the ground. Declan watched his enemy die with a cold satisfaction, yet he had no time to savor his victory.

Declan ducked, almost losing his balance on the root, one foot sliding off. Once he had both feet back under him, he jumped several feet into the air, then again, and a third time for good measure, avoiding a twisted black staff that was swung with an incredible force, buffeting him with a gust of air every time it passed by him. Landing on the bark and realizing the difficulty of his position, Declan jumped backward and onto the soft loam, the black staff slamming into the tree root right where he had stood just a second before.

A dark shadow leaped over the arcing root to stand in front of Declan. An Elder. The evil breast grinned at him, revealing his sharp, saw-toothed teeth.

The Elder swung his staff at Declan a fifth time, aiming for his head. This time, Declan ducked, and once clear of the stave, missing his head by no more than the width of a finger, he lunged for the Elder's side with his sword.

The Elder caught the blow with his staff, bringing the twisted wood back around with remarkable speed, jabbing with the sharpened tip for Declan's stomach.

Declan pivoted to the side and sucked in his gut, the rough, hardened wood scraping across his leather armor rather than through it and into his flesh.

Before the Ghoule could pull the staff back, Declan swung down with his sword with all of his strength, the steel cutting deeply into the black ash. He wanted to break the staff in two. Bryen had told him how the Elder he had fought on the coastal road had lost control of his Dark Magic when he fractured the beast's staff, and Declan was attempting to eliminate his adversary's greatest advantage the same way now. Unfortunately, unlike Bryen's combat, although Declan chipped a huge chunk of wood from the Ghoule's staff, the twisted black ash remained intact.

The Elder stumbled back a few feet in shock, realizing just how close he had come to losing the Dark Magic that the Ghoule Overlord had bestowed upon him. The beast examined the staff frantically, both terrified and enraged by the large gash about halfway down its length, the scar setting off a low snarl within the beast.

The Elder had wanted to play with the human, to make him experience a long, slow death for what he had done to the Ghoule. The beast realized then that he had made a mistake. This human was more skilled with the blade than he had anticipated, and he could not risk his hold on the Curse just to teach him a lesson.

He simply needed to kill him. Swiftly. Savagely.

Turning his black eyes back toward Declan, he grinned. A black mist began to seep from the top of his staff, spinning faster and faster as he gathered more and more of the Dark Magic for his use. He would still make an example of this human. The Elder would simply do it in a different way. In a way that demonstrated the power that he wielded.

Declan shook his head in irritation, knowing how close he had come to destroying the Elder's staff. One more good blow and the Elder would be nothing more than another Ghoule, a beast that, as he had demonstrated just minutes before, he could kill.

When he saw the Dark Magic beginning to revolve around the top of the Elder's staff, he resigned himself to his fate. Their combat had come to an end, because Declan had no way to protect himself against the Curse.

A SPHERE of incandescent energy shot from Rafia's palm, slamming into the trunk of a heart tree right where an Elder's head had been just a second before. She tried again and missed again, cursing with the acuity of a veteran soldier while still remaining focused on the task she had set for herself, another ball of fire spinning from her palm. Again the Elder was too quick, the beast diving behind a root that resembled a corkscrew before she could strike him with the Talent.

Rafia enjoyed games, just not in circumstances such as this. As they had been trained, the Company of Blood concentrated on the Ghoules, leaving the Elders to her, Sirius, Aislinn, and Bryen. At the start of the fight, the dozen Elders had not expected to find so many Magii in one place.

They had paid the price for that, half of their number flaking away into a black ash in just seconds thanks to the Talent. The Elders who survived that initial assault proved harder to kill, particularly this one.

While the battle raged around her, Rafia had spent the last five minutes trying to destroy this beast. He was fast. Faster than she anticipated. So far, he had either dodged out of the way or used his Dark Magic at the very last second to construct a shield that prevented Rafia from hitting him with the Talent.

She was getting frustrated. Unlike most people, however, she wasn't predictable when she became aggravated. Her exasperation instead helped her to achieve a new level of focus.

She had been trying to hit the Elder where he stood. He had escaped every one of her attacks. So time for a new strategy. She decided on one similar to what she did when she wanted to flush out a hare. To improve her chances of success, she couldn't concentrate on where the hare was, rather she needed to anticipate where the hare would be.

With that in mind, just as the Elder pushed himself up from behind the corkscrew, preparing to send a shard of Dark Magic toward Rafia, a dozen bolts of energy shot from her palm in just a few seconds, one right after the other.

Her latest attack caught the Elder off guard. Rather than ducking back down behind the tree root, the most sensible move, he sprinted to his left, Rafia's bolts following him, slamming one after another into the trunk of the heart tree as the Elder used his impressive speed to stay just a step ahead of the sizzling energy that tracked him.

The Elder responded exactly as Rafia hoped that he would, because just as the last bolt of power slammed against the bark behind him, so did the Elder, a spear crafted from the Talent impaling the beast through the chest and pinning him to the trunk of the heart tree. A blinding white light pulsed from the spear as it slowly dissolved, burning through the Elder from his core to his extremities, until there was nothing left but a swirl of cinders.

It was just a matter of timing, and hers had been excellent, aiming her throw for where she anticipated the Elder to be.

Nodding with the satisfaction of a job well done, Rafia surveyed the rest of the skirmish. She could only see so much of what was going on, the heart trees and roots hiding several of the combats that flowed around her. What she did see required immediate action.

Why Declan had decided to challenge an Elder, she didn't understand. The man was either stubborn, unlucky, or a fool.

Probably not a fool, she corrected, though definitely stubborn and unlucky.

The beast was about to kill the Sergeant of the Blood Company, Dark Magic forming just above the cap of the Elder's staff. That was something that she simply refused to allow.

Using what just had proven to be so effective in her duel with the now destroyed Elder, she shot a dozen bolts of power from her palm, the blazing energy streaking through the gloom and slamming into the back of the unsuspecting Elder right before he sent his Dark Magic streaming toward Declan.

One second the Elder was there. The next, he wasn't. The power of Rafia's strike left behind nothing but a swirling cloud of black ash.

Peering through the cinders, Declan caught sight of his rescuer, giving her a nod of thanks before he jumped over a tree root and drove his sword into the side of a Ghoule who was coming at Asaia from behind.

The gladiator had just used her barbed whip to decapitate one of the Ghoules, which was an impressive feat. Although she might have recovered in time to take on the stealthily approaching beast, Declan didn't want to take the chance.

Rafia watched Declan in action for just a moment more, impressed by his handiwork. Then she began walking among the trees in search of any other Elders who may have escaped her notice.

DAVIN AND LYCIA had cleared their small part of the battlefield with an efficiency that mimicked their time working together in the Pit. Fighting back to back, Davin with his spear and Lycia with her twin blades, they had taken on the handful of Ghoules foolish enough to challenge them.

The results of their work lay at their feet. Three dead

Ghoules, one missing his head because he underestimated Lycia's skill with a blade, not thinking that a woman could hold her own against the likes of him and paying for that miscalculation with his life.

The Ghoule who Lycia fought now was not as foolish as the last, taking her seriously from the start because he had seen what she could do with her steel. Still, that knowledge hadn't helped him all that much. Lycia had wounded the Ghoule four times already, and she wasn't done with him yet.

The Ghoule tried to rotate away from the slash that Lycia directed toward his midsection, realizing too late that he could not get his sword up in time to parry the cut. His several wounds were affecting him badly, the worst of them a slice across his gut that was bleeding profusely and forcing him to keep one claw against his belly, as he feared that the wound would rupture if left unattended.

Lycia took full advantage, the blade in her left hand cutting from the top of the Ghoule's chest down to his groin, taking the beast's claw with it. The wound now resembling a cross, and the beast down to one claw, the Ghoule's guts inevitably spilled out onto the forest floor. The Ghoule stood there for just a moment more, staring in horror at his stump that spouted a thick black blood, seeming to have forgotten the horror that was his midsection, before he crumpled to the ground, bleeding out.

Lycia spun around immediately, the Ghoules facing her dead or dying, to check on her brother as the sound of steel striking steel rang in her ears just behind her. Recognizing that Davin would be finishing the Ghoule he faced in just a few more moves, his spear a blur in front of him and the Ghoule already bleeding from a handful of serious wounds, Lycia scanned around her to see how the rest of the skirmish was playing out.

Aislinn Winborne fought two Ghoules just a dozen yards

away from her, the Lady of the Southern Marches caught in a vise between the beasts. Lycia judged that she was more than holding her own. Lady Winborne had gotten several good strikes in, streaks of blood apparent on both Ghoules, and she had yet to be wounded. Still, she was stuck between them with no easy way out.

Lycia growled in anger. A small part of her wanted to leave Aislinn Winborne to her own devices and allow her to extricate herself from the dilemma she faced. A larger part of Lycia, the compassionate part that she tried so hard to suppress most of the time, wouldn't allow her to do that.

Sprinting across the soft earth on silent feet, Lycia swept her blades from the inside out, two deep cuts leaking a thick black blood from the back of the neck of the Ghoule closest to her. His spinal cord severed, the beast collapsed, no longer able to move any of his limbs.

The Ghoule coming at Aislinn from the other side was distracted by the surprise attack, and his moment of hesitation gave Aislinn the opening that she needed. With a quick feint toward the Ghoule's leading thigh, she adjusted her grip on her sword and slashed upward with a backhanded cut, her sharp steel slicing through the beast's neck to the bone. With a soft gurgle, the Ghoule fell to the ground to join his brethren.

"My thanks," said Aislinn, turning toward Lycia. "These two were putting up quite a fight."

"I didn't do it for you," Lycia grumbled. "I just wanted to kill another Ghoule, and this one was the closest."

"Of course," nodded Aislinn, not believing a word that Lycia said.

Aislinn's gaze then shifted to a series of small explosions just past the heart tree a dozen yards to her front. Both she and Lycia sprinted through the gap, coming to a stop at the edge of a small clearing. Bryen stood in front of them, several dead Ghoules lying around his feet. The last Elder opposed him, and they were engaged not only in a combat of steel, but also of the Talent and the Curse.

Both were wounded, Lycia judging the Elder to have absorbed the worst of the fight so far, though the blood running down Bryen's side worried her. Bryen had infused the Spear of the Magii with the Talent, the two blades glowing brightly. Even so, he was having a difficult time breaking through the Elder's shield of Dark Magic, which swirled around the beast in a mist that solidified every time Bryen cut toward the Elder, keeping the shining blades from striking true.

Not one to give up easily, Bryen stepped back and instead of slashing toward the Elder with his Spear, he shot two streams of energy toward the barrier, the power proving too strong for the beast as the Dark Magic began to waver. Then, with a blinding flash and a resounding boom, an explosion ripped through the small clearing, kicking up a storm of dirt. When the grit finally began to clear a few seconds later, Bryen hadn't moved, the Spear still in his grip, but the Elder was gone.

Catching a flash of movement about fifty yards in front of him, Bryen sprinted after the beast, refusing to let the Elder escape, knowing and wanting to avoid the cost of doing so.

"Bryen, wait!" both Aislinn and Lycia shouted at the same time as he chased after the bolting Elder and lost himself among the heart trees.

BRYEN SPRINTED AROUND A HEART TREE, vaulted over a root that twisted almost five feet off the ground, cut to his left to avoid another root that had shattered into dozens of sharp spikes, then curled back around to his right. He stopped for just a moment, searching to his front.

The slice across his chest from the Elder's staff had scorched his flesh just like the mark that he had received on his cheek from the Ghoule Overlord when they met for the first time in the Sanctuary. He did his best to disregard the pain of his wound. He could deal with his injury once his opponent was dead.

Where was the Elder? He was certain that the beast had come this way. Bryen might not have gained on him because of all the obstructions in his path. Still, he couldn't be too far behind.

Bryen saw a hint of motion in the murk no more than a few dozen yards ahead of him, just off to his right. The Elder was fast. Very fast. Bryen caught a glimpse of him through the ragged breaks in the trees and the roots.

He was staying with Elder, he just wasn't gaining on the creature. Not willing to risk losing the beast, Bryen decided that he needed to do something to slow his target down.

Grasping hold of the Talent, Bryen shot a streak of energy from his palm that blazed through the gloom of the Dark Forest and slammed into a root that was just a few feet in front of the Elder. The blast of shattered wood, thousands of jagged splinters bursting into the air, caught the Elder from the side, throwing the beast off his clawed feet. He landed hard on his back, skidding to a stop against the trunk of a heart tree.

The Elder tried to push himself up. He couldn't, his strength failing. Looking down, he could understand why. Hundreds of shards of the destroyed tree root had shredded his chest just as well as if not better than a steel blade could have. The Elder realized that his end had come, so he settled back against the tree, waiting for the world to fade around him.

Bryen appeared before the Elder just a second later, taking in the result of his efforts. He held onto the Spear of the Magii, the double blades glowing with the Talent. Bryen realized that he would have little need to finish the beast. It was only a matter of time before the Ghoule went to the other side.

"You will not escape, human," whispered the Elder in a

raspy voice, a thick black blood beginning to bubble out of the creature's maw. "You will not escape."

Although the Ghoule spoke in his guttural language, Bryen understood every word.

"We come, human," continued the Elder. "We come for you. Your death is certain."

"Yet I'm the one still standing," replied Bryen in the Ghoule's language, not making the conscious decision to speak in the creature's tongue, never having learned how to speak it, yet knowing exactly what he had said, thanks to the Seventh Stone and the Dark Magic within him.

The Elder lying against the tree chuckled at that, the flow of blood running out of the beast's mouth accelerating.

"Not for long, human. We know who you are. We know what you have become. We come for you. We come for the Seventh Stone." The Elder then became silent for a time, Bryen staring down at him, thinking that the beast might have died, the pain of the burn across Bryen's chest becoming more insistent. Then with a start the Elder's glazed eyes gained a startling lucidity for just a few seconds more. "We come for you, human. We are here."

At the same time the dying Elder drew his last breath, a bolt of Dark Magic slammed into Bryen's chest, knocking him off his feet. He ended up on his back lying in the dirt ten feet from where he had been standing. His entire body burned with a cold fire, the Curse surging through him.

What had happened? It couldn't have been the Elder he had been speaking to. That beast didn't have the strength to call on his Dark Magic, not with his staff shattered by the blast of the Talent that also had killed the creature.

Bryen tried to push himself up, finding the task too much for him. He was only able to raise himself to one elbow and shakily at that before he dropped back onto the dirt.

Then two pairs of clawed feet appeared just to his side, and he realized that he had made a terrible mistake. He had focused so much of his attention on the escaping Elder that he had never considered that there might be others coming his way. He had run right into a trap, the wounded Elder nothing more than bait.

With the Dark Magic rushing through him, staining his body with an oily filth, Bryen knew that he couldn't make use of the Talent on his own. Not now. If he did, he'd resign himself to a fate worse than death. He turned his head to the side, finding the Spear of the Magii just out of reach.

If he crawled just a few feet, he could grab the Spear. With it, he could dispatch these two Elders. But when he tried to flip his body over so that he could dig his hands into the dirt and pull himself in the direction of his weapon, Bryen's strength failed him.

He was about to try again, realizing it was a futile attempt yet still needing to do it, when his greatest fear came to pass. The Dark Magic that he had gained through the Seventh Stone and had locked away was reaching for the Curse that had just struck him, trying to bring the two together.

The Dark Magic was pushing from both sides now against the barrier that he had created within himself to keep free from the taint, and as Bryen's stamina waned, his ability to maintain control over the barrier wavered.

Once the shield collapsed, he would be lost to the Curse forever.

He desperately sought to maintain the barricade, even though he knew that without the Spear he didn't stand a chance. If that wasn't bad enough, an even more immediate threat approached. Tilting his head forward, Bryen watched as one of the Elders came to stand right next to him, and there was nothing that he could do about it.

His first thought was that he was about to die, something that he didn't fear, though certainly regretted. Then he saw the second Elder call on his Dark Magic, the tainted black energy spinning across the top of his staff, the beast manipulating the corrupt power to form a portal.

The Elders didn't want to kill him, he realized. They wanted to take him. Now Bryen truly was afraid. The Elders wanted what was in him, which could mean only one thing.

They wanted to take him to the Ghoule Overlord, who could extract the Seventh Stone from him. Once that was done, the commander of the Ghoule Legions could then use the power of the artifact to destroy the Weir.

The faint mist that had been spinning behind the second Elder slowly coalesced into an opaque disk of black large enough for a Ghoule to walk through. With the portal ready, the Elder closest to Bryen reached down with his claws to throw him over his shoulder.

Desperate, Bryen reached for the Talent, just a trickle, any power at all, now more fearful of being brought to the Ghoule Overlord than being touched by the Curse. Better that he be destroyed by the Dark Magic than be used by his enemy.

He cursed silently in frustration. There was nothing for him to grab hold of, the fight within him between the Talent and the Curse consuming all the strength and energy he had left.

As the Elder's claw grasped Bryen's arm, a streak of scorching energy sizzled through the air, slamming into the other Elder from behind. The beast screamed in agony, his shriek cut short as his body turned to ash in just moments, the portal that he had created winking out as his staff dropped to the ground.

The Elder who had been reaching for Bryen snapped back up with his staff at the ready, seizing the Dark Magic that flowed within him. He was fast, just not fast enough. Another bolt of energy burned through the beast's chest and flung him back against a heart tree in a heap, his body a smoking ruin.

The next time Bryen looked up, Aislinn was there, her face

staring down at him and a welcome replacement for that of the Elder's.

Rafia stood next to her, using the Talent to search the area around them and ensure that it was free of any other Elders or Ghoules. Once she was satisfied, she released her hold on the natural magic of the world and she knelt down next to Aislinn.

"That was quite impressive," complimented Bryen in a weak voice.

"Rafia taught me," replied Aislinn distractedly as she examined the wound on Bryen's chest. "Rafia, please take a look at this. I don't know what to do."

Fear filled Aislinn's voice. She remembered what Bryen had looked like after being wounded by the Elder just outside the Aeyrie, and this injury appeared to be much worse, streaks of black already stretching from where he had been hit in the chest out to his arms. She assumed the Dark Magic had seeped down to his legs as well. The Curse was moving more swiftly than she ever imagined possible to make Bryen its own.

Rafia bent down for a closer look, ignoring the burn across Bryen's midsection. That was nothing compared to the thin tendrils of black that wormed their way up and down Bryen's body.

Davin, Lycia, and Declan appeared next, followed by Tarin, Jerad, and Sirius. No one said a word as Rafia took hold of the Talent once again and scanned Bryen, trying to figure out if there was anything that she could do to help him.

She identified the source of the problem immediately, yet that was the easy part. As she examined him more closely, a sick feeling in the pit of her stomach told her that there was nothing that she could do about the Curse raging through him. She couldn't help Bryen.

"Bryen," Rafia said in a quiet, calm voice that she hoped hid her fear. "You need to heal yourself. Just as you've done so many times before. I can't help you. None of us can help you.

You need to cleanse yourself of the Dark Magic the Elder struck you with."

"I know," Bryen replied through gritted teeth, his body beginning to shake uncontrollably, frightening all the people surrounding him. "I know. I just don't know if I can. The Dark Magic is calling to me. It wants me."

"Fight it, Bryen," said Sirius, who knelt next to the Protector and grasped his hand. "Fight it. You must."

Bryen looked up into Sirius' eyes, realizing that the real Sirius was with him now. The Master of the Magii, not the somewhat addled instructor. His eyes blazed with anger, and Bryen detected a hint of terror worming its way into his gaze. At first glance, Bryen thought that was likely because of what Sirius needed him to do with respect to the Weir, and that if he was taken by the Curse, Sirius instead would have to kill him if he didn't die on his own.

But the look in Sirius' eyes suggested that there might be more there than just that. That Bryen perhaps was more to the old Magus than just a tool to be used.

"The Seventh Stone, Bryen," said Aislinn, her words pulling his eyes to hers. "Use the Seventh Stone, just like when you were at the Aeyrie. It will give you the strength that you need. You must use the Seventh Stone."

"I can't," Bryen whispered, finding it harder and harder to talk.

The Dark Magic within him spread like a virus, weakening him, the boundary that separated the Curse contained within the Seventh Stone fraying, thread by thread. If he tried to use the Seventh Stone now, the barrier would unravel completely and the Dark Magic would gain dominance. When that happened, there would be no return.

It wouldn't be long now. It wouldn't be long before he was gone. Before the Curse stole who he was.

"You must!" shouted Aislinn, tears forming in her eyes. "You must at least try."

Bryen stared at Aislinn, seeing nothing else. He could let go right now. All the pain. All the fear. All the anger would disappear. He would be free from it all. Then a few soft words behind him shook him from the haze that threatened to engulf his spirit.

"Death doesn't choose us," Lycia said quietly.

"We choose our death," finished Davin.

"The Spear," Bryen mumbled, his breath increasingly difficult to come by now, clarity returning to his thoughts if only briefly. The shield within him was about to crack. Despite that, or maybe because of it, Lycia and Davin were right. He needed to fight until the very end. If he was going to die, it would be on his terms and no one else's. It would be with his weapon in his hands. "I need the Spear."

Lycia dashed to her left and was back at Bryen's side in less than a second, placing the Spear of the Magii on Bryen's chest and then helping him wrap his hands around the steel haft of the weapon.

In a flash, the Talent surged within Bryen, the Spear serving as a focal point, augmenting his strength a thousandfold, giving him a way to push back against the Dark Magic that was so close to consuming him. Yet, that would have to wait a few seconds more. He needed to do something else first.

Connecting the Talent that flowed through the Spear to the Seventh Stone within him, Bryen concentrated on the barrier that was only a few heartbeats away from fragmenting. He was done in an instant. The vault that he had constructed in the back of his mind to contain the Curse gifted to him by the Seventh Stone was made whole again.

Strong. Solid. Unbreakable.

For now.

That completed, Bryen turned his attention to the Dark

Magic that flowed through his veins because of the Elder's attack. Thanks to the power and unique qualities of the Spear of the Magii, the next change was almost instantaneous, the weapon helping Bryen to pull the Dark Magic from his body and destroy it in the welcome fire of the Talent.

Those surrounding Bryen watched in wonder as the entire Spear glowed a bright white, and as it did, the threads of black crisscrossing Bryen's body dissolved into nothing. When Bryen took a deep breath and then pushed himself up into a sitting position, Aislinn and Lycia both helping him, they all breathed a sigh of relief.

"Didn't you learn anything the last time you chased after a Ghoule on your own?" asked Tarin, not expecting an answer from Bryen, his words simply a way to release some of the tension that had been building within him.

"He's done this before?" asked Aislinn, her voice sharp because of the rawness of her emotions.

"After you left for Tintagel, Lady Winborne, Bryen pursued a Ghoule right into a trap just like this," confirmed Jerad. "He received just a scratch then."

"This was not just a scratch," Lycia said, her face red with anger. Not because of what Jerad had said, but rather because Bryen clearly hadn't learned from his previous escapade.

"I might have said too much," Jerad murmured, seeing both Lycia and Aislinn staring at him with daggers in their eyes.

"Perhaps you did, Sergeant," said Tarin. "Come on. Let's leave Bryen so that he can pay the piper. We need to check on the Blood Company."

"Sarcasm from the Captain of the Battersea Guard? I never would have guessed."

"Nice try, lad," said Tarin in response to Bryen's whispered comment. "You can't turn the conversation that easily. You made your bed. Now you get to lie in it."

"I think I'll go with them," said Sirius, who pushed himself off the ground, giving Bryen a companionable pat on the shoulder before he left.

"Definitely a death wish," murmured Rafia to no one in particular. "I knew it the first time I met him."

"You did this before?" demanded Aislinn. "When we were training in the practice yard at the Broken Citadel, what was the one thing that you kept telling me?"

"I'm not sure," said Bryen with a sheepish grin. "We talked about a great many things."

Bryen was tired, but he was stronger now. He felt more like himself. The Spear of the Magii had rejuvenated him to a certain extent, though he knew that he would be feeling the effects of his wound and the healing process for the next several days.

"Don't try to distract with humor," growled Lycia.

"I wasn't trying to be funny, it's just that ..."

"You can make a mistake, but you can only make it once. If you make the same mistake twice, you're dead," cut in Aislinn.

"Sounds just like Declan," confirmed Lycia.

"Good advice, don't you think?" Aislinn asked heatedly. "Why didn't you follow it?"

"It was just that ..."

"Why didn't you listen to your own advice?" Aislinn interrupted again, not having any patience for Bryen's attempted deflections. She had something to say, and she was going to say it. "You almost died because you made the same mistake twice."

"I didn't want anyone else to be hurt or killed because of me!" shouted Bryen. Although his tired voice wasn't very loud, it did stop Aislinn's diatribe. "Too many of the Company fell today. I didn't want that last Elder to hurt anyone else. To reveal where we were. I thought I could take him."

"Clearly that wasn't the case," said Lycia quietly, her eyes still blazing with anger at her friend's foolishness, though understanding his motivation.

Aislinn offered her hand to Bryen, who accepted it. After she helped him to his feet she didn't let go. Instead, her grip tightened as she pulled Bryen in close to her.

"You are the Seventh Stone. You are the only one who can repair the Weir."

"Yes, even though I don't even know if I can do that."

"That doesn't matter," said Aislinn, her voice returning to a less agitated level. "We believe in you even if you don't. And even if you fail, it doesn't matter. You're the only one who gives us a chance to hold back the Ghoules. You. Just you. We are here to help you get to the Sanctuary. Succeed or fail, we are only here to help you try to rebuild the Weir. If we fall, we fall. If we fall, you continue on. We don't matter. Only you do."

"That's not true ..."

Lycia cut him off, agreeing with every word that the Lady Winborne had said.

"She's right. We're here for you, not the other way around. Don't do something that stupid again, or I'll kill you myself."

With that, Lycia nodded to Aislinn. Then they both turned and followed after the others back toward the Company. Lycia grabbed Davin by the arm to take him with her, the Crimson Giant shrugging his shoulders apologetically to Bryen as he trailed after the two women.

Watching them go, Bryen didn't know what was worse. Being chewed out by both Aislinn and Lycia or the two women agreeing with one another.

With everyone else gone, Declan finally came up to Bryen. He could see the emotions raging across Declan's normally taciturn features. Anger. Irritation. Fear. Relief. Apparently even some satisfaction at the lecture that Aislinn and Lycia had just given him.

"You acted the fool," admonished Declan, now that it was finally his turn. "You're not the only one here who can fight. You're not the only one here who can take risks and get things done. Don't do that again. The Lady Winborne is correct, whether you like it or not. All of us can die, and it won't matter. The only thing that matters is that you stay alive and do whatever it is you need to do at the Weir. Are we clear?"

Bryen nodded, feeling like when he was a child and he had first entered the Pit, the Master of the Gladiators taking him to task for the tiniest of mistakes that he had made while he fought on the white sand, Bryen feeling ashamed for days afterward.

"Yes, Declan."

"Good." Declan nodded grouchily, not feeling the need to say anything else as he struggled to hide the terror that had surged within him when he'd seen the wound that Bryen had received. Declan cared about fixing the Weir, though not as much as he cared about Bryen. With that in mind, he shifted his focus to their next challenge. "Once the wounded are cared for, we'll get moving again. We need to assume the Ghoules know we are here."

"You're right about that," agreed Bryen, as he and Declan started to walk slowly back to the Blood Company, Bryen taking his time as his legs felt a bit wobbly. Declan stayed at his side just to make sure he was there if the young man he viewed as his son needed his help. "I'm beginning to worry that we won't be able to make it to the Sanctuary. We're less than a week out from Tintagel, and the Ghoules have already found us. I knew that this would be difficult. I knew that we would face challenges. I just didn't expect to face those challenges so soon."

"Could I offer you one piece of redvice?"

"I doubt I could stop you," Bryen replied with a grin. "What would that be?"

"We've been hit in the mouth and knocked to the ground a couple times. When that happens, there's only one thing to do."

"What would that be?"

"You get back up."

"And you hit whoever hit you harder than they hit you."

"There you go," confirmed Declan. "I guess you did listen to me on occasion."

"How could I not?" asked Bryen with a short laugh. "You make it very hard not to." Bryen reached across and grasped Declan's arm warmly, nodding his thanks for his guidance. "On to the Sanctuary?"

"On to the Sanctuary."

4

———

FROM A DISTANCE

"Are they in place?"

"Yes, they moved into position last night," replied the Elder, his clawed hand squeezing his twisted black staff every few seconds.

Nibli stood on a ledge on the last mountain at the southern tip of the Winter Pass. From here, the Breakwater Plateau spread out before him. For as far as he could see, there was nothing else but the long grass of the steppe, which resembled a brown ocean as the winds swept down from the Shattered Peaks and across the broad expanse.

Far below him and to the east, he could see tiny specks coming toward him. Soldiers. They were emerging out of the Spine not too far away from where the Winter Pass began. He had confirmed it with his Dark Magic just the other day, that the humans were close and approaching far faster than he anticipated. Somehow, the humans had defeated Nezgul and his packs and were continuing north at a rapid clip.

It should not have happened. Nezgul should not have failed.

He should have destroyed the human vanguard and caught

the main force on the plain.

Nibli grumbled to himself in irritation. *Should* and *should not* had no place during a war. Circumstances changed too rapidly, and there were never any guarantees.

With that thought guiding him, Nibli had worked to remove any uncertainties from what he had ordered his Ghoules to do next.

"Then go now. Do as I have instructed, as our Master has instructed. The humans will reach you before the sun sets."

The Elder nodded, then took his leave, racing down the slope.

Finally alone, for several minutes Nibli simply stood there, ignoring the cold, the wind, the flakes of snow that began to fall from the heavy, moisture-laden clouds. Then an awful grin broke out on Nibli's face that revealed his sharp, pointed teeth.

The approaching soldiers did not worry him. No, his Ghoules would be ready for them.

Instead, they excited him.

The humans wanted to defend their land. Their homes. Their families.

He understood that, but it didn't change his opinion of them.

They were fools.

Wasted effort. Wasted lives.

Nibli had forced three Legions through the Weir already with more to join him in the next few days.

The humans could hope all they wanted. It would do nothing for them. When his Legions marched down the Winter Pass, his Ghoules would snuff out that hope as if they were no more than candles in the wind.

The humans didn't know it, but they had already lost their Kingdom. Once Nibli pushed ten Legions through the Weir, and the Overlord took the Seventh Stone, the fate of the humans would be sealed, and the Ghoules would feed.

5

FROM BENEATH

"Has the situation changed in any way, Duchess Stelekel?" asked the Blademaster.

The Captain of the Royal Guard had adhered to the Caledonian General's order, waiting for her to arrive when the dark, thin slash signifying the southern entrance to the Winter Pass came into view. The Duchess of Murcia had ridden ahead with a small guard, the bulk of the Caledonian Army no more than a half-day behind.

Klines was glad that he had listened to her. His advance guard was about to enter treacherous ground, worse than what they faced a few days before when they battled against the Ghoules and Elders sent to waylay them. Then, they had fought on a lonely plateau on the western side of the Northern Spine that at least gave them cover at their backs. Here, the open land sloping down from the peaks to the grassland played to the Ghoules' strengths.

It was a forbidding sight, thought Klines, as he examined where the mountains rose on both sides to his front, seemingly touching the sky. There was no gradual incline to the towering heights, the plain giving way to just a few lonely knolls and bluffs scattered haphazardly about before the soaring spires of the Shattered Peaks thrust out of the ground with barely any preamble.

They would have to journey slightly more than a league through the narrow gap between those towering crests, the entrance to the Winter Pass no more than a few hundred yards wide the entire time, before the gorge finally opened up to a mile or more in width. For much of the way, the sides of the stone spires shooting up from the ground appeared to be shear.

But appearances could be deceiving.

There was the ever-present threat that loose boulders, shale, and scrabble jarred free by the wind from the north that screamed through the gap would bring tons more stone, ice, and snow crashing down onto the gulley floor.

Add to the mix the Ghoules who were waiting for them just outside the crack between the mountains, and the Caledonians' already dangerous circumstances became even more alarming.

"No, it has not," replied Noorsin, using the Talent once again to search in the direction the scouts had reported seeing Ghoule activity, then extending her search for leagues around them just to be certain that no potentially deadly surprises would be coming their way. "For whatever reason, rather than blocking the mouth of the gap, the Ghoules are a few hundred yards out in front of the Pass, a fast-running stream at their backs. There are several small hills on each side, more rocky outcroppings with flat tops than anything else, I'm assuming the result of the rockslides so common to these peaks, yet not a single beast is on top of any of them. Because of those knolls, I doubt that the Ghoules can see much to either side of them. With their placement, there's enough room to flank them if we go far enough out on the flanks. We might even have a chance to come at them from behind."

"But why there?" asked the Blademaster.

He understood that the Ghoules were not inclined to build

defensive fortifications, preferring to fight in the open. That approach allowed them to use their speed and agility to their best advantage. It was strange, though, and from a military perspective almost criminal.

If these Ghoules had aligned their positioning with the entrance to the Winter Pass, he and the advance guard of five hundred soldiers would have had a very difficult time forcing their way past them. He probably wouldn't have even tried until the Caledonian Army joined them.

"That's an excellent question," replied Noorsin, more bothered than pleased by her discovery.

The one hundred or so Ghoules and the handful of Elders with them were a formidable force. Yet there was no accounting for the Ghoules' decision on where they wanted to make a stand, as it gave the Caledonian advance guard an advantage that they could put to immediate use.

Yes, she was worried. There was an aspect to this situation that bothered her. Then again, there were no other immediate threats near, and she and the other Magii could negate the additional danger presented by the Elders, which meant that the Blademaster could bring his numbers to bear.

Even if the Ghoules preferred the open space, the advance guard certainly was large enough and had the experience needed to clear the path for the Caledonian Army coming up behind them. So perhaps she was thinking too much about what might actually be a gift, courtesy of the Ghoules' arrogance.

"I feel like this is all a bit too easy," Klines said. "Like we're missing something. Something important. It's almost as if the Ghoules want us to come forward, and not just because of the additional space they can make use of when they face us. I feel like there is something else going on here."

"Or perhaps we simply arrived at the right time and can take advantage of the Ghoules' mistake."

"Do you really believe that, Duchess Stelekel?" asked Klines, a raised eyebrow the only hint of his disagreement.

"No, I don't," replied Noorsin with a grimace. "Even so, we have the right numbers and two other Magii are with us. We should be able to handle the Ghoule vanguard. I don't really see a better alternative. We can wait for our host to arrive, but we need to get into the Winter Pass as quickly as we can. More Ghoules are coming down through the canyon from the north. If we allow too many of the beasts to dig in here, we may never get through."

Klines considered her words for a few seconds, then nodded his head. Although he still felt uneasy about the opportunity presented to them, he agreed with her, and he had found no good reason not to move forward with their original plan.

"Benin, you know what to do?" asked Klines.

"Yes, Blademaster," the broad Sergeant replied, nudging his horse forward so that he was right next to the Captain of the Royal Guard.

A small smile broke through Klines' normally taciturn countenance. The Sergeant had rewoven his beard, replacing the war hammer that had been there for the last several days with crossed daggers. Klines had to admit that Benin truly had a unique skill. Best of all, it seemed to help keep him and his soldiers relaxed and ready to fight, many of his troops growing out their beards so they could try their hand at what was one of their Sergeant's more unique talents. That was a necessity right now, because he had a feeling that this supposedly straightforward skirmish that they were about to initiate would prove to be anything but.

"Then off you go, Benin. Stay sharp. We'll meet you in the middle."

"Yes, Blademaster," Benin replied, the Sergeant wheeling his horse to the west, motioning with his hand for several squads of soldiers to follow as he headed toward the far edge of the outcroppings, staying out of sight of the Ghoules the entire way.

Klines watched Benin lead the soldiers away, then he turned his attention back toward Noorsin.

"Shall we begin, Duchess Stelekel? There's really no reason to keep the beasts waiting."

"Yes, let's do so. There certainly is no time like the present."

THE BLADEMASTER PUSHED the advance guard forward to a point where they were no more than a few hundred yards from the Ghoules. Surprisingly, the beasts did nothing in response, remaining right where they had been when Duchess Stelekel had checked with the Talent just an hour before, arrayed in front of the stream that zigzagged across the terrain a quarter mile in front of the entrance to the Winter Pass.

That nagging worry that had annoyed him when he first glimpsed the Ghoules started to buzz louder in the back of his brain. Nevertheless, he ignored it for the time being and formed his cavalry into two lines, the first separated from the second by ten yards.

The soldiers kept their mounts under good control even though many of the horses could smell the Ghoules now, the scent making them nervous. The men of the Royal Guard held their spearpoints toward the sky, knowing that those weapons would dip toward the ground soon enough.

The beasts lined up across from them started howling and roaring, a few even beckoning with their claws, what Klines could only assume was their attempt to urge their enemy forward. To have their meal come to them rather than the beasts having to hunt.

Several of the Ghoules gnashed their serrated teeth and pounded their chests with their claws as they readied for battle.

Perhaps they thought such bravado would terrify his soldiers, put them on edge, force them into a mistake. Maybe even make them turn and run.

Klines wasn't worried. His soldiers understood their fates if they fell to the creatures from the Lost Land. These soldiers had trained with him in Tintagel. They knew what they were about. They knew what needed to be done.

Klines believed that his troops would give the Ghoules more than they bargained for. All the soldiers required was the command to advance so that they could wipe these creatures from the face of the earth, because they also knew what would happen if they failed to do so. Yes, their Kingdom was at risk. What worried them more, however, was the fate of their families and loved ones if the Ghoules were permitted to invade Caledonia.

"Anything Maria?" asked Noorsin. "I have this nagging feeling that I'm missing something."

Maria scanned around them for the hundredth time with the Talent, starting with their current location and then expanding her search for several leagues, pushing her senses between the two towering peaks that marked the beginning of the Winter Pass and well beyond just to be sure. She shook her head when she was done, even though she too felt like something was amiss.

"Nothing, Noorsin. Nothing for leagues but this one group of Ghoules and Elders. It doesn't seem right, I agree, but there's nothing else around us that I could see."

"Telly?"

The gangly, awkward looking Magus shook his head as well.

"I didn't find anything either, Noorsin. Maybe it's just nerves?"

"And Benin?" asked Noorsin, ignoring the Magus' suggestion as to why she might be feeling as she was.

"Exactly where he should be," replied Maria. "The Ghoules don't have a clue."

Noorsin nodded her head in thanks, then turned her pensive eyes toward the Blademaster.

"Everything is as it should be, Captain Klines. You can begin when you're ready."

"Thank you, Duchess Stelekel."

He could tell that something was troubling the Duchess of Murcia, yet having no cause and not wanting to delay the next step, Klines pulled his sword from the scabbard attached to his saddle, raising the blade above his head. The steel caught the sunlight of the afternoon, shining brightly.

"We fight for Caledonia!" Klines shouted, his voice carrying down both sides of the two rows of cavalry arrayed behind him. Then he cut through the air with his blade. "Forward!"

Klines and the soldiers in the first row began at a walk that rapidly turned into a trot, the cavalry on both sides and behind keeping pace with their Captain. Within seconds, Klines urged the Royal Guard to a gallop, their powerful war horses digging big clumps of dirt out of the ground. The second wave of cavalry followed right behind, maintaining the recommended separation from the soldiers just in front of them.

As one, the soldiers in the front rank tilted their spears down until they were parallel with the ground rushing past, their horses racing across the rough terrain, undeterred, eating up the distance separating them from their foes in just seconds. The soldiers didn't bother to shout or scream. They didn't offer any yells of rage or fear. There was only the sound of their horses' hooves pounding into the turf to accompany their calm focus.

The soldiers had taken on the persona of their Captain, adopting the cold-eyed gaze and the hardened purpose of the Blademaster as their own. There was no need for drama. There was only a need for hard work. There was only a need for killing the Ghoules.

With a resounding crash, the front rank of the Royal Guard slammed into the raging and hissing Ghoules. Employing the training that they had received from Tarin Tentillin, they used their horses as weapons.

The soldiers in the front were less interested in striking the Ghoules with their spears. Instead, they wanted to ensure that the beasts couldn't escape their powerful mounts, which knocked to the ground the creatures too slow to get out of the way, crushing flesh and bone with their steel-shod hooves.

The second rank of soldiers followed right after the first, galloping over any beasts attempting to rise while using their spears or swords to engage the many Ghoules who had dodged out of the way of the attack, most often leaping right over the charging horses.

The Blademaster had hoped to wheel back around for a second charge, wanting the massive war horses to do their work for them again. It wasn't to be. The Ghoules who avoided the first charge were too fast, closing with the mounted soldiers with inhuman speed.

Much to the Blademaster's displeasure, it seemed that these beasts had learned some new tactics as well, thereby neutralizing to a very large extent the advantage provided by their war horses. It was not an unexpected development, though it certainly was unwanted, especially now, because it made their task that much more challenging and dangerous.

Although this change forced Klines to adjust his tactics, he was thankful that the Ghoules still failed to offer much in the way of a coordinated defense, their approach to battle synonymous with the combats in the Colosseum in which each warrior sought to demonstrate their skill at killing. Furthermore, the beasts were not interested in cutting down trees to carve spikes to be placed in the ground or in building bulwarks or digging moats or constructing any other type of defensive fortification that would prevent his soldiers from using their horses as their primary weapon of war.

The Ghoules still preferred to make use of the open space, to employ their natural strengths to the best of their ability, fighting from a defensive position apparently anathema to the Ghoule warrior culture. The beasts were naturally aggressive. They wanted to attack. They always wanted to be fighting from the front claw, dictating the parameters of every clash.

In fact, this was the primary reason the Legions failed when they first invaded the Kingdom a thousand years before. The Ghoules didn't view the humans, other than perhaps the Magii, as a major threat. As an opponent that required them to change their approach to battle. The beasts believed that no soft human from the south stood a chance one on one against a blooded Ghoule.

During the Caledonian charge, the Elders who had been standing at the back of the Ghoule line waited, not feeling the need to rush in, leaving the soldiers to the Ghoules, as they looked for the right time to join the fight. That was a mistake that several of the servants of the Ghoule Overlord paid for with their lives.

Noorsin, Maria, and Telly put in play the plan that they had discussed, coordinating their attack by concentrating on the Elder on the far right for their first assault.

Maria started the combat by sending a streak of energy across the battlefield. The targeted Elder raised a shield of spinning black mist to deflect the strike. The creature was quite pleased with himself, cursing his defiance toward Maria, even taunting her because he had defended against her assault so easily.

The Magus simply smiled at the Elder and gave him a wink just as two distinct streaks of sizzling energy ripped through him from two different directions at the exact same time.

Noorsin and Telly had moved away from Maria, making it appear as if she were the only Magus the Elder needed to worry about. Timing their attack perfectly, the beast collapsed to the ground before he could finish issuing his challenge.

For just a moment, the other Elders stood there in shock, never expecting to see one of their number fall right at the start of the fight. They recovered swiftly, however, and soon the Magii were engaged in separate combats with the four remaining Elders, the Duchess of Murcia forced to hold off two of the beasts on her own.

As the misty black of the Curse and the blazing white of the Talent shot across the battlefield, the soldiers of the Royal Guard, unable to wheel back around for another charge, employed another tactic that they had learned from Tarin Tentillin. The Ghoules favored fighting on their own, only fighting in unison when the Elders forced them to do so. The soldiers now sought to take advantage of that preference in another way as they broke off into their assigned squads of three or four fighters and attempted to take on one Ghoule at a time.

That strategy worked well at the start, the beasts not really aware of what the Caledonians were doing because of the swirl of the fight around them. The Blademaster's troops worked through the Ghoules methodically. Each squad first tried to isolate their targets, and then once they succeeded in doing that, they demonstrated a great deal of skill by maneuvering their war horses so that they could trap the beast between them.

The Ghoules were fast. That couldn't be denied. But they were not fast enough to avoid two or three pieces of steel being thrust at them at the same time from different directions. In this way, the Royal Guard reduced their enemies' numbers in a systematic fashion.

When the beasts finally figured out what was happening to

them, ignoring their instincts to continue to fight, many of the Ghoules jumped over the war horses and retreated toward the stream, forming once again into a larger group.

No longer able to take on the Ghoules singly, the soldiers reformed their lines, preparing for the next charge.

A sound strategy on the part of the Ghoules, Klines had to admit, and also unanticipated. His soldiers had done an excellent job of cutting down the trapped beasts much like a farmer using a scythe to harvest wheat.

Even so, quite a few had escaped. Too many in his opinion. Unfortunately for the Ghoules, he had assumed that would happen, which was why Benin and the several squads under his command had navigated around the rocky outcroppings to the west and circled back around to come at the Ghoules from the rear.

The Blademaster watched with a distinct surge of pleasure as the several dozen soldiers galloped through the shallow stream and crashed into the beasts with their war horses. So intent on the soldiers standing to their front, many of the creatures didn't realize that they were under attack from behind until after the soldiers' mounts had smashed them into the rocky terrain.

With Duchess Stelekel and the other two Magii keeping the Elders busy and the Ghoules to his front in growing disarray, Klines sensed that now was the time to finish the beasts. If they could do that, the Winter Pass would be open to them.

Klines was about to order his soldiers to charge a second time, his well-trained troops eager to join their comrades who had just cut through the Ghoules, when an unwanted pinch of concern along the back of his neck, a primal warning that he always listened to, made him look over his shoulder.

A touch of fear shot through him. His and Duchess Stelekel's initial worry had been legitimate, and they were about to pay a high price for their miscalculation.

"Duchess Stelekel! To our rear!"

Klines hoped that the Duchess heard him. He couldn't be certain, though, because her gaze never left the two Elders facing off against her. The Duchess of Murcia maintained a shield of bright energy that was attached to her left arm so that she could defend herself while she flung spheres of blazing power with her right hand.

"Second rank, about face!" shouted the Blademaster, realizing that the Duchess and the other two Magii wouldn't be able to assist until they had eliminated the Elders opposing them.

The soldiers in the row behind him moved quickly to obey, pulling on their horses' reins to turn toward the more than one hundred Ghoules who were sprinting across the open ground toward them. A neat trick on the part of the Ghoules, Klines thought. How the beasts had avoided the Magii's searches, he'd really like to know. But that would have to wait until after this fight, assuming there was an after.

The soldiers recognized the danger immediately. They couldn't allow the creatures to break through their line, because if they did it meant the Ghoules would catch them in a vise that would be almost impossible to escape, the two sides applying pressure until the soldiers were crushed between them, ensuring their deaths. So the soldiers nudged their horses together and lowered their spears, preparing to absorb as best as they could the attack that rushed toward them.

At the Captain's call, Noorsin glanced behind her for just a moment when one of the Elders opposing her faltered in his attack, driven back a few feet and needing to duck when she threw a few bolts of energy his way when he thought that she was focused on the other Elder. What she saw in that split second chilled her and angered her at the same time.

She had been incredibly thorough, as had Maria and Telly, and none of them had identified anything that suggested that there were any Ghoules near them but for those by the stream. Quietly cursing up a storm that would have made any soldier who overheard blush, she could only hope that the ploy they had agreed to just that morning would allow them to stave off annihilation, because at the moment she couldn't do anything to help the Blademaster and his troops. She needed to kill these Elders before they killed her.

❧

"Quietly now. Not a sound. Slowly. Carefully. No sudden movements. This won't work if they spot us."

Kevan Winborne urged his scouts forward in a soft voice. His several hundred soldiers, all from the Battersea Guard, were making their way through the spotty cover provided by the small groves that dotted the hills leading down from the Northern Spine less than a quarter mile east of where Noorsin and the Blademaster currently battled with the Ghoules.

It didn't take the Duke of the Southern Marches and his troops long to reach the verge of the trees where they looked out across the rough terrain that led toward the mouth of the Winter Pass. Why the Ghoules decided to fight by the stream rather than use the entrance to the gap to their advantage, he didn't know. He also didn't care, as he was more than willing to exploit that error for his own gain.

To do so, however, he needed to wait until the right moment to join the fight, and he knew that now wasn't that time, no matter how much he wanted it to be. So he remained hidden among the trees even though every fiber in his being urged him to charge out from the copse and finish the beasts.

Noorsin and the Blademaster were managing the skirmish exactly as they had planned they would, and from where he sat on his horse the two appeared to have matters well in hand. Hopefully that would continue to be the case.

But battles were fickle things, just like toddlers. Well behaved one moment, a terror the next. So better to be prepared.

He and his scouts were a rear guard, just in case. If playing that role didn't prove necessary, then they would join the fight. He and the Blademaster had discussed it the night before. With them both in agreement on the need to ensure that no Ghoule surprises waited for them, it had been an easy thing to convince Noorsin, even though Kevan chafed at having to delay his entry into the battle.

Soon, he promised himself. Very soon. He refused to leave Noorsin on her own against those two Elders for any longer than was necessary.

"Now, Duke Winborne?"

Dani Langston sat on her horse right next to her lord. She was anxious just like he was, although her agitation was more visible than his. He had more experience than she did at keeping emotion in check before a fight.

She wanted to get at the Ghoules just as much as he did. It was obvious. Her hands flexing on her reins. Her lifting herself up on her saddle as if she wanted to urge her horse into a charge right then.

He liked that about her. Still, now, she needed to demonstrate some restraint, because just like her, the scouts with them were itching to go after the Ghoules, and if they went too soon any edge they hoped to enjoy would be lost.

"Just a moment more," replied Kevan. "Make sure the scouts are ready, but also make sure that they don't do anything to reveal our position. This only works if we take the beasts by surprise. So no mistakes."

"Of course, Duke Winborne," replied Dani, who pulled her horse out of the line and walked slowly behind the anxious soldiers, issuing a series of quiet commands.

Kevan continued to watch the fight as it played out in front of him. The Blademaster's Sergeant appearing with several dozen soldiers behind the Ghoules curled his lips into a feral grin. A nice move on Klines' part, and it would help to bring the battle to an end that much sooner when he and his troops now came at the beasts from the sides to close the trap.

Kevan was about to send his soldiers forward to do just that when, as he expected, the unexpected reared its ugly head. More than a half-dozen Ghoule packs led by several Elders burst out of the ground just a few hundred yards behind the Caledonian lines, the beasts sprinting toward the soldiers of the Royal Guard at a frightening pace.

How the beasts had gotten there Kevan had no idea, but that didn't matter right then. This was a worrisome, potentially momentum-changing development. Even with the advance guard's greater numbers and three Magii already in the skirmish, these new arrivals could turn the tide in a matter of seconds, especially those other Elders.

He breathed a brief sigh of relief when he observed the second line of the Royal Guard turn their horses to face the fast-approaching threat. This latest surprise just magnified the importance of the Battersea Guard's role in this fight. So the timing of their involvement just became all the more critical.

"What happened?" hissed Dani.

"They came out of the ground," said Kevan distractedly, watching intently as the Caledonian soldiers now battled Ghoules to their front and their back.

"How could they come out of the ground?" Dani asked in shock.

"A good question, and one to answer when this is over. Not before."

Dani nodded, agreeing with the Duke. "Now?"

"We wait," Kevan grumbled. "We let things play out a few seconds more. We want the Ghoules fully committed, not thinking of what might be coming at their backs."

Kevan could see what was happening, what he had feared would come to pass as the Caledonian lines began to bend inward like two crescents facing away from one another that threatened to touch at the very center as the pressure increased, the Ghoules not only seeking to envelop the soldiers, but also to split the advance guard in two.

It was bad. He couldn't dispute that. Still he waited. He had been a soldier for a long time, and the voice of experience that he tended to listen to in times like these was telling him that he needed to delay just a little bit longer.

"But Duke Winborne, if we wait then the Ghoules may sweep them up. They're almost surrounded and the center on both sides is weakening."

"We wait," Kevan repeated, hating having to do so, even though his gut told him that it was the right decision.

The Ghoules had almost completed their encirclement. He needed the Ghoules to finish what they had started, because as soon as they closed the trap around the Caledonians, the Ghoules would be at their weakest. Their lines would be stretched thin, and it wouldn't take much to break that bubble and put those beasts in a very difficult position.

Considering how fast his heart was beating, it felt like the waiting was killing him. He watched the Blademaster rally his troops and regain control of the center of the lines on both the north and the south. At the same time, Noorsin and the other Magii continued to use the Talent to keep the Elders they had been dueling and the new ones to arrive on the battlefield from turning their attention to the soldiers. The discipline and commitment that were on display truly was an impressive sight.

"Duke Winborne," urged Dani, knowing she was speaking out of turn though unable to stop herself, the situation growing more dire as the Ghoules began to press forward again, compressing the Caledonians' cracking formation. "We need to do something to ..."

"A few seconds more," replied Kevan. Then he sat straighter in his saddle. He saw what he had been looking for. The Ghoules had finished their maneuver. The Blademaster and his troops were surrounded. Completely. As a result, the Ghoules now were heavily overextended and vulnerable.

"We ride for the General!" roared Kevan, pulling his sword from the scabbard attached to his saddle.

When the Duke of the Southern Marches burst from the trees, urging his horse to a gallop, the dozens of scouts hiding in the grove joined him, steel flashing in the bright sunlight, the Battersea Guard racing to join the fight.

NOORSIN HELD her shield constructed from the Talent to her front, blocking another shard of Dark Magic flung at her by one of the two Elders trying to kill her. She had been doing this for the last few minutes, defending against the Elders' coordinated attack, and it was growing tiresome.

She wanted to attack. She wanted to help the Blademaster and his troops. She didn't want to focus all her effort on protecting herself. Yet, she had little choice. Until Maria or Telly defeated the Elders challenging them, she could do nothing other than keep doing what she was doing.

The Elders were smart. One of the beasts stayed right in front of her the whole time, unconcerned by the fighting going on around him, his eyes never leaving hers. This Elder had a very simple task. Send blast after blast of the Curse at her. Whether shards, bolts, or spears of the Dark Magic gifted to him by the Ghoule Overlord, it didn't matter. And it didn't matter if he failed to penetrate her shield. His job was straightforward and critical. Keep her pinned in place.

Noorsin tried to attack the beast a few times, if only to throw him off his stride. She enjoyed little success, because every time she sent a bolt of blazing energy toward the Elder who gazed at her with a frightening intensity, the second Elder who always was just at the edge of her vision tried to catch her off guard, sending a shard of Dark Magic toward her to see if he could kill her when she was distracted, and if not that flank her.

Recognizing the danger of allowing this second Elder to come at her from the side or, even worse, from behind, she sent three bolts of the Talent straight at the feet of the beast whose job it was to keep her engaged. The explosions of dirt right in front of the creature forced him to turn away, finally ending his assault, if only for the next few seconds.

That was all the time that Noorsin needed as she nudged her horse toward the other Elder, who was attempting to sneak up on her left side. The beast almost realized the danger too late, the surprised Elder using his staff of black ash to spin a shield of Dark Magic as quickly as he could, never anticipating that Noorsin would throw a spear of searing energy straight at him. The spike made of the Talent slammed into his shield with such force that it knocked the Elder onto his back, the beast dazed and coughing grit.

Hacking out the last of the dirt, the beast pushed himself up off the ground as quickly as he could. He realized his mistake too late. The shield he had used to protect himself was gone, the power of Noorsin's attack not only knocking him to the ground, but also knocking the staff from his claw.

The Elder frantically scanned the rough terrain for his staff, his heart sinking when he saw the twisted length of wood lying in the dirt and muck thirty feet to his side. The beast gulped. Too far to retrieve it in time.

His failure to hold onto the black ash cost him. With no shield, the second blazing spear that Noorsin threw at him sliced across his knee, the Elder diving to the right just in time to escape the full brunt of the attack. With a hiss of pain and the scent of burning flesh in his nostrils, the injured beast leaped in the direction of the other Elder, who was only now turning his attention back toward the Duchess of Murcia, the gritty cloud of grime that had swirled around him finally dissipating to the point where he could see again.

Noorsin cursed herself for her ineptitude. She should have killed the Elder when she had the chance, the beast recovering faster from her initial strike than she thought possible. Still, she had wounded him, and she had prevented him from getting behind her, which was the most important consideration now that the first Elder was again sending shards of Dark Magic toward her in a constant barrage that forced her back on the defensive.

Noorsin growled in anger. This wasn't working.

Something needed to change, otherwise these two Elders would be the death of her. Yet, that was out of her control at the moment. She could not join the larger fight until she finished her own combat.

Her irritation and concern over her circumstances began to dominate her thoughts, and when she heard the Blademaster's strong voice issue a series of commands designed to bring the Royal Guard together into a defensive shell, her hope of turning the tide faded.

The Ghoules had closed their trap. They were surrounded.

KLINES REALIZED that they had reached the crux of the battle. With the cavalry charges complete and his squads now in a punishing fight against the Ghoules, he knew that the next few minutes would be critical. This was the moment when the fight could turn against them more than it already had, and if it did, he feared that they wouldn't be able to turn the tide back in the direction that favored them.

His soldiers were doing well against the Ghoules, so long as they kept to the tactics that he had been drilling into them for the last several weeks. Yet there was no accounting for the physical attributes of the Ghoules. Several of the beasts succeeded in breaking out of the traps his soldiers set for them, either leaping right over a horse or shooting through a gap when two soldiers didn't close the space between them fast enough.

When that happened, the Ghoules used their newly gained freedom wisely, attacking individual soldiers while the squad tried to regain its order. If the squad reformed and came to the aid of their comrade quickly, there was a chance that the soldier might survive the encounter with the Ghoule.

More often than not, however, the Ghoules employed their astonishing speed to great effect, making quick work of the isolated soldier by using their spears and claws to rip through their leather armor and into their flesh before moving on to the next victim, stalking any unwary soldiers who might not be keeping an eye on their backs.

That's what Klines was hoping to prevent right then, Ghoules getting easy kills against his men, as he rode through the battle looking for just those situations, coming to a soldier's aid when necessary with the hope that the man's compatriots would join the combat soon thereafter and trap the beast once again.

He had given himself a difficult assignment, he knew. By his count he had killed three Ghoules who had escaped from his squads and tried to come at individual soldiers from behind, and even still, his efforts hadn't been enough. The Ghoules were too fast, too many, and too skilled.

He couldn't be everywhere at once, and he feared that he wouldn't be able to help the soldier just ten yards in front of him. The man was so focused on working with his team to keep a Ghoule within the noose they set that he wasn't even aware that another of the beasts was creeping up on him from behind. Nevertheless, Klines had to try.

Urging his mount to a gallop, the war horse dug its hooves into the dirt and rock and raced toward the Ghoule. Klines had no intention of using his sword against the beast, the odds of a killing strike low. Instead he slammed into the beast from behind, the horse's shoulder knocking the creature to the ground, its steel-shod hooves crushing the beast's head into a bloody pulp with a good kick.

Through a stroke of luck, Klines didn't even need to change direction to make his next attack, his horse galloping toward the squad just thirty yards ahead of him. The trapped Ghoule was in the midst of jumping right over the soldier who had been stalked by the beast that was now no more than a crumpled mass of broken bones and flesh. Exactly when the Ghoule's clawed feet touched the ground outside the noose, the Blademaster was there, slicing across the beast's throat with his steel.

Klines' attack had been so fast and such a surprise, the Ghoule didn't register the wound he had received for several seconds. When the beast did, he dropped his sword and clutched at the bone-deep slash as a thick black blood seeped down his chest.

The Ghoule was dead, it was just a matter of time. But to speed the process along, the soldier the beast had jumped over turned his mount deftly, plunging his spearpoint through the beast's back and out through his chest.

Klines nodded to the soldier as the man pulled his spear free from the Ghoule, the young man pleased to have been noticed by the Blademaster. His soldiers managing the clash as well as could be expected on this section of the battlefield, Klines moved on, looking for another chance to assist his fighters.

What he saw when he scanned the rough country troubled him. It was just as he and the Duchess of Murcia feared would come to pass if they became engaged in a prolonged struggle.

Despite their best efforts, the Royal Guard was becoming more and more disconnected. Many soldiers were having to take on the Ghoules on their own now, the beasts escaping or evading the traps with an alarming frequency. If that continued, and Klines had no doubt that it would, soon their position no longer would be tenable. They needed to adopt new tactics. Immediately. Otherwise, the Ghoules would sweep them from the field.

Fortuitously, Benin appeared right in front of him.

"Sergeant!" called Klines. "Into a square! As fast as we can!"

Benin didn't even bother to respond, instead just issuing a stream of orders, understanding what his commander had in mind and the necessity for the adjustment in their approach. The other Sergeants repeated Benin's commands as they moved across the battlefield, urging the soldiers to pull back from the Ghoules and assume their place in the slowly coalescing formation.

It was a difficult maneuver at the best of times. Their success at forming a square was made all the more impressive because they accomplished the task while also disengaging from the Ghoules, who were intent on forcing their way in between the soldiers as they wheeled their horses into formation.

After the passage of several agonizing minutes, during which Klines worried that they wouldn't be able to do it, the square finally took shape. Through it all, the Ghoules continued to attack, trying to push their way past the soldiers, lunging with their spears, swords, and claws for flesh, human and horse, the Caledonians fighting desperately to hold them off.

The double line of soldiers, spears to the front, swords in the back, prevented the beasts from breaking through. Even more important, the Ghoules had little chance of success if they tried to leap over the first line of soldiers to get into the square.

The few who tried it landed on the steel of the second rank of soldiers who were waiting for just such an opportunity.

Still, Klines' worry grew. Noorsin and the other two Magii appeared to be holding their own against the Elders opposing them, the individual battles between those skilled in the Talent and those cursed with Dark Magic a stalemate. So, thankfully, his soldiers remained free of that fight. For how much longer, however, he couldn't say.

That combined with the fact that the Ghoules' pressure was not going to lessen in any way -- in fact, that pressure appeared to be increasing as a pack of the beasts massed right in front of him for the next attack -- suggested that time was not on their side.

Eventually, no matter how hard or how well they fought, the Ghoules would break through. Of that, Klines had no doubt. And when the beasts did, that would be the beginning of the end.

Klines wracked his brains, searching for something else that he could do to improve his soldiers' chances of surviving this fight. The change to this new formation, although it gave his soldiers more protection, also limited their choices. They had nowhere else to go with the Ghoules swarming around them.

Kill or be killed. Why one of Declan's many sayings popped into his head at that moment, he didn't know. But it certainly seemed appropriate. Klines was about to urge his soldiers on as they went toe to toe with the beasts when the words died in the back of his throat.

He felt it before he heard it. It was barely perceptible at first because of the din of the clash, the ground beginning to rumble gently as if they were experiencing a tremor. That rumble quickly became a deafening roar, confirming what the Blademaster had been hoping for, Klines allowing a menacing smile to crack his grim countenance.

Heavy hooves pounded the earth, the rhythmic thumping growing louder with each passing second, small stones and dirt bouncing up off the shaking ground.

What the Royal Guard needed to turn this battle in their favor had arrived.

~

"Are you ready, Corporal?" shouted the Duke of the Southern Marches.

Kevan rode right next to Dani at the head of the long row of soldiers keeping pace with them, one hundred fighters to Kevan's left, the other hundred soldiers who had been operating as scouts for the Caledonian Army on Dani's right. They galloped directly at the Blademaster's square, what Kevan viewed as the front of the formation because of all the Ghoules massing there for their next assault under the direction of the Elders who had led these beasts out of the ground.

"More than ready," Dani shouted in reply, the steady pounding of hooves on the rough ground making it difficult to hear.

Kevan nodded, expecting nothing less than that answer from her. She had been chomping at the bit to get into the action since they had taken their places in the grove, watching the battle unfold.

"Good. I'll meet you on the other side of the formation. We break ... now!"

Dani immediately raised her spear and pointed it toward the right, guiding her horse in that direction, the soldiers on her side adjusting to her movement effortlessly. In less than a minute, she rode in the center of the front rank, fifty soldiers strong, a second rank ten yards behind them having just as many soldiers.

She glanced quickly to her left, seeing that the Duke's

troops had performed the same difficult maneuver just as efficiently as she and her soldiers had. Good. Just as she had assumed would be the case.

Captain Tentillin was a stickler for doing everything exactly the way that he wanted it to be done. Rather than becoming aggravated by his expectations, or making fun of his peccadilloes behind his back, the men and women of the Battersea Guard worked hard to meet their Captain's standards, because they had learned time and time again that his acute attention to detail and his exceedingly stringent requirements helped to keep them alive.

They appreciated that, and they respected him for it. Because he wouldn't put in the effort, he wouldn't be so demanding, if he didn't care.

Dani turned her focus back to the battle they were galloping toward. Although they were seconds away from attacking the most dangerous foes that any of them had ever faced during their time in the Battersea Guard, she couldn't stop herself from smiling.

No more waiting. She hated waiting. Now it was time to fight, and that was something that she excelled at. There were few better than her in the Guard.

Rather than targeting the front of the square, the Battersea Guard put a subtler plan into motion. One designed to break the Ghoules' encirclement and leave the beasts at a decided disadvantage.

At least that's what Kevan hoped would happen. As he had already discovered once that afternoon, the only thing to expect during a fight with the Ghoules, other than a ferocious and lethal opponent, was the unexpected.

Even so, the beasts had played their card already. Now, it was his turn to flip over his and hopefully take the Ghoules by surprise.

The charging cavalry raced across the uneven ground,

approaching the Royal Guard's square swiftly. The horses competed with one another to go faster as Kevan and his troops angled toward the left side of the formation.

Kevan grinned viciously. The Ghoules hadn't even noticed yet what was coming at them.

They were so focused on trying to take down a few of the soldiers on the perimeter of the square so that they could break into the center that they couldn't be bothered to pay attention to what might be going on behind them or on their flanks. That lack of tactical awareness, mixed with a confidence that bordered on arrogance, was about to cost them dearly.

"For the Marches!" Kevan yelled, pointing his sword toward a Ghoule who stood right in his way, no more than twenty yards in front of him. The beast didn't even realize that he faced a new enemy until he heard the shouts from the soldiers riding with the Duke of the Southern Marches.

By then, it was too late. The war horses were too close. There was no way that the Ghoules fighting on that side of the square could get out of the way in time. In an instant, they became no more than stalks of grass to be mowed down.

Just as the Royal Guard had done at the beginning of the fight, the front rank of the Battersea Guard didn't bother to use their steel, their massive war horses doing more damage to the Ghoules than the soldiers ever could with their blades. The towering beasts were swept away much like a sand dune when one of the massive waves so common to the Silent Sea slammed into the shore and surged up the beach, taking with it every-thing that couldn't withstand its powerful pull.

KLINES' menacing smile turned feral while he watched the soldiers of the Battersea Guard sweep down both sides of the square and then curl around the back of the formation. Duke

Winborne and his troops proved to be exceedingly thorough in their work.

The only thing that could be seen in the wake of their charge were the broken and crushed bodies of the Ghoules, including several Elders who were caught up in the vicious and unyielding storm. The speed of the assault was so fast that the servants of the Ghoule Overlord didn't even have the time to turn their Dark Magic toward the charging cavalry, their bodies and staffs shattered in the sortie and scattered about the churned up ground.

Excellent work. Excellent work, indeed.

Even better, the Duke was kind enough to leave a few Ghoules for the Royal Guard right where he wanted them. Right where his soldiers could cause the beasts the most harm.

"Soldiers of the Royal Guard!" Klines called in a loud voice. "Shift formation on my command!" Klines waited just a few seconds, wanting to give his troops time to process his order and prepare for what was to come next. Most of the soldiers, all of them experienced, having watched the charge of the Battersea Guard, already knew what they were about to do.

"Front wedge!"

The soldiers responded without thinking, having practiced this maneuver until it was second nature. With no pressure on the sides of their formation anymore, and the Battersea Guard eliminating the Ghoules at their rear when the two wings of the cavalry met behind them, the Royal Guard shifted into a triangular formation several rows deep that now faced off against the only Ghoules still standing on the battlefield. No more than a few dozen as best as Klines could tell, supported by only three Elders.

Their next assignment was not necessarily a simple one, though certainly it was one that his soldiers should be able to manage quite well. And they were certainly ready for it, having had enough of the beasts who had threatened to overwhelm them.

"Charge!"

Noorsin crouched down, then raised her left arm so that her shimmering shield protected her entire body. Just in time. A blast of Dark Magic slammed into her, the power of the strike so strong that it almost knocked her off her feet.

To keep her balance, Noorsin took a step back. Then she took one more step back as another blast of the Curse smashed into her shield, the Dark Magic dancing across her barrier before slowly dissipating. And then a third hit, following so closely after the second that her latest step back became a stumble, which she deftly turned into a roll, coming back to her feet with her shield still in front of her so that she was ready for the fourth bolt of Dark Magic the Elder shot at her with his staff.

The Elder she had been battling since the fight began seemed to be less than pleased that she was able to regain her feet so easily, so she took some small pleasure from that fact. Still, she growled in anger. This combat had been going on for far too long.

She was a patient person. She had to be if she was going to function effectively as the Duchess of Murcia. She had a great deal of power, yes, but it could only be exercised in certain ways if she wanted her Duchy to thrive. That required working with others and more often than not building consensus rather than just issuing edicts.

Yet her patience was not an endless well, as those who had pushed her too far in the past had learned to their detriment. And now it was wearing thin. Paper thin, in fact.

The second Elder who had pinned Noorsin in place by

attempting to flank her while she fought the Elder she had just aggravated had become less of a factor as the fight wore on, in large part due to the wound she had inflicted on his leg. The injured beast was beginning to flag, unable to move as well as he had at the beginning of the combat, the injury clearly more severe than he originally thought.

So much so that the beast was now spending most of his time standing in one place, putting most of his weight on his other leg, and when he needed to move, dragging the useless appendage behind him. Every once in a while the beast sent a shard of Dark Magic toward Noorsin just to demonstrate to her that he was still there, that he could still be a danger.

Those reminders had little effect. She deflected his strikes with ease, nothing he did threatening her now so long as she didn't allow herself to get distracted.

She had worried about what might happen when those other Elders who had emerged from underground had joined the fight, admitting that she couldn't take on more than two Elders at a time. Thankfully, Telly and Maria killed the Elders they had been fighting right before these other servants of the Ghoule Overlord appeared, so they were able to step in and hold off these new entrants into the fight for a time. Even so, the three Magii still faced poor odds with five Elders still alive.

And it was the Elder she had been battling since the start of the clash who continued to cause her the most problems. The beast had yet to tire, sending shards of the Curse toward her in an almost constant stream, forcing her to hold onto her shield, barely giving her the chance to attack. In fact, as the minutes passed, the Elder appeared to be getting stronger despite the huge quantity of Dark Magic that he employed.

Noorsin found that fact to be incredibly aggravating. She wanted to kill this beast. She needed to kill this Elder. Because she couldn't join the larger fight until she did. Yet she had not found the crack that she required so that she could disrupt her aggressor's strategy.

With the two Elders holding so much of her attention, Noorsin didn't even notice Kevan and the Battersea Guard joining the fight until they swept right by the front of the Royal Guard's square and then down its sides, scraping those spaces free of Ghoules. It was an impressive sight and one that gave her a brief charge of exhilaration. Best of all for her, the charge swept up the injured Elder, a soldier of the Battersea Guard guiding his mount right at the beast, trampling the Elder and freeing her from having to worry about an attack from behind.

With that threat removed, Noorsin felt lighter, as if a weight had been lifted from her shoulders. She finally shifted from the defensive to the offensive, doing so in the blink of an eye. With the Elder facing off against her distracted by the charge for just a moment, Noorsin let go of her shield and pulled in more of the Talent than she had managed in years, the scalding energy surging through her blood, slightly painful, even more so invigorating.

When the Elder finally looked back toward her, preparing to send another blast of the Curse her way, a streak of blazing energy shot through the air directly toward him. The Elder dodged out of the way, then ducked and moved again, humiliated as he rolled and scrambled through the dirt and the grass, struggling to escape the bolts of power that followed right after him.

The Elder almost made good on his escape, if not for the Ghoule who got in his way.

With the cavalry charging down both sides of the formation, the Ghoules were forced together like fish in a barrel as they desperately tried to avoid getting crushed beneath the war horses' hooves. In the midst of trying to escape the melee, one of those Ghoules was knocked to the ground, his legs tangling with the Elder's so that both of the creatures tumbled to the dirt.

Bad luck for the Elder, good luck for Noorsin, who sent three bolts of energy in quick succession toward her adversary. With a desperate swipe, the beast blocked the first with his staff. After that, his luck ended.

The second bolt slammed right into his chest when the Ghoule who had taken him to the ground tried to scramble back to his clawed feet. With a flailing claw, the beast inadvertently knocked the staff from the Elder's hand, ending any hope of defending himself.

The third bolt slammed into the Elder's back. The fourth wasn't necessary, the Elder and the Ghoule having already collapsed to the soil with smoking holes in their chests.

Her combat with the Elder finally completed, Noorsin didn't take even a second to savor her victory. Instead, she turned her focus toward Telly and Maria. The two Magii had their hands full, working together to prevent three Elders from breaking through the shield that they had created with the Talent that they used to protect not only themselves, but also the soldiers around them from the Dark Magic the beasts sent their way with annoying regularity.

Some situations required delicacy. Others demanded brute force. Having assessed the state of affairs, and her patience long gone, Noorsin decided that there was only one path to take.

Adopting the approach favored by Rafia, Noorsin fixed her gaze upon the three Elders. Raising her hands to the sky, feeling the Talent surge through her, she slashed her hands down to the ground.

An electric charge filled the air, and then a split second later one lightning bolt after another, a half dozen in all, slammed down into the earth, an inescapable procession of power that obliterated the Elders and any Ghoules unfortunate enough to stand too close to them.

That done, Noorsin finally took a deep breath and scanned around her. She and the other Magii had removed all the Elders from the battlefield, Kevan and the Battersea Guard had cleared the Ghoules from three sides of the Royal Guard's square, and the Ghoules remaining to her front were well on their way to being destroyed, the Blademaster having shifted his troops' formation to a wedge, the soldiers just then crashing into the last of the disorganized beasts.

It had been a much more difficult battle than it should have been. They could examine the mistakes they had made later. Now, she needed to focus on the wounded, so she began to walk among the many soldiers lying injured on the ground, assisting those she could, Maria and Telly joining her in her efforts.

"I WAS A FOOL," said Noorsin, muttering a few choice curses under her breath.

"We were all fools," replied Kevan. "We trusted in only what we could see, not thinking about what could be."

"Maybe so," grumbled Noorsin, her anger at herself still hot after spending the last few hours healing the wounded and burying the dead. She knew that her thinking might be slightly irrational as a result. Still, she blamed herself for the outcome of the day's battle. They had won, yes, though at a terrible cost, losing more than a third of their fighters. "But I'm the fool with the Talent who failed to detect the second wave of Ghoules. I'm the fool with the Talent who searched right over where these beasts were hiding and didn't find them."

Noorsin continued to berate herself in her own head. How many of these soldiers would still be alive, how many of these soldiers would not have been wounded at all, if they had known of the Ghoules who had hidden themselves below the ground to their rear?

Yes, she hated being made to look the fool. Even more, she hated the price that these soldiers had paid for her folly.

Kevan didn't bother to respond, understanding that nothing he said at the moment would help her. Instead, he thought about all that had occurred during the battle.

The soldiers had performed admirably. They had been taken by surprise and fought through it, measuring themselves against the Ghoules and the Elders and coming out ahead. Most important, despite the losses suffered, despite the challenges of the clash, they had defeated the Ghoules placed to block their entry into the Winter Pass.

Because these Ghoules had been put right here. He had no doubt of that. Clearly, they were bait so that the Ghoules buried beneath the ground would have a chance to come at them from behind.

That ploy had failed in the end, and the entrance to the Winter Pass now stood open. They could begin moving into that forbidding space once the bulk of the Caledonian Army reached them later that evening.

They had also learned a great deal regarding their enemy's tactics and strategy. The beasts' surprise attack had worked. Yet because of the trap that they had set, the Ghoules had been overconfident, and the beasts had never expected that their opponents would set out to inveigle them as well.

That was useful information.

Along with the fact that everything that he had learned from Tarin and those who had already fought the Ghoules in larger skirmishes had proven accurate. The Ghoules were stronger, faster, more agile. They could leap over a mounted soldier with relative ease if they were given the space to do so. They were vicious fighters. Surrender was never a consideration, nor was mercy, either giving or receiving.

Furthermore, although the Caledonians took the initiative at the start of the fight and had the larger force -- more than three times as many fighters, in fact -- the Ghoules hadn't been concerned in the least, recovering from the initial assault and then almost turning the tide entirely. If the Battersea Guard had not arrived when they did, the victory would have gone to the Ghoules, and the soldiers of the Royal Guard would already be in the beasts' cook pots.

So it had been a much closer fight than any of them would have liked and what had happened during this battle would affect their strategy going forward. Perhaps most important, this clash confirmed just how critical it was to have the assistance of the members of the Order of the Magii whenever engaging with a large number of the beasts or when facing off with Elders. Without the Magii, the Caledonians stood no chance against the Ghoules because they had no way to defend themselves against the Elders' Dark Magic.

Assuming that more Magii heeded Noorsin and Sirius' call for aid and came to the Winter Pass, once the practitioners of the Talent began to appear they would need to use the Magii's unique skills wisely. There were more Elders than Magii, so making sure that they always had Magii to oppose the Elders would take some work.

And they would need to avoid any engagements with Elder Ghoules if Magii weren't available, though coordinating that might prove difficult when they entered the gorge. The terrain with the mountains pressing on their sides also might require a shift in tactics, and Kevan could tell just from this one battle that they would need to be creative if they were to have any chance of keeping these beasts from flooding the Kingdom.

"Are you done yet?" Kevan finally asked, giving Noorsin a wink to show that he wasn't upset with her, rather he was simply trying to gain her attention.

Noorsin and Kevan had walked back to where the Ghoules

had emerged out of the ground behind the Caledonians, the Duchess of Murcia still cursing up a storm.

For just a moment, Kevan thought that Noorsin was going to offer a few choice words in his direction, her raptorlike gaze suggesting that, in fact, she was not done berating herself and that she didn't appreciate his interruption. After several heartbeats, though, she sighed, which seemed to release a good bit of her anger. Then she nodded toward what they had found, turning her mind toward the Ghoules' ruse and away from her perceived failings.

"They didn't just do this in a day. It took them several weeks. They've been planning this for quite some time."

"Yes, I certainly didn't expect this," admitted Kevan, staring down into the darkness of the hole. He judged its circumference to be about ten feet wide and just as deep. It would be difficult for a man to climb out of the pit. For a Ghoule it was an easy jump. In one corner he saw a slightly lighter coloring to the darkness. The beasts had dug a tunnel into the side of the hole. "How did we miss this?"

"The Ghoules dug the hole, tunneled deeper underground, and then the Ghoules who were waiting for us at the stream filled the hole in with the dirt. The Elders we fought at the beginning of the battle used the Curse to tell the Elders waiting in the tunnel that it was time to join the fight. The Ghoules then dug themselves free in a matter of minutes."

"Buried alive," mused Kevan. "A scary thought unless you can dig yourself out from ten feet down without any trouble at all. How far down does the tunnel run?"

"On the eastern side of the hole that tunnel runs more than fifty feet beneath the ground to a larger chamber that's been hollowed out," explained Noorsin, having used the Talent to map out in her mind the subterranean construction. "It's large enough to hold several hundred Ghoules. I assume that's where the Ghoules waited until the time was right for them to make their appearance."

"Clever. Much too clever." The Ghoules weren't very good at building fortifications, yet they had done an excellent job of digging a tunnel and chamber that the Magii had failed to notice. "We'll need to keep this tactic in mind when we move into the Winter Pass. If they can dig this here, they can do it anywhere. I would hate to have these beasts coming at me from both sides while in the Pass. We also need to think about what else they might have in mind with these tunnels."

"Agreed," said Noorsin. "I'll speak with the other Magii and make sure that they're all aware of what they need to look for now when they're searching with the Talent." She shook her head, biting her lip, her irritation rising once again. "This was my fault. When I searched for threats, I never thought to scan below ground. I never considered the possibility that the Ghoules could be so wily and might take such an approach."

"You can't beat yourself up about it."

Kevan would have liked to have pulled Noorsin into his arms, to comfort her, to whisper in her ear that everyone had made mistakes, not just her. But he couldn't. Not at that moment. Because at that moment, she wasn't Noorsin, the woman who he had yet to tell he loved. Rather, she was the General of the Caledonian Army.

"Why not? It was my fault."

"Because that doesn't help anyone."

"I should have …"

"We had no cause to believe that the beasts would dig below us. We didn't even know that they were capable of doing something like this. From everything we've learned so far, we believed that the Ghoules employed few tactics at best. Now we know differently, and we can use that information in the future."

"Still, I should have …"

"Enough, Noorsin," Kevan said, his voice a bit harsher than he wanted, though it did cut her off and made her look at him. "You made a mistake. You made an assumption, an assumption that we all made in fact, and now we know not to make that assumption again. The next time you search for the Ghoules, you'll need to look below ground. Simple as that."

"That may be, but ..."

"Duke Winborne is correct, Duchess Stelekel," said the Blademaster, who had walked over after making sure that the soldiers had gotten a good start on setting up their camp for the night, focusing in particular on the sentries. They had decided to move into the wood that Kevan had used to hide the Battersea Guard, not wanting to be caught in the open if any Ghoules decided to attack during the night. The Caledonian Army would follow the advance guard and enter the Winter Pass in force on the morrow. "We had no idea the Ghoules would do this. We had no idea they could do this. There's quite a bit we don't know about them. Now we know this. Now we can use this to our advantage, just as Duke Winborne said."

Noorsin reluctantly grumbled her agreement. "I still don't like being fooled by the Ghoules. I promise you both that I won't allow it to happen again."

"Of that we have no doubt," said the Blademaster with a nod, in his mind the matter closed. "We must remember as well that we stand no chance against the Elders without you and the other Magii."

"Captain Klines has the right of it," agreed Kevan. "You put on quite a display against those Elders."

"Now you see why I'm here," Noorsin replied, her dry humor rising to the surface once again, working its way past her self-recrimination. "I'm not just a pretty face."

"I never thought that you were a pretty face, Noorsin."

For just a moment, Noorsin stared at Kevan, his words bringing a quirk to her lips. It took him a moment to realize how what he had said could be interpreted, Captain Klines smiling at his sudden discomfort, having instantly caught his gaffe.

"I am your General -- not by choice -- and I am also a healer and will do all that I can for the wounded," said Noorsin. "But I hope that you see that I'm also a fighter."

"You made that abundantly clear," nodded Kevan, amazed at how easily she had destroyed the Elders who were challenging Maria and Telly. "Frighteningly so, in fact."

6

TAKING STOCK

She didn't want to, but it might prove necessary. If she had no choice, would she be able to kill him?

And even if she had the stomach for it, which she did, could she?

She feared not.

Not because she didn't have the drive to do it. Not because she actually liked him.

If there was a need to kill him, she would do everything in her power to make that happen. She would do what was required.

No, rather, she discovered much to her chagrin that she didn't have the strength.

She had watched in amazement at what he had done, astounded by how much power he had exercised at one time. She had never seen the like, only hearing of such things from Sirius when he regaled her with stories of the Ten Magii.

It had given her hope that he could complete the task that only he could attempt.

It had also made her afraid. With that much power, it

wouldn't take much to push him over the edge. It wouldn't take much for the Curse to take him.

That couldn't be permitted. For his sake and for their own.

She was certain that Sirius would help her if there was a need. But she was a realist.

Even combining their strength in the Talent, she didn't think that they could do it on their own.

They would need help.

Blast it! Why did they have to contemplate this? Why couldn't everything work out in the end just as she wanted? Without any complications?

But she knew why. Life didn't work that way. It was never simple. It was never clean.

She simply couldn't escape the fact that no matter how much she didn't like it, in this instance he was a tool to be used ... and to be discarded if circumstances warranted.

He wasn't just the young man she had met on the pier at Haven. He was much more than that now.

A possible savior of the Kingdom and also the potential catalyst of its destruction.

Which one he would be had not yet been determined.

Both, perhaps?

Grumbling in disgust as she worried about things that she didn't want to worry about, Rafia pushed herself up from the log that she had been sitting on, grabbing a large metal spoon that lay on a rock by her feet and giving the stew she had set over the small fire a few stirs. She then took a careful taste, blowing first to cool it, careful not to burn her lips. She smiled.

Cooking was one of her hobbies, something that she enjoyed and excelled at, and the vegetable stew simmering in the cast-iron pot was no exception. She added just a pinch more of the spices that she always carried with her, then sat back down. A few minutes more and it would be done.

A welcome distraction, although cooking wouldn't give her the answers she needed.

Frustrated, she turned her thoughts away from her dilemma, taking in the pinpricks of light that dotted her vision.

Several other campfires dimly broke through the unrelenting gloom of the Dark Forest. After the skirmish earlier in the day, the conversations around those other fires were muted at best, most of the soldiers of the Blood Company eating quietly, reliving in their own minds their combats against the Ghoules.

Many of the gladiators called this unavoidable introspection the Curse of Declan, having continued the practice they learned in the Pit from the Master of the Gladiators. It was an exceedingly personal and contemplative exercise that all of the gladiators had come to value, because taking the time to replay in their minds their combats right after their conclusion often provided insights that they would not have discovered otherwise. And, as Declan had shown them, everything they learned, they could use to keep themselves alive during future engagements.

When Bryen had explained the process to her, Rafia had been impressed by the Master of the Gladiators' thoroughness. Everything she learned about Declan confirmed that he had done all that he could to ensure that the gladiators consigned to the Pit had the best possible chance of living to see another day.

Rafia smiled again, a rare occurrence for her these days. It was nice to be thinking about someone other than Sirius for a change. She and the old Magus had too much history. Too much baggage. Every conversation they had now always transformed into an argument.

Every day. Guaranteed.

Admittedly, there had been a time when she enjoyed the

constant give and take between them. The disagreements. The clashes.

The challenge of engaging with him had excited her. Made her feel alive.

Rafia sighed wistfully. Not anymore. Now she just felt tired. She didn't want to fight with Sirius. She just wanted to move on. Yet she was finding it incredibly difficult to make the necessary break.

She wasn't sure how Sirius felt, so she wasn't certain of how to raise the issue with him. She was good in a confrontation when the knives came out or the Talent was required, but not when she wanted to protect the other person's feelings.

Trying to settle her nerves, Rafia decided to engage in the Curse of Declan herself, her thoughts drifting back to the fight against the Ghoules not too far from where she sat now. For her, it had been a straightforward affair. Once the Ghoules had seen through her and Sirius' illusion, she had jumped right into the clash, turning one Elder to ash before the fight really even began and then taking on two other Elders.

She killed one in less than a minute with a bolt of energy that had ripped through the beast's chest and then struck two more Ghoules who were standing behind the beast before the energy finally smashed into the trunk of a heart tree, leaving a large scorch mark on the bark. Again, there had been little challenge in that combat, and there was little for her to learn, other than the fact that attacking first before your opponent was ready was the right thing to do.

The last Elder had proven more difficult to kill. That combat had stretched on for several minutes longer than it should have, beginning as expected with the Talent as she sought to counter the beast's Dark Magic. She had held off the Elder's attacks fairly easily. Even so, she had failed to penetrate the beast's defenses.

Thinking back on that portion of the duel, she couldn't

identify anything she could have done that would have allowed her to remove the Elder from the fight with greater speed. The only weapon that could have helped was the lightning bolt that she so preferred. Unfortunately, the terrain and the flow of the combats around her didn't permit her to employ that tactic against the beast. She feared that too many of the soldiers of the Blood Company would be caught in the blast.

So rather than allow the combat to continue longer than was safe, Rafia had drawn the short sword that was always sheathed in a scabbard across her back, infused the steel with the Talent, and then charged the beast. That had proven to be a good decision, her quick change in tactics leading to the Elder's demise.

Still, thinking on it, she had chosen a risky way to end the fight, placing herself in greater danger than she needed to. So a good decision though perhaps not the only decision that she could have made.

Her charge had caught the Elder by surprise, the beast so focused on using the Curse against her that he was slow to get his staff in a position to stop her thrust with her short sword, which slid cleanly through his heart. Of course, if she hadn't surprised the Elder and he had responded more swiftly, perhaps the beast would have realized that she had left herself open to a counterattack along her exposed ribs, which thankfully never came. So a lesson learned, and she promised herself that she would never make that same mistake again.

Eliminating the Elders so quickly had given her a few moments to watch the end of the fight among the heart trees between her comrades in arms and the Ghoules. She had to admit that she was impressed by what she saw. The Company of Blood demonstrated a great deal of skill and experience, a backbone and composure that she had rarely seen during her centuries of observing the clash of arms and was absolutely essential when fighting these monsters.

The Company enjoyed just a little bit of luck as well. None of the creatures escaped. So they had a day or two now to regroup and prepare for what was likely coming their way as they continued toward the Trench and the Sanctuary.

Needless to say, no one had enjoyed better luck earlier that day than the Protector. Bryen had been a fool to pursue the Elder on his own. It was too risky, even for him. Because of his recklessness, he had almost died. He would have if not for the Spear of the Magii and his ability to harness the power of the Seventh Stone so that he could heal himself.

Cursing his stupidity under her breath as she reviewed what had happened, Rafia hoped that Bryen was himself engaged in the Curse of Declan, reliving the fight. If he wasn't, she feared that his recklessness would lead if not to his premature death, which was something that none of them could afford to allow at the moment, then to a fate worse than death, a fate that had put her thoughts on the bleak path on which she had been traveling for far too long that evening.

That last fear gave way to a more immediate concern. Bryen had used the power of the Seventh Stone to heal himself. The Ghoule Overlord's servants strong in the Curse, if they weren't too far away from the fight, would have sensed it. Because of that concern, she had been using the Talent to check around them periodically, extending her senses more than a hundred leagues or more.

She did so again right then, identifying the Ghoules who were near the Shattered Peaks. They posed no immediate threat as they were a good distance away. Several packs were farther to the east as well; however, those beasts appeared to be more interested in the Caledonian Army that was marching toward the Winter Pass. So the Company of Blood was safe enough for now. For how much longer that would prove to be the case she simply didn't know.

What irritated her the most was that her worry refused to

go away, and when it burdened her like it did now, she had learned through hard experience to listen to it. Whatever was bothering her, beyond her concerns regarding the Ghoules and the Curse and the Seventh Stone, and was giving her this feeling that something was crawling up her spine, would remain with her until she identified the cause, her inability to do just that souring her mood even more.

Not knowing how else to address this niggling worry, she was about to use the Talent to search around them once again with the hope that she could finally discover what was troubling her when she sensed a presence standing behind her. It was hidden among the shadows that were being thrown up against the trunk of the heart tree and the thick roots that curled away from it by her small cooking fire.

It was not the person that she perhaps naively hoped would visit her fire that evening. But it was the person she needed to speak with after Bryen's scare earlier in the day, for Bryen's sake and theirs.

"You can come out of the darkness, Aislinn. No reason to hide there. I won't bite."

There was a quiet shuffle in the darkness, confirming for Rafia that the Lady of the Southern Marches was unsure of herself, struggling with why she had come there. After several seconds had passed, Aislinn walked into the light, her hands in her cloak, twisting the edges of the fabric. It was her biggest tell, Rafia had discovered. When she was nervous, her hands always needed something to do.

"I'm sorry. I didn't mean to disturb you. You seemed to be enjoying the quiet."

"You're not disturbing me at all," replied Rafia, choosing to keep to herself that Aislinn was correct. She had been enjoying the quiet quite a bit because it was so rare these days. Still, Rafia was glad that she had come to talk because they had much to discuss. "Would you care to join me for dinner? I am quite a good cook even if Sirius doesn't agree with me."

"That's very kind of you. Thank you." Aislinn smiled hesitantly, her expression then returning to the slight frown Rafia had noticed when she had walked into the light. "I'm sure you're a much better cook than I am."

"Let's hope so," replied Rafia with a grin, trying to help the Lady of the Southern Marches relax just a bit. Clearly, she had something on her mind.

Rafia rose from where she was sitting on her log, gave the stew a final stir and a quick taste, glad that she had added that last small pinch of spices, and then with a nod of silent congratulations to herself spooned out enough for two bowls, handing one to Aislinn, who sat across the fire from her, before she returned to her own seat.

For the first few minutes, they ate in silence, famished as a result of the day's excitement and enjoying one another's company. It wasn't until Aislinn was scraping the bottom of her bowl that she revealed why she had come to visit with the Magus.

"Do you mind if I talk plainly?"

"Not at all, I'd prefer it," Rafia said, placing her empty bowl next to her on the log. "You didn't come here just for my cooking."

"No, sorry, I didn't. Although the stew is delicious."

"That's kind of you to say. It took me several years to perfect the spice blend. Once I did, I have to work really hard to ruin the stew."

Aislinn smiled wanly and nodded, still struggling with how to begin, delaying just a bit longer before raising the topic that had brought her to Rafia's campfire. "I have little experience in cooking. Perhaps I could learn a thing or two from you."

"I'd be happy to teach you what I know," Rafia replied, understanding that Aislinn was still searching for the best way to raise the issue that was at the top of mind. The Magus decided to give her a gentle nudge, just to help her out. "I know you didn't come here for my cooking. What did you want to discuss?"

"Well, I really wanted to get your thoughts on …"

Aislinn stopped herself. Was she prepared for where this conversation could lead? For what might be required of her if her suspicions were correct?

"I was curious as to your perspective on …" she tried again.

Her discomfort regarding the issue plaguing her caught her midbreath again, her face flushing furiously. She was thankful that it was difficult to see in the flickering firelight, as it helped to hide her embarrassment.

Aislinn grumbled at herself in irritation. She was the Lady of the Southern Marches. She had faced down Marden Beleron. She had held her own against Tetric. She had won the respect of the Blademaster and the Royal Guard. After doing all that, why couldn't she talk about the issue that had been bothering her ever since Bryen had saved himself from the Curse.

"I'm just not certain what to do …"

"Just spit it out girl," urged Rafia, her patience, never good to begin with, already coming to an end. "We don't have all night."

"What am I supposed to do about Bryen?"

Aislinn almost shouted, requiring the quick burst of emotion to eject the words. She was uncomfortable revealing the primary cause of her issue, but she was also relieved to have finally done so.

Rafia didn't reply right away. Instead, she studied the young woman sitting across the fire from her. She had already proven her mettle many times over. And Aislinn demonstrated many of the same qualities that her Protector exhibited as well.

Strength of spirit. Implacability in the face of difficult odds. A lack of fear when difficult decisions needed to be made. As well as a natural reluctance or perhaps even fear when needing to discuss matters of a more personal nature.

"That's a loaded question, Aislinn, and it could be interpreted many different ways." Rafia believed that she understood Aislinn's meaning, though she couldn't be certain. And she knew that she couldn't be the one to raise the issue. So she had decided to come at it from a more roundabout way that might make it easier for Aislinn.

"Rafia!" protested Aislinn, catching the Magus' slightly inappropriate grin and wink.

"All right, all right. I was just having a little fun with you. What's the problem with Bryen?"

"It's just that he ..."

"It's not the scars, is it? On his neck and cheek? On most of him, actually, which isn't surprising considering how long he fought in the Pit. Some women find scars to be quite attractive. It makes them feel like they're getting into something dangerous ..."

"No, it's not the scars," answered Aislinn quickly, "and I think we can both agree that Bryen and danger are essentially synonymous. It's the fact ..."

"The fact that he's so quiet? Some women like that too, you know. They like a man to stay quiet so they can talk up a storm, you know, demonstrate who's really in charge." Rafia took a moment to think about that, seeing that she had thrown her visitor for a loop based on Aislinn's expression, which had been her intention. "That doesn't really fit Bryen, does it? He's more of the strong and silent type. Which do you prefer?"

"The fact that Bryen tends to be quiet doesn't bother me. The reason I'm here is that ..."

"He's always there for you. Helping you. Looking out for you. That has got to be really annoying after a while."

"No, that has nothing to do with it," said Aislinn, knowing Rafia was teasing her to lighten her mood, and for some other reason as well that she couldn't quite figure out. Strangely, it seemed to be working. "I like the ..."

"The looks he gives you and the light touches, almost as if he cares about you beyond just the connection that you had when he was your Protector?"

"Not the looks and the touches," said Aislinn, distracted by Rafia's last comment, which broke her train of thought. "Although I do worry at times about how he would perceive me if he hadn't been forced to be my Protector."

"That's a wasted thought," said Rafia, setting the joking aside. "The fact is that he was your Protector and nothing can change that. He was your Protector and you were his charge. That's the way it was. Simply accept it and move on. Whether that played a large or small role in how your current relationship with Bryen developed isn't important, other than the fact that without that interaction you probably wouldn't have a relationship with Bryen at all. He'd still be on the white sand or dead and you'd probably be married to Marden Beleron, so although I disagreed strenuously with what your father did, in the end it actually proved beneficial for both you and Bryen as well as the Kingdom."

"I guess you're right about that," said Aislinn.

"So we're done," said Rafia. "I'm glad that I could help."

"That's not really why I'm here," protested Aislinn. "You didn't give me a chance to ..."

"It's his relationship with Lycia, isn't it? They're close. I know. It was likely unavoidable considering how intense it must have been for the two of them in the Pit."

"Yes," Aislinn replied, then quickly corrected herself as she tried to keep up with Rafia. "I mean no."

"Which is it, Aislinn?" huffed Rafia with just a touch of vexation. "Yes or no?"

"It's both. You're not giving me a chance to answer."

"I disagree. You seem to be having a great deal of difficulty saying what you mean. What do you mean?"

"I am trying to say what I mean," replied Aislinn, her temper swelling. This wasn't how she expected this conversation to go. She knew by reputation that Rafia could be difficult, yet she hadn't prepared herself for this, and they hadn't even gotten to the real issue yet. "What I mean to say is that yes, Lycia worried me some because of her previous relationship with Bryen. I know that will never go away, the closeness they have, but I spoke with Bryen about it and he explained where he stands now. Where we stand now. I feel good enough about that conversation to believe that their relationship has changed since Bryen left the Pit and that his feelings for Lycia have changed as well. But that's not why I came here to speak with you."

"Then what's the problem?" demanded Rafia, allowing her exasperation to show, although it was actually more to drive the conversation along than anything else. To move it in the direction that she needed it to go. "Obviously, you like him. Obviously, he likes you. It's pretty simple when you have those two variables fixed in place. Unless, of course, it's the fact that Bryen has become the Seventh Stone and no one has any idea how this little adventure of ours is going to play out."

"Yes, that's why I'm here," Aislinn finally admitted, sighing in frustration. "I didn't come here to speak with you about my relationship with Bryen. It's of little relevance compared to the larger issue of his fight against the Curse. I'm afraid for him."

Rafia nodded sagely. "That's what I thought. It was as clear as day."

"If it was as clear as day, why did you bring up all that other stuff?" demanded Aislinn. "Really, Rafia, maybe this was a bad idea."

"The delay came from you, Aislinn, not me."

"But you were throwing out ..."

"I was throwing out a few things that came to mind that I knew would at least get you thinking so that you could get beyond the barrier that has been keeping you from having this conversation. I figured we would get there eventually. I just wasn't sure when as my raising the issue wouldn't have helped you."

"You say that with such confidence," replied Aislinn. "I don't know if I should believe you. I still think that you ..."

"Aislinn, let's focus on why we're here and not allow ourselves to get sidetracked as you did at the beginning of this conversation."

"I didn't," protested Aislinn, her voice containing a touch of pique. "That was you. You were the one who ..."

"Now you are primarily concerned about the fact that Bryen is the Seventh Stone and that he faces a task that no Magus has ever accomplished on his or her own before."

"Yes, that's right," growled Aislinn, realizing that continuing to argue with Rafia about who was really responsible for all the tangents in their conversation was a waste of time, understanding slowly dawning within her as well.

Rafia's cross examination was a masterclass of manipulation. She put that to the side. She would think on how she could add that skill to her repertoire later.

"Are you worried that Bryen is going to die?"

"Of course I'm worried about that. Aren't you?"

"Are you worried that you might be the person who has to kill him?"

"Why would I have to kill him?" asked Aislinn, her shock obvious.

"Because if he makes even the tiniest of mistakes and the Curse takes him -- just as almost happened today -- we have no choice but to kill him." Rafia's voice was hard as she learned across the fire toward Aislinn, locking eyes with her, wanting to make sure that every word she said registered with the Lady of the Southern Marches. "Since Bryen is the Seventh Stone, not only can he repair the Weir, at least theoretically, but he also can challenge the Ghoule Overlord because of the Curse contained within and the special properties of the Seventh Stone. That burden or ability, depending on your perspective, also means he's at greater risk because of what the Seventh Stone is and can do for him and to him. If Bryen turns to the Curse he becomes something worse than the Ghoule Overlord. We will have no choice but to kill him then, because once the Curse takes him, it will never let him go. He will no longer be himself. He will be a tool of the Dark Magic against which we will have no defense."

"I had thought about that but hadn't taken it to its logical conclusion as you just so starkly portrayed it," Aislinn said softly. "I just hoped that ..." Aislinn shook her head dejectedly, the full ramifications of what Rafia had just said hitting her.

"I didn't think you had," Rafia replied sadly, commiserating with Aislinn. "Clearly, your mind was focused on a different dynamic of this equation."

"Yes, but don't you think that there's a way ..."

"Can you do it?"

"Can I do what?" demanded Aislinn, the sharpness of her tone demonstrating that she was getting tired of the Magus interrupting her.

"Can you kill Bryen if you need to?"

Aislinn allowed several seconds to pass before responding, her hands twisting the cloth of her cloak. "I don't know," she said in a whisper.

"You don't know because of how strong he is in the Talent and how much stronger he will be with the Curse or you don't know because you love him?"

"I didn't say that I loved him," protested Aislinn. "I care for him. I'm not sure that ..."

"Aislinn, you must stop beating around the bush. Even if you love him, you may need to kill him."

"That's a terrible thing to say."

"Nonetheless, it's true. If circumstances don't play out as we hope they will, if he makes just one mistake and allows himself to be seduced by the Curse, killing Bryen will be an act of kindness."

"Can we just start over please?" pleaded Aislinn. "I came here with what I thought was a simple question and you've spun up so much detritus around it that I'm not really sure what I'm asking anymore."

"That's not my fault, that's yours."

"But ..."

"I'm only speaking the truth. You haven't considered all the issues that are related to the question for which you are in search of an answer. You've only focused on you. Not on him."

"I didn't think that ..."

"That's the point, Aislinn. You're the Lady of the Southern Marches. You need to look at the challenges we face, the challenges that Bryen faces, from a much broader perspective. There is nothing simple about any of this. There is no easy solution. There rarely is."

"I see that now," she said quietly, finally understanding what Rafia was saying. She didn't like it. But that didn't really matter in the larger scheme of things.

"Now what was your question again?" asked Rafia, her bright eyes flashing in the firelight as she stared intently at Aislinn.

"So what should I do?"

"With respect to Bryen?" asked Rafia, wanting to confirm.

"Yes with respect to Bryen," Aislinn almost shouted before she gained control of her emotions. "We've been talking about Bryen the entire time. What should I do if I can't help him fight the Curse? If you ask me to help you kill him?"

"I can't tell you what you should do," replied Rafia quietly.

"But that's what I need from you," demanded Aislinn.

"I can't tell you what to do because you already know what to do," said Rafia.

"But you just said you're not giving me advice."

"I'm not giving you advice. You don't need my advice. You know what to do."

"You're not being very helpful," growled Aislinn, feeling as if she had just wasted a half hour of her life. "I don't know what to do."

"You might think that now," said Rafia sagely. "But you'll see. I helped you a great deal with this conversation. You just don't know it yet."

"I still find it a bit disconcerting."

"Find what disconcerting?" asked Lycia, the gladiator sitting next to her twin brother on a large root at the very edge of the small clearing that the Blood Company was using as their campsite for the night. She was trying to relax, to let the stress of the day go. Davin wasn't making it easy.

After the day's fight with the Ghoules she had unbraided her red hair, combed it out, then braided it again so that it now rested over her right shoulder. It was a habit that she had developed after each of her combats in the Pit and that she continued to follow, as she found the repetitiveness of the activity calming.

"What Bryen can do with the Talent," replied Davin, scrubbing his hands through his spiky hair. "Even after watching him do it so often, it's still kind of frightening, and he was scary enough as it was on the white sand." Davin held up his hands, wanting to clarify what he had just said. "Not that he can do it, but that one of our friends can do it. I never thought we'd get mixed up with a Magus. Does that make sense?"

"It does," Lycia agreed, "though having a Magus as a friend does prove quite useful, doesn't it?"

"It does."

Davin and Lycia had just visited with Bryen, waiting until he, Rafia, Aislinn, and Sirius had seen to all the other wounded first. The two had suffered nothing more than a few minor scrapes except for the long slash across Davin's forearm courtesy of a Ghoule's claw. After Bryen had used the Talent to heal the wound, Davin was left with a pink scar that he was certain would fade quickly over the next few days.

So his sister was right about that. Without the Talent, it would have taken weeks for his wound to heal naturally, to say nothing of the more serious injuries Bryen had helped with after the fight.

He had been amazed when he watched Bryen use the Talent on him, the natural power of the world closing the wound and knitting the flesh back together after his friend had cleaned the slash with fresh water and then applied a foul smelling paste that Rafia said helped to ensure that there would be no infection.

"Even so," continued Lycia, "I wonder what it might have been like if he had not learned that he could use the Talent."

"He would have discovered the ability one way or the other, Lycia. Eventually he would have realized the truth even if it hadn't been forced upon him the way it had been thanks to Sirius."

"I know," Lycia sighed. "I was just wondering. That's all. It would have made life much easier. It might even have meant a different life altogether."

"I know," Davin said quietly, then whispered to himself, "though quite a bit less exciting."

He looked at his sister closely, taking in her slumped shoulders and downcast expression. He knew her moods as well as he knew himself, and this was not normal behavior for his sister, the always pugnacious Crimson Devil on the white sand. Her combative personality had followed her from the Pit when they were freed. Now it was strangely absent.

He thought that she might be feeling sorry for herself, though Davin understood that he couldn't ask his sister whether she was or not. She'd as soon as stick a dagger between his ribs as give him a hug if he did, so he needed to approach what was bothering her delicately, if he even dared.

A challenge for him, because he wasn't exactly very good at approaching anything, whether a combat or difficult emotions, delicately. Not liking to see his sister in such a mood, and not really knowing what to say, he chose to be as blunt as he usually was, because he had learned long ago that he couldn't be anything other than himself.

"You don't have a hold on him anymore, Lycia. He's not the person he was when he was with us. You need to let go of him."

"What are you talking about?" demanded Lycia, her hands crunching into angry fists. She looked like she was about to leap from her seat and pounce on him.

Davin could tell that she was trying to regain some of the fire that played such an important part in who she was. But in this moment, Davin understood that his sister's reaction was more bark than bite, the fire no more than a spark, and barely one at that.

"You know exactly what I'm talking about," he replied in what he hoped Lycia took to be a calm voice. "You don't have a hold on Bryen anymore. The world is different now. Bigger. There is more going on now than just what we faced in the Pit. In the Pit it was simple: kill or be killed."

"It still is," countered Lycia, "just as we experienced today. Kill or be killed."

"Yes, but strange as it may sound, now the ramifications of

our actions affect an entire Kingdom, not just ourselves. This isn't just about us surviving. It's about all of Caledonia surviving."

"What if I don't want to let go of him?" mumbled Lycia deflatedly, the tiny spark that she had just displayed winking out meekly, her shoulders sagging even further. "What if I want to keep hold of him no matter what?"

"Lycia, I understand why you feel this way," said Davin, extending his arm around her shoulders and pulling her in for a hug. "I'm sorry this is so difficult for you."

Davin understood that he was taking a risk by doing so, assuming that his sister would elbow him in the ribs to make him let go of her. She always had been stronger than him when they lived on the streets of Tintagel, begging or stealing for food before they were swept up by the City Watch and deposited in the Colosseum. Always looking out for both of them. Never having any doubts. Never backing down from a fight. Never allowing anything to get in her way. Instead, unexpectedly, she folded into him.

"How could you?" Lycia whispered into his shoulder. "How could you have any idea what I'm feeling?"

"I do, really," continued Davin. "I feel for you. You and Bryen were quite close. It's just that we're not in the Pit anymore. Everything changed when Duke Winborne took Bryen from the Pit."

"It didn't have to change," Lycia protested, pushing herself up off Davin's shoulder and wiping her eyes.

Davin pretended not to notice. He was catching a glimpse of a side of his sister that he had never seen before. A sensitive side. And he still wasn't sure what to make of it. So he decided that he needed to continue to tread carefully.

"It did, Lycia. I'm sorry, but it did. Bryen wouldn't have survived leaving the white sand if he didn't change. If he didn't adapt to his new circumstances. A lot has happened since we were in the Colosseum together. You can't expect everything to just go back to the way things were."

"Why not?"

"The world doesn't work that way."

"It should," scowled Lycia, that tiny spark returning once again. Davin wasn't certain if it would last, though he hoped that it would.

"That's unrealistic at best and unfair at worst."

"Unfair to me."

"You don't have to like it, Lycia. You do have to deal with it."

"Why? Why do I have to deal with it?"

Lycia's voice had become little more than a whisper again. Davin took that as a positive sign, so long as that fire within her didn't release her very well-known and sometimes destructive temper.

"Too much is at stake. Caledonia is at risk."

"Why should I care about Caledonia? Caledonia never cared about me. Never cared about us. Caledonia put us in the Pit."

"Bryen is at risk as well," Davin replied in an exceedingly quiet voice, thinking about all that had been placed on his friend's shoulders, because he certainly didn't disagree with his sister's perspective. After all that had happened to him and Lycia, he felt little loyalty to the Kingdom. "I'm in the same boat as you. I don't really care about Caledonia. I do care about Bryen. We wouldn't be alive today without him. He's our friend. He deserves our help, because if we don't help him Caledonia dies. And if Caledonia dies, Bryen dies too. I might not be able to keep him alive, but I mean to do all that I can to ensure that he gets to the Sanctuary and can at least try to do whatever it is he needs to do. He deserves nothing less from me, from us."

"Words of wisdom from the Crimson Giant," Lycia murmured, her lips curling into a slight smile. "I never would have guessed."

"Every once in a while I do have a good thought, you know."

Davin wasn't certain whether to take Lycia's comment as a compliment or a veiled insult. He chose compliment, because after the fight among the heart trees, he was too tired to engage in a war of words with his sister.

"That you do."

"Is that agreement?" asked Davin, still a bit surprised that something that he had said might actually have resonated with his sister. Normally it was the other way around.

"For now," Lycia replied reluctantly. "So I should just let it go ..."

"Because he needs us. Yes."

"You're asking quite a lot, Davin. And Bryen shouldn't get a free pass on this. We need him too."

"You're right, but not in the same way that he needs us."

"Fine. I get it. You're right. I agree with you, even though I don't want to." This time Lycia did elbow her brother in the ribs. Not as hard as she ordinarily would, though his slight grimace brought a broad smile to her lips. "So how do we help him?"

"You know how he is," explained Davin. "When there's a task to complete, he's going to focus on that at the expense of almost everything else. He might ignore something important if he thinks doing so will get him where he needs to go that much faster."

"Like common sense?" asked Lycia. "Like not chasing an Elder by yourself through the Dark Forest?"

"Yes, exactly like that," agreed Davin with a nod.

Lycia had felt sick when she had seen the wound the Elder had inflicted upon Bryen, a spidery web of pulsing black spreading across his chest. She couldn't understand how he could manage the pain, let alone survive the ordeal. The Dark Magic had been consuming him so quickly and so completely that she doubted he had more than just a few seconds left before he died.

Yet Bryen had healed himself. She understood how he had done it, that this ability resulted not only from his skill as a Magus, but also because of his link to the Seventh Stone. Still, what he had done stunned her. It frightened her as well. Not for herself, but rather for him. Davin was right. They needed to do all that they could to help him.

"Bryen and I still need to deal with the issues between us."

"As you should," Davin agreed. "We have a long way to go before we reach the Sanctuary. Let's get Bryen there alive. Then once he does what he needs to do with the Weir, you and Bryen can have the conversation that you two need to have. Fair enough?"

"Fair enough."

"Good, now come on." Davin hopped off the root and offered his hand to Lycia. As he expected, she ignored his offer of assistance as she jumped down right next to him. "Declan asked us to check the sentries before we turned in."

"Why us?"

"My guess is that he's trying to infuse within us a stronger sense of leadership and responsibility."

"Why do you think that?" asked Lycia. "That seems a bit of a stretch."

"Because that's what he told me," Davin said with a grin. "There might be more to it than that, but do you really want to ask Declan why? You know how that will go."

"Not really. He's been more grouchy than usual this evening."

"Probably because of what Bryen did."

"Maybe," conceded Lycia, her tone suggesting that she wasn't quite convinced. "Although I'm not certain that's the only reason."

"What do you mean?"

"I think that there might be more to it than that. It might not just be Bryen."

Davin stood there for several long seconds, expecting Lycia to provide more detail. When she didn't offer anything else, he was forced to try again.

"How so?"

"I just think that there's something else going on that's bothering him. Something unexpected. Something that he's not quite sure how to handle."

"Could you be any more obtuse?"

"Probably," replied Lycia, who now offered her brother a broad grin. "It wouldn't take much more effort than it's taking now."

"Come on," grumbled Davin, realizing that the moment of vulnerability between them, which was so rare to begin with, had come to an end, and that they were about to fall right back into their normal squabbling and regular attempts to see who could irritate the other with the least amount of effort. "You can fill me in while we check the sentries."

THE STRAIN of the very long day, both on his body and his mind, had exhausted Bryen. Yet despite all that had occurred, his brain still refused to turn off. He blamed it on Declan, and he felt justified in doing so because the Master of the Gladiators had rooted this within him as part of his training and preparation for the white sand.

Bryen continued to obsess over every aspect of the fight against the Ghoules. His decision to pursue the Elder, which he admitted after the fact hadn't been the best choice he could have made in that situation. The cost that he had almost paid because of that impulsive decision.

He had located a quiet place just a few yards beyond their

campsite, stepping comfortably into the darkness and nodding to the sentries as he passed, where he could take a few minutes and hopefully gain the peace that he was seeking but was having such a difficult time finding. He pulled himself up onto a twisting root that burst out of the ground and leveled off at the perfect height for him to sit, letting out an involuntary groan as he dropped down onto his perch.

The fight with the Ghoules, the Elders in particular, was tiring enough. Having to use the Seventh Stone to heal himself after two of the Elders tried to take him to the Ghoule Overlord had drained him of what little strength he had left.

Only now, several hours after that terrifying experience had threatened to release the Curse within him, was he beginning to feel like himself again. To feel as if he wasn't being split in two and that once more, he had the competing energies gifted to him by the Seventh Stone back under control.

Because the Curse had almost broken free, trying to join with the Dark Magic with which the Elder struck him. And if that had happened ...

Well, if that had happened, he'd be dead now. Either at the hands of the Ghoule Overlord if the Elders had succeeded in taking him or Rafia and Sirius, who had been quite clear multiple times what would happen if the defenses that he had constructed within himself in order to maintain control over the Dark Magic contained within the Seventh Stone failed.

Taking a deep breath in an effort to clear his mind, despite the many challenges of the day, Bryen actually smiled. It hadn't all been bad. He had just finished visiting with every soldier of the Blood Company. The gladiators had been glad to see him, slapping him on the back, offering a few quick stories of the difficulties they faced in their own combats with the Ghoules.

The thread that had tugged at his heart was how often the hardened fighters told him how pleased they were to see that he was all right. They had heard about what had happened to him, and their concern for his well-being had been genuine. They had been more worried about him than themselves.

His friends from the Pit also were quite pleased that they had finished off the Ghoules with only a handful of their number taking serious injuries, and those few had been healed thanks to Bryen and the other Magii's skill with the Talent. Because of their assistance, all the gladiators would be fit for service on the morrow, none the worse for wear, all of them raring to go as they continued on their journey.

Initially, Bryen had worried that the gladiators would look at him with a touch of uncertainty, second thoughts making them question their decision to join him, now that they had faced their greatest challenge yet against the Ghoules. He was the one who had put them in danger. He was the one who had forced them to risk their lives.

His fears proved to be unfounded. The gladiators knew what they had agreed to do. They knew why they were there. They knew what was expected of them.

Their only desire was to meet the obligation they had made to him.

Asaia had been the first to notice the look of concern that had crossed Bryen's face when she had spoken with him. She had moved quickly to quell his fears by speaking just as bluntly as she always did: "We are here because we choose to be, Volkun. We are here because we choose to be with you. To fight with you. To die with you if necessary. That was our decision to make. You cannot take that from us, so don't try."

Remembering that exchange brought another smile to Bryen's usually grim visage. Asaia was correct, just as she usually tended to be. Bryen needed to stop worrying, at least about the Blood Company, because Asaia had helped him realize that his fears for them were simply a manifestation of his own. He needed to let those go because there were other matters that demanded his attention.

The attempt by the Elders to take him to the Ghoule Overlord had been quite terrifying. What he found even more frightening was the fact that Lycia and Aislinn had seen eye to eye in terms of his decisions. They both had agreed that he should never have taken the risk of pursuing the fleeing Elder on his own.

He hadn't expected the two to agree on pretty much anything, yet they had. About him, no less. That was an alarming development for many reasons. It also was a worry for later, and it didn't rise to the level of the many other pressing concerns that continued to flow through his mind, threatening to inundate him. One, in particular, stood out.

He was troubled about their chances of making it to the Sanctuary. He and the Blood Company had fought their way through these beasts earlier because they had benefited from the use of the Talent, giving them the chance to attack from the very beginning and never cede the initiative. That was essential when fighting Ghoules and Elders. You had to be on the front foot right from the start.

That wouldn't always be the case. Particularly now that the Ghoule Overlord knew exactly where they were, and Bryen was certain that his nemesis would be sending as many of his Ghoules and his Elders toward them as he could, doing everything in his power to stop them from reaching their objective.

They were less than a week from Tintagel. They had been hunted as soon as they had left the gates of the capital. They still had a long way to go. He expected even more severe challenges from the Ghoules hunting them, and that didn't bode well for their chances of success.

In his mind, because of that, the odds of making it to the Sanctuary, never good to begin with, were made that much worse. So what to do about that, if anything at all?

"You're thinking too much," said Sirius, the old Magus appearing out of the murk.

Sirius took a look at where Bryen sat about six feet off the ground. Then he approached with a confidence that was impressive for someone of his age, reaching up with his hands and attempting to pull himself up next to Bryen.

His first attempt failed, Sirius chalking that up to the lack of momentum when his hands slipped off the bark. He tried again, putting more effort into the attempt, this time with no better a result as he was unable to gain much of a grip. Maybe he wasn't as strong as he used to be. That thought sent a wave of irritation through him. He was about to try a third time when the old Magus looked up and saw Bryen offering him his hand. Swallowing his pride, Sirius nodded his thanks and then allowed the Protector to pull him up and help him take a seat on the bark next to him.

"Lycia and Aislinn would disagree with you," he replied quietly. "They don't believe that I think enough."

"Yes, well, I could say that that's normally the way of the world when a woman is concerned for your well-being. They tend to nit-pick your decisions ad nauseam."

"I'm assuming that you're only sharing that perspective with me," replied Bryen with a slight smile. "Because I don't think it would be wise to offer such a perspective in mixed company. Say, for example, if Rafia were here with us. I have no doubt she'd take issue with it. She might even set you on fire again. Although your comment does explain a lot about the state of your relationship."

"She tried to set me on fire," corrected Sirius. "She didn't actually succeed. She hit the trees behind me instead."

"I get the feeling after having come to know Rafia fairly well that if she really wanted to set you on fire, she would have set you on fire."

Sirius was about offer another rebuttal, then realized that once again the young man was baiting him.

"I'm old, lad. I'm set in my ways. But I'm not a fool."

"No, that you are not," agreed Bryen. "And how do you know that I'm thinking too much?"

"I can tell by your expression, lad. You're replaying everything that you did today, over and over in your head. Do it once. Identify your mistakes. Learn from them. After that, move on. You don't have time to be stuck in your head. You need to be in the here and now."

"Unexpectedly sage advice. Thank you, Sirius."

"You're welcome," Sirius replied with a slight frown.

Bryen expected Sirius to latch onto the gentle jibe that he couldn't resist offering. In fact, a small part of him almost hoped that the Magus would, as it would delay the real conversation that Sirius had sought him out for, yet the old Magus had let it go. Bryen shook his head in resignation. That was out of character for him, and that worried Bryen just a little bit.

Then he closed his eyes for a moment and cursed himself silently. He had no good reason to antagonize Sirius. His attempt to do so was childish and unbecoming, particularly after what he had seen earlier in the day.

Bryen recalled the emotions that the old Magus had revealed when Bryen was wounded. He had anticipated seeing the worry there, because Sirius needed Bryen to survive his injury so that he could do what he wanted him to do. Yet something else had been there as well. Something that he had found both surprising and a touch heartwarming, assuming he had interpreted it correctly.

Sirius seemed concerned for the person that he was and not just the function that he could serve. Bryen hadn't glimpsed that before from the old Magus. He thought that he never would, and it had caught him by surprise.

"How are you feeling, lad? It was quite the adventure earlier today."

"As well as can be expected," replied Bryen, a smile curling his lips. Sirius always did everything in his own time, and this conversation was no exception as the old Magus began to work toward the reason for him joining Bryen that evening.

"Your wound has healed?"

"As well as can be expected."

"And the Dark Magic within you is back under control?"

"You would know if it wasn't," confirmed Bryen. "I expect that if I had failed to prevent the Curse's release within me, you and Rafia would be meeting with me right now with but a single purpose in mind if you hadn't done the deed already."

"Just so, lad. You're right about that." Sirius nodded in agreement. Bryen knew what would happen if he lost control of the Dark Magic forced upon him by the Seventh Stone. As was his habit and predilection, Sirius kept a great deal to himself, but in that regard, he had been brutally honest with Bryen from the start. The Magus wouldn't hesitate to kill him if he believed that it was necessary. "No ill effects at all?"

"Nothing for you or anyone else to worry about."

"That's good to hear, lad."

Maybe it was because he was tired. Maybe it was because he didn't have a lot of patience as he just wanted to be alone and enjoy the peace and quiet of the night. But Bryen didn't want to continue waiting for Sirius to get to the real conversation.

"So let's get to it, Sirius. You came here for a reason."

Sirius' immediate thought was to protest his innocence, that he had only sought out Bryen to check on how he was doing. He realized that doing so would only undermine his efforts to speak with Bryen about the topic that he really wanted to discuss with him.

"You don't trust me," said the wispy-haired Magus.

Sirius already felt guilty because of his failure to save Bryen's parents from the Ghoules. He didn't want to feel guilty about losing Bryen as well, whether to the Curse or the Ghoule Overlord, without doing all that he possibly could to help him achieve his goal. Their goal, he corrected. Not his goal, but the goal of all who joined this expedition.

To do that, the Magus understood, he needed Bryen to trust him. Or at least ensure that Bryen didn't distrust him as much as he apparently did.

"What makes you say that?"

Sirius couldn't stop himself from smiling, Bryen's sarcasm unmistakable.

"Because you're so guarded at times. It's rare in someone so young."

"It's rare in someone who hasn't fought in the Pit."

"I stand corrected," acknowledged Sirius with a self-deprecating nod.

"Wouldn't you be wary if you were in my position?" asked Bryen. "Besides, trust is earned. It's not given blindly."

"I promised not to lie to you anymore. I've kept to that promise."

"I know you have, and I appreciate it."

"But ..."

"But that still doesn't mean that you've been completely honest with me. You're still holding things back."

Sirius was about to offer an immediate defense, then hesitated, realizing that he really had no defense. Bryen was right. And he was also right about one other thing. Trust was earned, not given.

"You're right. I'm sorry. It's a hard habit to break."

"As Master of the Magii."

"Yes," Sirius admitted grudgingly. "It's an affliction of having been a Magus for so long."

Bryen was going to challenge Sirius' statement. Noorsin and Rafia didn't seem to keep so much so close to the vest as Sirius did, yet there was little point in going down that road. Nothing productive would come from it and it would likely derail the conversation.

"So what's really on your mind, Sirius? I know you're not just here to check on my health or to tell me that you're worried that I don't trust you. You've known that my trust in you has never been strong since you were the one who locked the Protector's collar around my neck."

"Am I that obvious?" asked Sirius with a grin, trying to and not necessarily succeeding in keeping the mood light.

"We've been spending a lot of time together the last few months. I know your tells."

"What are my tells?" asked Sirius, irritated in part because Bryen could read him so well. Still, he was very interested to learn what they might be. If he knew what they were, he could do a better job of controlling them.

"I'm not going to tell you your tells."

"Why not?" Sirius protested, his temper, never really far from the surface, beginning to percolate.

"Think about it, Sirius," challenged Bryen. "How does my telling you your tells benefit me?"

"That's a very cold way of looking at the world."

"Maybe so," nodded Bryen in agreement. "I would argue that it's simply looking at the world as it is. Besides, such an approach has proven necessary."

"I guess I can't challenge you on that," replied Sirius, letting his irritation slide away as he didn't have a good response. "Look, I just wanted to let you know that I'm here to help you. I'll be at your side to the very end."

"Whether that means aiding me in my attempts to rebuild the Weir or killing me if the Curse breaks loose inside me."

"Just so," Sirius replied immediately, understanding the danger of trying to dissemble.

"Thank you for that. I do appreciate your honesty in that respect."

Both Bryen and Sirius sat there in silence for a time. The quiet didn't bother Bryen at all. It was making Sirius slightly uncomfortable, but the Magus kept his mouth shut, at least for a time.

As the minutes continued to pass, the darkness around them still, silent, the old Magus started to fidget in his seat like a toddler told to sit at the table quietly while the adults were finishing their evening meal. The need to talk growing more insistent within him, Sirius was unable to stand it any longer.

"We have a hard road ahead," Sirius began, hoping to use that statement to bring Bryen into the conversation.

Bryen only murmured his agreement, continuing to stare off into the darkness. He wasn't ready to let the silence go, not yet, though it didn't seem that he had much of a choice. Bryen assumed that Sirius would get to what he really wanted to discuss, just as he always did, despite Bryen's best efforts to get him there just a bit faster.

"We will face greater challenges than just these Ghoules and Elders."

Bryen murmured his agreement once again, at the moment not feeling the need to engage any further.

"Quite a bit will be demanded of you."

For a third time, Bryen murmured his agreement, which immediately set off the old Magus.

"Blast it, lad! This is serious!"

"I know it is, Sirius. Now get to what you really want to talk about so we can move on. You beating around the bush since you got here is getting tedious."

For just an instant, Sirius sat there slightly stunned. In all his centuries as the Master of the Magii, few people had ever demonstrated the courage to speak with him so directly as Bryen did. Sirius understood that Bryen didn't do it because he felt entitled or because of the burden of his responsibility. It was just who he was. It was who he had become after fighting on the white sand.

"Can you do it?"

"Rebuild the Weir?" asked Bryen, seeking some clarification. He shrugged his shoulders. "I don't know. I'll do my best. I can't make any promises beyond that."

"Not that. I know you'll do the best that you can with respect to the Weir. I would expect nothing less from you."

"Then what?"

"The Ghoule Overlord," replied Sirius quietly. "I have this terrible hunch that rebuilding the Weir might be the smallest and easiest part of the challenge you face. A key part, obviously, yet still only a part. I don't know why, but I believe that you'll also have to fight the Ghoule Overlord. Fight the Curse itself when the time is right."

"That sounds a bit ominous," replied Bryen with a forced smile. "Trying to scare me?"

"No. I mean yes. I'm sorry." Sirius shrugged his shoulders helplessly. "I'm not trying to scare you, and I agree, the possibility of confronting the Ghoule Overlord is a bit unsettling."

"I would suggest that fighting the Ghoule Overlord is more than just a bit unsettling."

"You're right," agreed Sirius. "We both have already faced him, I know, but not at his full strength."

When the Overlord revealed himself during the rebellion in Tintagel, shedding his brother Tetric's skin on the white sand of the Pit, Sirius had been filled by an almost uncontrollable rage and sadness, the two emotions building upon one another. That incident had left him feeling like a failure. Not only because he had not been able to save his brother, but also because he had failed to kill the Ghoule Overlord when he had the chance. Bryen had to join the combat to ensure that Sirius wasn't himself killed.

"I would simply ask that you not underestimate the Ghoule Overlord and his Dark Magic if you do face him," continued Sirius. "I'm sorry, I just can't escape the feeling. Do you think you can beat the Ghoule Overlord in a combat if that's what it comes down to?"

Sirius' question stopped Bryen short for several heartbeats. A bolt of fear shot through him. He immediately crushed it before that fright could settle within him and fester over time. Fighting the Ghoule Overlord would be no different than fighting any of the many beasts that he had faced off against in the Pit. The Ghoule Overlord was simply another opponent he needed to defeat if he was to stay alive. Or so he told himself.

Who was he kidding? Bryen scoffed. Of course it would be different. Challenging the Ghoule Overlord to a combat likely would ensure his death. Even with the Seventh Stone, he wasn't sure that he had the strength to give that monster a good fight.

So he wasn't surprised by Sirius' fear. In addition to the very brief confrontation on the white sand during the rebellion against King Beleron, Bryen had already come face to face with the Ghoule Overlord several times in his dreams. And as the thin, black scar across his cheek demonstrated, there was little difference between dreams and reality when it came to the Ghoule Overlord.

Just then one of Declan's favorite sayings filtered through Bryen's mind: "Everyone dies. Not everyone dies with honor."

Even though the thought of dueling the Ghoule Overlord frightened him, Bryen would do what was required of him. If he died, he died. He had never run from a fight, and he wasn't about to start now, no matter the odds. Not even if his opponent was the Master of the Curse.

"I don't know," Bryen finally replied, feeling no need to give Sirius a false sense of confidence. "I guess there's only one way to find out."

Sirius nodded. Then he and Bryen sat there on the tree root a bit longer lost in their own thoughts. Finally, Sirius pushed himself up from his seat, clapped Bryen on the back, then dropped down to the ground and walked back toward the light of the campfires.

Bryen watched him go with a raised eyebrow, finding his comradely action out of character for the old Magus. In fact, Sirius had been acting oddly ever since Bryen had been wounded earlier in the day.

He would have to think more on that. Maybe it had something to do with the unexplained emotion that he had seen in Sirius. Maybe not. Regardless, he needed to deal with something else first.

Bryen's thoughts immediately turned toward their next steps for reaching the Sanctuary. He needed to think about changing their strategy. About doing something unexpected. Something that would throw the Ghoule Overlord off the scent or at least slow him down. However, despite his best efforts at trying to figure out what that could be, nothing useful had come to mind.

Until he came up with something, they would need to press forward and be ready for what was coming for them. And they needed to remain wary. Because Bryen feared that the Blood Company would face much worse quite soon if they allowed the Ghoule Overlord to dictate the events to come.

Growling softly in frustration, this issue having remained an unsolved problem for the last few hours, Bryen used the Talent to extend his senses once again. He had been doing it every twenty minutes or so since he had healed himself.

His search with the natural magic of the world didn't take long. He found nothing of immediate concern. He sensed the locations of the Ghoule packs that were already converging upon them.

Bryen understood that these packs would become more of a concern in the next few days, just not yet. So he ignored them, if only for a time. Because something else had caught his attention.

He had found a presence off to the west near the border of the Dark Forest that made him feel distinctly uncomfortable. It was a feeling that he had never experienced before, and it gave him pause. It was a similar feeling as when he located Ghoules, but this sensation differed.

The taint of evil was stronger, mustier, almost ancient. He didn't know what could be causing it, because whatever it was, it was shielded with Dark Magic as was the case when he and Sirius had escaped the Ghoules pursuing them when they left Battersea and made for Haven what seemed like ages ago.

That worried him. Fighting Ghoules and Elders was bad enough. Whatever this evil was, it was not Ghoules and Elders. It was something worse.

Something that sent a primal shiver of fear down his spine every time he touched the cloud of evil hiding this latest predator.

7

OUT OF THE GLOOM

Rocco stood warily at the top of the waterfall. His gaze moved constantly from one shadow to the next, the gloom of the Dark Forest preventing him from picking out anything more than the faint outlines of the huge trunks of the heart trees and their entwining roots.

The large gladiator growled in frustration. He could see no more than a few dozen feet into the murk, which would give him barely enough time to react if a new pack of Ghoules decided to take up the challenge of defeating the Blood Company, a challenge at which they had failed just hours before.

The sluggish stream to his right ran off the ledge and fell about fifteen feet into a small pool and then rambled on its way, twisting and turning across the forest floor. The only light in the forsaken wood came from the embers of the handful of campfires scattered below him, the few shadows created by the small flames playing across his broad back. Dawn would only bring a slightly brighter shade of grey, but it would be a welcome change to what he dealt with now.

Spear in hand, he shifted from one foot to the other,

stretching the muscles across his back by flexing his shoulders, rotating his neck to relieve the kinks, raising himself onto his toes to stretch his calves, twisting his hips and jogging in place, doing everything that he could to ensure that he remained alert.

He was a soldier of the Blood Company, and he wanted to meet his responsibilities in a way that would make his comrades proud. He would be the first to admit, however, that fighting Ghoules was a lot easier than functioning as a sentry. He had been on duty for two hours already, starting right after midnight, and he still had another two hours to go. He knew from experience that at this time in the morning, staying awake and remaining aware of his surroundings became more and more difficult as each minute passed.

He'd much rather stand across from one of the many beasts that had died the day before than do this. Because then, when he was driving his spear into the throat of a Ghoule not too far from where he stood now, he felt an exhilaration, his adrenaline surging, that had stayed with him for hours. Now, he just felt tired, lethargic, not as alert as he wanted to be.

Rocco had selected a position far enough away from the small waterfall so that the sound of the water spilling over the ledge wouldn't prevent him from hearing any irregularities in the nighttime sounds of the forest, which were few and far between to begin with. Few animals made these forbidding trees their home.

He walked up and down the periphery of his assigned area, changing directions regularly, never following a pattern, something that he had learned while in the Royal Guard. His eyes scanned the darkness just beyond him, having memorized the shadows to his front as best as he could, looking for any differences when his eyes passed over the same silhouettes time and time again.

The Volkun had suggested just such an approach for scanning the gloom when they had first entered the Dark Forest. And when the Volkun offered him advice, he tended to listen, because so far whenever he did it had worked in Rocco's favor.

Finishing his latest survey of his area of responsibility, he shook his head in mild annoyance. Rocco understood why they were here. He knew the importance of their mission. He believed in what they were doing.

Still, he would have preferred to be somewhere else, almost anywhere else, where he could see the stars in the sky and use the bright light of the moon to gain a better sense of what might be lurking around him. Where the environment was more of what you would expect of a typical forest.

There was nothing typical about where he and the other members of the Blood Company had pitched their camp for the night. Night or day, the Dark Forest was always strangely silent, the infrequent and thus startling sounds of wildlife setting his nerves on edge.

He had been in among the heart trees for more than a week now. He had assumed that by now he would have gotten used to his surroundings. Not so. That sense of unease that had struck him as soon as he had walked beneath the intertwined branches that blocked the sun had stayed with him every second of every day.

Rocco had battled in the Pit for almost two years, believing that had been the hardest, most menacing environment that he had ever been in ... until now. He had fought more than one hundred combats against some terrifying creatures. None had made him as nervous as he felt now, staring into the black of the night, confirming once again that the shadows that he had examined for the last two hours hadn't changed since the last time he had examined them.

To free himself from this feeling of impending doom that had been building within him since he had assumed his night-time assignment, he tried to decide what had been his most difficult combat in the Pit. He concluded that it had to be the lizard that had been just as big as he was. The beast had been some kind of dragon. Declan had told him before the combat, noting in particular that the beast's wings had been clipped so it couldn't fly.

Rocco could no longer remember what they were called. He wished he could. He did remember that Declan told him these dragons were native to the Jagged Islands, an uninhabited archipelago far to the southwest somewhere in the Burnt Ocean. So how and why one had ended up in the Colosseum was a mystery to him.

Wyverns! That was it. The animal had been a Wyvern, a distant relative of the black dragons they were marching toward.

The Wyvern had been incredibly fast, its clawed feet digging into the sand and its large tail swishing behind the beast to push it along and keep it on course. Its sharp, needle-like teeth were bad enough, but that had been the least of his concerns when fighting the animal.

It was the saliva that he really had to worry about. The drool that dripped incessantly from the beast's maw contained a bacterium that functioned much like a poison. If it got into your blood, you died, because there was no known cure. So if the dragon bit him, even if it wasn't a life-threatening wound, he was a dead man.

Rocco still remembered Declan's suggestion offered in his usual raspy growl when he walked through the gate that led out onto the white sand.

"You know how to kill it, lad," grumbled Declan. "It's flesh and blood. Just don't let it bite you."

Rocco repressed a slight chortle upon remembering that exchange. Helpful as always. Declan always had good advice though he always gave it in a very dry sort of way.

It had proven to be a difficult fight, the animal smartly using its speed to its advantage. It didn't bother Rocco. He knew how to deal with that, and even though he had no real desire to do so, he had killed the Wyvern. Even better, he hadn't gotten bitten.

After having fought the Ghoules several times now, he believed that his combat with the dragon had helped to prepare him for the creatures that he was fighting now. The speed of the two was very similar. As was the aggressiveness. Neither beast demonstrated much creativity in battle, knowing only how to attack. And the goal when fighting both Wyverns and Ghoules remained the same. Don't get bitten.

Yet even with that experience under his belt and his success against the Ghoules so far, Rocco still couldn't escape the oppressiveness of the Dark Forest, the feeling of wrongness that plagued him. The atmosphere played with his nerves.

In just the last few minutes, it seemed as if his surroundings had gotten even quieter than they had been before. How that was even possible, he didn't understand. It appeared to be gloomier as well. Although the shadows that he had memorized still hadn't changed, for some strange reason he felt like he was being stalked, a few drops of cold sweat running down his spine.

"Everything all right, Rocco?" said a quiet voice right behind him. "You seem a bit edgy."

Rocco continued to stare out into the darkness, having heard the gladiator approach. Why did the wood still feel wrong? The Blood Company had killed all the Ghoules, and the Magii had confirmed that there were no other packs close enough to bother them that night. So what was it?

It could be nothing at all, of course. Just the result of being in the Dark Forest. Just him coming down from the adrenaline of the fight. Or could it be something else?

Those thoughts made Rocco appreciate that Dorlan had come by to check on him, if only for a few minutes. The very large, very muscular gladiator was also very smart and patient. The big man liked to think things through, always very tactical in his approach. Even better, he listened to the fighters he was responsible for. That's why Rocco liked the newly named Corporal of the Blood Company so much.

"Just a bit wound up, I guess."

It could be the Dark Forest. It could be that he was still feeling his nerves from the battle against the Ghoules. That had to be it, he told himself. If there was anything else out here in the murk with them, the Magii would have warned them.

"Anything you think we need to worry about, Rocco?"

Rocco took a few seconds before responding. Had that shadow to his right shifted a bit when he had glanced at Dorlan? He stared at the silhouette a while longer, then decided that the shadow was exactly as it had been just a few minutes before. Nothing to fret over.

"Not that I've seen or heard," he finally replied. "It's probably just because of where we are. I'm looking forward to seeing the sun again."

Dorlan stared at Rocco, his eyebrows drawing closer together as he frowned, slightly concerned because of Rocco's hesitation. Finally, he nodded.

The Corporal then looked out into the darkness for a time. There was no moonlight. Of course, there hadn't been since they entered the Dark Forest. So without torches there was nothing to reveal the heart trees and roots that were just a dozen feet in front of them. A darkness darker than a starless night.

"I'm with you on that. Keep an eye out," Dorlan said unnecessarily, but it made him feel better doing so. Then he clapped Rocco on the shoulder. "Keep up the good work. If you see anything give a shout. I'm going to check on the others."

Rocco nodded as Dorlan headed off into the darkness, the

Corporal in search of Kollea next, who was stationed down below the waterfall to the west a short way.

Dorlan could understand Rocco's nervousness. The Dark Forest made him feel uneasy as well. In fact, the Dark Forest made anyone who walked among the heart trees feel anxious, almost apprehensive.

But now? Now, it was making Dorlan feel like he did the few times he had walked out onto the white sand with a fear of his own imminent death hanging over him. That was something that he would sooner forget, because each time it happened he had almost died. And he had no desire to do so in this dismal wood.

THE SHADOW WATCHED as the large man started to work his way down the slope on the western side of the waterfall, his hand trailing along the rough bark of a heart tree so that he wouldn't fall. Although every fiber in its being demanded that it feed, even though it would have been so easy, the shadow waited as patiently as it could, resisting the urge to reach out for the tasty flesh with its claw, not detaching itself from a dark notch in the tree trunk until the man had passed.

Despite its huge size, the shadow moved silently around and over the roots as it slowly worked its way toward the guard who stood atop the waterfall. Taking its time, allowing the darkness of the wood to hide it. The shadow felt no need to rush. There was still plenty of time to accomplish the task that it had set for itself.

The humans had chosen their campsite well with the stream and the small waterfall running down into it, providing some protection on that side. Opposite the stream, the twisting roots had become so entangled over the centuries that nothing could approach from that direction without being noticed.

That left two sides to worry about, and on one the heart trees were bunched together so tightly that it would be difficult to make a silent advance from between the trunks. That left the western side, which was still a tangle of roots twisting and arching this way and that, no rhyme or reason to how they grew. Nevertheless, there was more space here, more of an opportunity to approach without being discovered, even with the sentries keeping a sharp eye.

The shadow had to admit that the humans had made a good effort to guard themselves. But it was wasted effort.

The shadow knew that as it came out of the pitch black of the early morning the humans stood no chance against it. Darkness was not only its sanctuary, it was also its home. The darkness moved with it. Shielded it. Protected it, although it rarely needed that protection.

The shadow reached its position in less than a quarter of an hour, gliding silently across the soft loam until it stopped no more than a few feet behind the human standing at the top of the waterfall, not making a sound, only taking a breath every minute or so. The human who continued to stare away from the camp and out into the darkness.

Then the shadow waited, again not feeling the need to rush, instead savoring what he knew was happening within its prey. The shadow could sense it. The tells were barely perceptible, barely seen in the darkness, but they were there, nonetheless. Besides, the shadow could see in the gloom just as well as if the sun was shining brightly in the sky at midday.

The human knew that the shadow was there, even though the human had not yet admitted it to himself, ignoring his senses, ignoring the terror that was rising within him.

The shadow shivered in pleasure, discerning the change in its prey. The human had stopped his side to side movement, standing stock still now. His hands gripped the haft of his spear more tightly, nervously.

It was almost too much for the shadow. The thrill sent a shudder of pleasure through it.

It wanted to kill. To feast.

But what the shadow was experiencing now was too exquisite to hurry.

So the shadow waited, despite the fact that it took every ounce of self-control for it to do so.

❧

Dorlan had been gone for only a few minutes, yet in that time Rocco felt as if everything had changed.

His whole body was shivering now, ever so slightly. His hands gripped the haft of his spear nervously, and despite the icy cold that had filled him, he had begun to sweat, frigid rivulets running down his back.

Then he knew why.

He wanted to deny it. To ignore it.

But he couldn't. Not now.

He was no longer alone.

Finally, unavoidably, Rocco slowly pivoted his foot to turn around. For just a split second, he stared at what he thought was just a deeper darkness.

Then his horror at what he discerned towering before him shattered his composure. He had glimpsed the sharp teeth when the shadow smiled and the blood-red eyes that blazed brightly in the darkness.

Before Rocco could scream a warning, the Slayer's fist shot out. His clawed fingers ripped through Rocco's leather armor, flesh, and ribs with ease. When the Slayer withdrew its talon, the beast showed the gasping human what it grasped.

His still beating heart.

Grinning even more broadly to reveal the fangs extending

from its jaws, the Slayer bit into the soft meat of the organ, tendrils of flesh still connecting the heart to the human.

With a deflating hiss, Rocco crumbled to the ground, the light leaving his eyes before he hit the dirt, the Slayer feeling a pleasurable charge surge through him as his prey died.

Rather than continue on to its next target, the Slayer remained where it was, eating the human's heart, enjoying the taste of the still beating organ, relishing the blood that dripped down onto its armored chest. The Slayer knew that its brethren would be eliminating the other sentries located around the campsite, so there was no need to rush.

The beast would finish its treat first, then get on with the killing.

~

Bryen was exhausted. Despite that he was finding sleep difficult to come by.

When he closed his eyes, he dozed for no more than a few minutes at a time, lying restlessly in his blankets. Inevitably, scenes of the fight with the Ghoules replayed through his mind, particularly the final combat with the two Elders.

Aislinn was right. He had acted the fool. His decision to pursue the Elder on his own had almost cost him his life and put at risk the entire purpose of their expedition.

He believed that's what kept him from sleeping. The doubt in himself, in his decisions, that had worked its way into his heart. He had allowed his instinct to take precedence over rational thought.

Such an approach had worked well for him in the past, since he was still alive, but he was beginning to understand that might not be the case in the future. That his instincts, if not balanced against reason and good decisions, could lead to his early demise.

Leaning back against the base of a heart tree, Aislinn lying just a few feet away from him, Davin and Lycia bedded down on the other side of the now glowing embers, Bryen drifted, not really awake, not asleep.

Images floated through his mind. At first, he thought it was a dream, realizing almost too late that it was actually a nightmare.

Three monstrous shadows stalked toward him, and with them came an overwhelming sense of approaching evil. He was drowning in it. He couldn't breathe, the taint filling his lungs. As the darkness closed in around him, threatening to smother him, all he could see were three pairs of bright, blood-red eyes shining in the darkness.

Bryen came awake with a start, his right hand tracing the black scar on his cheek that burned whenever a creature crafted from the Curse was nearby. That may have been a dream, but after experiencing several similar episodes involving the Ghoule Overlord, he knew that dreams were inextricably linked to reality. That they could exercise real power.

He was certain that his dream had connected once again to the world around him, because now he could detect the evil coming for him. It had something to do with the Seventh Stone, because this evil felt different from that of the Ghoules. There was an ancient quality to this foulness that he couldn't identify, as if this wickedness had come from a time that had no business mixing with the present.

Bryen's thoughts immediately turned to action when he glimpsed out of a partially closed eye a dark shadow distinct from those that had been around him for most of the night moving just above him, working its way carefully down the slope so that it would come at him from behind. He moved his right hand slowly to the side, wrapping his fist around the haft of the Spear of the Magii. Then he waited.

Bryen had picked a spot close to the base of the waterfall, the heart tree's roots spilling across the top of the stream. It gave him a good view as one of the creatures from his dream stalked toward him.

The shadow took its time, and with every foot that the shadow came closer, the sense of evil became more and more overpowering, so terrifying that it threatened to freeze him in place.

Bryen's first thought was to jump up and attack. Instead, he took a few seconds to think about that strategy.

If he gave in to his first instinct, it could put his friends at risk, all of whom were sleeping soundly. The shadow seemed to be focused solely on him, so he continued to wait and let the evil draw nearer, even as every fiber in his being resisted.

Bryen could barely contain himself, the corrupted stench wafting from the shadow making him feel slightly ill. He could just make out the shadow as it began to glide toward him along the tree trunk, the only clear confirmation of the creature's existence the blood-red eyes that glittered brightly whenever they were caught by the glowing embers of the fire.

The shadow was only ten feet away from Bryen now. Still, he couldn't really see what it was, unable to penetrate the murk, unable to identify what might be lurking within it. At least the shadow remained focused on him and not his companions, reducing the level of difficulty for what he needed to do next.

Although only a few seconds passed as the shadow drew closer, Bryen could barely contain himself. He watched through slitted eyes, the shadow finally coming to a stop, no more than a few feet away, looming above him. A bolt of adrenaline shot through Bryen. Still, he waited, not moving, scarcely breathing, trying to mimic the pattern of someone in a deep sleep.

The shadow remained where it was, in no hurry, its blood-red eyes staring down at him. Even now, despite his proximity to this ancient evil, Bryen failed to pierce the cloud of darkness surrounding whatever it was that had snuck into their camp. So he decided to take a slight risk, reaching for the Talent so that he could use the natural magic of the world to remove the glamour that hid the assassin sent to kill him.

That was a mistake.

As soon as Bryen touched the Talent, the blood-red eyes piercing the gloom widened, revealing that whatever hid in the murk had sensed what Bryen was doing. In a blur of motion, the shadow swung a massive claw down toward Bryen's chest, reaching for his heart.

Bryen responded without even thinking, filling the double blades of the Spear of the Magii with the Talent and swinging it across his body to knock the claw away from him. His attacker growled more from shock than pain, never believing that Bryen would stymie its attack. At the same time, Bryen used his momentum to roll to his feet, kicking himself free from his blankets then slashing across his body with his spear.

He missed whatever hid within the gloom, the assassin darting back faster than his size should allow. Yet the touch of that shining blade against the darkness surrounding the assassin caused a bright flash that swept through the clearing. The murk that Bryen hadn't been able to penetrate but for the blood-red eyes vanished, revealing a creature that made his heart skip a beat.

The monster was huge, taller than a Ghoule, its grey, black armored skin still making it difficult to pick the beast out of the darkness. The fangs that protruded from both jaws chilled his blood, though Bryen was more worried about the creature's claws. They were razor sharp, and he had no doubt that the beast could rip his head from his shoulders with a single swipe if he gave the assassin the chance.

"Rise! Fight for your lives!" Bryen shouted even though he knew that his friends were already on the move.

Bryen continued his attack, slashing and cutting with his spear, forcing the beast back toward the waterfall and away from Aislinn, Davin, and Lycia, who had all come to their feet with their weapons drawn.

Based on his dream, he assumed that there were two more of these assassins already past the perimeter guards. The shouts of battle coming from behind him confirmed that assumption.

He couldn't worry about that now. Not with the monster that stood across from him. The beast that continued to skip away from his glowing steel with a dexterity that was chilling.

Bryen realized almost immediately that his current strategy was a losing one, and not just because he was so tired. The beast wasn't afraid of him, even with the glowing blades shining brightly with the Talent. Instead, the assassin seemed to be playing with him, gauging him, figuring out how to kill him with the least possible effort.

Cautious, not afraid. Of course, Bryen doubted that this monster was afraid of anything.

The Spear of the Magii infused with the Talent appeared to be the only reason his attacker kept its distance, because from what he could hear happening in the campsite, the clangs that sounded like metal hitting metal that drifted through the air suggested that the soldiers' steel blades couldn't penetrate the monsters' armored skin, let alone the spikes that protruded from their forearms, thighs, and shoulders.

On top of that, although those sounds indicated failure on the part of the gladiators to fight as they would prefer against the assassins, there were far too few for Bryen's liking. The monsters were too fast. And the other two assassins probably were still masked by shadow, making it that much more difficult for the Blood Company to locate and drive off their attackers.

As he continued to spin the Spear of the Magii in front of him, keeping the monster at bay, he hit upon what he needed to do to shift the current dynamic in his favor. Because he was certain that if he did what was expected of him this monster would kill him, those needle-sharp claws ripping into his flesh.

Bryen spun around swiftly, aiming a backward slash for the beast's hamstring. But as he did so, he stumbled, his foot going out from under him as it slid through the mud of the stream.

The monster's eyes expanded upon seeing the opportunity that it couldn't ignore, the beast lunging forward with one massive claw, just as Bryen hoped the assassin would.

The Protector used the feigned stumble to roll beneath the lunge, continuing his motion so that he could bring his glowing blade across the beast's side with all the strength that he could muster.

The shriek of pain, anger, and surprise told Bryen all that he needed to know as the beast faltered, its left leg useless because of the deep gash in its hip that had also shattered the bone.

Bryen smiled mercilessly, his fear replaced by a growing confidence. It was as he guessed. Steel couldn't harm the beast, just as the soldiers of the Blood Company had discovered. The Talent could, however, and with devastating effect.

Just then, to aid the gladiators, Sirius used the Talent to craft a shimmering light below the lowest branches of the heart trees, the glow illuminating the campsite and putting the three assassins in stark relief.

"The Talent!" shouted Bryen. "You must use the Talent to harm these beasts!"

Bryen was certain that everyone else with him already knew that. Even so, better to issue the warning than not.

"Can you manage this one?" asked Aislinn, who had crept

up behind him, the injured beast struggling to remain on its clawed feet as a thick black blood poured down its injured leg and ran into the stream. She thought that the creature might try to flee, but she discarded the thought instantly. The roots winding above the murmuring water served as an exceedingly effective barrier.

"Yes, help the others."

With that, Aislinn was gone, running toward the sounds of battle, streaks of the Talent already blasting between the heart trees, Aislinn adding her strength to Rafia's as they went after the other two assassins, the monsters proving to be difficult adversaries because of their speed and agility.

To escape the bolts of energy, the assassins leapt onto the heart trees, hanging there with their sharp claws digging into the bark, then throwing themselves from one branch to the next with a remarkable speed, often just above the light that Sirius had created, using the shadows to hide themselves.

"What do you need from us?" asked Davin, he and Lycia spread out behind Bryen so that the assassin couldn't try to sneak around them.

Bryen studied the situation for just a few seconds. He realized that the fight was already won if he played his cards right.

The beast was trapped against the waterfall, and with its injured leg, the monster had no chance of escaping up the slope or through the tangle of roots on the forest floor or across the stream. Its only path for getting away was through him.

Besides, Bryen doubted that this creature would flee if given the chance. The monster had come for a very specific purpose, and it wouldn't leave until it had achieved that purpose.

So Bryen had no choice but to kill it, and that was just fine with him.

"Don't let the beast get past me," Bryen replied. "Steel can't cut through its armor but the Talent ..."

Then a thought struck him. If he could infuse the Spear of

the Magii with the Talent, why couldn't he do the same with his friends' weapons? He was a fool not to have thought of this earlier.

He didn't need to turn around to know that he had succeeded when he heard the gasps of surprise behind him.

"The Talent won't hurt you," Bryen called over his shoulder, his eyes never leaving the creature that he had cornered. "It will harm this beast."

"Fight it like a Ghoule," suggested Lycia.

"Fight it like a Ghoule," Bryen confirmed.

With that, Lycia moved to Bryen's left, Davin to his right. The wounded beast opposing them growled when he saw the maneuver, then roared a challenge, its huge claws scratching at the air. Judging from the way the beast could barely take a step, Bryen interpreted the rage demonstrated by the beast to be all bark and no bite, the monster frustrated by its unanticipated and debilitating injury.

Once his friends were in position, Bryen flashed forward and lunged toward the beast. The creature deflected the strike with its claw, pushing the Spear past its uninjured side. Even so, the glowing blade still cut through the monster's armored flesh, the beast releasing a groan of agony that was drowned out by its scream of unbearable pain when at the very same time Davin's spearpoint stabbed through the overextended creature's armpit and continued deep into its chest, the Talent-infused steel charring the assassin's flesh. Yet even with those terrible wounds, the beast still attempted to kill its prey, ignoring as best as it could the blade piercing its side.

"Down!" shouted Bryen.

Davin and Lycia dropped to the ground, Davin still holding onto the haft of his spear, the steel caught on one of the creature's ribs, as the beast's tail, which was as long as the creature was tall and had not been visible with the monster's back turned, shot through the air toward Bryen, its spiky tip aimed right for the Protector's heart.

Bryen sidestepped the strike and slashed down with his spear, the glowing blade slicing right through the appendage and taking off several feet of its length.

The creature's tortured shriek echoed throughout the heart trees. Lycia barely heard it, back on her feet in a flash, her twin swords slicing first across the beast's arm and scraping against the bone and then stabbing through the creature's other hip.

Already off balance, the new wound to the beast's hip was like the last stroke of an axe before a tree toppled to the ground, the creature collapsing face first into the water of the stream.

Davin never gave the creature the chance to rise again as he wrenched his spear free from the beast's side and drove the shining point of his weapon into the base of its neck. There was no scream, no moan after that, just a slight quiver. Finally, the monster was dead.

Bryen nodded his thanks to Lycia and Davin, and then the three ran toward the sounds of the fight taking place deeper among the trees. When they reached the skirmish, a deathly silence had fallen, the soldiers of the Blood Company having formed a large circle around the edge of the small clearing, Rafia, Sirius, and Aislinn positioned strategically around it, their eyes turned toward the branches several dozen feet above them.

"What happened?" asked Bryen.

"Those monsters decided to make a run for it," explained Declan, who stood next to Rafia with his sword drawn. "They leapt onto the heart trees and then scrabbled away with those claws of theirs, pulling themselves up the bark. They were gone in seconds."

"Just now?"

"Yes, just now," confirmed Rafia.

"Right after Davin killed the first beast," said Lycia.

"They made for the trees when they heard that shriek," Sirius nodded. "These two probably felt the death of the third and decided the odds were against them with so many Magii."

"How did Davin kill the beast?"

"I infused his and Lycia's weapons with the Talent," replied Bryen.

"Clever," nodded Rafia, who looked over her shoulder, taking in the shining steel. "Very clever. If we had thought of that we could have ended this here. Now we need to assume that these assassins will try again."

"What are they?" asked Bryen.

"I never got a really good look at them because they were moving so quickly, so I need to confirm," replied Rafia, who then walked back toward where Bryen, Lycia, and Davin had killed the lead assassin. "Although the tail certainly is distinctive."

"They'll definitely be back," confirmed Sirius, staring at the creature once Davin and Bryen had rolled it over onto its back, the size of the beast requiring the two to work together to accomplish the task.

"Why do you say that?" asked Aislinn.

"Because these monsters are Slayers," answered Rafia, who spit to the side in disgust. "They're supposed to be unstoppable, although this one clearly wasn't. They are relentless. Once given a target, they will do whatever is needed to kill it, even if that means sacrificing themselves. Although I doubt that's been required of them very often since they are such excellent killers."

Rafia had needed to take a good, hard look at the beast for her to figure out what it was, because she had never seen one in the flesh. She did recall paging through an ancient text that provided details and sketches of the monsters that had invaded Caledonia during the First Ghoule War. This was one of them. Rarely seen, for obvious reasons, and extremely deadly.

Usually tasked by the Ghoule Overlord with eliminating Magii.

"What's a Slayer?" asked Declan, who continued to remain at Rafia's side. "I'm assuming its name gives away its purpose."

"Exactly so," said Rafia. "A Slayer is the preferred assassin of the Ghoule Overlord. It's one of the deadliest creatures to ever come out of the Lost Land. A monster that's extremely difficult to kill. One hasn't been seen since the end of the First Ghoule War."

"What are they specifically?" asked Declan, wanting to learn as much as he could so he could prepare the gladiators for when they next came up against the monsters. "They're impervious to steel. Are they demons crafted from Dark Magic? Ghoules transformed into something worse by the Curse?"

"We don't know," replied Sirius, who continued to stare down at the dead beast. He never thought that he would see one of these monsters again. He realized now that had been a false hope. The Ghoule Overlord would do whatever was necessary, use whatever was necessary, to achieve his goal. "No one knows. We just know how dangerous they are. During the First Ghoule War, the Ghoule Overlord sent Slayers after the Magii, trying to winnow down our numbers. They were lethal then, killing several dozen of our brothers and sisters, and they remain so as we've seen this night."

"How many died during the attack?" asked Bryen.

"We lost three good gladiators," Declan replied somberly.

"But a credit to you, Davin, for killing this one," said Rafia. "I don't know anyone who can make that claim and speak true."

"It's not a claim to be made if we lost that many fighters," said Lycia. "Besides, if not for Sirius and that light, we'd probably all be dead. And we've still got two of those monsters to kill before they kill us. That won't be an easy task."

"It's an ugly beast, isn't it," said Declan. "Steel didn't affect it at all. All my soldiers could do was keep those two Slayers in place. The only reason that they didn't tear through us was the fact that there were so many Magii with us."

"That's all true, Declan, but you're leaving something unsaid," said Aislinn.

"How do you know that?" protested Declan.

"You forget, Declan. I have years of experience in dealing with people who have their own agendas, who want to achieve their own objectives, or who are trying to hide something or not reveal everything when dealing with the Lady of the Southern Marches. Besides, Sirius does it all the time, and I've spent the last ten years learning from him, so I've got a nose for it now."

"Now that's not fair," huffed Sirius.

"Maybe not," said Aislinn before Sirius could continue. "But it's true. Now out with it, Declan. What aren't you saying?"

"The other reason those beasts didn't tear us apart was because I think they were waiting. They didn't try to attack us right after they killed the sentries. They wanted to distract us. They wanted to keep us where we were."

"Why? What were they waiting for? What were they trying to do?"

"For that one Slayer to kill Bryen. That's why they were here. They came for Bryen. We just happened to be in their way."

Bryen felt a bolt of fear shoot down his spine, knowing that everything Declan said was true. He did his best to control it, though it was a struggle. He needed to accept the position that he was in. He was walking around with a huge target on his back. That was his life now. Until he repaired the Weir. Yet even if he succeeded in doing that, he had no doubt that he would remain a target.

There was only one way to free himself from being within the sights of the Ghoule Overlord, and that was to kill the Ghoule Overlord. Until then, he needed to do all that he could to keep alive the people who were willing to risk their lives for him.

"We need to go. Now." Rafia's voice was strong and certain. "Two Slayers escaped. They know where we are, which means the Ghoule Overlord knows where we are now. He'll be coming. If the Slayers can't finish us, he'll want to complete the task himself."

8

—————

NEW FRIENDS

"I assumed that fighting the Ghoules would be hard work, but it's worse than I had imagined," complained Cornelius Stennivere, Duke of the Three Rivers, rubbing his bald head and then tucking his red beard into his belt to keep it out of the way. He was known for his irascibility, which was on display at that very moment, as well as being fastidiously honest and trustworthy. "I never guessed that it would be this difficult. A wound that would kill one of us is nothing to them. They just shrug it off and keep fighting. It's incredibly irritating!"

The Duke sat on his horse just through the entrance to the Winter Pass. Duchess Stelekel had called for a strategy session now that the bulk of the Caledonian Army had appeared on the field, more than a dozen companies of soldiers already moving as fast as they could north into the dagger-shaped gorge that ran straight through the Shattered Peaks to where the Elders were forcing the Ghoules through the Weir.

Most of their companies, including those from the Royal Guard and the various Duchy Guards, were still on the Breakwater Plateau. The Duchess and the assembled Dukes wanted to get them off the plain and into the mountains as quickly as they could, the freak storms that ravaged the steppe at the top of their minds.

They had seen the black clouds beginning to form just a few leagues to their south and west. They hoped that the bad weather would continue to move away from them, yet there were never any guarantees on the Breakwater Plateau.

Of course, notwithstanding the storms, their ability to achieve their objective depended in large part on how quickly they could push the Ghoules deeper into the Winter Pass. So the sooner their troops marched between the imposing peaks that marked the entrance to the gorge and began moving north toward the Weir the better.

"If they'd stretched a few packs across the entrance to the Pass, we'd have a real battle on our hands and the army would be strung out worse than it already is across the Plateau," offered Wencel Roosarian, Duke of Roo's Nest.

Wencel was a short man with a goatee. Noorsin believed that the Duke waxed the tips of his mustache, which was so thick that it resembled the horns of the steers so common to his Duchy, simply so that he would have something to twist with his fingers when he was nervous, which he clearly was in that moment as she feared he might pull out a few too many whiskers if he kept at it.

"Still, it hasn't been easy just like Cornelius said," continued Wencel. "Far from it. We're paying in blood for every step that we take."

"We knew all this going into this enterprise," said Kevan. "We knew that it was going to be a hard fight." His unyielding gaze caught the eyes of all those assembled around Duchess Stelekel. "We're at the tip of the Pass, the narrowest section. Once we push through another few miles, the canyon opens up. Then we can bring more of our forces to bear. Our scouts report that the Ghoule resistance is scattered throughout the Pass, positioned at natural chokepoints. They haven't set up a defensive line that we'd need to fight our way across. They've essentially picked various locations that we need to leapfrog from one to the next. So, until circumstances change, our original plan is still in play. We can form as many columns as we need to and root out the beasts. Until then, it will be slow-going."

"So the Ghoules don't mind if we advance so long as we don't do it too quickly," said Noorsin.

"Exactly, and even after we root out the beasts it's going to be a slog," said Wencel. "The Ghoules don't like building fortifications, although they certainly know how to use what nature has provided them. The beasts are using the rockslides common to the Pass to stall us for as long as they can by forcing us to climb the rocks. We've been using the tactics employed by the Battersea Guard and the Royal Guard, but in these situations we're at a greater disadvantage when we're dismounted." Wencel nodded toward Kevan and Jurgen Klines, the Captain of the Royal Guard, to demonstrate his thanks for their guidance. "The tactics have proven useful. Still, it's a beast of a job – pardon the pun – to kill the creatures. With the rockfalls and mountains of snow littering our path, we've had to try a new approach."

"Yes, we can't go as fast as we would like," admitted Duke Stennivere, "but our strategy has saved lives and proven effective. We set mounted archers on the Ghoules first and try to come at them from multiple directions just as the Duke and the Captain suggested. We don't always hit them, and when we do it rarely kills them unless we are lucky enough to strike them in the eye because of that blasted natural armor of theirs; however, it does enrage them and they lose patience. It doesn't take much to get them angry, and once that happens, they lose what little self-control they have. Once the beasts scramble down the rocks and make a move for the archers, the spears come forward to trap them just as they've been trained. So it works. It reduces the risks we face. Nevertheless, it does take time and patience."

"Even that is exceedingly difficult work," continued Wencel. "So it is taking longer than we expected, just as Cornelius said. Based on our progress so far, and what we'll likely face in the coming weeks even when the gorge opens up in front of us, I don't know if we can clear a path in time to get to the Weir before the bulk of the Ghoule Legions make it through. The Ghoules don't surrender. They fight to the death. We have to kill them all to continue to move forward."

"Wencel is right," said Cornelius. "You can't break them. They don't run. And those Elders are even worse than I expected."

"Yes, they are," agreed Wencel, who nodded toward Noorsin with a great deal of respect showing in his eyes. "What you and the other Magii have done to aid us is much appreciated. But Duchess Stelekel, you and the other three Magii are stretched thin with all that we're asking of you, and it will only get worse as we continue to advance."

"We will do what is necessary, Duke Roosarian," replied Noorsin calmly and with more confidence than she felt. "Have no fear of that."

Nonetheless, Noorsin had to agree that their concerns were legitimate. She, Telly, Irelda, and Maria had gotten scarcely any sleep the last few days, as they were either fighting the Elders who led the Ghoules or trying to protect the soldiers from the Dark Magic against which they were defenseless. It was wearing all of them down, yet there were few other options from which to choose, because the number of Elders opposing them was increasing every day.

"Of that I have no doubt, Duchess Stelekel," said Duke Stennivere. "We just don't want you to push yourselves too hard. We have no chance against the Elders without you. If we need to slow our advance so that you and the other Magii can get some rest, we should take that into account. We can always have a go at the Elders ourselves if we need to. The Blademaster told us how he took down a few of those devils on his way here, so perhaps we could employ a similar tactic to improve our odds. Although admittedly that would be a temporary measure at best. I don't want to throw away lives if we can avoid it."

"That won't be necessary, Duke Stennivere, at least not yet," replied Noorsin. "I value your concern for us, but we must remember that time is not our ally. We cannot delay if we can avoid it. We must continue to advance as fast as we can. The longer it takes us to push deeper into the Winter Pass, the more time the Ghoule Overlord will have to force more Legions through the Weir."

"Perhaps we can help," said a nondescript man with short hair and glasses that were perched at the very end of his nose. "We can share the work with you and make the task that much easier."

The assembled leaders turned as one upon hearing the quiet voice, taking in the three men and one woman who stood there calmly just behind them.

"Benjin!" exclaimed Noorsin, who dropped down from her saddle and strode over toward the Magus. She gave him a hug, then did the same for the other three as well. "I am so glad that you are here."

Joining Benjin were three Magii who Noorsin knew quite well, having spent time with all of them during her apprenticeship with Sirius when they traveled throughout the Duchies of Caledonia.

Suzane looked like a kindly grandmother, her grey hair cut at her shoulders, yet there was nothing kindly about her. She spent most of her time in the Caledonian wilderness, preferring the quiet and ruggedness to the busyness of the cities and towns. She didn't talk much, and when she did, people tended to listen, because she wasn't the type of person who you wanted to anger by failing to heed what she had to say. She held grudges with the best of them, never letting them go unless amends were made. And even then she never forgot them.

Usil was short and stout, an irrepressible energy radiating from him in waves. He was always moving, always doing something. Even standing before the assembled leaders, he shuffled from one foot to the other, unable to stay still. And in the rare times that he wasn't moving physically, his mind was, his brain never turning off. He had fought the Ghoules several times before during his journeys through the Shattered Peaks, the scar peeking out from his collar that started at his shoulder and then cut diagonally down to his abdomen serving as evidence. The Elder had tried to gut Usil before he was dead. That had been a mistake, and Usil had never given the beast the chance to regret it.

And finally, Cinjin. With his long hair tied in multiple braids that ran down his back and his slightly raised eyebrows, he aways seemed to wear an amused almost mocking expression. However, his eyes never smiled. Ever. He had lost his entire family to the Ghoules, and he was always looking for an opportunity to pay back the beasts for the suffering that they had caused him.

"We are just the beginning," said Benjin. "The Order knows what we are up against. More are coming. We just happened to be the closest."

"I'm glad you arrived when you did," she said with a grin. "You heard the challenge that we face?"

"We did," he replied. "We should be able to alleviate some of the stress. We all have experience fighting the Elders."

"That would be greatly appreciated. We can certainly use the help."

"Yes, you are all most welcome," said Duke Winborne, dipping his head as a sign of respect, the other Dukes and the

Blademaster doing so as well. "We can certainly put your skill in the Talent to use."

"I doubt this lot of Magii could do more than I can with my Guard," shouted a young woman who galloped up to the group on a black destrier, pulling her mount to a stop with a harsh and unnecessary tug of the reins. "My soldiers can fight and kill anything put in front of them. I would worry that this group of elderly folk couldn't handle my laundry if it gave them a fight."

Before Benjin and the other Magii, who clearly didn't care for the woman's comments or attitude, could respond, Noorsin stepped in, hoping to defuse what had become a potentially explosive situation. None of the assembled Magii, other than perhaps for Benjin, were known for having much patience for anyone who challenged their abilities.

"You are Selecia Westgard, are you not?" asked Noorsin. "I am Noorsin Stelekel, Duchess of Murcia. We have not had the pleasure until now."

"You know me?" asked Selecia with a huge grin. "My exploits must precede me." Selecia's horse pranced around in a circle at her command. She wanted to give those assembled a brief show of her skills. "Tell me, is the Volkun here? I have heard much about him, first because of his combat against Stil Sheldgard -- a man who certainly deserved to die, if I might say -- and then because of his role in freeing the gladiators and leading the rebellion against Marden Beleron. I have not decided whether I want to duel him or employ him. Perhaps both."

"No, he is not here," said Noorsin, recognizing the tone in the Duchess Westgard's voice when speaking of Bryen and choosing to ignore it. The young woman had another interest in the gladiator that she had left unsaid, an interest that Aislinn would be less than pleased to hear about. "He is on a mission distinct from ours."

"That's too bad," replied Selecia. "I had hoped to learn for myself if the stories were true. Meet the man versus the myth."

"And returning to your original question, actually, no," replied Noorsin, deciding to offer a tiny barb with the hope of popping the bubble of arrogance that seemed to be permanently in place around the Duchess Westgard. "Never having met you before and not having been to the west coast of Caledonia in some time, I know you only by the markings on your armor."

Noorsin's honesty appeared to achieve her purpose, deflating the young woman for a few seconds. Noorsin watched as the Duchess' eyes chilled. With her dark chestnut hair and blue eyes, she was attractive even with her haughty demeanor. Westgard was one of the newer Duchies located just to the north of Roo's Nest that Corinthus Beleron created in recognition of the family's service to the Crown. Other than the one large town on the coast that was becoming a hub for fishing and commerce across the Burnt Ocean, the Duchy was still mostly wilderness.

"You'll know me soon enough," said Selecia, trying to recover quickly the dignity that she believed she had lost. "That I promise you. No one can beat me with a blade on the west coast, likely the entire Kingdom now that I think of it."

"That's good to hear," replied Noorsin, trying to calm the waters that continued to churn around her. "And thank you for joining us in this fight. I assume that you have brought your companies and not just yourself?"

"Just a day behind me," she replied. "Ten in all. Every soldier a master of the steel."

"A welcome addition," confirmed Kevan. "I am Duke Winborne. And these are the Dukes Stennivere and Roosarian, as well as Jurgen Klines, Blademaster and Captain of the Royal Guard. Perhaps at dinner tonight we can take you through our plan of battle and how you and your soldiers might best fit in."

"I look forward to it," said Selecia.

Selecia zeroed in on the famed Blademaster, taking his measure and thinking of how she might convince him to spar with her in the training circle so that she could show him her skill with the blade, which in her mind couldn't be rivaled. The Blademaster he might be, but he had never fought her.

She shifted her attention to the practitioners of the Talent. They appeared to be no better than commoners. If, in fact, they were all powerful Magii, they looked like anything but.

"Although I still have doubts about whether the old folks over there will be of much use. I don't see how they could stand more than a second against the Ghoules, much less the Elders."

"Selecia, I take it that you don't have a great deal of experience with ..."

"Duchess Stelekel, if I may," cut in Suzane, the Magus unable to control her simmering anger any longer. "As you know, sometimes a demonstration is much more effective than words."

Noorsin stared at her old friend for several seconds before finally nodding. Almost reluctantly, but realizing that it was necessary. She had seen this same scene play out before.

"Don't harm her, Suzane. We need all the fighters who we can get."

"I will simply broaden her perspective," agreed Suzane. "She will not come to harm."

"I doubt you could even do that, grandmother," chuckled Selecia. "But you are welcome to try."

"That I will," said Suzane, who stepped right in front of Selecia, unconcerned by the massive war horse that towered above her, the animal snorting in her face because the young woman sitting on its back was pulling too hard on the reins and the bit was digging into the animal's mouth. "Tell me, Duchess Westgard. You say you are good with a blade. Have you fought a Ghoule before?"

"I have not had the pleasure yet," she replied. "The beasts have not made their way to Westgard. That's why I'm here now. To kill Ghoules."

"An admirable and worthy goal, Duchess Westgard. But do you at least know how to fight a Ghoule? You just admitted that you've yet to come across one."

"They bleed just like anything else, don't they?" asked Selecia with just a touch of contempt in her voice. "A sword in the gut will kill anything alive."

"True, but trying to stab a Ghoule in the gut is a difficult thing. These creatures are fast. Much faster than we are. It takes several soldiers working together to take one down, especially since their armored skin makes it difficult to kill them if you're lucky enough to even hit one. You have to strike them in their few weak points to have any chance of killing them, and that's something at which you don't want to fail, because if you do, you likely become the beast's next meal."

"Are you trying to scare me, grandmother?" scoffed Selecia. "Because if you are, it's not working."

"No, Duchess Westgard, I am not trying to scare you. I am trying to educate you, although I fear you are not listening."

"I hear what you are saying, grandmother."

"Hearing and listening are two different things, Duchess Westgard. Since you are quite confident about your chances against a Ghoule, let's move on to the Elders. These beasts have been gifted with Dark Magic by their master, the Ghoule Overlord. Your steel will do nothing against the Curse."

"Yes. Yes, I know. It doesn't matter, though, because Elders are still flesh and blood. Stab them in the gut, and they die."

Suzane closed her eyes for just a moment, pinching the bridge of her nose with her fingers, trying to calm herself. This young woman was infuriating. So certain in what she knew, the problem being that she knew so little.

"You assume that you'll get close enough to an Elder to try

to pierce its flesh with steel. You won't. You must rely on the Magii to kill the Elders, or at least to hold them off, for you to have any chance at killing a Ghoule."

"Is there a point to this, grandmother?" asked Selecia with a scornful shake of her head. "Because I'm beginning to lose patience. Instead of talking so much and wasting my time, perhaps you could show me so we could move on to more important matters. You were going to do that, were you not? I am tired of words. I am a woman of action. A woman of valor."

"Are you?" questioned Suzane. "Action, that's obvious. You can't even sit still on such a beautiful horse that you are treating rather poorly. You've been twitching atop your mount ever since we started speaking. Valor? That's yet to be determined. I guess we'll find out soon enough. But what of intelligence? Are you a woman of intelligence?"

"How dare you ..."

"That's something that the stories tend to ignore," said Suzane, speaking right over Selecia. "The best fighters are brave, yes, that's a given. What's often ignored is their intelligence. So tell me, young Duchess Westgard. What would you do when faced with this challenge?"

"What challenge?"

Selecia stared at the old woman for several seconds, not understanding. Then she realized to her horror that other than her eyes, she couldn't move. She was frozen in place, as was her horse, whose eyes rolled wildly.

"Release me!"

"It's hard to act when you can't move. It's certainly a useful and necessary ability when fighting a Ghoule, who is stronger and faster than you. Yet if an Elder does this to you, then you're no better than a piece of meat."

"You will pay for this, you old ..."

"As a result, sometimes other actions are needed," continued Suzane. "Perhaps something like this."

A glowing white globe appeared just above Suzane's left hand, while she gestured with her right. Selecia's eyes bulged when she saw the dagger at her hip slip out of its sheath, hover in front of her eyes for several heartbeats, then drift in the air until it was just in front of the Magus.

With barely a flick of her finger, the ball of energy spinning atop Suzane's palm consumed the dagger, starting with the tip and working its way up to the hilt, the metal melting into liquid drops that splattered the grass at the Magus' feet. She then allowed the hilt to drop into the grass after releasing her hold on the Talent, freeing Selecia and her frightened horse at the same time.

"So I would suggest," said Suzane, her eyes blazing, "that intelligence is just as important as action or valor, perhaps even more so. I also suggest that you attempt to exercise your intelligence a bit more. Being the Duchess of Westgard will only get you so far. Do we understand each other?"

Selecia nodded without saying a word, struggling to maintain control over her spooked mount and her own fear and embarrassment.

"Good. You understand now of what we're about, do you not?"

"I do."

"You understand now of what we are made, do you not?"

"I do."

"Then off with you, lass. You're wasting our time, and we have more important matters to discuss. We'll let you know when we have need of you."

9

CHANGE IN DIRECTION

"North or west? That is the question."

"Sirius, you don't need to keep repeating that same statement. It's getting aggravating."

"Saying it helps me to focus. It helps me to mull the decision that I need to make."

"That we need to make," clarified Rafia. "You're not leading this expedition on your own."

"You're right, my apologies. Still, we need to make a decision. North or west?"

"Your one-track mind is driving me crazy," snapped Rafia. "Just like it did when we were together for so many years."

"I cannot be responsible for how you feel," countered Sirius. "Your emotions are your own."

"Not even when you are the primary cause for the emotions that I'm experiencing right now?" challenged Rafia.

"I can only be responsible for myself and not for how others feel about me. Isn't that what you told me right before we left Haven?"

"I may have said that, but I didn't think ..."

Rafia's retort caught in her throat. How was she supposed to respond to that? Sirius actually had been listening to what she had said then, which was rarer than a white buck in the Dark Forest.

Of course, knowing Sirius, he likely only remembered her words so that he could throw them right back at her at the most opportune moment. As he had just done. Perhaps even more aggravating, as she thought about it, was that she had to concede that he was right.

"Can you two push your bickering to the side for a moment?" asked Declan, although by the hard glare he gave the Magii, both Sirius and Rafia were quite aware that he wasn't making a request. "As Sirius has made nauseatingly clear, we need to make a decision, and we need to make it now. Once we've done that, you can go back to the arguing that you both seem to enjoy so much."

Sirius opened his mouth to protest then he closed it just as quickly. He had learned during his short association with the reticent Master of the Gladiators that he was not easily intimidated, Magus or no. Because of that, he was beginning to understand just how much of Declan had washed off onto Bryen. A good thing, for the most part, in his opinion. Infuriating on occasion.

Rafia simply stared at Declan appraisingly. Why did this gladiator intrigue her so? She pushed that thought from her mind. Declan was right, just as Sirius was. He just wasn't as annoying as the Magus. They needed to make this decision so that they could keep moving.

"You're right, Declan," said Rafia apologetically. "Allow me to put the question before everyone. North or west?"

It had been several days since the Slayers had attacked. Since then, they had not seen any sign of the two surviving monsters, although Bryen could sense them and knew exactly where they were. Strangely, none of the other Magii could find them with the Talent. So Bryen assumed his ability to identify that ancient evil came from the Seventh Stone.

Sirius believed that it was because the evil used to create these monsters may have predated the time of the Ghoule Overlord. Rafia disagreed, suggesting instead that the assassins of the Ghoule Overlord had an innate ability to hide themselves from the Talent that the Elder Ghoules lacked, which would explain why the creatures had been so successful at eliminating Magii during the First Ghoule War.

Once the dispute between the two Magii had devolved into another hours-long argument, Bryen had stepped in, having lost patience with both of them. The two Magii wisely decided to worry about how the Slayers could shield themselves so effectively later since Bryen could still locate the beasts.

At that moment, the Slayers were less than a league away, having stayed the same distance from them since the early morning fight. Never getting any closer, never falling behind. That suggested one thing to Bryen.

The Slayers had been instructed not to attack again, at least not yet. Instead, the monsters were tracking them. Rafia's theory that the Ghoule Overlord had to be the one to take the Seventh Stone rang too true to disbelieve until proven otherwise.

With the Slayers staying at their backs and no Ghoules close enough yet to be an immediate threat, although several packs were moving toward them through the Shattered Peaks from the east, the Blood Company had reached the north-eastern corner of the Dark Forest.

Having quieted the two Magii at least for a time, Declan stepped to the verge of the wood, looking out upon the long grass of the steppe that led all the way to the southern boundary of the Shattered Peaks. For too brief a moment, he stood there, enjoying for the first time in several weeks the glare of the sunlight and the warmth of its touch.

The Dark Forest certainly was aptly named for many reasons, he thought, and perhaps the one most ignored but most telling was how the gloom and silence of the grove worked to crush a person's spirit. As soon as you walked into the murk, it was as if you had been placed in a grape press, and as each day passed there was another turn of the machine's lever so that it bore down on you just a little bit more. After a few days of this there was nothing left within you but loneliness, paranoia, and an impending sense of doom.

Declan was well aware of the dangers of the Breakwater Plateau, having crossed the steppe several times when he served as a soldier in the Royal Guard. The deadly storms appeared without warning, and he knew from experience that if you got caught in one of those, you were placing your life in the hands of what was a very fickle and frequently harsh nature.

In the Dark Forest, you had more control. What you gained by avoiding the peril of the long grass you had to balance against the slow progress you made through the wood as well as the impact the murk could have on your mental health.

Of course, for him, north or west was an easy decision. He was tired of the gloom, the shadows, the feeling that you were never quite alone among the massive and soaring heart trees. He wanted to walk back out into the light, come what may. If he was to die, whether at the claws of the Slayers or the Ghoules hunting them, he wanted to see his death coming and preferably with the sun shining.

"If we go north, do we make straight for the Shattered Peaks?" Declan asked, turning around to face the others who had gathered around him. The Blood Company had settled among the tree roots at the very edge of the wood, enjoying the first glimpse of the sun in almost two weeks, though not yet stepping into the light.

"We do," replied Rafia. "Straight across as fast as we can."

"And what of the Ghoule packs coming at us from the east?"

"You're assuming, Declan, that we can even make it across the Breakwater Plateau without any unforeseen difficulties," said Tarin. "Now, the steppe appears calm, peaceful. There's no guarantee that it will remain so. In my experience, it won't stay that way for very long."

"Do you want to remain within the Dark Forest, Captain?" Declan asked, already knowing the answer.

"No, actually I don't. I simply raise the concern we are all thinking about. Better to have all the facts in front of us before moving forward."

"And a valid concern it is," agreed Declan. "I would argue that without a little risk, there is no reward."

"Another of Declan's sayings?" asked Rafia quietly, who nudged Bryen with an elbow, the Protector sitting next to her.

"Yes, but keep in mind that he comes up with sayings all the time. Some of them are his, some he's picked up from others."

"Still, I find that very fascinating, indeed," murmured Rafia.

"Can we focus on the task at hand?" hissed Sirius, redirecting them back to the conversation.

"Stop being a grouch, Sirius," Rafia hissed back at him, giving him a much sharper elbow to the ribs than she had given Bryen.

"In addition to the obvious, of course," said Declan, "the steppe gives us a better chance to stay ahead of the Slayers. If we move fast enough, we might even be able to avoid those Ghoule packs coming at us from the east."

"What would be the reward if we crossed the Breakwater Plateau?" asked Tarin.

Bryen smiled. It was almost as if the Captain of the Battersea Guard and Declan already had decided what needed to be done and were now working the rest of them through the same process to ensure that they reached the decision that they believed was the correct one.

"The Haven," replied Rafia. "If we stay in the Dark Forest, we have few options for defending ourselves. The gloom favors the Slayers. If we make it across the Breakwater Plateau and worse comes to worse, we can use Haven either as a defensive fortification or a rest stop before we make for the Trench. It might add a few days to our journey, though I would argue the extra time might be worth it, because we might have a way to cut some time from our journey if we can reach the Library of the Magii."

"What of the Slayers?" asked Jerad. "What if they stop tracking us and come at us when we're crossing the Breakwater Plateau? I don't mind fighting them, I'd just prefer to do it when we have more working in our favor."

"You can be certain that they will come at us again, Sergeant," said Sirius, looking at Rafia, who was ignoring him, trying to puzzle out her last comment. "The Slayers are tracking us now because we're going the direction that they want us to go. If that changes, if the Ghoule Overlord gets close to us, they likely will attack us."

"How can you be so certain of that?" asked Tarin.

"If I was the Ghoule Overlord it's what I would do. He wants to be the one to take the Seventh Stone. He won't risk losing his chance to destroy the Weir. So he uses the Slayers to herd the Seventh Stone where he wants it to go at the pace that he wants it to go. And if we veer off course, then the Slayers push us back on the right track if they don't kill us outright."

"Then how do you explain the Slayers attacking us a few nights ago?" asked Declan. "The Ghoule Overlord wasn't anywhere near us then."

"They were instructed to test us," replied Sirius. "To see what we were made of. Perhaps even to try to take Bryen and bring him to the Ghoule Overlord. That would make the most sense."

"You aren't sharing all that you believe, are you, Sirius?"

asked Aislinn, her tone suggesting that she knew there was more going through his mind than just that.

"No, I'm not," replied Sirius with a grin. Clearly, the Lady of the Southern Marches knew him too well. "I think it might be much simpler than all that."

"How do you mean?" asked Rafia, irritated that Sirius couldn't even provide a complete answer without being nudged.

"The Slayers have not been seen in the Kingdom for a thousand years, and there's a reason for that," explained Sirius. "Even during the First Ghoule War those monsters were difficult for the Ghoule Overlord to control because they are driven by an insatiable hunger. A drive that they can't ignore, and that they can't alleviate no matter how many they kill. I wouldn't be surprised if the Overlord locked those creatures away when he didn't have need of them because they aren't picky in what they eat. Ghoule or human, it doesn't matter to them if they're desperate."

"Just spit it out, Sirius," Rafia urged, struggling to maintain control of her rising temper.

"They wanted to feed."

"Thank you for that frightening and morbid perspective, Sirius," said Bryen with a nod. He had little desire to replay in his mind as he'd been doing ever since the fight against the Slayer what the attack really meant for him, having already guessed at what Sirius had suggested. He had more than enough to worry about as it was. "Going back to Jerad's original question, we have more space to fight on the Breakwater Plateau, and the Slayers will have fewer opportunities to escape if they decide to come at us."

"And with that trick that Bryen has taught us," said Rafia, "we can make sure that every soldier in the Blood Company has a Talent-infused weapon. The Slayers will be vulnerable to all of our blades."

"So our steel will penetrate their natural armor?" asked Jerad.

"That it will," confirmed Rafia.

"I like the sound of that," said Jerad.

"So do I," confirmed Tarin. "No one likes fighting something that you can't kill."

"Bryen, Davin, and Lycia took down one of the creatures," reminded Declan. "If the other two Slayers decide to come at us again on the long grass, we'll be ready for them. We should be able to give them a better fight, one that they'll likely regret."

"Always looking for a fight, are we, Master of the Gladiators?" asked Sirius.

"No, I'm simply considering options," replied Declan, ignoring the use of his old, now defunct title. He could understand the tension between him and the Magus, stoked in large part by Rafia. But he didn't have time for such childishness. He was there to help Bryen in any way that he could. It was as simple as that. "If we don't have to fight and can escape the Slayers, then all the better."

"Even so, there are no guarantees," offered Rafia. "We can fight them now, though I'd prefer that we don't. Those monsters were made for a reason. We'll be better prepared for them, but they're still deadly creatures. I'd like to avoid losing anyone else to them if we can."

"As would I," agreed Declan.

"So better to escape if we can," confirmed Tarin. "Speed is all important now, which means that there is no need to continue this discussion. There's only one direction to go."

"Which could be more dangerous than fighting the Slayers," suggested Sirius. "At least with the Slayers we know what to expect. On the Breakwater Plateau anything could happen."

"A valid point that has already been made, Sirius," confirmed Tarin, "and as Declan put it so eloquently, without a little risk, there is no reward."

"We have no choice," agreed Rafia. "We head north. If we make it across, we turn west when we hit the Shattered Peaks. We have Haven as a refuge if we need it. Hopefully we won't."

Understanding that the decision had been made, Sirius turned his mind toward reducing the risk of crossing the Breakwater Plateau. He was not a gambler by nature, although he did agree with what Declan had said, so if he could mitigate that danger in any way, he wanted to give it a try.

"There's something that I might be able to do that could give us a better chance of success. More of a head start with respect to the Slayers, and perhaps keeping the Ghoules off our backs for a while longer, if nothing else."

"What did you have in mind, Sirius?" asked Rafia.

"I can use the Talent to create a false trail."

"How would you do that?" asked Aislinn.

"I provide a scent of the Seventh Stone that continues in the Dark Forest toward the west while we mask our new path to the north."

"Will it work?" asked Rafia. "These Slayers are made of an evil older than the Ghoules."

"For a time, I believe it will work," replied Sirius. "Unfortunately, I can't say for how long. Eventually, we'll be found out. But even if we only gain a couple days, that could prove useful."

"Then speed is our best friend at the moment," said Declan.

"That it is," replied Tarin. "It's time to get moving."

Declan nodded, then stepped away from the group, issuing a series of commands as he worked his way through the resting Company of Blood. He understood the dangers of the Breakwater Plateau, so he wanted to make sure that every one of the gladiators knew what they were doing, why, and what was expected of them.

After most of the small group had gone their separate ways to complete their preparations, Bryen remained sitting on a thick tree root that allowed him to look out over the plain and watch the wind gust through the long grass. Aislinn stayed with him. He had that look on his face that had become so familiar to her. He was contemplating something important.

"What's on your mind?" she asked finally.

"Quite a lot of things," Bryen replied with a smile. "More than I probably should be thinking about."

"You know Noorsin has a saying about that."

"Thinking never hurt until you thought too much."

"She shared it with you?"

"She did," confirmed Bryen. "I had gone to check on her to make sure she was healing well when we were back in Battersea, and we spoke for a time on several matters. I guess she saw that I was conflicted about a few issues, so she left me with that saying."

"It's good advice."

"I know."

"You're not rethinking all this again, are you?" asked Aislinn. "You're not worried about everyone else like you were before, I hope. We've discussed this already. We're here because we want to be. We choose to be. You can't take that away from us."

"No, of course not."

"You're a terrible liar, you know that?" replied Aislinn with a smirk.

"I do now," said Bryen in a soft chuckle.

"I hope you realize that if you tried to skip off on your own and make for the Sanctuary by yourself, I'd be right behind you, as would the rest of the Blood Company. We're with you to the end."

"Of that I have no doubt."

Aislinn studied him for several heartbeats. Bryen was quiet to begin with, yet at the moment he seemed to be stuck within his own mind.

"Then if you're not thinking about that, what are you thinking about?"

"Whether I can do this," he replied softly. "Whether I have what it takes. Whether I'm leading you and everyone else on a fool's errand, because even if we reach the Sanctuary, I still have no idea how to repair the Weir. Even with what the Seventh Stone showed me, I just don't know if I can do it."

Aislinn nodded, understanding his concerns. It was this more vulnerable side of her Protector that had drawn her to him when they were forced together, once she realized that they both were dealing with the same challenges because of the silver collar placed around his neck.

When she had first met him, she had simply assumed that coming from the Colosseum, he was a cold-blooded killer. Nothing more. She had realized over time that there was so much more to him than that.

"I can understand why you have doubts," said Aislinn, reaching for his hand and taking it in her own. "We all do, whether we want to admit those doubts to ourselves or not. You worry about repairing the Weir, I worry about what's expected of me as the Lady of the Southern Marches and what might be required of me if my father isn't there. Whether I can manage the responsibilities that will fall to me when that happens."

"How do you deal with all that?"

"I try not to think about it, of course."

"But ..." Bryen prodded with a laugh.

"But I also understand that I won't be ready for it when it happens. I can't be ready. Even with all that I've done to prepare myself, all that my father has done to make sure I'm ready, I still worry about whether I have what it takes to do what needs to be done." Aislinn gripped his hand just a little bit tighter. "Just as you've been doing."

Bryen nodded, appreciating her viewpoint. "Thank you for that. It helps to put things in perspective."

"Now what else is on your mind?" she asked, giving him a gentle nudge with her shoulder.

"Why do you think that there's something else bothering me?"

"Because I know you."

"Because of the collar?"

"No, because I know you," Aislinn replied in a slightly offended tone. The certainty of her voice caught his attention, drawing his eyes to hers, and when he saw the sparkle there, he couldn't stop himself from smiling.

"It's the Slayers," Bryen revealed finally.

"What about them?"

"Right now they're our biggest concern. No matter what direction we go, they'll catch us. Even with what Sirius is doing, they'll figure it out eventually and come at us again."

"That's why you're worried? We can fight them now thanks to you."

"Even so, it won't be an easy fight. So I'm also thinking about what we can do about the Slayers. We might be able to use their hunger to our advantage."

"You want to bait the assassins of the Ghoule Overlord?" asked Aislinn, slightly incredulous.

"In a word, yes."

10

FALSE TRAIL

The Dark Forest was still and silent, the pall of the grove resembling a shroud that consumed even the loudest sounds within the wood. The gurgling of the small streams that meandered beneath the corkscrewing roots. The few squirrels, foxes, and rabbits that skittered across the forest floor. The birds flitting from branch to branch during the day. The owls waiting for the slightest sign of movement at night. The snap of a dead limb cracking off a larger branch. The wind rushing between the heart trees and rustling the leaves that were as large as a small buckler. All of those noises were muffled at best, unheard most of the time because of the suffocating air of the wood.

Yet now, that soul-crushing mood took on a new note. Menace. Not a sound whispered among the trees, not even a single breath of the wind.

Not with the predators that sprinted across the soft loam, easily leaping over the towering arched roots and launching themselves onto and then from the bark of a heart tree to fly fifty or more feet through the air and continue their pursuit.

The beasts increased their pace, their sharp claws scarring

the massive trees, cutting out huge splinters, as they chased after their quarry.

All to no avail. The hunters followed a scent that with each step they took, no matter how fast they moved, grew fainter and fainter, slipping from their grasp.

Until the scent simply disappeared.

The hunters had reached the far northwestern corner of the Dark Forest, the western section of the Breakwater Plateau less than a league away.

Howling in frustration, their terrifying shrieks lost in the gloom, the Slayers continued on for another mile, taking their time now, ranging from north to south and back again, hoping that they would pick up the scent that had tickled their nostrils since their Master had freed them from their cells beneath the Temple of the Ghoules.

No such luck. The trail had gone cold.

With nothing left to do, the two Slayers perched on a huge root that shot out of the ground twenty feet into the air, ran above the forest floor for another twenty feet, and then plunged back down into the earth. Their large, clawed feet dug deeply into the bark, holding them in place. They used their roost to scan the forest around them, seeking any kind of movement. Anything to suggest that their prey had come this way.

There was nothing but the unnatural stillness of the wood.

Nor was there any hint as to where their prey may have disappeared. No trail. No scent. Nothing.

For the first time in more than a thousand years, the two Slayers had lost their quarry.

Confused, angry, hungry, the Slayers roared in unison, their howls of rage and anguish bursting free from their broad chests and battering off the heart trees, the sound of fury mixed with a deep craving traveling for leagues within the grove.

Their Master had commanded that they take the Seventh Stone and bring it to him.

They had failed.

A trickle of unease seeped into them.

They feared nothing in this world, except for their Master.

Worse, they had not eaten in days. They had expected to find their prey by now. To feast on the humans that they were hunting. Now they were hungry, ravenously so. They needed to feed, that demand dominating their thoughts.

They had seen nothing to eat as they had stalked through the wood following what they believed now to be a false scent, and that likely meant several more days of the hunger that was more painful than the scorching energy of the Talent. The starvation that left a hole in their gut and that would remain there until they finally found the fleeing humans.

Unless ...

About to leap down from the root, the Slayer on the right was knocked from its perch by a staggering blow to its head, its sharp claws ripped free from the bark, the monster too surprised to adjust to its fall and landing hard on its back in the dirt. The beast struggled for air, its breath knocked from its lungs.

Blood trickled down the side of its jaw, the long tear of a three-taloned claw shredding its armored flesh. Even though the Slayer was dazed, it managed to roll out of the way when it saw through its clouded vision the massive shape leaping down from the branch.

The other Slayer had hoped to crush the chest of its brethren with its clawed feet, but it had been too slow. Its partner now prey jumped back up, recovering faster than the attacking Slayer had thought possible after the blow it had struck.

The two monsters faced off against one another.

Whether it was anger at losing their prey, the always-present hunger, or the fact that one of the Slayers had failed to murder the other, neither of the beasts really cared. They had been hunting for more than a week now with little success and they had lost their leader.

Now they just wanted to fight. Now they wanted to kill. Now they wanted to eat.

If that meant killing one of their own kind to do so, then they would. The blood and flesh of their brethren was no different than that of their prey when their stomachs begged to be fed.

The wounded Slayer dove toward the other beast, slamming into its brethren's legs as it tried to knock the Slayer that had hit it across the jaw to the ground. The wounded Slayer ignored the pounding on its back as the other monster dug its clawed feet into the turf and struggled to free itself from the crushing grip, its sharp claws cutting needle-thin furrows in the Slayer's muscular flesh.

The wounded Slayer held on, ignoring the pain. Pushed on by a fury that made its blood-red eyes flash with rage, the hurt monster locked one large claw around the other creature's waist, holding the monster there, then plunged its free claw into the beast's thigh.

The Slayer howled in pain as the beast's claw dug deeper into the flesh of its leg. For almost a minute, the two creatures remained fixed in place, moving no more than a few inches in either direction as they pushed against each other.

Then, instead of pounding its claws against its brethren's back, the Slayer reached below the beast, wrapping its arms around the other monster's waist, ignoring the pain as its brethren's claw scraped against the bone in its thigh. Gaining the momentum and leverage that it needed, the Slayer lifted the other beast into the air upside down and slammed it against the ground as both beasts fell backward.

With both Slayers now on the ground, the fight turned into a wrestling match, the Slayers' natural aggressiveness and debilitating hunger driving them on.

Sharp claws dug into flesh as they rolled around in the soft loam, crashing into tree trunks and roots, dozens of bloody wounds spotting the dark flesh of each Slayer.

As they tussled in the dirt, each beast trying to cut the throat of the other, the scent of blood from the injuries they had suffered made them salivate, the smell too much for either to ignore.

The hunger pulsing within them pushed them to kill. To feed.

Then, shockingly, just as swiftly as the fight began, it ended. With low growls, the two Slayers, bloody and bruised, deep gashes marring their flesh, released their hold on one another and reluctantly pushed themselves up off the ground. They turned toward the east, bowed their heads, and waited, the slight touch of fear that had been buried by their hunger raising its poisonous head once more.

Out of the gloom that lurked between the heart trees walked the Ghoule Overlord, several packs of Ghoules appearing with him and surrounding the Slayers, the Elders massing at their Master's back.

For several minutes, the Ghoule Overlord simply stared at the Slayers, the deadly assassins trying to appear meek, even cowed, in front of their Master, although it was a difficult thing to do, the monsters terrifying even when they themselves were afraid.

When the Slayers finally lifted their heads, the Elders and Ghoules stepped back several feet, clearly uncomfortable in the presence of such dangerous, unpredictable creatures, even with the Ghoule Overlord standing imposingly in front of them. They knew that these creatures were not particular about what they ate, and the Ghoule Overlord had been known to gift these beasts with a Ghoule or two when it served his purposes.

"I am disappointed," rumbled the Ghoule Overlord. "You

have lost one of your number. You have not done as I commanded."

The two Slayers stood their ground, though their eyes returned to the dirt, knowing that to do anything other than listen to their Master's tirade and demonstrate their obedience would mean their deaths.

"You had a simple task," continued the Ghoule Overlord, his voice rising as his rage burst forth. "The only task that you were created for. The only task that needed to be completed to ensure that you would be given free rein to terrorize and feast on the soft humans who populate this land. Yet you couldn't even do that. And now you have lost the scent, you have lost the Seventh Stone, and one of you has been slaughtered like an animal!"

The Ghoule Overlord stepped forward until he was no more than a finger's breadth away from the beasts, his Dark Magic swirling above the black diamond set in his staff, spinning faster and faster as his fury increased.

"How is this even possible?" the Ghoule Overlord demanded in a whisper. "No human should be able to kill one of you. Yet one of them did."

The Slayers feared nothing within the world, but for their Master. The quiet dread that radiated in waves from the Ghoule Overlord as his harsh words washed over them made the two assassins whimper softly with terror.

"So now I must do this myself," continued the Ghoule Overlord, with each passing second the Curse rotating more swiftly around the top of his staff. "I will find the scent again, and you will follow it no matter where it takes you. You will find the Seventh Stone, and you will take him for me. Kill the other humans. I don't care. But you will bring the Seventh Stone to me. You will bring the Protector to me. Alive."

The two Slayers growled their acceptance of their Master's command.

Their fear had dissipated. They would be given a second chance. They would hunt once again. And they understood that this time they could not fail.

In a flash, the Dark Magic shot from the Ghoule Overlord's staff and seized one of the Elders standing behind him, the creature dropping his own staff as the Curse surged down his mouth and nose, forcing itself into every cell of the beast's body. With a flick of his wrist, the Ghoule Overlord lifted the unfortunate Elder into the air with the Curse until the beast was suspended above the small clearing so that all the assembled Ghoules could observe.

The scent of the Seventh Stone was so faint that the Ghoule Overlord could barely sense it, even with the huge reservoir of the Curse that the artifact contained. From here, he had no idea which direction to go. To have any hope of regaining the Seventh Stone that had been free from his grasp for so long thanks to that thieving Magus, to find the trail once again, he needed to take a much more direct approach.

Unable to speak, the Elder's terror at what was happening to him was evident in his eyes as more and more of the Ghoule Overlord's Dark Magic spun around the beast. Once the swirling black enveloped the Ghoule, pinpricks of the Curse jabbed into the beast's flesh, the Elder arcing his back, the overwhelming pain eliciting a silent scream of torture, unable to do anything but exist within the torment thrust upon him.

Through it all, the Ghoule Overlord stood still as a stone, his eyes closed, the Dark Magic revolving faster and faster until the Elder above him was barely visible in the wisps of black. Using the additional power that he had taken from his disciple, the Ghoule Overlord extended his senses, infusing his memory of the Seventh Stone into his search.

There was nothing but hushed silence among the Elders and the Ghoules as they watched, transfixed, as one of their number slowly died. The Elder suspended in the air was losing his very essence, the beast's skin tightening around his bones, his eyeballs drying up and turning to dust, and when it seemed like all the creature's blood had been sucked into the Curse, the Elder began to shrivel into a dried up sack of bones that didn't make a sound when it fell to the soft loam that covered the forest floor.

When the Elders and Ghoules looked upon their Master once again, the Ghoule Overlord was grinning. He had found what he was looking for.

The Seventh Stone was on the Breakwater Plateau and still a good distance from the Shattered Peaks. If they moved fast enough, they could catch the humans before they reached the mountains.

Clever. Whatever trick the Protector had used to disguise himself was clever indeed. But not clever enough.

The humans had extended their head start. They had gained several days on him. Nonetheless, his Slayers and Ghoules would gain on them quickly.

The Ghoule Overlord knew from previous experience that hunting the Protector would be difficult. He had assumed as much. And he did not expect an easy fight when he caught up to the Seventh Stone.

Even so, the Ghoule Overlord was good at solving problems. And now, not only could he take the Seventh Stone, but he could also kill the Magii who were helping the Protector, in the process reducing the number of those skilled in the Talent right when his Legions were about to march down the Winter Pass.

He nodded to himself. A complication, though not an insurmountable one.

The Ghoule Overlord could live with this additional delay. It would give him more in the end than he had expected to gain when the chase began, assuming that his Slayers accomplished the assignment given to them. Assuming they did not meet such a disgraceful end as had been the case with their leader.

"You have failed me once," the Ghoule Overlord said to the two monsters as he used the Curse to give them once more the scent of the Seventh Stone. "Do not fail me again. If you do, I will feed on you."

With a nod of their Master's head to the east, the two Slayers launched themselves over the gathered Ghoules and sprinted through the Dark Forest, racing around the heart trees and over the roots. They were angry at having lost their brethren to the human. And they were terrified of their Master, which only increased the rage boiling within them.

Yet even more so, they were hungry. So hungry. They hadn't eaten in days. They needed to catch up to the humans. They needed to feed.

11
____

STANDING STRONG

The Company of Blood was two days out on the Breakwater Plateau, all of the soldiers pleased to have escaped the oppressing murk of the Dark Forest.

With the excellent weather, only a few wispy clouds drifting lazily above them, they were making good time across the steppe. They stopped for one hour out of every five, night and day. The gladiators didn't mind the grueling pace. They could rest when they were in a better position to defend themselves and got into the mountains, which were still two days away, the dark smudge to the north their goal.

As soon as they had walked out onto the grasslands, Aislinn had assumed responsibility for tracking the Ghoule packs, which had followed the same trail Sirius had placed for the Slayers, the beasts having crossed the Breakwater Plateau with a remarkable speed from the northeast and then entered the Dark Forest and moved toward the far west of the wood. She was thankful that the Ghoules had fallen for the deception, because every time she searched to confirm the beasts' location, she sensed an evil with them that threatened to suffocate her every time she touched it with the Talent.

It was like an endless pool of wickedness that once she fell in, Aislinn knew that she would never be able to escape, drowning in the taint and the corruption. She hadn't asked Bryen what this evil was. She didn't need to. She knew what it was, and she knew that it was coming for her Protector.

Rafia had stated with absolute confidence that the Ghoule Overlord would be joining the pursuit himself, and it appeared that she had been correct. So Aislinn was more than happy with the pace that the Company of Blood was maintaining, Tarin and Declan with an almost annoying regularity actually urging the gladiators to move faster this afternoon after she informed them that the Ghoules had turned back to the east just a few hours before, leaving the Dark Forest and moving out onto the steppe far to the west so that they could avoid the obstacles of the wood and make better time in their pursuit.

While Aislinn concentrated on the Ghoules, Bryen focused on the Slayers since he was the only one able to track them. The monsters had turned back to the east just minutes before the Ghoules, which indicated that the false trail that Sirius had laid had served its purpose for as long as it could. Now their passage across the Breakwater Plateau had become a race. It was just a question of when and where they would meet those monsters again.

"Are they always like this?" asked Lycia, who strode rapidly through the long grass of the Breakwater Plateau just a dozen feet in front of Rafia and Sirius, unable to block out the constant, repetitive dialogue between the two Magii.

Davin walked next to her, Bryen and Aislinn right behind. They were near the front of the column, Jerad and Tarin at the point, soldiers of the Blood Company on their flanks, Declan bringing up the rear with Dorlan and his squad, Kollea sticking right next to the huge gladiator as was her wont.

"Pretty much," replied Bryen. "They were like this on

Haven, always going at one another, and they haven't stopped since. I can only assume that this is how they usually are."

"How did you survive?" asked Lycia. "Having to listen to these two day in, day out, I'd lose my mind after the first hour. They never stop."

"I got away from them as much as possible, although it was a bit of a challenge at times because Haven isn't a very large island and the two of them spent quite a bit of time training me in the Talent."

"It must have made you miss your cell in the gladiators' barracks," suggested Davin with a smirk. "At least it was quiet there. You could actually think rather than having those two voices droning on in the back of your brain."

"Almost, but not quite," Bryen replied with a chuckle. "I'd pole across the lake and wander the mountains when I could, and I did find a few quiet places along the shore where I could take a few hours for myself."

"That doesn't surprise me," replied Davin with a knowing grin. "You were quite good at finding those quiet places where you could while away your free time."

"Just what does that mean?" demanded Lycia, her face beginning to reveal a bright red flush.

"It means that Bryen was very good at finding quiet places around the practice yard," Davin responded hesitantly, realizing that his dry humor may have either struck his sister the wrong way or perhaps it had hit too close to the truth that he was hinting at. He also realized that antagonizing his sister in that moment, intentionally or otherwise, probably wasn't a good idea. Her temper was never far from the surface, and it could be sharper than the steel of her twin blades when she let it loose. "You know, so he could read for a few hours."

Lycia gave her brother a very long look, one that turned his already pale face even paler. She had been grouchy ever since they had left the Dark Forest. Davin corrected himself.

Grouchier than usual. To try to relieve some of the tension, he gave his sister a big smile, hoping that she would accept his explanation.

Lycia stared at her brother for just a little while longer, her eyes narrowing. Then she nodded. Although she wasn't really satisfied with Davin's smile or his quick recovery, she didn't have any desire to pursue what he had been implying any further. She knew where it would lead, and she certainly wasn't prepared to engage in that conversation.

"Well done, Davin," Bryen whispered. "You got out of the hole you dug for yourself all on your own."

"Thanks," he replied in an even softer whisper, breathing a bit easier. "But I think you were in that hole with me."

"Why is Lycia so upset?" asked Aislinn in a quiet voice, having just finished searching for the Ghoule packs once again. Still coming directly toward them. Still coming fast. She hoped that they reached the mountains before the beasts and the evil leading them reached them.

Bryen's face colored slightly, a tinge of worry striking him.

"Davin just has a habit of rubbing his sister the wrong way." Bryen certainly wasn't ready for the discussion that inevitably would follow if he offered a more detailed response, so he didn't.

"Is that so?" asked Aislinn. She studied Bryen for a few seconds. "Why do I feel as if you're not telling me everything?"

Bryen gave her his best smile, hoping that Davin's solution to his problem with his sister would work for him now. "Because you have a very suspicious nature."

Aislinn simply stared at Bryen a little longer. "For good reason, it seems," she finally said. "I hope you do realize that at some point we will need to address this."

"Wonderful," he grumped under his breath, then in a louder voice so that Lycia could hear as well, Bryen suggested, "Let's move a little closer to the front and see if we can catch up to Tarin and Jerad. Lycia's question about Rafia and Sirius has instilled within me the desire for a bit more peace and quiet, and we won't have that here."

With Bryen and his three friends moving farther ahead, and the Blood Company having gotten used to the constant bickering between the two Magii and adjusted to it by staying as far away from them as possible, a space opened up to the front and back of the Magii of a hundred paces. Not the best discipline, having a huge gap in the middle of your column when you knew that your enemies were pursuing you, but even Tarin and Declan were willing to allow it for now because no one really had any interest in hearing the same arguments being rehashed time and time again by Rafia and Sirius -- the value of the entertainment having degraded the more they had to listen to it -- other than the two Magii, of course.

"I asked you to marry me because I thought you wanted me to," said Sirius, trying to explain and not realizing that he was only digging a deeper grave. "I wasn't interested in marriage. I've never really believed in the concept. I just thought that you wanted me to ask you, so I did. I was just trying to do the right thing."

"You thought that I wanted you to ask me?" replied Rafia, flabbergasted and having a hard time grasping Sirius' reasoning. "You should have asked me to marry you because you wanted to marry me, not because you thought that I wanted you to marry me. How could that be good for either of us?"

"Now you're just playing with words," argued Sirius. "What you're suggesting is a difference without a distinction."

"It's a huge difference," countered Rafia, focusing her sharp gaze on Declan, who was walking just a few feet behind them now. Against his better judgment, he had given in to his military instincts and pushed the rear guard forward to close the distance to the two Magii, although he was now regretting that decision as the argument became more heated and the Magus sought to bring him into it. "Wouldn't you agree, Declan?"

"You can leave me out of this," replied the Sergeant of the Blood Company. He had no desire to involve himself in this seemingly endless spat. "I only engage in fights that I know that I can win."

"Really?" asked Rafia, studying Declan closely. "From what I've learned from Bryen, you have a keen sense of justice, of right and wrong, and that you won't hesitate to involve yourself if you believe that it's necessary. Regardless of the odds."

"Perhaps so," replied Declan with a shrug, unable to disagree with what the Magus had said. "In this case, however, with you two talking at one another and never talking to one another, I would suggest that having heard both your arguments, multiple times might I add, in fact more times than any sane person would care to, that you're both in the right and ..."

"Ha!" declared Sirius. "He just said that I was right."

"He just said that we were both right," corrected Rafia. "And you didn't let him finish. We're both in the right and ..."

"And you're both in the wrong," Declan concluded, his eyes not bothering to touch on the two Magii, instead always scanning around them, never resting on one spot for more than a second. He trusted in Bryen's and Aislinn's abilities with the Talent, knowing that they would give the Company sufficient warning if they were to be -- Declan corrected himself, as it was just a matter of time -- when they were about to be attacked. But he was a ten-year veteran of the Royal Guard, and old habits die hard.

"Wrong!" protested Sirius. "How could you possibly suggest that I'm in the wrong?"

"Yes, tell us, Declan," said Rafia, her eyes sharpening to the point where Declan thought that they resembled those of a hawk just about to launch itself at its prey. "Tell us how we're both in the wrong."

"You really want to know?" he asked, apparently unperturbed that the Magii's anger, previously directed at one another, was now pointed toward him.

"We do, indeed, Declan," nodded Rafia. "Please tell us why you believe that we're both in the wrong. I'm dying to hear what you have to say."

"Sirius didn't want to ask you to marry him, though he thought that he should because he believed that you wanted him to. You didn't want him to ask you to marry him, and you lost your temper with him when he did. Sirius is angry because of how you reacted to something that he thought you wanted him to do. You're angry with Sirius because he did something that you didn't want him to do. Where does the fault lie in that?"

"Sirius," replied Rafia quickly.

"Rafia," responded Sirius just as fast.

Declan's lips twisted into a smile as he shook his head. He wasn't surprised by the answers that he had received, although he was disappointed by them.

"It lies with you both," Declan continued calmly. "This whole situation could have been avoided if you'd spoken with each other about what you both wanted rather than making false assumptions about what the other wanted. Neither of you wanted to communicate with one another, or perhaps you were both too afraid to be honest with one another. I don't know. But it was the lack of communication that placed you both in this ridiculous mess."

Declan finally brought his eyes away from the long grass that swayed around them at the whim of the wind, taking in the hard glares that both Magii threw his way. They didn't bother him in the least. Obviously, neither Rafia nor Sirius were pleased by his words, but truly, it just didn't matter to him. There were more important issues to deal with than the ridiculous behavior of two Magii who were acting like jilted lovers.

"I don't really care, either," he continued. "But because you both didn't communicate honestly with one another, you've both walked down a path based on what you believe rather than on what is. And you've walked that path for so long that you're both afraid to admit that it was the wrong thing to do. Neither of you have the courage to acknowledge the mistakes that you've made and move on. Instead, you keep belaboring the same points, acknowledging at least to yourselves that nothing will change, because then you don't have to take a risk."

"And what risk would that be?" asked Rafia, her words frighteningly quiet.

"Of telling each other the truth."

Sirius could only stare at Declan, his expression suggesting that he was either trying to process what Declan had just said or he'd eaten a fly and was attempting to get it out from between his teeth.

"Tell me, Declan, do you have a death wish?" asked Rafia.

"No more than Bryen does," the Master of the Gladiators answered, Bryen having taken him through his first encounter with the Magus when the Protector had arrived on Haven on the back of a Griffon.

"You like to live life on the edge, don't you, Declan?" suggested Rafia. "You have no worries whatsoever over angering two Magii."

"Not really," Declan replied with a tired expression. "To both your statements."

"Then what do you worry about?" asked Rafia, clearly intrigued.

"Of having to engage in the same conversation over and over. Life is too short to become stuck in place. You need to keep moving. Sometimes forward, sometimes to the side, unfortunately sometimes you need to take a step or two back. Regardless, you need to keep moving. Whatever direction it might be at any particular point in time, you need to keep moving."

"Is this another of your sayings, Declan?"

Declan finally turned his gaze toward the Magus and offered her a brief smile, one that put a pin in the bubble of anger that had risen within her since this conversation had started, the rawness of her emotions fading.

"It can be, if you want. I don't think I've said it before. If I have, I don't remember. I'm sure that if you repeat it enough, it'll stick with time."

"Yes, it likely will," agreed Rafia. "Thank you for your thoughts, Declan."

"Always a pleasure," he replied absently, his eyes once again scanning around them.

Rafia then turned right back to Sirius, who still appeared to be trying to figure out how to deal with what Declan had told them. She could restart the same argument that they had been having for the past decade. That certainly was the easiest path. However, she realized now, thanks to Declan, that she had been acting foolishly, and it was time for her to stop.

Or rather, she knew that she had been acting foolishly for quite some time, and that she hadn't wanted to do as Declan had said. She hadn't wanted to take the risk of telling Sirius the truth. However, it was time to do just that. It was time to take a risk. It was time to stop acting the coward.

"I didn't want to marry you, Sirius. You're right. And I don't mean for this to sound harsh, but I've never wanted to marry you. I was just enjoying our time together, no more than that." Rafia smiled as she recalled some of the better experiences that they had enjoyed together, as well as the many more that were not so good but at least were lively, in part because she and Sirius had a unique ability to rub each other the wrong way. "We're too different. And, despite the fact that we're working together now, we had different responsibilities back then. I needed to be at Haven. You needed to be in Battersea with Aislinn."

"I didn't want to marry you either. And you're right." It was Sirius' turn to grin, allowing his anger to ebb, as he too thought of the time that they had spent together as a couple, a time that had been both good and bad, and clearly now was over. "I did what I thought you wanted, even though we had never discussed it. We should have. If we had, we wouldn't be where we are now. We could have parted from one another without any animosity a decade ago."

"Thank you for your honesty, Sirius. I do appreciate it."

"And thank you for yours. If we both agree that it was a mistake, that we're both at fault, and that we should not be together, why are we still fighting about it?" Sirius asked after letting out an exasperated sigh.

They both stared at one another for a moment until two small grins broke out.

"Because we're good at it," said Rafia.

"And it's fun," added Sirius. "It's also certainly easier than being honest, just like Declan said."

Their grins broadened into smiles, and then they laughed together for the first time in a decade.

"I think we've drawn out the drama as long as we can or should," said Sirius. "Are we done?"

"We're done," agreed Rafia.

Sirius nodded. "I'm going to walk up ahead. I wanted to talk to Bryen about something."

"That was a bit awkward," Rafia said, breaking the silence that had dragged on for several minutes once Sirius had left, Declan still walking next to her. The Master of the Gladiators didn't seem to have paid much attention to the final exchange between the Magii. She had expected him to comment on it, yet he hadn't said a word.

"That's one way to put it," said Declan gruffly.

"You don't talk a lot, do you, Declan?"

"Only if I need to."

"Why is that? From all the sayings that I've picked up from you through Bryen, and this last conversation with Sirius, it seems to me that you have a lot to say. Perhaps you should say something more often."

"That's kind of you to suggest, Magus. But I think not."

"Rafia," she corrected. "And why not?"

"Because the people who tend to speak a lot usually aren't saying all that much. They just enjoy the sound of their own voices."

"Are you suggesting something?" asked Rafia, her eyes flashing, whether with the beginnings of rising anger or something else that he thought could be even more dangerous, Declan wasn't certain. Still, it wouldn't keep him from saying what he wanted to say.

"No, Magus. I am simply offering my perspective based on my experiences in life."

"Rafia," she corrected again.

"Rafia."

"So regarding those experiences."

"I gather, Rafia, that you are not one to travel quietly, lost in your thoughts."

"Whatever gave you that idea, Declan?" Rafia replied with a sharp laugh.

"Nothing at all, actually. I was simply hoping."

"A joke," said Rafia with a raised eyebrow. "I am learning more about you than I ever could by walking in silence. That's why I prefer conversation. It is one of the best ways to learn about the world, about other people."

"As is listening."

"You are quite correct in that respect."

"So tell me, Magus."

"Rafia."

"So tell me, Rafia, how is it that you became the Keeper of Haven? From what I've discovered, you were in line to become the Master of the Magii, which would have meant the Aeyrie instead."

"Do you know much about the ways of the Order of the Magii to have an answer to your own question?" asked Rafia, looking at Declan in a new light. She understood that he was educated, having confirmed that fact time and time again when working with Bryen since Declan was responsible for his education. Yet how could he have known so much about the Magii and her own history with the Order?

"I know enough to know that based on your skills, either you went there by choice or you were sent there for a reason."

"Which do you think it might be?"

"You don't seem the type who would want to assume responsibility for the Aeyrie and managing the affairs of the Magii," said Declan. "That would be better left to someone like Sirius, who likes to tell people what to do. I believe that you prefer to be out in the world, doing. So I believe that it was probably a bit of both."

"Indeed it was," Rafia replied with a nod, not feeling the need to be circumspect with Declan. "The Ghoules were stirring in the Shattered Peaks. The Haven gave me a chance to track their movements, see what they were doing and why. Maybe have a little fun with them as well since they have a habit of coming too close to the island."

"And?"

Rafia's look became more appraising. Yes, Declan was a fighter, yet he was so much more, apparently having the ability to sniff out when the whole truth wasn't being shared.

"And it would allow me to learn more about the Seventh Stone."

"You knew what was coming?"

"No, not for certain. Sirius and I, as well as a few others in the Order, suspected. We wanted to be ready. But I assure you, we didn't know what would happen regarding Bryen and the Seventh Stone. That was unexpected."

"I assumed as much. I just wanted to confirm." Declan turned to Rafia with a grin. "Honesty is the best policy after all. Especially when it comes to Bryen. He means a great deal to Caledonia, but he means a great deal more to me. He's like a son to me."

His smile brought out hers, and it was then that she realized that he had turned the tables on her. She had wanted to learn more about him, to get him talking, but he had directed the conversation toward her. And she couldn't miss the full meaning of what he had just said. The warning he had just given her.

"You have done well by Bryen. I wanted to thank you. I knew his parents before they were murdered. They would be proud of the man that he has become."

"I have done what I should have done," replied Declan. "I have done no more for him than I have for any of the other men and women forced into the Pit."

"You are fooling yourself and nobody else if you believe that. I spent a great deal of time with that young man on Haven and since. He is much like you. You have had a tremendous influence upon him, and he would not be here now if not for you."

"Much of what he has earned he has earned on his own."

"Yes, that's true. But not all."

"And your point, Rafia?"

"No point really. Just seeking some honesty myself. Is that not what you prefer? Is that not what we have been discussing this entire time? The need to be honest with one another."

That last comment brought another smile to Declan's lips, this one slightly more mysterious. "Indeed, I do, Rafia. Thank you for the reminder."

"Why the smile?" asked the Magus. "You're making me think that you know something that I don't."

"That's not my intention," said Declan. "But I did figure something out. I know what you're doing."

"What do you mean?" asked Rafia, her confusion plain, though it appeared a bit forced to Declan.

"I'm not a fool, Rafia. If you're interested in me, then be interested in me. You tried to use me against the Magus. Now that you two have parted ways, you can't do that anymore."

"How could you even think that I would be …"

Rafia blushed a furious red. She had never expected Declan to be so direct, though she should have. She should have known, because it wasn't in his nature to avoid an issue or conflict. He went at the world with a fearlessness that likely terrified others. It certainly frightened her now that she was his target.

"Now I admit that Sirius is not my favorite person, though he has done right by Bryen, at least when it was necessary, so that more than makes up for his faults. But if we're going to get to know one another any better, then we need to be honest with one another just as you said."

"I was not attempting to …" she tried to protest. The words died on her lips when she caught Declan's look. Why did this man make her feel so excited and so unsure of herself at the same time? She was centuries old, blast it! She should be well past all this.

"You're a beautiful woman," continued Declan, "though a bit distracted at times by the games that you try to play. If you want to become more than friends, just say so and we can have a real conversation."

"I am a Magus, Declan, one of the most powerful in Caledonia," she said, trying to regain control over the situation. "Don't presume to know me just because we've spent some time speaking together."

"I presume nothing, Rafia. I know you're a Magus. I know what you can do, having seen it with my own eyes. I also know that you're an intelligent, beautiful woman. I'm too old to play games, and I don't have the time for it. Let me know if you'd like to talk again."

With that, Declan strode ahead, shifting his attention to Bryen, who had just completed a conversation with Sirius, the two having expressions on their faces that in Declan's opinion were cause for serious concern.

Rafia stopped walking for a moment, a shocked expression on her face, then she chuckled lightly and resumed her trek. What was it about this man that appealed to her so much?

He challenged her. He scared her. He told her the truth. He told her what he wanted.

Maybe that was it. Maybe she, too, was done with the games. She just hadn't realized it until that very second.

12

DISTRACTIONS

"Do we need to worry about that?" Jerad asked.

He and Tarin walked at the head of the Blood Company, the mountains gaining greater clarity with each step that they took, although they were still at least a day away from reaching the rocky ground and evading unscathed the dangers of the Breakwater Plateau. Pitch-black storm clouds were beginning to form to their south and west, a few streaks of lightning ripping through the darkness that put the gloom of the Dark Forest to shame.

The Captain of the Battersea Guard stared at the weather front slowly coming toward them. He didn't like the look of it. He had traveled on the Plateau several times before, never enjoying the experience. He knew what the result would be if they were caught out in the open by the driving rain that could scald flesh, the lightning that could incinerate you, or the hail that was the size of a man's head that could smash through a raised steel shield and crush the person beneath.

Every time he saw the lightning blast through the murk, he glimpsed a touch of green as well. That was never a good sign. A tornado brewing. They already had crossed several massive tracks in the long grass a league or more wide that revealed the paths of some of the previous storms that had ravaged the steppe. The grass had been ripped from the earth, nothing remaining but large furrows of dirt and sometimes the perfectly concentric circles in the loam that showed where a whirlwind had touched down before moving across the grassland on its devastating route.

"We do," replied Tarin reluctantly. That storm was coming toward them whether they wanted it to or not, and it wouldn't take long for the tempest to gain the speed needed for it to become a monster, the swirling black mixed with green already beginning to rotate at a faster pace. The front was too broad, blotting out everything to the west, for them to hope that it would pass them by. The best that they could do was try to outrun it. Just another incentive for them -- besides the Slayers and the Ghoules chasing them, as if those weren't enough -- to cross the Breakwater Plateau as fast as they could. "We should pick up the pace. Try to beat it to the mountains."

"Even if we do, will we make it in time?"

"Probably not," replied Tarin with a grin. "But where's the fun in life without a challenge."

"It seems that all life is, is a challenge," grumbled Jerad, the normally loquacious and grinning Sergeant of the Battersea Guard grumpy and out of sorts that afternoon as a new difficulty was added to their list, one over which they had no control.

"I couldn't have said it better myself, Jerad," replied Tarin. "Would you mind telling the others that we'll be moving faster and cutting out the breaks? We might not escape the storm, although we will at least give it a try. And please make sure the column tightens up. We don't want to be strung out across the plain with that cyclone coming our way."

"Are you ready to try again, Aislinn?"

"Yes, just give me a moment."

"Take your time. This is delicate work and it needs to be managed effectively. Otherwise ..."

"Otherwise you can die," Aislinn finished. "I know. That seems to be the most likely result whenever you make a mistake with the Talent."

"Correct," replied Rafia. "That's why caution and concentration are just as important as power and precision."

"Do you think what you're teaching me will be necessary when we reach the Sanctuary?"

"I don't know," Rafia replied as she considered the question, both she and Aislinn lengthening their strides as Jerad had requested, the Sergeant of the Battersea Guard working his way down the column to bring everyone closer together. They had seen the clouds slowly coming toward them as well. "I do know that the Ten Magii had to link their power so that they could craft the Weir. I wouldn't be surprised that even with Bryen employing the energy of the Seventh Stone that he might require some additional reservoirs of the Talent or our help in rebuilding the barrier. But who can say? Learning this skill might prove useful for other reasons as well."

"So better to be prepared. I understand."

"Remember, Aislinn. A delicate touch. You and Bryen are the two most powerful Magii in Caledonia. Oftentimes when such power meets for the first time, there is a natural resistance. Your Talent and his may attempt to repel one another."

"I have no fear of that," replied Aislinn with a grin. "Bryen and I connect quite frequently and easily now."

"Do you?" asked Rafia, one of her eyebrows raised. "Would you care to share?"

Aislinn's face turned a bright red when she realized how what she had just said could be interpreted. She needed to be more circumspect.

"No, I was just saying that since we've spent so much time together, we know each other quite well now," she replied, trying to recover as quickly as she could. "So I don't think that we'll have too much of a problem linking with the Talent if doing that proves to be necessary."

"Well, if you believe that it's so easy, show me now," challenged Rafia.

Aislinn nodded. She felt the welcome warmth of the Talent surge within her, filling every cell of her body and bringing a broad smile to her face as she experienced the world with a greater clarity.

She sensed that Rafia had taken hold of the Talent as well, so she did as the Magus had explained, reaching out carefully, tentatively, for the thread of the Talent that Rafia offered to her. The Magus was right. When Aislinn first attempted to connect to Rafia's thread with her own, she met with some difficulty. Rather than connecting on the first try, both threads turned away from the other, refusing to link.

"Remember, it requires a gentle touch," said Rafia. "You can't force it. You must be patient. Just get as close as you can and then allow it to happen on its own."

Aislinn nodded absently, her focus still on the two threads. Taking Rafia's advice, she brought her thread of energy as close as she could to Rafia's, no more than a whisker away, then left it there, afraid to push any farther having seen what had happened during her first attempt. One second passed. Then another. Then one more. Then another ten as Aislinn counted in her head. A full minute more. And another minute besides that.

The urge to bring her thread closer became more powerful as the time passed. She wasn't a patient person to begin with, and this exercise was testing her in an excruciating fashion. Even so, she forced herself to keep the cord where it was.

Then slowly, ever so slowly, Rafia's strand drifted closer to her own. Not wanting to interfere, not wanting to miss out on the chance, Aislinn kept her thread in place. Finally, after several more minutes passed, the two strings touched, then began to weave themselves around the other until there was now just a single thread. Through that new, powerful connection she could sense the deep pool of the Talent that belonged to Rafia.

"Well done, Aislinn," said Rafia, ignoring Davin as he jogged past them toward the front of the column. "Very well done. Few achieve a connection on their second try. Now let's move on to the more difficult task of giving another Magus permission to use your Talent. After you master that, we'll flip the focus to asking another Magus to use their Talent."

DAVIN IGNORED Aislinn and Rafia as he went by, realizing that they were clearly engaged in something that he had little knowledge of and no desire to interrupt. Rafia had a temper that he would prefer to avoid whenever he could, and he knew from experience that bothering her when she was teaching was the best way to set it off. Unless you were Sirius. Then it just took the Magus appearing at the wrong time, saying the wrong thing, giving Rafia the wrong look ... it really didn't take much for the two Magii to go at it.

"You needed some time away I take it?" asked Tarin.

"How did you know?" asked Davin.

"Your sister doesn't do a very good job of hiding her emotions, even at the best of times. Earlier this morning she looked more explosive than those storm clouds coming our way."

"You're right about that. She's in a worse mood than usual."

"Bryen?"

"Bryen. Aislinn. The two of them together. It's been the same story since we freed ourselves from the Pit."

"Yes, the Protector used to have the same effect on me," said Tarin. "Every time I interacted with him, he put me in a bad mood."

"Not anymore?"

"No, not anymore."

"Why not?"

"Once I got to know him, I began to like him," said Tarin. "Of course, his saving the Lady Winborne's life, my life, and the lives of many of the Battersea Guard made the adjustment in my perspective much easier."

"That makes sense," replied Davin. "I just hope that Lycia changes her perspective soon. It's getting old."

"It's bothering you."

"I wouldn't have come up here so quickly if it wasn't," Davin replied. "No offense meant, of course."

"None taken," replied Tarin. "Your sister will change her perspective or she won't."

"And if she doesn't?"

"Then there's nothing that you can do about it. It's her issue, not yours. You trying to make it your problem to solve doesn't help you, and it certainly doesn't help her. She needs to be the one to handle this."

"Then what would you suggest?" asked Davin, hoping for some advice on how he could manage what for him was becoming a much more difficult situation with each passing day. He hated feeling as if he were being pulled in two different directions by the two people that he cared about the most.

"You can tell your sister what the tension that's coming off her because of her feelings for Bryen is doing to you," said Tarin. "Just make sure you aren't too close when you do. She might try to put a few holes in you with those swords of hers."

Davin chuckled for the first time that day. "You know, you

sound just like Declan. You give advice, but when you offer it, I can't really tell if it's good advice or just something that popped into your head and you're telling me it just to get rid of me."

"I can only offer you my opinion, Davin. What you do with it is up to you."

"That's something else that Declan would say."

"Which is why I like the Sergeant of the Blood Company. Similar experiences. Similar minds."

Davin looked back down the column, grimacing slightly. He decided that he'd stay at the front for a little while longer. Whatever Declan was telling Lycia was turning her face into a thundercloud darker than the storm that slowly but inexorably drifted toward them, pushed on by the winds swirling from the west and colliding with the gusts coming down off the Shattered Peaks that towered to their front.

"It's not as easy as you thought, is it?"

"What do you mean, Declan?" asked Bryen, as there was very little going on with him right now that was easy.

"Life beyond the Pit."

"I don't know about that," replied Lycia. "It's a nice change not to have to worry about who or what you'll be fighting on the white sand every week."

"True," agreed Declan, "although I would argue that life in the Pit is fairly simple compared to what we're dealing with now."

"Kill or be killed," said Bryen.

"Exactly," said Declan. "Kill or be killed. That inescapable dynamic requires you to view the world through a unique lens. One that offers greater clarity, greater certainty, than what we face now."

"What's your point, Declan?" asked Lycia. "I get the feeling that there's a point hiding somewhere within whatever it is you're trying to tell us."

"Why do you think that I'm trying to offer you another lesson? Maybe I'm just trying to engage in a conversation."

"Because you always have a lesson for us," replied Bryen with a grin, offering his support to Lycia. "And you rarely engage in a conversation just for the sake of conversation."

Declan tried to keep the smile that threatened to crack his stoic countenance from breaking free. They knew him too well. He looked at his two former charges as they moved more quickly through the long grass, the three having passed Jerad and increased their pace at his request. They could see the wall of black to their west as well, and they had no desire to be caught within it.

"My point is that life in the Pit is more dangerous, but it is simpler. Fewer choices. Fewer issues. Fewer concerns. Beyond the Pit, life gets more complicated. You have more decisions to make. More issues to deal with. It becomes more confusing."

Declan gave both Bryen and Lycia a meaningful look. But Bryen simply stared back at him as if he didn't understand a word of what he was saying and Lycia, the faint tinge of red breaking out on her cheeks suggesting that she knew exactly what he was driving at, choosing to ignore his point by shifting the topic of the conversation.

"You've been spending quite a bit more time with the Lady of the Southern Marches," Lycia said to Bryen, her tone accusatory.

"She's been teaching me more about the Talent and how to use it," he replied with a shrug of his shoulders, as if it wasn't really that big a deal.

"Is that the only thing that she's been teaching you?" Lycia asked with a wink, her tone joking but her hard expression betraying her real reason for asking. "I'm beginning to think that you are spending time with her for more reasons than just the Talent."

"Be careful, Lycia," said Declan softly. "You're moving into dangerous territory. You might not like where it leads."

Instead of responding immediately, Bryen just looked at his friend, his face darkening. Then the mask that she and Declan were both so familiar with slipped over Bryen's visage, the mask that had become so well known in the Pit. An emotionless, dangerous expression.

"Is this the conversation that you want to have right now?" asked Bryen, his words clipped, said without feeling. "Because Declan is right. Life is more difficult outside the Pit. It can hurt just as much as it can on the white sand, though for a host of other reasons beyond a steel dagger sliding into your gut."

"What conversation would that be, Bryen?" asked Lycia harshly, unwilling to back down from her friend's challenge. She couldn't say that she was ready for where the discussion might lead; however, it was too late to turn away from the issue between them and it wasn't in her nature to do so.

Before the conversation could turn down a road that both Bryen and Lycia might regret, Declan stepped in. There were ways to handle the concerns that were circulating between the two gladiators, and this wasn't one of them.

"And what of you, Lycia?" asked Declan, placing her in the same position that she had placed Bryen. "You seem to have taken quite a fancy to the Sergeant of the Guard. Jerad. You certainly had eyes for him when he walked by."

"I do not ..."

"Come now, lass. It's obvious to everyone. Instead of teasing Bryen because it's the easy thing to do, why don't you go walk with Jerad and talk to him a bit."

"How can you presume to know ..." Lycia's anger was beginning to build. This certainly wasn't what she had expected when she had set out to tease Bryen just a moment before.

"I know you better than you know yourself, lass," cut in Declan. "I've seen you at your best and at your worst. I know your strengths and your weaknesses. Just as I do for your brother and for Bryen. Now, as I suggested, why don't you find Jerad and talk with him a bit. It'll do you good. Perhaps distract you from the issue that's truly bothering you but you're not ready to discuss quite yet."

"Another woman has a claim on Jerad," replied Lycia quietly, "and I won't interfere with that. I promised her. That's why I'm here and not there."

"Lycia," said Declan. "You're not breaking your promise to the other woman. Talking with Jerad isn't a confirmation or a hint or a promise of anything. Besides, it'll do you good. Help you get your mind working on other things for a time."

Lycia's face now matched the bright color of her hair. Without saying a word, she stalked off toward the back of the column where Jerad was urging the rear guard to push a little faster and tighten ranks.

"THAT WAS a brave and dangerous thing to do, Declan," said Bryen.

He knew Lycia's propensity to use the knives that were hidden in various places around her body, particularly when she was angry. And she clearly was getting angry, her fingers having started to twitch.

"It was necessary," said Declan. "She wants to move on, she just doesn't know how. So I just gave her a little nudge. She'll figure it out when she's ready, and then she'll be the better for it."

"Just as always, acting like the mother hen that you are," said Bryen with a grin. "Always trying to help everyone else solve their problems."

"I am not a mother hen," protested Declan vehemently, his eyes blazing with disagreement.

"You are a mother hen, among many other things, Declan. I meant it as a compliment. I wouldn't have made it this far without you looking out for me."

"That's kind of you to say, lad. I did what I could. You did the rest. You made the decisions. You did the work."

"You can deflect all you want. I'm here because you gave me the path that I needed to follow. You didn't have to do that."

"Maybe not," agreed Declan, who wiped at a speck of dust that had gotten into his left eye, making it tear. At least that was what he told himself. "But it was the right thing to do."

Bryen smiled, not saying a word, just giving the man he viewed as his father a clap on the back.

"Speaking of doing the right thing," Declan continued. "You owe Lycia the truth. You need to talk to her. Not doing so is more than unfair."

Bryen's mask immediately dropped back into place, his emotions draining from his expression. "What do you mean?"

"You know exactly what I mean. Don't act like a child."

"I am not acting like a child," Bryen protested, a flash of anger appearing behind his cold grey eyes before vanishing just as quickly.

"Are you listening to yourself, lad?"

"Of course I'm ..." Bryen shut his mouth, the emotions he had repressed so effectively racing to the surface. He growled in anger as he stewed on what Declan had said.

He was angry with Declan for maneuvering him so adroitly into this dialogue, which he really didn't want to have. Even more so, he was angry with himself because Declan was right. Lycia did deserve an honest conversation, and he'd been avoiding it. A confrontation based on steel was nothing to him. An emotional confrontation, however, terrified him.

"You know you really can be a pain in the ass, Declan," grumbled Bryen.

"Of that I have no doubt, lad ..." Declan stopped talking when he saw Bryen's faraway look. Based on his expression, whatever he had discovered couldn't be a good thing. "What's the matter, lad?"

Bryen took a moment longer before responding, wanting to make sure. When he released his hold on the Talent, having searched to their rear well into the Dark Forest and not liking what he had discovered, his expression darkened to the same color as the approaching storm. The ancient evil that only he could sense was coming for them at an almost impossible speed.

"Slayers. They've gained more ground on us than I thought possible. They'll be here sooner than I hoped they would be."

"How far away?" asked Declan.

"Ten leagues. Maybe a bit farther. Not much more than that. Based on how fast they can move ..."

"They'll be here in just a few hours. I'll tell Tarin and Jerad so that we can try to get a bit closer to the mountains before we need to make our stand. I was hoping that we would get across the Plateau before those monsters caught up to us. We could use the rocky ground at the edge of the Shattered Peaks to our advantage because it's much more defensible. But if those monsters are coming as fast as you say, we may have to take a different approach."

Bryen could only nod. He agreed with Declan. He didn't think that they would make it across the grassland before the Slayers confronted them again. They had too far to go and the Slayers were too swift.

There was nothing for it now, Bryen thought. Not unsurprisingly, that didn't bother him. Not in the least.

It was now just as it was during his years in the Pit. Kill or be killed. A simpler reality than the one that he and Declan had been discussing.

With that thought running through his mind, rather than try to escape, it was time to become the bait. It was time to lure the Slayers where he wanted them to go, and then use their innate aggressiveness against them.

13

STORM COMING

The black clouds tinged with flashes of green, blasts of earth-shaking lightning ripping through the inky darkness, hurtled closer, the wind gusting from the west pushing the storm across the long grass of the Breakwater Plateau at an inescapable pace.

They could hear it now, the roar of the wind sounding like the shrieks of so many of their victims, as strong as any gale that swept over the sea.

It didn't stop them. It didn't make them consider turning around. It didn't make them think to delay their pursuit and allow the storm to pass before continuing on.

The coming storm only gave them the incentive to run that much faster.

Not because they were afraid of getting caught in the lethal weather. Rather, the Slayers feared that the storm would hide their prey from them. They could not permit that, not after losing their quarry once before.

The Slayers understood what the clouds meant. They understood how bad the storm would be.

The monsters didn't care.

They only cared about one thing.

The Seventh Stone.

They had to catch the humans they hunted before they could escape in the storm.

Already gliding so swiftly through the long grass that they were no more than a blur, the Slayers sprinted even faster, the advancing weather driving them on. Fear of their Master's rage giving them an even greater sense of urgency.

They had been running for more than a day, all the way from the far western boundary of the Dark Forest. Still they kept their pace.

Never stopping. Never flagging. Never doubting that they would achieve the goal that their Master had set for them.

The scent of the Seventh Stone growing stronger with every step that they took. They were close.

And with every stride through the long grass, they got that much closer to what they craved. To what they deserved. To what they required.

The beasts hungered for their quarry, thoughts of the soft flesh of the humans making the monsters drool in anticipation. The Slayers hadn't eaten since they had killed those humans when they were so close to the Seventh Stone the first time, and then it had been just a few bites before they had been interrupted, the three Magii preventing the slaughter and ruining their fun.

The huge beasts could still taste their prey's flesh and blood. So sweet. So succulent. So energizing. So necessary.

They were desperate to taste the flesh of humans again. And they would.

Even so they would wait before they gave in to the urge that consumed them, no matter how much the delay pained them. They would do as their Master commanded.

It would be hard. Excruciating. But they would obey.

Both Slayers turned their heads to the northwest, hearing

the powerful rumble of thunder as the storm bore down on them. They both increased their pace once again, racing across the steppe at a speed now well beyond that of a galloping horse.

The approaching storm would rip into the ground, tearing up the long grass, sending down pellets of rain that would slice into the skin and hail that would crush bone.

The Slayers didn't care. They didn't fear the weather. Their armor would protect them.

No, they feared the Ghoule Overlord. They feared their Master.

They feared disappointing him because they knew the price that they would pay for doing so.

So they would not fail.

They did not fear death at the hands of their Master. No, they feared being returned to their cells far beneath the Temple of the Ghoules. They feared being left there for another thousand years. Unable to feed. Unable to satiate their insatiable hunger.

So they continued across the steppe, not caring about what approached, not caring about what might be going on around them, only caring about catching their prey.

Because their Master was not too far behind them.

They needed to get to the humans first. The needed to get the Seventh Stone. They needed to please the Ghoule Overlord.

Then their Master would give them what they wanted. What they craved. What they needed.

The Ghoule Overlord would give them the humans. And then they would feast.

14

HAVING NO CHOICE

"How close are they, Protector?"

Tarin Tentillin stood next to Declan, the two soldiers conferring as the Company of Blood took a few minutes to rest. They were fatigued. Worn down. But still focused, ready, and quite tired of running. Even as a touch of anxiety at what was coming for them played in the back of their minds, the gladiators viewed this threat as no worse than what they had faced in the Pit.

They had been trotting through the long grass without complaint for almost the entire day, never faltering, never giving in to the exhaustion that beckoned to them with every step they took, staying ahead of their pursuers. Until now.

Stopping on the long grass could mean only one thing. The fight that they had been trying to avoid was coming for them. So be it. That's why they were there. This is what they did. And it would give them a chance to exact some revenge on the beasts that had killed three of their comrades.

They had all survived in the Colosseum. They knew what was expected of them. They knew what would be required of them. These might be the most fearsome creatures that they had ever fought, still it didn't daunt them in the least.

Kill or be killed. That was the mantra of those who stepped onto the white sand.

Besides, Davin had proven that you could kill these monsters. If he could do it, so could they.

When he didn't reply immediately, the Captain of the Battersea Guard looked at Bryen's troubled eyes and saw the truth there. He nodded, acknowledging the reality they faced. They had run a good race, but now the race was run. There was no way that they would make it to the foothills of the Shattered Peaks in time.

"Minutes," replied Bryen, confirming Tarin's suspicions. "No more than that. They're coming faster than they were before."

With late afternoon upon them, the light of the day was beginning to fade, and with the ominous thunderclouds, which resembled dark plumes rising in the sky, surging toward them across the Breakwater Plateau, they found themselves in a weird grey dusk that had washed out all the color in their world. The wind was picking up as well, the explosive bursts rushing across the steppe making it hard to hear. If the gusts picked up in intensity, just as Tarin and the others assumed that they would, if they weren't careful they'd be knocked off their feet.

Even so, the approaching tempest was a secondary concern. The Slayers were the immediate threat. The monsters needed to be dealt with first.

"Then we fight here," said Declan. It didn't matter to him where the battle occurred. A combat was a combat.

"It seems that we do," agreed Tarin. "With the light fading, the Slayers will have the advantage over us."

"They'll have the advantage over us with or without the light," said Bryen.

"Anything you can do to improve our odds?" asked Tarin.

"We'll do what we can," Bryen said, motioning to the three other Magii who stood in a cluster not too far away from them discussing their strategy for dealing with the Ghoule Overlord's assassins. "Have the Company form into a square, but a few ranks deeper facing the west."

Declan nodded. "You're going to try to herd them."

"Try being the key word," confirmed Bryen.

Declan took one last look at the snow-capped mountains rising to the north. They had pushed hard. So close, yet so far. If they had just one more hour, they might have gotten there. They might have found a more defensible position at the base of the peaks. "Hoping doesn't make it real," muttered the Master of the Gladiators under his breath, having picked up the saying from Sirius. Then he cleared that useless thought from his mind and turned his focus to what needed to be done.

"Blood Company, form square!" shouted Declan so that he could be heard above the howling wind. "Third line facing west!"

The gladiators hurried to obey, rapidly getting into the formation that Declan had ordered, shields locking in place, spears facing outward, the Magii placing themselves in the center of the hollow square with Declan and Tarin.

"Aislinn, you up for this?"

"Are you doubting me, Bryen? Because if you are that would be a very dangerous mistake to make."

"Not at all, Lady Winborne," he replied, offering Aislinn a tiny nettle in her breeches by calling her by her formal title. "I haven't doubted you since you set my shirt on fire."

Instead of responding with a barb of her own, Aislinn grinned at the memory, then took hold of the Talent and infused the spearpoints and sword blades of all the soldiers of the Blood Company with the natural power of the world. Now, none of the men and women waiting impatiently on the steppe had to worry about finding a way past the Slayers' natural armor. If any of the fighters got in a solid blow, their steel would slide into the beasts' flesh without any resistance.

With Aislinn completing the first task, it was time for Bryen to put in place the next step that he had been planning, which he hoped would limit the Slayers' angle of attack. Reaching for the Talent himself, Bryen did as Sirius had done when they were escaping the Ghoules during their journey from Battersea to Haven.

Needle-sharp strings of white-hot energy that were thinner than a hair spun out from Bryen's fingers and drifted through the air. Resisting the wind's gusts, the cords took on the shape of a loosely formed spider's web along both sides and the back of the Company's formation, leaving the west open to the Slayers, although Bryen also had narrowed significantly with the deadly strands that avenue of approach, the Protector seeking to funnel the monsters exactly where he wanted them to go.

"Ready?" Bryen asked, turning toward the other two Magii standing with him.

Rafia and Sirius nodded, neither feeling the need to respond with words. Instead, they both took hold of the Talent, linking to one another so that a dome of light started to form around the Blood Company that extended from the center of the formation for several hundred yards in all directions out onto the plain.

They could have hardened the dome so that it became solid, preventing the Slayers from reaching them. But they knew that solution was really just a trap. They didn't want to be stuck in place. They knew what was following closely behind these monstrous assassins, and they had no desire to face the Ghoule Overlord with all his resources in play.

No, better to kill these monsters now. The Company could then try to escape the pursuing Ghoules in the mountains. At least in the Shattered Peaks they'd have a better chance of defending themselves if they did, as they feared would be required, cross blades with the Master of the Curse.

The two Magii finished their work just as two massive shadows burst out of the gloom and into the light.

THE SLAYERS ROARED IN ANTICIPATION, slashing their claws in the air, their pleasure at finding their quarry igniting their ravenous hunger and their desire to kill.

The light didn't bother them. The steel weapons glowing brightly didn't bother them either.

These humans were weak. The Magii were weak, these Slayers having feasted on the practitioners of the Talent before. But it had been a long time ago. And they wanted to taste again that flesh marinated in the natural power of the world.

Strangely, rather than attacking right away, the Slayers chose to wait, ignoring their natural urges. Instead, they took a few seconds to study their quarry.

The monsters could see it. The sweat dripping off the humans' brows. How their hands opened and closed repeatedly on the hilts and hafts of their weapons. How their feet shuffled from one side to the other, many unable to stand still.

They could sense it. The elevated heart rates. The uncontrollable shivering.

The fear.

The Slayers savored it, raising their fang-filled maws to the sky and howling with a rapacious craving, the almost intolerable shriek forcing many of the humans to cover their ears and turn away.

The instinct to hunt and the desire to kill ruled them now.

The Slayers would feast on the humans. That was a given. First, though, they needed to take the prize their Master desired.

They could sense exactly where the Seventh Stone was, who it was, their blood-red eyes locking onto the tall human holding a double-bladed spear and standing coolly in the center of that steel, clearly unaffected by their appearance.

Then, and only then, could they give in to their urges. Then, and only then, could they give free rein to their baser needs.

The Seventh Stone first, and then the Slayers would feed.

"WILL THIS WORK?" asked Aislinn, a streak of ice running up her spine as she stared at the two monsters standing across from them.

It was the first time that she had gotten a good look at their pursuers, the light created by Sirius and Rafia illuminating the Slayers with a blinding clarity so that she and the gladiators could finally see what they were battling. She almost wished that they were back in the Dark Forest fighting in the gloom. At least then she didn't also have to combat the terror rising up within her, thoughts of those daggerlike claws and whiplike tail punching into her flesh almost making her teeth chatter.

"It should," replied Bryen, her Protector seemingly unconcerned by the monsters.

For a brief moment, Aislinn hated him for that, then pushed away what she viewed as an unbecoming emotion.

"It should?" Aislinn's incredulous tone suggested that wasn't the answer she was looking for.

"It will," Bryen corrected quickly, hoping his words would give her the comfort she was seeking.

He said it confidently, even though he was anything but, keeping his worries about these monsters to himself. Then again, these Slayers were still flesh and blood. So what he had done should work, just as it had for Sirius against the Ghoules.

The Slayer that was just a few steps in front of the other

barked sharply, the second Slayer responding instantly with a growl of acknowledgment, the beast shifting his course toward the southern side of the humans' formation. The first Slayer would attack from the front and hold their prey's attention. The second Slayer would seek to break through from the side or the back. Once the second Slayer got in among the humans, the beast could take the Seventh Stone, while the first Slayer attacking from the west took advantage of the inevitable chaos its brethren would cause.

Then the rules that the Ghoule Overlord had established for the Slayers would change. Then they could do what they really wanted to do. What they needed to do.

And now it was time to put their plan into action.

The two Slayers separated. One standing right across from Bryen, glaring at him hungrily, the other disappearing back into the gloom.

Bryen recognized what was about to happen. The Slayer that sought to hold his attention was about to launch himself into the air, the monster crouching, digging his clawed feet into the grass, likely so that the beast could crash down among the soldiers facing him, seeking to create a gap in their front rank right from the start that would require the gladiators to shift their positioning and weaken the area where the other monster planned to attack. Even with the light Sirius and Rafia had created to illuminate the battle space and the Talent infusing their blades, the gladiators likely would have a difficult time defending themselves because of the speed of the monsters' assault.

In the blink of an eye, the Slayer did as Bryen guessed he would, surging forward, taking two big steps before a shriek of pain tore through the darkness from the other side of the dome. The monster abruptly skidded to a stop no more than a few dozen feet from the shield wall.

Bryen smiled, watching as the surprise in the Slayer's terrifying face turned to rage as another shriek, followed by another, and finally one more, rang out from the east.

Just a few seconds later, the Slayer tasked with coming at the gladiators from the rear stepped back cautiously into the light, long streaks of blood coloring its body. The monster stopped right next to the first Slayer, who still stared directly at Bryen. His cocky grin seemed to be angering the Slayer even more so he added a touch of contempt to his gaze.

"Are you trying to antagonize that monster?" Aislinn asked, taking in Bryen's taunting smile.

"And if I am?"

"You're not facing off in the Pit against Marden Beleron. This is an altogether different opponent. An assassin of the Ghoule Overlord."

"Maybe so, but that doesn't mean trying to push these beasts into a rash decision still isn't a bad idea. What I'm doing here is no different than what I did in the Pit."

Aislinn shook her head in both wonder and concern. "Rafia is right. You do have a death wish."

"Probably, but what I'm doing is working."

"Not anymore," corrected Aislinn.

She had caught the subtle shift in the Slayers, the quiet one in particular, who appeared to have been thinking through the challenge that Bryen had set for them. Judging by the glint in the beast's blood-red eyes and its hungry smile, the monster apparently had found the answer it had been seeking.

WITH FOUR THIN streaks of blackish red marring his armored skin along his arm, hip, and thigh, the wounded Slayer howled in fury, his tail, as long as the beast was tall, whipping about behind his head. The monster wanted to lash out at the source of its pain, but it couldn't. Not being able to do so was fueling his rage. Because it had failed to identify the source of its injuries.

While the angry Slayer continued to roar its displeasure, the other beast ignored the gladiators but for the Seventh Stone, not having moved an inch, its mind clearly working through the challenge set before it.

The beast finally shifted its focus to the direction his brethren had gone before being forced to return. The monster didn't understand how the other Slayer could have been hurt. There was nothing there. The Magii had not attacked and its brethren had not gotten close to the humans. But maybe that assumption was wrong. Maybe the Magii had ...

When it looked again, the Slayer caught it, though it was barely perceptible because the flicker was so fast. A brief flash of light. Then another not too far away from the first.

The Slayer nodded, more out of pity than respect. The beast understood what the Magii had done now. It still wouldn't stop them from claiming what was theirs.

The Slayer hadn't seen something like this since it had hunted Magii when their Master first set them upon the humans.

Just as they had done centuries before, the Magii among the humans had created some kind of barrier with their power, and it was so thin and finely done that the Slayer could only see the weave when the light struck it in a certain way. The beast assumed that the Magii had created the same defense along the other side of their formation, probably along the back as well.

The Slayer returned his gaze to the humans standing to his front, ignoring the other Slayer as the beast continued his tantrum, gnashing his teeth in frustration. As far as the more calculating Slayer could tell, there was nothing in front of them. No sign of the flashes that would signify the barrier the Magii had constructed.

His blood-red eyes narrowed shrewdly, latching once again

onto the Seventh Stone. The humans seemed to think that they knew how to fight against killers such as them.

But the humans were foolish as well. They were too overconfident. And they would die because of that.

These humans might be clever. They might have power. It still wouldn't be enough to save them. Because these humans were nothing more than meat.

The Slayer whose gaze remained fixed on Bryen howled then, the second quickly joining in, the haunting sound combining an anger, pain, and incessant hunger that drowned out the roar of the rapidly approaching storm, the grey murk turning a darker black just beyond the Magii-crafted light.

In the blink of an eye, the two beasts rushed forward, tails lashing just above their shoulders, claws outstretched, their movement nothing more than a blur even with the bright light hovering above them.

"You are gladiators!" Declan shouted, his voice carrying above the gusting wind. He realized straight away that what he had just said was a bit of a misnomer. The men and women fighting with him were soldiers now. They were free, no longer consigned to the Pit. Still, it was true. Once you were a gladiator, you were always a gladiator. You could never escape the white sand no matter how much you tried. "You stand! You fight! You die!"

The Company of Blood shouted their agreement, and then they got down to the bloody work with which they were so familiar. Archers from within the square shot Talent-tipped arrows over their compatriots' heads. Soldiers in the front rank lunged with their spears, the shield bearers standing strong. Fighters in the gaps between the spears slashed down with their swords over the shoulders of their friends.

The gladiators fought with their customary precision and viciousness, a deadly combination that had proven effective time and time again in the Pit and also against the Ghoules. Yet in this instance, several of the men and women took wounds in just the first few minutes of the fight, and none of the gladiators got a good strike in on the two monsters stalking them.

Many of the soldiers of the Blood Company cursed in frustration at only being able to gain a few scratches and nicks against their attackers. They had the means to kill the monsters thanks to their Talent-infused weapons, yet they were having little success. The Slayers were fast. Very fast. Faster than anything that they had ever fought before.

Even Bryen and Aislinn struggled. They used the Talent carefully, not wanting to hit any of the gladiators who stood before them, which was a distinct possibility because of how the Slayers darted forward erratically.

The beasts often tried to rip the spears from the gladiators' hands, the Slayers shooting forward and back, never standing still, at the same time their deadly tails shooting over their shoulder in search of flesh. So far, Bryen and Aislinn had succeeded in gaining only a few glancing blows against the beasts, who continued to search for a way to get in among the gladiators.

That was good in one sense. It meant that the Blood Company's defense was holding. But they needed more than that. They needed to kill these monsters if they were to have any chance of getting into the mountains, and these incredibly agile beasts were preventing them from doing that.

THE SLAYERS TOOK turns lunging toward the humans.

They had learned quickly that their quarry was fixated on their sharp, elongated claws. So they used their claws as a distraction, instead employing their tails, which struck faster than the eye could see, to deadly effect. The sharp point at the end of the appendage punctured flesh with ease, and every time those tails hit home it was followed inevitably by the sickening sound of the serrated, spiny scales on the end tearing out large chunks of meat as it was ripped free.

Whenever the Slayers heard that noise they shivered in pleasure, redoubling their efforts.

Several times after the Slayers had wounded one of the humans, the smell of blood that permeated the air almost caused the beasts to forget the discipline that they had demonstrated since they first engaged their prey.

The Slayers were hungry. They wanted to eat. They were desperate to feed.

Not yet though. Soon. They just needed to be patient.

Their Master followed them. He wasn't very far away, he and his packs catching up to them quickly. Once their Master arrived, they would eat their fill. So there was no need to rush their kills. They just needed to keep the humans in place. They just needed to make sure that the Seventh Stone didn't have the chance to flee.

But then an unanticipated opportunity opened up right in front of the wounded Slayer, and the beast couldn't resist, his instincts and rage taking hold.

When the human holding a shield stumbled, caught across the neck by its tail, the wounded Slayer charged forward, slicing into two humans at the same time, the one on the right with its claws, the one on the left with its whiplike tail. With the two humans losing their grip on their spears because of the severity of their injuries, for just a split second there was a small gap in the square. The Slayer took full advantage, leaping over the human with the sword now blocking its path, the woman missing the Slayer with her steel by just a hair.

The monster had made it to the center of the square.

The Slayer roared in triumph, finally free to wreak the havoc the beast thrived upon, its bladelike tail shooting out toward the humans standing just a few feet away.

DECLAN SLASHED down with his glowing blade at the exact same time that the beast that had broken into the square shot its tail toward the broad back of an unsuspecting soldier. He didn't get as much flesh as he wanted because of the speed of the monster's strike, but he got enough, slicing off the last six inches of the spiky appendage, the Slayer pulling back its wounded tail in a flash and releasing an ear-splitting scream of pain and anger that rose above the shrieks of the howling wind.

Before the wounded Slayer could turn its full attention toward Declan, Tarin came at the beast from its blind side. His shining sword was a blur of sizzling energy, slicing into the monster's flesh a half-dozen times before the Slayer lunged forward and finally forced the Captain of the Battersea Guard to take a step back.

Declan rejoined the attack then, cutting into the creature's forearms, thighs, and back, always cognizant of the lightning-fast tail that, although missing the very end and spraying a thick black blood as it whipped through the air, was still a deadly weapon thanks to the spiny scales lining the sides of the appendage.

And so it continued for several minutes, the two veterans dancing around the Slayer, spending as much time avoiding the beast's vicious attacks as attacking themselves. By coordinating their actions, Declan and Tarin succeeded in marking the beast's flesh several dozen more times. Even so, the injuries didn't appear to be slowing down the Slayer. Instead, their attacks only served to infuriate the beast.

Nevertheless, they maintained their focus, keeping with

their strategy, until they finally saw the chance that they had been waiting for.

The Slayer spun around, irritated by a cut across his side that Declan had landed, reaching for the Sergeant of the Blood Company with his skeleton-like claws.

Declan got his blade up just in time, knocking the beast's attack to the side.

With the monster distracted, Tarin jumped over the Slayer's tail as it sliced through the air toward his knees, then cut down with a backward blow that almost severed the beast's leg at the knee, his Talent-infused blade cutting deeply into the creature's flesh and bone.

The Slayer's instinctive response was to try to launch itself at the human who had injured it so grievously. But the monster hesitated, the beast realizing that its ability to move had been curtailed severely because of its wound. Now just remaining upright was a challenge.

Before the monster could screech in rage at its circumstances, Declan and Tarin heard a shout from Bryen that made them drop to the turf.

"Down!"

A stream of the Talent streaked right above their heads, the blazing hot energy blasting the Slayer twenty feet through the air, the monster crashing onto its back and now no more than a smoking, charred wreck.

Less than a second later, Declan and Tarin heard a shriek of rage from just beyond their formation.

Somehow the last Slayer knew that the humans had killed its partner.

∽

SIRIUS GROWLED IN FRUSTRATION, chomping at the bit to get into the fight. He understood that what he and Rafia were doing with the Talent to light up the space around the Blood Company was absolutely essential and had to take precedence over his desire to join the skirmish.

He didn't like it, however. Even though Bryen and Aislinn were more than capable of assisting against the Slayers, he wanted to get in the mix.

"Focus, Sirius!" called Rafia, shouting over the din of the battle and the roar of the wind, which was worsening steadily, the gusts coming from the west now flattening the long grass as the strength of the fast-approaching storm intensified.

"I am focused!" he shouted back, having to set himself again in the grass so that he didn't get blown backwards.

"Of course you were!" agreed Rafia, a smile breaking out despite the increasing severity of their current circumstances. The Company of Blood remained where they were, engaged with Slayers, a deadly storm bearing down upon them, and the Ghoule Overlord just hours behind the tempest. It wasn't exactly the position that any of them wanted to be in.

Sirius reluctantly admitted to himself that Rafia was right. His concentration had shifted toward the fight right behind them, Declan and Tarin taking on the Slayer that had jumped into their midst. Hearing Bryen's shout and catching the tremendous flash with his peripheral vision, as well as the scent of charred meat that lasted for a few seconds before the wind blew it away, he assumed that one of the monsters would no longer be bothering them.

Still, he was itching to go after the last Slayer. They had to kill it. Soon.

Because he had realized immediately what the Slayers were doing when this battle started. This was not normal behavior for these monsters, seeking to keep the Company's attention on them rather than trying to slaughter every human within reach as fast as they could, and he had no doubt as to the cause.

Aislinn had been tracking what was coming behind the

Slayers, keeping them all up to date. Every minute the Company of Blood stayed on the Breakwater Plateau brought the Ghoule Overlord that much closer to them.

Sirius didn't fear going up against the Ghoules and Elders who were now only a few hours to the northeast of them. However, he wasn't certain that the Company of Blood was prepared to challenge the Ghoule Overlord. Not yet, at least. Even with Bryen having become the Seventh Stone, the Master of the Ghoules had a reservoir of evil that was almost endless and against which Bryen stood little chance.

The old Magus shook his head, the motion a mix of frustration and bemusement. He was worried about the Company. He was worried about Bryen. Yes, that couldn't be denied.

He was also worried about himself. He had challenged the Ghoule Overlord once before, and he had failed.

What would happen if he took on the Master of the Curse again? For just a second, he acknowledged that the most likely result frightened him.

Not that he might die taking on the Ghoule Overlord. No, that didn't worry him in the least. He had lived through more than ten centuries. There was little else for him now.

No, what bothered him, what terrified him, was a scenario in which he failed to protect Bryen from the Ghoule Overlord. He had failed to protect his parents. He wouldn't allow the same thing to happen to their son. He couldn't.

So he would do all that he could to protect Bryen, even from himself.

So much better to stay ahead of the Ghoule Overlord and focus on repairing the Weir. Once Bryen completed that task, they could worry about this other threat presented by the Master of the Lost Land, a solution to which he had yet to discover. But a threat that could be dealt with much more easily if there was no risk of Ghoule Legions overrunning Caledonia.

Well, there was a partial solution that had come to mind.

Once Bryen rebuilt the Weir, the Seventh Stone was no longer needed. Sirius could remove that piece from the puzzle, no matter how much doing so might pain him. But he didn't want to contemplate that unless it was absolutely necessary.

So the question continued to play through his mind even as he and Rafia worked to maintain the dome of light above them. How do you kill a creature with the capacity to manage as much Dark Magic on his own as all the Seven Stones combined?

The old Magus was pulled from these worries by a new concern, sensing that the squall was coming directly toward them at a much faster speed than it should. Granted, these storms on the Breakwater Plateau moved quickly. But not this swiftly. Not unless something was driving it forward. Not unless some other power was guiding this tempest right at them.

Was that even possible? If so, that could only mean ...

Sirius glanced quickly behind him when he sensed the immense amount of energy suddenly put into play. Aislinn and Bryen stood right next to each other, eyes closed, a swirling mist of white spinning around both of them. They couldn't be, but they were. From that swirling haze, a stream of light shot up into the sky like a beacon, blasting through the pitch black of the tempest.

How did they learn how to connect their power?

Rafia! Blasted woman! Had she even considered what it would mean if these two Magii, the two most powerful in Caledonia, shared their strength, to say nothing of the fact that Bryen also could harness the tremendous power of the Seventh Stone to aid their efforts?

Too late now. There was nothing that he could do to stop them. If he tried, he would probably kill them all. Better just to let it all play out and hope for the best.

What were those two doing anyway? he wondered.

When he figured it out a second later, it all made sense.

Even so, his eyes expanded until they almost popped out of his head. By then there was no time to do anything other than prepare as best as possible for what was about to crash down upon them in just a few seconds.

"Company of Blood, tighten your square!" yelled Sirius, using a small stream of the Talent so that he could be heard above the howl of the storm.

The soldiers obeyed, beginning to step back toward him. But they were moving too slowly. Much too slowly. Sirius' fears increased. He understood the challenge they faced. If they moved too quickly, the breaking storm and its gales might sweep them away. The last Slayer might find a weakness to exploit in the shield wall.

Davin appeared right next to Sirius. "We need more space to fight this beast," argued the gladiator, his red hair in disarray and matching his emotions. "We need space to move. If we get too close together, then we lose that ability! We cede the advantage to the Slayer."

Sirius ignored him, turning his head toward the west.

Declan followed the old Magus' gaze, and he understood immediately what needed to be done. The inky black surging toward them, mixed with purple and green, flashed with dozens of lightning strikes every second, the energy ripping into the ground and leaving fires blazing in the long grass that the powerful gusts of wind coaxed into a blazing conflagration.

"Faster!" Declan shouted. "On the double time! Form the testudo!"

The soldiers moved as swiftly as they could to obey their Sergeant's command, stepping backward carefully, weapons always pointing to their front, compressing their flanks until they were in a shell so tight that they scarcely had any room to breathe much less move.

The Slayer remained standing to their front, not yet making a move toward them, apparently not understanding why its prey did what it just did. Then the monster noticed for the first time the power of the tempest rushing across the plain, the beast digging its clawed feet into the ground in an effort to stay in place.

"Rafia!" Sirius shouted.

"Bryen!" Rafia called to the Protector. "Now! You and Aislinn need to do it now!"

With a flash that momentarily blinded any who looked at it, Bryen and Aislinn's stream of energy curled toward the ground in all directions, covering the Blood Company and hardening into a see-through, semicircular shell.

And just in time as the tempest that had been careering across the Breakwater Plateau consumed them, the Slayer fading into the darkness, the Blood Company protected by a thin though almost indestructible layer of the Talent as a jet black darker than the night swirled above them, gale force winds shrieking in their ears. They heard, as well, the rapid chatter of the hail, some pieces as large as a small boulder, smashing against the barrier and shattering into millions of pieces, the rate of the strikes so constant that it sounded like the rush of a tidal wave crashing against the shore.

And then the lightning joined in, slamming down, faster and faster, until for several minutes the impenetrable darkness around them disappeared, replaced by the rapid-fire flashes of the bolts of energy striking the shield, naturally drawn to the power that Aislinn and Bryen had used to craft the shield and illuminating the long grass around them in a gut-wrenching display of light and shadow.

Although for many of the gladiators it felt like the bombardment continued for hours, it was actually only minutes. Just as quickly as the storm came upon them, it passed them by, continuing on its way to the east, plowing through the long grass. The tempest's track was more than a league wide, the soldiers, staring out from their protective shell, awed by the destructive power of the squall.

The grass around them had been flattened with huge, smoking holes pockmarking the ground, the result of hundreds of lightning strikes smashing into the earth. Also scattered across the landscape were thousands upon thousands of pieces of hail. Some so small that they weren't any bigger than marbles, others so large that they couldn't see beyond them.

"You took a huge risk," Rafia said, approaching Bryen and Aislinn exactly when they released their hold on the Talent, she and Sirius having done the same, the protective dome and light no longer necessary in the bright light of the day.

The Slayer was gone. Hopefully dead, taken by the storm as even a monster such as that couldn't have survived such a demonstration of natural power, though Bryen would have to check, just in case. He wouldn't believe that the beast was dead until he saw its remains.

"It was the only way," said Aislinn.

"I'm not disputing that," said Rafia. "I'm simply saying that you two took a huge risk by bringing that storm right down on us so quickly. I want to talk to you both about that when we have a chance." Both Aislinn and Bryen sighed in resignation, not looking forward to the conversation until they caught the last of what Rafia had to say. "I want to know how you did it."

"When we have a chance," agreed Bryen. "Right now, though, we have other concerns. We can't stay here. We need to get to the mountains."

"And fast," added Aislinn. "The Ghoules are only a few hours behind us thanks to the efforts of the Slayers. And with the Ghoules ..."

"Yes, we know," finished Rafia. "The Ghoule Overlord. Let's get going. Bandages for now. We'll heal the wounded when we reach the foothills."

15

TWO KILLS

"Your soldiers fought well, Declan," said Tarin Tentillin. "I don't think they view themselves as gladiators anymore."

"They will always see themselves as gladiators, Tarin," Declan offered in a tired voice, knowing the truth of fighting in the Pit, something that could only be understood by those forced to compete on the white sand. "It's unavoidable. Once a gladiator, always a gladiator."

"Maybe so, though I would argue that they didn't look like gladiators during the fight. They looked like soldiers. Grizzled veterans, in fact. They were better disciplined than any soldiers I've ever had the pleasure of training."

"Thanks in large part to the time and effort that you and Jerad put into working with them," replied Declan. "Credit should be given where it is deserved."

"They already knew how to fight. For that, the credit belongs to you. Jerad and I just instructed them in some of the formations that have proven so effective against the Ghoules. They mastered the knowledge that we gave them with a speed that I still find remarkable."

"In the Pit you either learn quickly or you die."

"A useful skill," admitted Tarin, "as was just demonstrated."

"Maybe instead of trying to deflect the credit that each of you is trying to give to the other, perhaps you should just accept it so that we can move on. This humility is getting more than just a bit tedious. In fact, this self-deprecation is making me feel slightly nauseous."

Both Tarin and Declan stared at Sirius for a few heartbeats, their already flinty eyes turning harder still, the old Magus having joined them atop a small knoll that they had selected because it gave them a good view of the Shattered Peaks. The Company of Blood was taking a short break after their final sprint across the Breakwater Plateau before they continued their race into the imposing, snowcapped mountains that towered to their front.

"Sirius might actually have a point," Tarin finally said with a nod that seemed to suggest that the Magus rarely had a point.

"What do you mean *might*?" demanded Sirius with a touch of heat in his voice. "And what do you mean *actually*?"

"He might indeed," replied Declan, ignoring Sirius' protests, using the same tone as Tarin. "From what the Magus Rafia has told me, this can happen on occasion, although it's exceedingly rare."

"What do you mean by *rare*?" challenged Sirius.

"Rare indeed," agreed Tarin, also ignoring the old Magus. "Nevertheless, I must agree with Magus Rafia. It does happen from time to time."

"If you listen to anything that Rafia says," began Sirius, his voice rising in relation to his anger, "then you're wasting more than your time. And I'll have you know that ..."

Sirius' building rant died in his throat when he noticed the huge grins plastering Declan and Tarin's faces. His eyes, which had blazed with fury, mellowed just a touch to a low burn.

"You've been spending too much time with Bryen, his

habits are washing off onto you," muttered Sirius. "You're playing with me."

"We are," chuckled Tarin. "But only because you make it so easy for us."

"Well, I hope you enjoyed your fun."

"I did. Did you, Declan?"

"I did, Tarin. Thank you."

"And now that you've gotten all that childishness out of your systems, why did you two come up here other than to sing each other's praises and aggravate me?"

"We wanted to get the lay of the land," answered Declan. "We need to decide on the route that we should take into the Shattered Peaks. We can't afford to make a mistake with the Ghoules so close behind us."

"Unfortunately, we're not seeing many options from here," concluded Tarin. "Nothing but a hard slog no matter what path we take, and we want to avoid that if we can."

"What do you see with the Talent, Sirius?" Declan asked.

Rather than responding, Sirius immediately took hold of the natural power of the world, extending his senses out among the stone spires that soared majestically into the sky.

"If we hike about a league to the west, we can pick up a trail that should take us a good distance into the mountains. It doesn't seem to be a hard trail, so we should make good time. Once we're in among the peaks, we can figure out when to head to the west."

"Don't listen to Sirius," said Rafia, who had climbed up the hill without making a sound and spoke right into Sirius' ear.

"Blast it, woman! You're no better than Bryen, sneaking up on me every chance that he gets trying to give me a heart attack."

"It's not my fault that you didn't hear me coming," replied Rafia, attempting to shift the blame, though the spark in her eyes suggested that she was quite pleased by Sirius' reaction and his comparing her to the Protector.

"Why shouldn't we listen to Sirius?" asked Declan.

"Because he doesn't know these mountains like I do. I admit that what he's found looks like the best bet when you start on that trail, but it will only slow us down the farther we take it. It's a narrow path that ends deeper within the Shattered Peaks than he probably searched and would place us in a very dangerous position."

"I'll have you know that I searched five leagues into the mountains."

"And if you had searched a league further on you would have found where that trail is blocked thanks to a rockslide that we'd never be able to get across in time with the Ghoule Overlord pursuing us." Sirius gave her an angry look, so with a raised eyebrow Rafia offered him a challenge that she knew he couldn't resist. "If you don't believe me, search again and tell us if I'm right or wrong."

Sirius grumbled a few choice words to himself, then he reached for the Talent once more and extended his senses to the distance and location Rafia suggested. He looked at her with a touch of astonishment that was accompanied by a flash of irritation across his face.

"I hate when you're right."

"Even when my being right proves helpful to us?"

"You've got me there," admitted Sirius, his receding anger deflating him. "How did you know?"

"As I said, I know these mountains better than anyone. They're my home."

"So then what route would you suggest?" asked Declan, trying to keep his amusement at the interaction between Sirius and Rafia out of his voice. There was no good reason to irritate an already irritated and irascible Magus.

"We head west along the edge of the mountains for three

leagues, then we follow the game trail we find there to the north. We take that trail until it ends, which will be about ten leagues within the peaks when we come to a small valley that opens onto a large glacial lake. We turn to the west there on another trail. It's a straight shot from there to Haven as long as we stay on the path heading in that direction. And, we'll have ample opportunity on this route to offer some surprises to the Ghoules that I believe will help to slow down the Overlord and his packs and hopefully give us the time that we need to escape them."

"I admit that if we get to Haven before the Ghoules that gives us a strong defensive position that we could certainly use. Even so, we need to consider the downside to that, as it also means that we're giving the beasts the opportunity to corner us. We won't be able to escape the island once the Ghoules get there."

Rafia nodded her head at Sirius' comment. He wasn't wrong. It was a valid concern. He wasn't entirely right either. As the Keeper of Haven, there were a few secrets that she knew about the island that no one else did that could prove quite helpful if they made it safely to her home.

"Let's focus on getting to Haven. Leave how we get off the island to me. I've got a few tricks up my sleeve."

"That works for me," said Tarin before Sirius could continue the conversation, which the Captain of the Guard could see the old Magus really wanted to do after Rafia's final comment. He could understand. He had several questions himself that he wanted to ask Rafia about what she had in mind. Nevertheless, time was working against them, and they needed to get moving. Now. So they could have the necessary conversations while they made their way to the trail that Rafia suggested. "Let's check on how Bryen is doing with the wounded. Every minute we wait brings us that much closer to the fight that I would prefer to avoid for as long as possible."

"Agreed," said Declan. "And since I doubt that we can avoid the fight, I'd at least like to decide where it's going to take place rather than having it forced upon us. From what Bryen has told me, Haven might be our best bet."

"That's it," said Bryen. "Take your time."

"This is harder than I thought that it would be," Aislinn admitted as she concentrated on using the Talent to heal the long gash along Kollea's right arm.

She was the last of the Blood Company who needed to be healed. One of the Slayers had cut across her flesh to the bone with its claw. Yet despite the severity of the wound, she hadn't said a word, simply continuing on as if it were no more than a scratch. Dorlan's fussing about it had finally convinced Kollea to let Bryen take a look at her injury once they exited the long grass.

Bryen had helped all the other gladiators with their wounds, leaving them as good as new. Even better, the use of the Talent gave them an extra burst of energy that they could certainly benefit from after their struggles of the last few days.

As he worked his way through the gladiators, Aislinn had stayed at his side, observing how he used the Talent and then learning how to apply the healing energy herself.

Bryen was pleased by her work. She was a quick study, picking up everything that he was teaching her with a remarkable acuity. Even so, she was right. It wasn't an easy skill to learn. In addition to needing a natural inclination, it took patience and practice.

Dorlan anxiously watched everything that Aislinn and Bryen were doing. He knew the laceration running along Kollea's arm wasn't too serious a wound. In fact, she had dealt with much worse in the past. Still, it worried him.

Kollea found his angst to be quite amusing. It was as if the broad and burly Corporal believed that she had been gutted and her intestines were strewn about the long grass rather than just having to manage a clean slice across her arm.

"You're acting like an old maid," said Kollea, making fun of Dorlan in an attempt to remove his frown. "This is nothing compared to some of the injuries that I suffered in the Pit."

"I know, it's just …"

"Besides, it's going to take more than a Slayer to kill me."

"I know, but …"

"Then what is it? Why are you so worried? When I was hurt in the Pit you never acted like this."

"I'm just worried about you," replied Dorlan quietly, the large man finding it difficult to express his emotions.

"And I thank you for that. Yet as I've said, there's nothing to worry about. It's no more than a cut that the Lady Aislinn is healing quite nicely."

"Maybe it's watching the woman I love get patched up so many times that's bothering me. In the Pit, death was a certainty. Here, death is a possibility."

Kollea was about to offer an immediate response, telling the massive gladiator that he needed to stop worrying, but Dorlan's unexpectedly honest statement stopped her cold. He loved her. She had guessed as much. He had never said it before, though. Not until now.

"You'll need to get used to this if we're going to stay together," said Kollea, not addressing directly what Dorlan had just revealed, as she didn't do well expressing her emotions either. "You're a fighter. So am I. No matter how you feel about me, how we feel about each other, that won't change."

"Then we'll fight together," said Dorlan. "Just as we've been doing."

"I look forward to it," replied Kollea with a grin.

Bryen only half listened to the exchange, focused instead on the work that Aislinn was doing.

"You're right. With the Talent everything is always harder than you think it will be," said Bryen. "A little slower. You don't want to rush it now. Let the Talent do the work for you."

"So with a more serious wound, you take a similar approach," Aislinn said. "It's just a higher level of difficulty. Same approach, just more patience and more focus. More of letting the body heal itself. You're just guiding that healing process along faster than it would go without the application of the Talent."

"Yes, it's very similar," Bryen explained. "There are some aspects that need to be handled differently as you saw when we started with the more critical wounds, but all in all healing a wound like Kollea's is much the same as healing a serious injury."

"Just don't rush it."

"Right, don't rush it," agreed Bryen. "The more you do this, the more you'll get a feel for the pace. With a life-threatening wound like a nicked artery or a slice across the gut you'll probably have to work faster than you want to. You'll have no choice. The same concepts apply, though. The body can heal itself. The body will want to heal itself. All you're trying to do is speed the process along at a measured rate. You're just accelerating what the body wants to do on its own."

In just a few more seconds, she was done.

"Good as new," Aislinn said, who released her hold on the Talent and helped Kollea to her feet. "Nothing but a thin scar to remind you of the wound."

"Thank you, Vedra," said Dorlan solemnly. "This will not be forgotten. I am in your debt."

"Dorlan, will you stop being so serious," said Kollea, punching him in the shoulder with the arm that had been injured to show him that she wasn't feeling any ill effects from the wound. "You need to relax."

"It's just that ..."

"I know, I know," said Kollea. "You were worried about me. I love you for that. Now let's leave the Volkun and the Vedra be and grab some food while we can." The gladiator gave Aislinn a nod of respect. "Thank you, Lady Winborne. I very much appreciate what you've done for me."

"Aislinn, Kollea. No need for formalities."

"Aislinn," Kollea replied with a smile.

Aislinn knew that her informality with the gladiator would do more for her than the fact that she had healed Kollea's wound. The gladiators had not accepted her yet as the Blademaster and the Royal Guard had, their perspective on her clouded by what her father had done to Bryen. The process would take time, though this was certainly a good step in the right direction.

"Kollea, you look no worse for the wear," said Declan, who strode through the long grass, his mind focused not only on where the Company needed to go next, but also several stops down the road. It was a habit that he had picked up in the Royal Guard, focusing on the task at hand, although not without also taking into account the many other tasks that would need to be completed after the first was accomplished. The job was never done, it simply shifted into another job, and then another, and another. At times it was an exhausting way of looking at the world, but it worked for him.

"All thanks to Aislinn," Kollea replied, pleased to call the Lady of the Southern Marches by her given name.

"Good to hear. Would you and Dorlan please make sure that the Company is ready to go?"

"Of course, Sergeant," said Dorlan, reaching for Kollea's elbow to guide her back toward the other gladiators, and instead finding that she had slipped her hand into his as they walked away. That clever move didn't seem to bother the big man in the least, squeezing her fingers tightly with his.

"Will you two be ready soon?" asked Declan.

"We're ready now," replied Aislinn.

"Ten minutes then," nodded Declan. "I just want to give everyone a few more minutes of rest. We'll need to make the most of it, because who knows when we'll get another chance. We won't be stopping until we're well within the Shattered Peaks and have found a more defensible position."

"And the route?" asked Bryen.

"Rafia found a path for us that begins a few leagues to the west. We'll make our way to Haven. If we need to fight, better to do it there than in the mountains."

"Haven is still a long way off," said Bryen. "It will be difficult to stay in front of the Ghoules even with our lead."

"That's why we need to get moving soon."

"A good plan," Bryen agreed, "though that still doesn't give us the time and distance that we require. The Ghoules are too fast. We won't make it to Haven with them so close. We also don't know if the Slayer is dead or was only swept away by the storm."

"Can you feel the Slayer?" asked Aislinn.

Bryen reached for the Talent, extending his senses all around them for more than thirty leagues. He located the Ghoule packs coming toward them swiftly from the southeast along with that darker taint of evil that Bryen could only assume was the Ghoule Overlord. The ancient evil of the Slayer was nowhere to be found. He didn't identify anything else around them that worried him, as if the Ghoule Overlord coming for him wasn't worry enough.

"Not at the moment, though I'm not going to believe that monster is dead until I see it with my own eyes. Separate from that, we have a more immediate concern. The Ghoules are less than three hours behind us now and closing faster than we would like."

"I can tell by the look in your eye that you have something in mind," said Declan. "What is it?"

"Sirius showed me some tricks that I can use that should buy us some more time and put off the fight that we know is coming," replied Bryen. "You go on ahead, and I'll catch up."

"We'll catch up," said Aislinn.

"I can handle this," Bryen protested. "There's no reason for you to take this risk."

"I'm sure you can," said Aislinn. "I want to learn what Sirius showed you, and the only way to do that is to go with you. Besides, we've talked about this before. I and everyone else here are less important than you. You are the reason we're here. You're not gallivanting around in the mountains having fun while we run from the Ghoules."

"I don't gallivant."

"That may be," Aislinn replied, unable to stop a smile from curling her lips. "But you're still not going off on your own."

"We'll go with them," said Lycia, she and Davin walking up behind Declan.

"Yes, we'll do our best to keep them out of trouble," added Davin.

"As if you two don't get into enough trouble yourselves," grumbled Declan.

"Then we can all keep each other out of trouble," said Davin with a big grin.

"You all don't need to put yourselves in danger for me ..."

"Bryen, you need to let this go," said Aislinn. "You're not going off on your own. Trouble seems to find you. When it finds you this time, we'll be there to help you get out of it."

"Yes, but I can still ..."

"Bryen, it's easier just to agree with her," said Lycia. "She's tougher than she looks, and we're not going to let this go. So instead of wasting more time, let's get started."

"Do you really think that it was a good idea to let Lycia go off with Aislinn?" asked Bryen. "Whether she'll admit it or not, her feelings toward the Lady of the Southern Marches are fairly obvious. I get the sense that she's just as likely to speak with her as stab her."

"Lycia is like that with most people," said Davin, his tone hinting at his complete lack of concern. "You know that. It takes a while for her to warm up to you. Besides, they're just on the far side of this knoll. What could happen?"

"You know what could happen."

Davin shrugged. "Lycia was adamant. You know what it's like trying to push back when she's already made up her mind."

"I do," Bryen admitted, having experienced it many times in the Colosseum. "I just don't think it's a good idea to have those two off on their own."

"Maybe not," agreed Davin. "But it's too late now, and we have more pressing issues to deal with. What are you planning?"

"Something similar to what I did to force the Slayers to come at us from one direction," replied Bryen. "And I promise you, the Ghoules are not going to like what they find when they come to the end of the channel here. Then we're going to move a bit farther to the west when Aislinn is done with her traps. No matter which side of the knoll the Ghoules select, they're going to run into some obstacles that they are going to wish they hadn't."

"Some more nasty surprises? Good. They deserve no less." Davin would be the first to admit that he had a mean streak. It was one of his characteristics that had allowed him to survive for so long in the Pit, although he tried to apply that mean streak judiciously. Here, and now, seemed a very appropriate place for it.

"Yes, I wouldn't have it any other way. I've got several other traps in mind that should kill a good number of the beasts before they catch up to us. Just don't hold your breath. With the Ghoule Overlord running with them, anything could happen." Bryen poured a few more streams of the Talent into the air around them, then let go of the natural magic of the world. "If nothing else, some of these tricks should slow the beasts down and give us a better chance to make it to Haven."

"That's all that we can hope for," agreed Davin, "and of course that Lycia doesn't do something that she shouldn't to Aislinn. My sister does have a strange and strong affinity for her knives."

∾

"You're awfully quiet," said Lycia.

Aislinn and Lycia hadn't spoken since they had separated from Bryen and Davin. Neither was entirely comfortable in the other's presence, so Aislinn was quite surprised when Lycia was the first to break the silence that had settled between them. She thought that the gladiator was simply going to give her incisive perhaps even intimidating looks the entire time that they were together that Aislinn couldn't entirely interpret, although her initial impression was that none of Lycia's looks meant anything good for her.

"I'm not ignoring you, Lycia," replied Aislinn. "I'm just concentrating. That's all. Much of what Bryen showed me is complicated, and I need to do it right."

Aislinn had already put in place three traps that Bryen had shown her how to craft out of the Talent, and she was working on the fourth right then. It was the most difficult of them all, a thin stream of the Talent spinning out of her palms and settling onto the ground behind them. If any of the Ghoules wandered into this ambush, they would have little time to regret it.

"Are you done?"

"With this trap, yes. Let's move a bit farther along the trail. I have one more to set."

If the Ghoules were taking the fastest route in their pursuit, they would need to choose which side of the knoll to take. Now, after what Aislinn had done, and what Bryen was leaving for the beasts on the other side of the hill, the Ghoules would have little to no chance to avoid what waited for them.

"You're a better fighter than I expected," said Lycia.

"That's kind of you to say, thank you." Aislinn responded warily, not sure why Lycia was so interested in engaging in a conversation and why she had started with a statement such as that. Lycia was quiet to begin with, and in the past she had avoided speaking with Aislinn as much as possible, apparently the gladiator's only desire to get her onto the white sand to test her mettle. So their engaging now in a conversation was a bit of a surreal experience for Aislinn. "Is that because I beat your brother?"

Lycia smirked at that, remembering the combat that had taken place in the Pit that the now deceased King of Caledonia had disrupted at its conclusion.

"Davin would probably say that it was a tie."

"Davin can say what he wants, but he would be wrong," said Aislinn. "I had him right where I wanted him. I won that combat."

"I'll give you that," agreed Lycia with a soft chuckle. At first, she had thought that Davin had taken it easy on the Lady of the Southern Marches when they dueled with quarterstaffs, Declan refusing to allow the use of steel. As time passed and she replayed the practice combat in her mind, she realized that she had been mistaken. "With what Bryen has taught you, you might even survive in the Pit."

"You think I'd survive in the Pit?"

Lycia studied Aislinn for a few seconds, then smiled. She liked Aislinn's spark, although she wasn't ready to admit it because there were still so many things about the Lady of the Southern Marches that grated on her nerves. "A few minutes at least."

"High praise coming from you," said Aislinn, smiling now.

"Has Bryen told you much about me?" asked Lycia, deciding to just dive right into the topic that she had been wanting to discuss with her competitor for quite some time.

"Some," Aislinn admitted, working to keep herself on an even keel just as her emotions threatened to knock her into the water. "He told me that you used to spend a good bit of time with him."

"I did." Lycia chose not to offer any more detail than that, allowing Aislinn's mind to move in any direction it cared to.

"You love him," stated Aislinn, her heart in her throat. She wanted to get right to the crux of the matter. Better to do that than to allow her worry to continue to grow and fester as it had been for several months now.

"I do," Lycia confirmed. "I did." Lycia sighed. She didn't have to make this easy, in fact her initial instinct was to make it as difficult as she could. Yet if she did, that wouldn't help either of them. Better to be honest. "I did. Just not like you do."

"I don't understand ..."

"Don't play the fool with me," said Lycia. "The others might not see it, but I do. Of course, Davin does, which is a miracle in and of itself because he rarely notices anything like this. I'm sure Rafia does as well. She might come across as distracted, a little loopy, but she's sharper than the edge of my blade."

Aislinn didn't know what to say, so she didn't say anything

for a minute, trying to gain control over the rush of emotions welling up within her.

"You're being honest. I should be as well." Aislinn sighed, taking a moment to gather herself. "I do love him."

"Thank you for that," replied Lycia, though the words felt like a small slice had been cut from her heart upon hearing them. She had wanted to know the truth, even though she had feared it as well. Now that it was out in the open, it still didn't make confirmation of her greatest fear any less painful.

"Is it that obvious?" Aislinn asked.

Her voice was strong even though admitting the veracity of her feelings made her feel incredibly vulnerable. She couldn't hide from the truth. She refused to. Even if it put her in conflict with the woman standing just a few feet away from her who had a real rapport with the various pieces of steel situated on her body.

"It is. As I said, many of us see it."

"Which means that Bryen ..."

"He'd be a fool not to see it as well."

"And he's not a fool."

"No, he isn't." Lycia stopped when Aislinn did. Not because Aislinn didn't want to continue the conversation, rather because they had reached the place where she wanted to set the last trap. "I will admit, if you haven't figured it out, that I didn't trust you when we first met. Especially when I learned about the Protector's collar. What it meant. What it did to Bryen. Why it was there."

"That wasn't ..."

"Stop fussing, Aislinn. I know you had nothing to do with it. Bryen was quite clear about that as well as the fact that you hated the collar as much as he did."

"I did hate it. I do hate it. I still haven't forgiven my father for what he did."

"I'm just trying to say that I'm beginning to feel differently about you," acknowledged Lycia with a sharp nod. "I won't say that I trust you completely. That would be lie, and I don't want to tell a lie when we're being honest with one another. I do see that you're more than just your title and the privilege and power that goes with your rank."

"Thank you," murmured Aislinn. "I appreciate that."

"You've done well by him," Lycia admitted with a half-hearted nod. "Since we're being honest, I want to tell you this as well." Lycia stepped in close so that they were no more than a foot apart from one another. "Bryen deserves more from life. As you know, he has had to deal with more than most. When this is over, he deserves a better life. He deserves to pursue the life that he wants."

"Something else that we agree on."

"Good. Just remember, if you hurt him, I'll kill you. So don't take that risk unless you're willing to pay the price."

Aislinn and Lycia locked eyes, neither willing to be the first to break the hold the one had on the other. For most Lycia's comment usually would have been taken humorously. Aislinn knew that the gladiator was dead serious. They had been speaking frankly to one another, so she took Lycia's last statement for the truth that it was.

"So what will it do?" asked Davin.

He and Bryen were on the other side of the knoll and almost back to where the two paths came together. Davin had spent the last few minutes watching Bryen use the Talent as he set a variety of traps for the pursuing Ghoules. At first, what his friend was doing unsettled him, still not used to the fact that Bryen, the Volkun who had helped him survive in the Colosseum, could tap into what he viewed as a dangerous, though admittedly useful, power.

Yet the more he thought about how what he and Aislinn were doing could potentially impact their hunters, the more enjoyable it became for Davin to watch Bryen at his work. The likely result for the Ghoules from these snares appealed to him.

Bryen continued to stare at the ground, streams of the Talent swirling from his palms as he coated the dirt and the grass with the natural magic of the world, the threads of white settling and then fading into the landscape. For a moment, Bryen ignored his friend, needing to concentrate. When he was done, he released his hold on the Talent, and they both continued along the trail to the west so that they could catch up to Lycia and Aislinn.

"Think of them as hunting traps," explained Bryen. "If the Ghoules come through here, the Talent that I wove into the ground will snap closed like a vise, except rather than catching on ankles, those traps I just crafted will slice all the way through the beasts' midsections, flesh and bone."

"What if someone else comes through? A trader maybe?"

"They have nothing to worry about. The trap can only be activated by the taint of Dark Magic that's associated with Ghoules and Elders."

"Very thorough," Davin nodded with approval. "Very final."

"I try my best."

"Do I sense a mean streak?" teased Davin. "I like people with mean streaks."

"When it comes to Ghoules, yes," said Bryen after pretending to take a few seconds to consider the question.

"You know, you don't look it, but you really are a quite forbidding fellow."

"Everyone keeps telling me that I look dangerous," scoffed Bryen, as if he didn't believe it himself. "What do I look like to you?"

"More like a baker to me." Davin got the words out without breaking into a smile, though his twinkling eyes betrayed him.

"If only. A much safer and less complicated profession."

"Yes, life would be a lot simpler," Davin agreed, "though probably a whole lot less fun."

"You call this fun?" asked Bryen. "Fighting in the Pit. Overthrowing the King. Battling Ghoules and Elders. Escaping the Slayers and the Ghoule Overlord."

"In a word ... yes," Davin grinned. "A cinnamon roll every now and then certainly would be appreciated, but I need something more than that to get me through the day. You as well, I know, whether you're willing to admit it to yourself or not."

"You really have a strange sense of fun."

"Think of it less as fun and more as the desire for adventure. What baker would ever have the chance to do what we're doing?"

"What baker would ever want the chance to do what we're doing?"

"You've got me there," admitted Davin. "Still, despite the challenges, I much prefer this than the life that Lycia and I had before we entered the Colosseum."

"You and me both," Bryen admitted quietly.

"Yes, you are never one to run from a challenge, are you? Even if running makes the most sense."

"Well, you know what Declan likes to say, and what I borrowed from him in the gladiators' barracks before the uprising. You must do what you must do."

"I'm glad you said that," replied Davin as he and Bryen continued along the base of the knoll, the wind beginning to pick up again. "Truer words I've never heard."

For just a second, Bryen stopped, looking around them. There was really nothing to see in this rugged land, the long grass to their south rippling in the wind, the Shattered Peaks rising to their north, yet something had tickled the hair on the back of his neck. Something that wasn't quite right.

"You all right?" asked Davin.

"Yes," Bryen replied, staring back the way that they had come. He thought that he had caught a flash of movement in the long grass, and he had, though it wasn't what he had feared was coming after them. Rather, it was a large fox who had leapt out of the stalks and then sprinted through them for about twenty yards. The fox stopped abruptly, slinking down into the grass. Either the animal had caught whatever it was pursuing or it had missed and was waiting to see what other prey might come its way. Or could the fox have stopped its hunt for another reason? Could it be hiding from something? "Sorry, just got distracted for a moment. You were saying?"

"I was saying that you never walk away from challenges."

"I'm assuming that there's a point to all this, Davin? You're taking a really long time to get to whatever it is that you wanted to speak to me about."

"I'm just trying to approach the topic in the appropriate way. It's a delicate matter, and I didn't want to upset you."

"Lycia is anything but delicate."

"How did you know that I wanted to speak to you about Lycia?"

"The better question is why do you feel the need to speak to me about Lycia? It's none of your business."

"She is my sister," Davin protested. "You two were close in the Colosseum."

"We're still close, I believe," replied Bryen, really not wanting to get into this conversation with Davin right now, though seeing no good way to prevent it.

"Yes, but in the Colosseum you two were really close," Davin hinted. "Really close."

"Just what do you mean by that?" demanded Bryen, his face turning slightly red.

"You know what I mean."

"No, I have no idea what you mean."

"Come on, Bryen. You and Lycia spent a great deal of time together when we were in the Colosseum."

"So did we," said Bryen. "What's your point?"

"In the Pit for us," replied Davin with a smile, enjoying the fact that he was making his friend uncomfortable. He was a natural instigator, after all. "Not in the barracks."

The slight blush on Bryen's cheeks deepened, and despite the chill in the air, he began to sweat. He felt more nervous now than he did when fighting a Ghoule.

"Lycia and I simply enjoyed spending time with one another."

"I'm well aware of that, Bryen," said Davin.

"Davin, you're beginning to irritate me more than usual, and that's saying quite a lot. Would you please just get to the point of all this?"

"I want to know what's going on between you and my sister. Or what went on. Both, actually. It's weird being around you both now. There's this tension that wasn't there before."

"Why do you want to know?" demanded Bryen. "It has nothing to do with you."

"It has everything to do with me."

"Where are you getting that from?" asked Bryen with a touch of incredulity. "Whatever is between me and Lycia is between me and Lycia."

"I'm her brother," said Davin calmly. "I have the right to know what's going on between you. It's as simple as that."

"Really?" asked Bryen with a raised eyebrow. "What would Lycia say if she heard you say that?"

"She'd probably try to stick me with one of the daggers she's got hidden in her armor or in her boots."

"Exactly," said Bryen, his face darkening, becoming more menacing. "And knowing that, why wouldn't I do the same?"

Noting the change in Bryen's voice and his expression, Davin realized that he may have pushed his friend a bit too far or perhaps a bit too quickly. He knew from experience that Bryen wasn't as testy as Lycia, though he did have that mean streak as he had already noted. And he did hold onto grudges. For quite a long time. So maybe now was the time to take a step back and try a different approach, since clearly his first attempt at engaging on this topic wasn't working.

"I'm sorry," said Davin. "I didn't mean to get you worked up. But you need to speak with her."

"I know," said Bryen with a sigh, shaking his head miserably. "There just never seems to be a good time."

"There never will be a good time."

"First you push me, doing your very best to get under my skin. Now, all of a sudden, you're a font of wisdom."

"What, you didn't think I could give good advice?" asked Davin, feeling slightly offended.

"I never said that."

"That seems to be what you're suggesting."

"If I was suggesting it, I would say it."

"Then why don't you say it?"

"I would say it if I thought I should say it," Bryen replied with a bit more heat, his anger beginning to simmer once again.

"So you're saying that I give good advice?"

"You want me to say that?"

"I would like you to say exactly that, yes."

"You know, you really can be a pain in the ass."

"I know. It's one of my finer qualities. Now would you please just say it."

Bryen stared at his friend, slightly amused though his temper continued to simmer. He allowed the seconds to pass as Davin stared back at him, clearly desperate for the words that he craved to hear.

"All right. Yes. You just gave me good advice."

Davin whooped, extremely pleased by Bryen's comment, and then he found himself face down in the dirt trail, Bryen having launched himself into his friend's back upon seeing a flash of movement behind them.

The Slayer flew through the air, claws outstretched, the beast screeching in anger as it missed its prey by no more than a hair. The monster rolled on its shoulder and got back to its clawed feet in an instant, its whiplike tail hovering just above its head.

Bryen stared at the beast, expecting the Slayer to attack immediately. Apparently, however, since they had killed two of its brethren, the creature was demonstrating more restraint than it normally would.

Still, Bryen could see it in the monster's eyes. The Slayer wanted him. Desperately. The beast wanted the Seventh Stone because that's what its Master wanted. And now it finally had its chance without having to fight its way through a wall of steel.

"Like fighting a giant scorpion?" asked Davin, who rose to his feet, spear in hand.

"Like fighting a giant scorpion," confirmed Bryen, who took hold of the Talent, infusing the tip of Davin's spear and the double blades of the Spear of the Magii with the energy needed to cut through the beast's armored skin.

Bryen shifted toward the right, slowly spinning the Spear of the Magii in front of him, trying to pull the Slayer's attention in his direction as Davin moved to the left. The beast stood perfectly still, obviously unconcerned by their actions.

Davin feinted a lunge with his spear. The Slayer didn't move. As Bryen and Davin separated from one another, the Slayer's eyes stayed locked onto Bryen, having a preternatural sense of where Davin was at all times.

So Bryen wasn't surprised when the Slayer tensed, bent its knees, and then sprang toward him. Bryen swung with his left hand, bringing his Spear up in time to deflect the beast's claw, and then doing the same with his right to catch the creature's other claw, which had swept toward his hip from the other side, missing his flesh and slamming against the steel haft of the Spear of the Magii instead.

The Protector ducked as the Slayer's spiked tail shot through the air right where his face had been just a second before. And then again, this time the sharp tip aimed for his chest, forcing Bryen to flip backwards in the air to avoid the strike.

Surprised by what he had done and happy that he didn't even stumble when his feet hit the ground again, Bryen didn't have the time to congratulate himself as the Slayer was on him in a flash, the beast's claws swiping for his flesh in a deadly rhythm. Bryen danced back, the Spear always in the right place at the right time to parry every lunge, jab, and slash the monster sent his way.

Still, it wasn't the situation that Bryen wanted to be in when fighting such a dangerous creature. He wanted to attack. He wanted to force the beast onto its back foot. And then he realized that he might get that chance when he caught the movement just behind the Slayer's right shoulder.

Davin lunged with his spear, aiming for the center of the Slayer's lower back. His aim was good, the glowing steel just a finger's breadth from striking true, when the Slayer leapt into the air and spun, its long tail cutting around behind the beast and slamming into Davin, knocking him off his feet and sending him sliding through the grass.

Bryen watched in horror as Davin hit the ground and stayed there, his friend an unmoving figure in the long grass.

The Slayer turned back toward him, a deep growl emanating from its throat, pleased that now it had the Seventh Stone all to himself. The creature gnashed its teeth a few times.

If the Slayer's intent was to intimidate, then it failed. All it did was strengthen Bryen's resolve.

This was no different than a combat on the white sand. And

there was only one possible result. Kill or be killed. So better to be the one doing the killing.

With that thought in mind, Bryen took the fight to the Slayer. He attacked with a speed that surprised the beast, forcing it to dodge backwards, then duck and step back again. Bryen slashed at the creature, his glowing steel blades a blur, doing all that he could to ensure that the Slayer's attention remained fixed on him rather than on his fallen friend.

Bryen refused to allow the Slayer to attack. Rolling to his left, Bryen swung backwards with the Spear of the Magii, the tip of the blade slicing across the monster's shin. The wound wasn't deep, but it was enough to anger the beast, which launched itself toward Bryen with an uncontrolled abandon.

Bryen smiled upon seeing the effect that single wound had on the Slayer. This was the chance that he had been looking for, the Slayer no longer in control of itself, its instincts and drive crushing its reason.

The Slayer initiated a wild assault, claws slashing for Bryen's face, chest, and hip, its tail seeking to puncture his flesh. This is what Bryen wanted. The Slayer allowing its anger to rule meant poor decisions on its part, of which Bryen took full advantage.

The glowing blades of his spear sliced through the creature's armored flesh like a hot knife through butter, leaving the Slayer with more than a dozen gashes marring its body, the beast's thick black blood streaking down its chest and legs.

Despite the physical toll of its mounting wounds, the Slayer continued to attack. Maddened even more by each injury it received, its reason was replaced by rage, its desire to obey its Master subsumed by its ravenous hunger and the domineering need to kill.

Bryen was more than happy to continue the game he played, weakening the monster one cut at a time. He knew, however, that now was his best chance to end this combat. He was about to go back on the offensive when he heard a rustle behind the Slayer. A sound that he had been hoping to hear though he had feared that he wouldn't.

He smiled grimly, that sound telling him exactly what he needed to do next. Rather than shifting to the attack, Bryen instead played the part of the prey, permitting the monster to attack, catching both of the Slayer's claws on the steel shaft of the Spear of the Magii.

The Slayer grinned at him from no more than a foot away, revealing its serrated teeth that were so perfectly formed for ripping into human flesh. The beast pushed down on the metal, its drool dripping onto Bryen's leather armor, the Slayer screaming in his face in rage and expectation, believing that it was finally going to take the prey it had been stalking since its release from the Temple of the Ghoules.

Instead, the Slayer's screams turned into a surprised grunt, followed by a whimper of pain, a sharp, glowing spearpoint appearing right through the monster's chest. The steel was pulled free, and then pushed through again, and again, until the Slayer's chest was nothing more than a bloody mess of broken bones and torn and charred flesh.

After the sixth and final lunge, the Slayer's strength evaporated, the beast's claws slipping from the haft of Bryen's weapon as the monster slid to the ground on its mutilated chest, its back no better. Yet even with the spear removed, the Talent that had been infused within the point continued to do its work, burning swiftly through the monster until there was nothing left but a pile of ash.

"You all right?" asked Bryen.

"Yes, fine," replied Davin, who dug the butt of his spear into the dirt and used it to hold himself up so that he could catch his breath. His ribs were sore from where the Slayer's tail had struck him, and the sharp pain that he felt every time he breathed made him think that he might have broken a few.

"Just a little banged up is all. Got the wind knocked out of me."

"What happened?" demanded Aislinn, who came running around the other side of the knoll, Lycia right behind her with both of her blades in hand.

"Slayer," said Bryen.

"You killed it?" asked Lycia, directing her question to Bryen.

"Not me," Bryen replied with a grin as he wiped off the black blood streaking the double blades of the Spear of the Magii in the long grass. "Davin."

"Davin?" asked Lycia. "He killed another Slayer?"

She wasn't upset that her brother had eliminated the Slayer, rather she was more annoyed. She had no doubt that he would take every opportunity that he could to remind her that he felled two Slayers and she none. Of course, after coming up against these monstrous beasts already, she probably could live with that. For now.

"That's the second Slayer he's killed," said Aislinn. "Very impressive."

"I like to think so," agreed Davin, although he had trouble speaking because of the pain in his midsection.

"What happened to him?" asked Lycia.

"A few broken ribs," replied Bryen. "Nothing to worry about. We can fix those up before we move on. But we have a more important matter to deal with?"

"You mean other than the fact that your friend needs to be healed?" asked Aislinn, hands on her hips and a sharp look in her eyes. In her opinion, now was not the time for games.

"Yes, something far more important."

"And what would that be?"

"The Crimson Giant needs a new name. After his latest exploit, he needs a name that represents his latest successes against the assassins of the Ghoule Overlord."

"Monster Killer?" suggested Lycia.

"Something snappier," said Bryen. "It needs to roll off the tongue."

"Monster Man?" offered Aislinn against her better judgment. She wanted to heal Davin and get going, but that name had popped immediately into her mind and she had offered it before she could stop herself.

"A good thought," said Lycia. "Of course, that could be interpreted several different ways. Many of them deserved, I'll give you that."

"Hey, now wait a minute ..." Davin started to protest, but the pain of breathing cut off the flow of his words.

"True," Aislinn admitted.

"The Slayer of Slayers," said Bryen. "I think that has a nice ring to it."

"That one," Davin whispered before his friends could offer any more names and keep him from receiving the medical attention that he wanted. His ribs were beginning to hurt even more with every breath that he took.

"It might be a bit too long for a good catchphrase, though," said Bryen, enjoying his friend's discomfort and more than happy to prolong it after the conversation Davin had forced him to endure just a few minutes before.

"I think it sounds good," said Davin, gritting his teeth from the pain. "The Slayer of Slayers."

"Wonderful," murmured Lycia. "Something else that's going to go to his head. Big enough as it is already, just what we need."

"With that settled," said Bryen, "Aislinn, did you want to try your hand at healing Davin's ribs. Once done, we need to catch up to the Company. The last Slayer is dead, but the beast did succeed in slowing us down. The Ghoule Overlord is no more than an hour behind us now."

16

CAUGHT IN A TRAP

"What have you learned, Gurzen? How far ahead are they?"

The Ghoule scout skidded to a stop in front of the Ghoule Overlord, staring with wide eyes and a feeling of awe for just a few seconds at the shape of the black diamond carved into his Master's forehead before pulling his gaze away and falling to a knee.

"No more than an hour away, Master," reported the Ghoule. The scout regained his feet with a sharp motion from his Master.

"Still to the west?"

"Yes, Master. Still to the west. Ten leagues to our front, no more. It is the only direction for them to take now. The trail only leads that way."

"No breaks? No chances for them to cut back around a mountain or take another path?"

"No, Master. The trail is too narrow, the terrain too rough, and the peaks here are too steep to climb. Even if the humans tried, it would only mean lost time for them and a worse position to defend themselves. They cannot escape us going in this direction."

The Ghoule Overlord nodded as he contemplated the information that his scout had just provided. If what Gurzen said was accurate, then there was only one reason for the humans to be moving so quickly in that direction. His prey believed that if they reached their redoubt hidden away within the Shattered Peaks that they would have a better chance of fending off his pursuing packs of Ghoules.

Perhaps the humans understood that they couldn't escape. They could only hope to find a place to hide or hole up, forcing his Ghoules to dig them out of the earth like the worms that they were.

"They are only trying to escape us for a short while longer, Gurzen," explained the Ghoule Overlord.

"They will stand against us?" asked the Ghoule scout, not believing it possible. He had crossed the Weir several weeks past. During that time, he had come to view the humans as weak, as no more than cattle to be slaughtered when there was need.

The Ghoule Overlord ignored the Ghoule scout, reviewing his options. It wouldn't matter if the Seventh Stone reached the bastion of the Magii. The Protector stood no chance against him. Even so, better that he takes his quarry before he reached the island. Then he could turn his attention to destroying the Weir that much faster.

"Stay with them," the Ghoule Overlord finally commanded Gurzen. "Get your eyes on them. When you catch up, don't go after them. Not yet. I can't afford to have anything go wrong. Do what you need to do to keep them in place. I must be there when we reclaim the Seventh Stone. I will be right behind you. Do you understand?"

"Yes, Master," Gurzen nodded, the Ghoule scout running off quickly, his clawed feet digging deeply into the rocky ground and helping to propel the beast down the trail at an incredible speed.

With a sharp bark from the Overlord, the Ghoules who had been resting along the side of the trail stood once again, preparing to continue the chase. They were hungry, insatiable now after not eating since they first entered the Dark Forest almost a week before.

The Ghoule Overlord and his dozen packs of hunters had made excellent progress across the Breakwater Plateau, the massive yet incredibly agile creatures loping across the ground at a blindingly fast pace. Never tiring. Never questioning.

The Ghoule Overlord hoped that he and his hunters would have caught the humans by now, having been only a half dozen leagues behind the massive storm that had ripped across the grassland, thinking the tempest would slow the humans and force them to confront his Slayers.

He had been right about that, although what the Ghoule Overlord had found when he had come upon the hours-old scene had surprised him.

One of his Slayers lay dead in the long grass of the steppe, the monster's body nothing more than a charred husk, still smoldering and smoking from the staggering power used to destroy it. Not just the Talent, the Ghoule Overlord realized. The power contained within the Seventh Stone as well.

That discovery concerned the Master of the Ghoules. Was the Protector learning how to manipulate the power of the artifact?

Two Slayers dead in just a matter of days. That shouldn't have been possible. His assassins were the deadliest creatures in the Lost Land. The humans should not have been able to kill them without losing many of their own fighters at the very least. But he and his Ghoules had found just a few bodies where the first fight had occurred in the Dark Forest days before and none on the Breakwater Plateau. Surprising, though not impossible, the Ghoule Overlord had to admit.

Perhaps his worry was misplaced since there were Magii with the Seventh Stone. When last he had sent Slayers after the members of the Order of the Magii, on occasion the practitioners of the Talent had managed to kill one of his assassins. Rare, but not an impossibility. Just concerning. Just another factor to consider when he finally caught up to the Protector.

The question now was, with two of his Slayers dead, where was the third?

He wasn't certain. For some reason, he couldn't locate the beast, something that he should have been able to do quite easily with his Dark Magic. Yet each time he tried to connect with his last remaining assassin to check on the Slayer's progress, he couldn't do it. His assassin had disappeared just like the others had.

That could mean only one thing. Again, not an impossibility, just slightly more concerning.

Still, even if all his Slayers had perished at the hands of the Magii, it was an acceptable loss. The Slayers had slowed down the humans just as he wanted them to, allowing the Ghoule Overlord and his packs to make up ground faster than they would have otherwise.

And he could feel it now, the faint signal becoming stronger with every step that he took toward the west. The Seventh Stone was close. The power that he had been seeking for so long finally was within his reach.

That realization sent an almost uncontrollable impulse surging through the beast. The Ghoule Overlord wanted to move. To sprint down the trail as fast as he could, to give in to his urges and push forward with the chase. But he had learned the hard way the cost of such impetuousness.

He had begun to lose Ghoules, already more than a dozen, to the ingeniously crafted and hidden lures set by the Magii not soon after he had reached the southern edge of the Shattered Peaks and turned to the west.

Three of his Ghoules had been cut in half by blazing white scythelike bands of energy sweeping up from the grassland, several more certain to be killed if he had not acted quickly with the Curse. A few more of his beasts had shredded themselves by sprinting through razor-thin, almost invisible threads of power. And even more Ghoules had fallen victim to discs of energy set in the dirt and rock that activated when a creature touched by Dark Magic came near, beams of energy shooting into the air and incinerating the trapped Ghoules in just seconds.

What the Ghoule Overlord found most exasperating was the fact that despite his incredible power in the Curse, there was nothing he could do to detect the Talent used by the Magii, which meant he couldn't identify a trap until it had been triggered.

Even so, no matter how frustrating the experience proved to be, the number of Ghoules lost during the pursuit so far was acceptable. He didn't want to slow down. He couldn't afford to slow down, not when he was so close.

Speed was the most critical factor now. Nothing else mattered but reclaiming the Seventh Stone, the sense of urgency within him pounding faster and faster in a rhythm that matched his racing heartbeat.

He and his Ghoules needed to do all that they could to obtain the Seventh Stone before the boy reached the island. If the boy made it across the water, it would only make the Ghoule Overlord's task that much more difficult.

So throwing caution to the wind and ignoring his own instincts, he and his Ghoules bounded along the narrow trail at an unmatched pace.

The Ghoule Overlord had traveled no more than a few miles when he felt the first fleeting touches of the Talent, those fleeting touches instantly morphing into bonds as strong as steel as the trap confirmed the Dark Magic surging through his blood and that of his Ghoules.

The lure placed along the trail would allow one or two Ghoule scouts to pass unharmed. Not several packs at once. A trigger set for a certain quantity of the Curse. Ingenious and infuriating both at the same time.

The Ghoule Overlord was losing patience and vowed that he would kill the Magii very slowly to repay them for all the aggravation they had inflicted upon him. He would make these practitioners of the Talent feel an unimaginable pain and suffering, and then he would feed on them while they still lived. A fitting end for those foolish enough to challenge his power.

A welcome thought, but now, the Ghoule Overlord needed to extract himself and his hunters from this latest trap, a white mist having surged up from the ground, wrapping around the Ghoules' clawed feet, upending and yanking them to the dirt and the grass. No matter how violently the beasts moved, fighting frantically to break free, nothing worked, the white mist contorting around them, responding with a unique intelligence to their movements and holding them in place.

The Ghoule Overlord remained perfectly still as the mist curled around him, understanding what would happen next. There was no need to struggle because there was no chance to break free. Not yet.

His Elders should have known that. The fools! Better to let this infernal mist settle over them and save their strength for breaking the bonds that held them once the snare had been closed.

"Stop!" shouted the Ghoule Overlord, bringing the packs following behind him to a halt before they too fell into the trap.

In spite of his shout, the Ghoule Overlord hadn't been fast

enough. Several dozen of his Ghoules were caught along the trail before they could heed his warning.

The Ghoule Overlord growled in anger. It would take time, time that he couldn't afford to lose, to free them all.

Then the Ghoule Overlord's eyes widened. He cursed himself for only seeing what was most obvious. There was more to this trap than he had suspected. Whichever Magus had set this lure had added a loathsome twist, because now the mist began to flash brightly, and with every flash his Ghoules began to scream, the Talent burning through their leather armor and then into their flesh.

Even the Ghoule Overlord began to feel the first tingles of pain as the bonds holding him flared and began to bite into him. A clever trick, indeed, yet not one that could hold him for long.

Ignoring the agonizing screeches and pleas for help that grew louder and more insistent around him, the Master of the Ghoules drew on the Dark Magic that flowed through his blood, a black mist spinning around the top of the black diamond set in his staff, that mist swirling faster and faster, expanding rapidly until it covered the Ghoule Overlord entirely, sweeping the Talent clean from the beast.

Free from the grips of the trap, the Ghoule Overlord swept his staff in a broad circle, taking in the dozens of screaming Ghoules who struggled hopelessly against the bonds holding them, unable to break free, unable to stop the incessant burning.

The mist poured out rapidly from the black ash, smothering the pulsing bonds of white. Yet for most of the trapped Ghoules, it was too late. The Talent did its work too quickly, searing flesh and bone, the white-hot energy turning a beast to ash in less than a minute, much as would happen if the Ghoules had been caught in the Weir, and leaving in its wake the sickening sweet smell of scorched meat.

Frozen in place, not from the bonds of the Talent that had played across the trail, but by the cold, incensed eyes of their Master, the Ghoules not caught in the trap counted the dead. At least two dozen Ghoules lost.

None of the surviving Ghoules dared move, afraid to attract the notice of the Ghoule Overlord, his growing rage made obvious by his flashing black eyes and the bolts of Dark Magic that sparked intermittently from the top of his staff.

17

REACHING THE REDOUBT

"A good location," said Declan. "We can work with this."

He stood on the small, rocky beach beneath one of the tallest spires in the Shattered Peaks, a dozen mountains towering all along the shore, draping the rocky coastline in a hazy shade even though it was only early afternoon and giving the air a chill, making it feel as if it were fifteen degrees colder than it was in the sun.

Directly across from him, less than a mile distant, a rocky island sat in the middle of the glacial lake, the pellucid stone tower that was the Library of the Magii gleaming brightly. The water leading out to the isle was so clear that he could see the undisturbed sediment and rocks resting on the bottom just a few dozen feet beneath the surface, several large fish darting about the trees that had once stood on the lakeshore and that because of the ravages of time had settled into the ice-cold water.

Haven.

Hopefully the island would prove worthy of its name. Although Declan wasn't one to place too much faith in hope. In what might be. Not after all that he had experienced in his life.

Instead, he believed in a reality filled with surprises, some good, some bad, some critically important, some with little meaning. As a result, he assumed that the circumstances of life never played out as you would like, so better to be prepared for those unforeseen eventualities, because hoping too much for something could lead you to an early grave. In short, what was, was more important than what could be.

That's why he believed in himself, his gladiators, and his steel, and he was ready for what was to come, whatever that might be. If they got off the island, then that would be a happy occurrence. And if not, it was as good a place to die as any other.

A fatalistic perspective, he admitted. But it had served him well in the Royal Guard and then in the Colosseum, so he saw little cause to adopt a new way of looking at the world.

The Company of Blood had reached the lake just a few minutes before. Tarin and Jerad weren't wasting any time on getting the gladiators across the water to the island, breaking the Company into teams and sending the first two across on the skiffs that they had found tied to broken tree stumps that slowly were being reclaimed by the lake.

With two skiffs available, and the small boats only able to carry at most ten people at a time, perhaps a few less than that depending on which gladiators crammed themselves onto the boat, the process for escaping the beach took a lot longer than anyone would have liked, what with the Ghoule Overlord and his packs coming at them fast from the east. Yet there was nothing for it. They would simply need to work as fast as possible and hope they all made it across in time.

Long poles in hand, the gladiators assigned the task went to work with a will as they transported the troops across the placid surface of the lake. The flatbottomed boats glided swiftly through the gentle waves. The gladiators were thankful for that. True, the water wasn't very deep, but it was frigidly cold thanks to the constant runoff from the surrounding snow-capped mountains, and none of them had any desire to go for a swim.

"Yes, we should be able to defend ourselves fairly well against the Ghoules," said Rafia. "Assuming we get everyone across in time."

"But?"

"How did you know that there was a but?" she asked.

"Because there's always a but," said Declan. "Especially when it comes to Magii."

"You know, your view of the world could be described as quite cynical if you're always looking for the but," the Magus' expression challenging though also curious.

"I get the sense that we might be speaking about more than one topic at the moment."

"Maybe," said Rafia with a wink. "Maybe not."

Declan chose to ignore what Rafia might be implying with her play on words, focusing on her original comment instead.

"That's one way to think about it," said Declan, "always looking for the other shoe to drop. I would argue that a touch of cynicism ensures a more realistic view of the world."

"We'll have to continue this conversation later," said Rafia, intrigued and not a bit surprised by Declan's thinking, not after what he had gone through in his life. Even better, her dry humor didn't seem to affect Declan, something that appealed to her and that she wanted to test further when the time was right. "I must say as well that I can't disagree with you, because there is a but."

Declan watched as Asaia and Jenus ordered their teams into the skiffs for the trip across the lake, the pier sticking out from the island beckoning to them, promising them a brief respite if nothing else. In less than a minute, their squads were all aboard and the two gladiators were making good time as they poled their way across. At this pace the entire Company actually might make it to the safety of Haven before the pursuing Ghoules arrived.

Still, better to be skeptical and assume the worst. Such an approach helped to ensure that when the worst did happen you weren't taken by surprise, and when it didn't, you felt a bit better about life than you might have otherwise.

"But even though we can defend ourselves on the island, that also means we're on an island, which limits our options for escape."

"Exactly," said Rafia, "and we can assume that the Ghoules will attack across the water. The beasts did the last time that Bryen, Sirius, and I were here."

"Judging by the state of your pier," said Declan, motioning toward the island and the several broken sections of wood and splintered logs that stuck out of the water, "you three did quite well against those Ghoules."

"We did," replied Rafia. "Thanks in large part to Bryen. He was able to come at the Ghoules sneaking across the lake from behind. He was very thorough in his work."

"I would expect nothing less from him," confirmed Declan with a grunt of satisfaction.

"You're quite proud of him, aren't you?"

"Of course I am," Declan replied with a smile. "How could I not be?"

Rafia stared at Declan for several seconds, wanting to say something more, then choosing not to. Several questions had come to mind, though she didn't feel that she knew Declan well enough to ask them, at least not yet. And with her questions came a niggling touch of concern.

How would Declan react if he learned that she and Sirius needed to act against Bryen if he touched the Curse or the Ghoule Overlord was about to take him?

She realized that she was asking herself a foolish question.

She already knew the answer. She was wasting her time hoping for something else.

Declan's primary loyalty was to Bryen. Turning her thoughts away from such an unpleasant challenge, she returned her focus to the challenge set before them.

"We faced fewer attackers then. And we did not have to deal with the Ghoule Overlord himself. That monster complicates our current situation more than I would care to admit."

"How long can we hold against the Ghoule Overlord?" asked Declan.

"Not as long as we would like," said Rafia. "Even with Bryen being the Seventh Stone, wielding the power that he can, to expect him to keep at bay a creature such as the Ghoule Overlord, a beast that has threatened Caledonia for millennia and is the Master of the Curse, is asking too much of him. He doesn't have the knowledge or the training to do that. Not yet. Besides, Sirius would argue that Bryen must concentrate on a more important task first."

"Rebuilding the Weir."

"Yes, and though I'd like nothing more than to take on the Ghoule Overlord, now is not the time. Not with so much else hanging in the balance."

"So we're back to the need for an escape route, because once the Ghoules make it to the island – and they will, it's just a matter of time, it's not just me being cynical – we'll be fighting a losing battle."

"Correct," said Rafia, who gave Declan a wink and a nod. "Does that worry you?"

Declan stared at the Magus for a moment, his hard eyes boring into hers. Then his expression softened, which took her by surprise, because she didn't know how to interpret that look. And she didn't like not knowing what she didn't know.

"No, it doesn't," Declan replied. "You wouldn't have brought us here if you didn't have a way to get us off the island when it came time to do that."

"You believe that, do you?" asked Rafia, who turned to face Declan, her eyes sparkling with pleasure. "Sirius has been bothering me about that ever since the Breakwater Plateau, pushing to know what I had up my sleeve. But you haven't asked me about it at all."

"I do believe that," replied Declan, who stood toe to toe with the Magus, no more than a finger separating them. The tension building between them was equal parts discomfiting and pleasurable. "I trust you. I figured you'd tell us what we need to know when we need to know. Better to focus on getting through the mountains and to Haven first. We can worry about escaping the island once we're actually on the island."

"Thank you," said Rafia, her lips curling into an inviting twist. "For your trust."

"You're welcome."

"Do you really think that you know me so well as that, Declan?" asked Rafia.

She felt the need to challenge him, in large part because of her concerns about Bryen and the Curse. What might be required of her. What she might need to do to Bryen, that thought souring her stomach.

"I'm not Sirius, Rafia," replied Declan, standing his ground, refusing to back down. "I haven't known you for long. But what I have learned about you since we've met is that in addition to having a mean streak when it comes to fighting Elders – something that I must admit that I appreciate, value, and admire – you also have more than one card to play at any one time. You always ensure that there is more than one path to take, no matter how dire the circumstances. So I am absolutely certain that you wouldn't have brought us to Haven unless you had at least one other option in play that would ensure that we weren't trapped on the island by the Ghoules."

For several heartbeats, Rafia stared at Declan. Every time she spoke with him, she learned something new. Something that appealed to her. Replaying his words through her mind, she concluded that what he had just told her might be the nicest thing that anyone had ever said to her.

"Perhaps you know me better than I assumed," Rafia admitted grudgingly.

"Perhaps I do," Declan admitted, "though I would never presume to say so."

Declan's last comment earned him a brief laugh from Rafia. Before she could say any more they were interrupted.

"If you two are done doing whatever you are doing, and honestly I'm not really certain that I want to know what you're doing, perhaps we could get a move on," suggested Aislinn, who had watched with an amused expression for a brief time as Declan and Rafia squared off.

The two had been dancing around one another since Tintagel. It'd be nice if they'd finally dance together. It would eliminate some of the tension that seemed to follow the two around. Of course, others could probably say the same of her and Bryen, though she chose to quash that thought before it gained traction in her mind.

"Even with the traps that we set, at least ten packs are coming this way with a few more approaching from the north to join them," continued Aislinn. "They're all coming fast. To say nothing of the Ghoule Overlord, of course."

"How far?" asked Rafia, reluctantly breaking Declan's hold on her and directing her attention to the Lady of the Southern Marches.

"Less than an hour away," replied Aislinn, who used the Talent to search around them one more time just to confirm that her estimate was correct. "Their scouts will be here sooner than that."

"Then you're right," said Declan. "We need to get moving,

or some of us are going to be stuck on this beach, and I really don't feel like dying just yet."

"WHAT WAS ALL that on the beach with Rafia?" asked Bryen with a grin that he knew would irritate Declan. "It seemed quite intense."

Bryen stood in the flatbottomed boat next to Declan, Dorlan and his squad of fighters poling them across, the other skiff well ahead of them on the water. They were the last of the Company of Blood to make it off the beach and head for the safety of Haven. While Dorlan and the others kept their focus on the pier to their front, Bryen watched the beach they had just left a minute before, knowing that it wouldn't be long now. He had been tracking the Ghoules just as Aislinn had.

"What do you mean?" Declan asked innocently. He, too, kept his eyes on the shore that they had just left, not really wanting to have the conversation that Bryen appeared to be intent on starting, though Declan assumed it was either for his own amusement or his own distraction. Probably a bit of both. It was one of Bryen's habits that he had developed when fighting in the Pit, a way to calm his nerves before an impending combat.

"You know exactly what I mean. What's going on between you and Rafia? It was like watching two lovestruck teenagers who didn't know what to do next. For a moment there I thought that you were going to pull her close and kiss her."

"I was not," spluttered Declan, wondering if humoring Bryen had been a mistake. "What gave you that idea?"

"Bryen's right," said Dorlan, the large man not bothering to turn around as he poled the craft through the gentle waves of the lake. "I thought you were going to kiss her, too. Didn't you, Kollea?"

"I did, Dorlan. You're right. I thought Declan was going to do it. He probably should have. The Magus wanted him to kiss her. You would have had to have been a fool to miss the signs she was giving him."

"I was not going to kiss her," protested Declan. "And how could you even have any idea what the Magus might want? We were just having a conversation."

"If you say so," said Kollea, who worked a pole on the other side of the boat across from Dorlan, although clearly by her tone the hardened gladiator believed that Declan and the Magus had been engaging in more than just a conversation, whether Declan knew it or not, whether he was willing to admit it.

"I do say so," grumbled Declan.

"Quite the conversation, though. So much being said without actually saying anything."

"Dorlan!"

"Sorry, just trying to help."

"You're not trying to help," said Declan. "You're acting like Davin. You're instigating because you have nothing better to do."

"Sorry," said Dorlan. "That wasn't my intention, and I'm not trying to pry into your business. But thinking about it now, I really think you should have kissed the Magus. Kollea is right. I think she wanted you to kiss her."

Declan's face turned a bright red. Whether from embarrassment or anger Bryen wasn't sure. He was certain that he was enjoying Declan's discomfort more than he probably should have been because it was so rare to see the Master of the Gladiators in this position, one in which he didn't seem to be able to exercise complete control. If Bryen knew anything about Declan, it was that he preferred to be in control.

"Can we just let this go?" asked Declan, his request more a

command rather than a plea. "I really don't need the aggravation, and we have more important issues to deal with."

As if to make Declan's point, Bryen stated without emotion, "The Ghoules have arrived."

Declan looked away from Dorlan, who continued to pole the craft toward the pier, the large man hiding his grin, and followed Bryen's gaze. More than a hundred of the towering beasts stood in silence on the rocky beach, staring across the water at the prey that continued to evade them.

Dorlan, Kollea, and the other gladiators on the craft began to pole faster, not bothering to look behind them, not needing to since they could sense the malice and hate being directed toward them. They wanted to get off the water as soon as possible, as they felt more exposed on the lake than any of them would care to acknowledge.

Even from this far away, Bryen could sense the hunger driving the beasts. The overwhelming desire to catch their quarry. To kill. To eat.

"Can Ghoules swim?" asked Declan.

"Not that I'm aware of," replied Bryen. "I expect that they'll build rafts so that they can attack in force. That's what they did the last time I was here."

Bryen had assumed that some of the Ghoules would at least howl or scream their anger at missing out on their quarry after such a long chase. He understood the silence when the massive, robed Ghoule, who stood at least eight feet tall, walked down to the water, his twisted staff of black ash, black diamond set into the top, almost as tall as he was.

The beast looked just as he did when Bryen confronted him first in his dream and then again in the Pit when Sirius required his assistance. A malevolence radiated from the Ghoule Overlord that curdled Bryen's stomach.

For some unknown reason, Bryen wondered how much substance there was to the Master of the Curse. Yes, the beast was flesh and blood. That much was obvious. But how much of what made the Ghoule Overlord who he was really was just a manifestation of the Curse? He didn't have the chance to pursue that thought further because Declan turned his mind in another direction.

"Do you ever wonder what life would be like if it wasn't one challenge after the other?" asked Declan, taking in the Ghoule Overlord with a hard glare.

Just like Bryen, he had fought more monsters and beasts on the white sand than he could recall, so very little worried him. Even so, the creature standing on the far shore did. He was the only opponent that with a single look could send a wave of cold fear washing over the Master of the Gladiators.

"You're asking me that question?" said Bryen. "Now? Have you suddenly found a sense of humor?"

"I've always had a sense of humor. It's just that so few people have been able to recognize it."

"Right," said Bryen with a nod that suggested that he didn't necessarily agree with what Declan had just said. "In all the time that I've known you, I've never really seen you display much in the way of a sense of humor. Usually you're just grouchy."

"I've always had a sense of humor," argued Declan. "I just never had cause to use it. And I was grouchy because I had to deal with the likes of you and the other gladiators every day." He turned back around to measure the Ghoule Overlord, the beast just standing there, his malevolent gaze like a weight on his shoulders. "You still haven't answered my question."

"You want me to answer the question now with the Ghoule Overlord staring us down? It's like we're back in the Pit, the combat about to begin."

"Yes."

"About challenges?"

"Yes, about challenges."

"What's life without challenges?" countered Bryen, pointing toward the leader of the Ghoules who, though standing calmly on the beach, radiated a deep agitation that he couldn't help but sense. "I can't think of a time when I didn't have to deal with a challenge, whether it was fighting on the white sand, overthrowing the King, or dealing with a monster like that."

"This isn't the Pit anymore," continued Declan. "This is something else entirely. Even with that Spear of the Magii augmenting your use of the Talent, can you defeat the Ghoule Overlord when he challenges you?"

"You really want to know?"

"I wouldn't have asked otherwise."

"You want the truth?" asked Bryen. "Because I think you already know the answer, you just want me to say it."

"Maybe so," replied Declan with a grin. "But I do want to hear from you, and I do want the truth."

"Even with the Spear of the Magii, even with me being the Seventh Stone, no, I don't know if I have the strength or the ability to fight the Ghoule Overlord and win," Bryen admitted reluctantly. "Not yet. Maybe not ever."

Declan nodded. "I think you're doing yourself a disservice."

"Why's that?"

"Because you spent ten years fighting in the Pit. You didn't lose once, and I don't think you're going to lose this combat. You may not believe in yourself just yet, but I do believe in you."

"Why so confident?"

"Because I'm the one who trained you."

Bryen laughed at that, Declan's statement helping him to release some of the tension that had been building up within him.

"Funny. I guess you do have a sense of humor after all."

～

"I am sorry, Master," said Gurzen, the scout standing next to the Ghoule Overlord, head bowed, a tremor of fear making the beast shake ever so imperceptibly. Scouts were the best fighters in the Ghoule Legions. They didn't experience fear. Not unless they believed that they had disappointed their merciless leader. "We did not get to the shore as fast as we thought we would. There were several more traps that forced us to scramble along sheer cliffs and avoid the trail. By the time that we did make it here, the last of the humans were on the water."

The Ghoule Overlord did not reply for several long seconds as he stared at the last boat being poled through the water toward the dock.

He and his Ghoules had pushed hard. So close, yet still his prey escaped him.

A seething rage swept through the Ghoule Overlord, his black eyes flashing as he gripped his staff of black ash tightly in his claws and considered the chase of the last few weeks. He was not accustomed to failure. So close, and still so far.

Then again, perhaps not too far. The lake wasn't very deep. Perhaps there was still a chance to take what belonged to him before the Seventh Stone set foot on the island.

"The fault is not yours, Gurzen," rumbled the Ghoule Overlord, his words allowing the scout to breathe easier. "I told you to follow them, not take them. You obeyed me. Our delay was not of your making, it was of the Magii we pursued. The Magii will be made to pay the price for the difficulties and delays of our hunt."

"Do you want me to take my scouts across, Master?" asked Gurzen. "We can have log rafts made in just a few hours. The water will not delay us for very long."

The Ghoule Overlord ignored Gurzen for a moment, his sharp eyes focused on the last boat, and then on the island less than a mile distant. The tower of the Magii, the translucent stone shining at the barest touch of the sun, served as a beacon for anyone looking down into the hidden valley. It was a reminder of the power once exercised by the Order of the Magii, a power still exercised, though not to the extent that it had been in the past, as it had been during the War of Remembrance when the Magii had played such a critical role in preventing his Ghoule Legions from conquering the Kingdom.

Yet even with the passage of time, that power, though weaker, still proved potent. Even from here, he could feel the energy emitted from the island, the defenses still in place that would hinder his Ghoules' efforts to take the Seventh Stone. Weaker, yes, but still a formidable redoubt, even for one such as him and the power that he wielded.

A low growl of anger escaped the Ghoule Overlord that made Gurzen and the handful of Ghoules standing near him take a few steps back, not wanting to be the target of his wrath.

The Ghoule Overlord could sense the Seventh Stone now without restriction. The power called to him, wanting to be used. After hunting for weeks, after craving the Seventh Stone for weeks, he had missed by less than an hour the chance to recapture the artifact so important to him and the future of the Ghoules. And now nothing but a half-mile of flat water separated him from his quarry.

So close, yet so far.

The Ghoule Overlord had no doubt that as soon as the Protector set foot on the island, it would prove difficult to take him. The defenses the Magii had set around the tower and the border of the island tingled at the edge of his awareness, making his skin feel as if he had been struck by thousands of tiny pins all at the same time and warning him that much worse was in store when he sought to breach the island's perimeter.

Landing on the island would be no easy task. The power of the Magii may have dissipated over time, but that deadly energy was still strong here. It would be difficult to penetrate without paying a great cost.

It could be done. But it would take more time than he cared to spend in this hidden valley. Time that could be better spent elsewhere, preparing the way for his Legions.

"Take two packs with you, Gurzen. Build as many rafts as you can by the fall of night. We will have need of them as you suggest. The Magii and the humans with them will pay for their insolence, for thinking that they could escape me."

Gurzen nodded, then ran back up the trail toward the trees that grew farther up the slope, issuing commands as he went, several dozen Ghoules following him.

The Ghoule Overlord considered his options. The scout was correct to ask about rafts. They would have need of them. Rafts were the only way for his Ghoules to take the island. Yet, perhaps there was something else that he could try that would ease the press of time upon him. Something that would allow him to achieve his primary goal and then eliminate the Magii and the remaining humans at his leisure.

The massive Ghoule lifted his staff above his head, the black mist seeping slowly from the black diamond, the wispy threads forming a cloud of darkness that swirled faster and faster above the Ghoules gathered on the rocky beach. When the Dark Magic blotted out the sun, leaving the beasts in shadow, he flicked his wrist. The Curse streamed across the water toward the last skiff, the inky threads curling through the air, resembling the twisting roots of the heart trees that ran across the floor of the Dark Forest.

The Ghoule Overlord grinned malevolently, revealing his sharp teeth. Perhaps the Seventh Stone hadn't escaped him after all. If the Protector ended up in the lake, his Ghoules could still retrieve him. Gurzen could manage the task once the first few rafts were complete.

Besides, better to get the Seventh Stone now. Before the Protector reached the temporary safety of the island.

"Just looking at that monster makes my skin crawl," said Declan. The Sergeant of the Blood Company then turned his attention to Dorlan and the other gladiators poling the skiff across the lake. "Let's pick up the pace if we can. I feel like a sitting duck out here."

Having experienced the same feeling as Declan when the Ghoule Overlord appeared on the lakeshore, the gladiators did as he asked, working their poles more rapidly into the soft sand at the bottom of the lake, propelling the small craft forward at a faster rate, even earning a small wake as the bow cut through the water.

Bryen stared at the Ghoule Overlord as the skiff glided more swiftly across the almost flat surface, nary a breeze sweeping down from the surrounding mountains to ruffle the water as had occurred so frequently the last time that he had been here.

This wasn't their first meeting, of course. He remembered their confrontation in the Sanctuary, his hand involuntarily touching his cheek, feeling the thin burn, the blackened scar that never really healed, a flash of pain shooting through him whenever he thought about the creature who had given it to him.

Bryen understood the dilemma that he faced. He understood that the challenge placed before him likely was an impossible task and one that would lead to his death. Still, that didn't bother him. The Ghoule Overlord didn't intimidate him.

He was wary, yes, just as he should be. He wasn't frightened, though. He was anxious more than anything, a touch jittery. Just as with Davin, for him the worst time before any combat in the Pit had been waiting to walk out onto the white sand.

Once the duel began, his anxiety melted away, replaced by his training, his instincts, his intelligence, and his intuition. So a small part of him just wanted to get it over with. To fight the Ghoule Overlord as Bryen believed would be required so that he could release the tension that swept through him as he stared at his antagonist.

He might die. He probably would. He was a realist after all, just as Declan had taught him to be. Still, he preferred the fighting to the waiting.

"Lad, watch out!" shouted Declan, who ducked down upon seeing the streaks of black coming toward them. "Everybody down!"

Bryen realized that the combat that he preferred might begin sooner than he expected when he saw hundreds of black threads swirling faster than a tornado head straight for their raft.

Heeding Declan's command, the gladiators dropped as low as they could, though they had only so far that they could go, the water just a few inches below the deck of their small craft.

In an instant, a dome of white energy formed above Bryen, the young Magus using the Talent to protect the gladiators with him, shielding the boat just as the Dark Magic slammed down upon them from above.

It was as if a boulder the size of a small hill had been dropped on them, the tremendous power of the strike pushing down on the shield, forcing it to sink into the lake despite Bryen's efforts to keep the hardened energy above the surface. Because the force displaced the water around the magical barrier, one geyser after another shot up into the air just along the edge of the shield, releasing the pressure within the protective dome that threatened to burst the gladiators' eardrums.

Through it all, Bryen maintained his hold on the Talent.

Although the surface of the lake beyond the shield roiled dangerously, the water within the shield remained strangely still as huge waves rushed out from the edges of the protective dome and surged toward the island.

The sudden whitewater almost submerged the other skiff. It did send several of the gladiators into the water, although all of them succeeded in grabbing hold of the side. Thanks to Tehana's skill at maneuvering the craft through the froth and how her unnatural calm only deepened during times of danger and stress, the gladiators on the second skiff were able to ride the ten-foot swell all the way to the island's shore, beaching the craft before they were swept under the waves.

Relieved that Tehana and the others had made it safely to the island, and that he and the gladiators on his skiff had survived the first attack, Bryen looked back toward the far lakeshore. The Ghoule Overlord stood on the rocky beach, Dark Magic continuing to swirl above his head and those of his Ghoules. The beast grinned maliciously, gnashed his teeth, then nodded toward Bryen. He took it as a promise of what was to come.

Whether his adversary was impressed or amused by Bryen's quick thinking, or simply trying to relay the message that when this was over Bryen would be the one in the cook pot, he wasn't sure. Bryen was certain that this fight wasn't over. It was just beginning, because with a second nod and a glare that Bryen took to be a challenge, the Ghoule Overlord sent stream upon stream of Dark Magic toward him, the twisting flows of darkness blotting out the sun as they streaked across the water.

Not knowing what else to do, Bryen kept the dome in place, pulling in more of the natural power of the world to strengthen the barrier, using the Seventh Stone within him to harness more of the energy than he could manipulate on his own, because he knew exactly what was going to happen next, and he dreaded it. He could only hope that what he had done with the Talent was enough to keep himself and his comrades alive.

The first blast of Dark Magic struck, followed in quick succession by the others, the onslaught never stopping, until it felt like and sounded to Bryen as if a constant flood of the Curse slammed into his shield. Each blast of tainted power echoed throughout the valley when it struck, the Curse seeking the one tiny crack in his barrier that would destroy the craft and send them all broken and burned by a cold fire into the lake.

Struggling to maintain the shield, Bryen dropped down to one knee, the force being applied by the Ghoule Overlord almost too much for him. The thousands of threads of darkness lingered after they hit the barrier, wriggling across the surface, not yet able to find a way through though not giving up.

Bryen understood with a rapidly growing resignation that it was only a matter of time. Even with the additional power gifted to him by the Seventh Stone, the Ghoule Overlord was too strong for him, too powerful, too knowledgeable.

Too deadly.

As the Ghoule Overlord's Curse pressed down on his barrier, the energy that Bryen used to protect against his nemesis' attack began to heat the water, making it boil, great gouts of steam blasting into the air. The top of the shield was no more than a foot above Bryen's head now, the choppy water within the shield churning dangerously, massive geysers blasting across the surface of the lake just beyond the dome.

The beast had failed to break through Bryen's defense, something that pleased him. Yet, that small victory wouldn't matter if the Ghoule Overlord succeeded in crushing them against the surface of the lake. And that, unfortunately, was very close to happening. Bryen had to duck farther down, now crouching just as Declan and the other gladiators were as they tried to stay clear of the shield that inch by inch pressed closer.

Because of the constant pressure that the Ghoule Overlord was applying, the lake around the skiff resembled the whitewater of the Eastern River. The flatbottomed craft rocked precariously at the mercy of the turbulent water, the gladiators holding on for dear life, stretching themselves across the wood in a desperate attempt to keep the small boat balanced and on the lake's surface rather than beneath it.

Through it all, Bryen could do nothing more than send a constant flow of the Talent into the dome above him, seeking to keep the Dark Magic at bay for a little while longer, the Curse continuing to search for that one tiny crack that would burst the magical barrier that he had created. Bryen hated the position in which the Ghoule Overlord had placed him. He wanted to attack, to force the Ghoule Overlord to retreat from the lakeshore and put a stop to the maelstrom that raged within the shield.

He couldn't. He didn't have the strength.

For the first time, Bryen realized that he had acquired an adversary he could not defeat. The Ghoule Overlord was proving to be too much for him.

The Ghoule Overlord continued to send wave after wave of the Curse across the lake to crash down on Bryen's shield, the beast clearly pleased with his results. As the pressure on the protective dome intensified, water poured up the stern as the skiff started to tip over backwards, dousing the gladiators lying prone on that end of the craft as a rush of whitewater lifted up the front of the raft.

At the same time, Bryen saw that his dome was flattening and starting to crack, the heavy weight of his enemy's Dark Magic too much for him. Watching in horror, he concluded that he was only seconds away from losing control over his shield.

Bryen closed his eyes in thanks when he heard a sound that gave him a hope that he thought had long faded, explosions echoing repeatedly throughout the hidden valley, the shock-waves starting several landslides that cleared away the loose rock and shale from the sides of several of the surrounding peaks. Much to his relief, the churning water slowly died down, the large whirlpools that had begun forming on the surface of the lake slowly dissipating and the skiff, now with its stern almost a foot beneath the water, settling back onto its bottom with a large splash, the raft once again rocking gently on the surface.

Bryen breathed deeply, thankful that he and his friends were still alive. They had survived, but it wasn't his doing, at least not entirely.

Turning his head toward the beach, the Ghoule Overlord still stood on the lakeshore. The beast wasn't grinning anymore, however. Far from it. Although Bryen couldn't hear what the Ghoule Overlord might be saying, he assumed it was a string of curses and threats.

Glancing toward the island, Bryen understood why. Aislinn stood on the dock with Rafia and Sirius, bolts and spears of blazing energy shooting across the lake and disrupting the Ghoule Overlord's attack, forcing the beast to focus more on defending himself and his Ghoules rather than killing Bryen.

"Dorlan, Kollea," said Bryen quietly, pushing himself back to his feet, keeping the shield in place just in case, "let's get back to it. Fast as we can. This is a fleeting opportunity at best. We want to make the most of it."

Not bothering to waste any energy on words, Dorlan and the other gladiators scrambled up as quickly as they could, many slowed by the seasickness playing havoc with their stomachs. It wasn't long before their poles were back in their hands and the small skiff resumed its journey toward the island.

Happy to be back under way, with an impudent grin, Bryen waved to the Ghoule Overlord. The beast's indignant reaction made him smile, the Ghoule Overlord's countenance a shade darker than the Dark Magic that he had just sent toward them during his attempts to sink the skiff.

His enemy had almost succeeded, and he would have if not for the intervention of Bryen's friends. Still, he didn't want the Ghoule Overlord to become too confident, so Bryen decided to give the Ghoule Overlord something else to think about.

Allowing the shield to dissolve, he raised his arms to the sky, the energy from the Seventh Stone surging within him. Bryen whipped his arms down.

A bolt of lightning shot down, blasting through the barrier the Ghoule Overlord had constructed to protect against Aislinn, Rafia, and Sirius' attacks, obliterating a Ghoule standing just a few feet away from the Master of the Curse, leaving nothing but ash to twist in the wind that finally began to drift down toward the lake. Satisfied with his first effort, Bryen continued his assault, the flares of power slamming down into the Ghoules and Elders, killing more than a dozen of the beasts before the Ghoule Overlord finally directed enough of the Curse into his shield to prevent the supercharged energy from cutting past his defense.

Sensing the change in momentum, Rafia, Aislinn, and Sirius accelerated their own attacks. Even though they had little chance of breaking through the barrier that the Ghoule Overlord had strengthened, the incessant lightning bolts pulled the beast's attention away from the skiff that was now moving swiftly toward the island.

The three Magii, standing calmly on the pier, did not end their assault until Dorlan, Kollea, and the others finally brought the waterlogged boat to the shattered pier.

"That was not an enjoyable ride," muttered Kollea, her face a sickly green.

Although she maintained control over her stomach, many of the other gladiators who stumbled out of the craft, including Dorlan, could not, the soldiers of the Blood Company leaning over the side of the dock and expelling whatever little remained in their stomachs into the lake.

"Not the finest moment for the Blood Company," said Declan after he pushed himself back to a standing position, having used the frigid water to clean his mouth of the acrid taste of his last meal.

"Perhaps not," agreed Bryen, who stood on the pier unaffected by what they had all just experienced. "Then again, we're all still alive. That's all that matters. At least for now."

"Too true, lad," agreed Declan, who began walking unsteadily down the pier toward the island, having to reach out to a log every few steps so that he didn't tumble into the lake since his balance was still off. "Too true. The best fight is the one that you can walk away from."

Before striding down the pier toward the Library of the Magii, Bryen took one last look across the lake toward the far shore. The Ghoule Overlord had released his hold on the Curse, the barrier made of Dark Magic vanishing.

His adversary wasn't smiling now. No, all Bryen saw in that single glance was anger and hatred. And one other quality that Bryen hadn't expected to see.

The Protector smiled. The Ghoule Overlord was a powerful adversary as had just been demonstrated. But though Bryen's nemesis controlled a tainted energy that few could defend against, the Ghoule Overlord had demonstrated a weakness that Bryen might be able to use against him later.

Desperation. All of the Ghoule Overlord's schemes were dependent on one thing and one thing only.

The Seventh Stone.

Without it, the Ghoule Overlord's plans for his Legions and Caledonia would come to naught.

To regain the Seventh Stone, the Ghoule Overlord needed to kill Bryen, and he had proven, thanks in large part to the help of his friends, that once again that would be no easy task.

No doubt the Ghoule Overlord would take great pleasure in gutting him and extracting the artifact that had merged with him, probably wanting to make the process as painful as possible. But Bryen realized that he could inflict some pain on the Ghoule Overlord as well.

The longer he stayed free, the longer he stayed alive, the more difficult he made it for the Ghoule Overlord to take the Seventh Stone, the greater the chance that the leader of the Ghoule Legions would make a mistake.

Because that's what desperation did. It affected your thinking. It made a bad decision seem like a good one. It made you rush when you should go slow. It made you take risks that you wouldn't take otherwise.

And when the Ghoule Overlord made that mistake, whatever it might be, when he allowed his desperation to take control over his better judgment, Bryen would be ready to return the favor and inflict as much pain on his enemy as he could.

18

TESTING THE WATERS

The Ghoule Overlord stood on the beach, unmoving, staring across the water at the gleaming tower constructed by the Magii as the sun began to set. He watched as the humans left the sagging and damaged dock and entered that edifice, believing that they were safe, protected by the power of the Magii.

He snorted in derision.

That was a false hope. The humans had simply found a temporary refuge. It wouldn't be long before that refuge became their prison, and then soon after that their crypt.

His Ghoules would see to that. They were eager. They were hungry. And they understood the penalty for failure.

With barely a flick of his wrist, a long streak of the Curse broke free from the cloud of evil that spun above his staff and shot across the surface of the lake. The shard struck the tower with a flash and a low rumble as the Curse slammed into an invisible barrier that was briefly revealed as a shimmering white dome. The barricade receded into the falling night once the shard of Dark Magic played itself out against the surface of the shield.

The Ghoule Overlord flicked his wrist again and another sliver of Dark Magic cut free from the intensifying whirlwind and streaked toward the tower, followed by another, and then a handful more.

Each time one of the bolts of Dark Magic hit the shield, the same thing happened. A flash of light followed by a deep rumble that reverberated throughout the hidden valley.

When the Curse slammed into the barrier constructed of the Talent, the protective dome allowed the Dark Magic to tire itself out across its exterior as it slowly absorbed the energy. Once the process was complete, the barrier became invisible once again.

A neat trick, the Ghoule Overlord thought. But it wouldn't stop him for long, because he was only getting started.

"So any thoughts on how to keep the Ghoules from reaching the shore?" asked Rafia. "The longer we can keep those beasts out on the water, the better it will be for us."

The curly-haired Magus had fallen in with Tarin, Jerad, and Declan when they left the gleaming tower after the Ghoule Overlord had tested the power of the shield protecting the Library of the Magii and began a circuit around Haven, the three soldiers wanting to become familiar with the territory that they would be defending come the morning. Most of the Blood Company except for the scouts remained in the tower, eating, trying to sleep, and sharpening their steel.

As they walked around the shoreline, Rafia picked out several of the gladiators who were hidden among the trees and rocks, the men and women keeping an eye on the lake and the far shore just in case the Ghoule Overlord decided to attack during the night. She was certain that she had failed to identify all of them, which she viewed as a good thing. If she couldn't find the lookouts, neither could the Ghoules, and they would need all the advantages, however small, that they could muster when the beasts came for them.

Rafia and her escort all believed that the Ghoule Overlord would wait until dawn to attack, needing the time to build the rafts required to bring his Ghoules across the water. Still, better to be cautious. Better to be ready against any eventuality. That seemed to be the mantra that Declan lived by, and it would certainly come in handy now, as Rafia doubted that their enemy had much patience left.

The Ghoule Overlord desperately wanted the Seventh Stone. He had already demonstrated multiple times that he was more than willing to sacrifice as many of his fighters as necessary if it meant he could achieve his goal. So who was to say what the leader of the Ghoule Legions might try and when?

"I was hoping that you and the other Magii could just use the Talent to keep the Ghoules from getting across the lake," Jerad joked with a grin. "You do like killing Elders, and this is the perfect opportunity."

"That I do, Sergeant," replied Rafia with a nod of satisfaction. "And I hope to kill some Elders tomorrow. But hoping doesn't make it real."

"One of Sirius' sayings," said Tarin. "He used that one quite frequently when we were in the Southern Marches."

"Actually it's one of my sayings," corrected Rafia. "He took it from me, though I won't hold that against him. The words are true no matter who speaks them."

"So no relying on the Talent?" Jerad asked again, his voice carrying a tinge of disappointment.

"We can use the Talent, and we will, but no, we can't rely exclusively on the natural magic of the world in this battle that we can't avoid. Not with at least a dozen Elders coming for us with the Ghoules. Those Elders will be more than enough to keep me, Sirius, and Aislinn busy, and let's not forget the

Ghoule Overlord. You saw what that beast did on his own to the shield. Bryen is the only one among us who has a chance against the Ghoule Overlord, and though I have no doubt that the Protector will put up a good fight, I fear it might be a doomed fight. The best that we can hope for from Bryen if he must engage with the Ghoule Overlord is that he holds that monster off and gives us some additional time."

"But hoping doesn't make it real," said Jerad.

"I couldn't have said it better myself," replied Rafia with a smile.

"So you, Sirius, and the Lady Winborne will take on the Elders," said Declan, who had walked at the rear of the small group deep in thought as he considered their current circumstances. "Bryen is expected to take on the Ghoule Overlord if that beast decides to come across with his Ghoules. The Company of Blood focuses on the Ghoules. A fairly simple strategy, though any way you look at it, it doesn't end well for us. The numbers aren't in our favor."

"Does that bother you, Declan?" asked Rafia. "The long odds?"

Although Rafia hadn't known Declan for long, in that short time she had come to appreciate his fatalistic approach to life. He wasn't suicidal, not by a long shot, but after spending so much time on the white sand, just like all the other gladiators who made up the Blood Company, he wasn't afraid to die. He just wanted to approach death on his own terms. A fair demand, in her opinion.

"No, it doesn't," he replied in a soft but strong voice. "I just want to make sure we're in a position to cause as much harm to the Ghoules as we can before we take our leave of Haven, either by passing to the other side or ..."

"You haven't told the others?" asked Rafia, somewhat astonished.

"No, Magus," Declan replied. "I assumed that you'd want to be the one to reveal the surprise."

"What surprise?" asked Jerad.

"Magus Rafia has another way off the island," explained Declan. "We wouldn't have come here otherwise. Always better to be on the move than cornered."

"Rafia, Declan. You may call me Rafia. We've been over this before. Many times. It's as if you do this just to aggravate me."

"Yes, Magus," Declan replied with a quick lift of his eyebrows, knowing that his reply would irritate her. "I'll try to remember in the future."

"You can be a difficult man, can't you?" asked Rafia.

"When it suits a larger purpose," he replied.

"And what purpose would that be, Declan?"

"Making sure that everyone knows what we're about," he replied. "It's the only way to ensure that we survive what befalls us on the morrow."

Rafia used the moonlight to study Declan, her gaze shrewd. This gladiator liked to challenge her. He kept her on her toes. With Sirius, she found these challenges irritating. With Declan, it didn't bother her. Rather, it fascinated her. Why that was the case, she had yet to determine, though she had a strong urge to find out.

Although a small part of her already knew. She just wasn't ready to admit the truth to herself. Not yet.

"Fair enough. I do have a way that we can get off the island when the time is right. Assuming, of course, that the way remains clear."

"Why not go now?" asked Jerad. "Take advantage of the darkness and put some distance between us and our pursuers."

"Because the Ghoule Overlord can sense the Seventh Stone, sense Bryen," explained Tarin. "We need to bloody his nose first. Get him angry. If we can reduce his numbers, when he comes after us again, he'll either be more cautious, which gives us more time, or he'll be overly aggressive, which means he might make a mistake that we can use against him."

"Correct, Captain Tentillin," replied Rafia. "We can't escape the Ghoule Overlord entirely. We can, at least for a time, dictate the terms of our engagement. Haven is the perfect place to do that if we're smart about it."

"I don't disagree with you, Magus Rafia," said Jerad. "We have limited the options the Ghoules might use against us by making Haven our battleground, but the island limits our options as well."

"Yes, you're right, Jerad," agreed Declan. "Our choices are fewer than we might have elsewhere. Even so, the opportunities we have on the island are better than the ones we had on our way here."

"What do you mean?" asked the Sergeant of the Battersea Guard.

"The situation we face now is similar to one that I experienced while in the Royal Guard," explained Declan. "I was a Sergeant at the time, and I was sent with a squad of soldiers to the Dark Forest in search of a small band of brigands, no more than a handful supposedly, who had attacked a merchant's caravan coming down from the mines in the Shattered Peaks. We found them."

"But you didn't find what you expected," offered Tarin, sensing where the story was going.

"We did not," confirmed Declan, "as what had been reported as a handful of brigands actually proved to be more than a hundred. My soldiers were excellent fighters, but as the Magus noted, hoping doesn't make it real."

"Rafia, Declan. You can call me Rafia."

"Yes, Magus," said Declan with a grin and a slightly bemused expression. She might be one of the most powerful Magii in Caledonia, yet there was no reason not to keep her a little off balance. She was so certain of herself at times that

Declan believed that challenging her every once in a while in little ways was necessary. "My soldiers and I knew the likely result if we took on so many bandits. We had little chance of surviving if they came at us all at once, which was the smart play for them of course."

"You didn't allow that to happen," offered Rafia, ignoring the challenge that Declan had set before her, or at least trying to. Engaging with the Sergeant of the Blood Company filled her with an exhilaration that she hadn't experienced in quite some time.

"No, Magus, we did not. When we discovered our predicament, night was falling. So we used the darkness to our benefit, splitting into smaller groups to make the brigands think that they fought a much larger number of Royal Guard than they actually did. Then we shifted our approach. After we'd cut down a good number of the bandits through a series of hit-and-run attacks coming from multiple directions, we let them come at us. Then we ..."

"Narrowed the battlefield," said Tarin with a wicked smile.

"Exactly so," replied Declan with a satisfied nod. "I believe that we can do the same here."

"The first step is to use the water," said Tarin.

"Leave that to Sirius and me," replied Rafia. "We won't be able to stop them all from landing. The Ghoule Overlord will make sure of that. However, we can certainly make their attempts to do so much more difficult than they would be otherwise."

"Done," replied Declan. "I assume, Magus Rafia, that there is a storeroom in the tower."

"There is. In all honesty, though, I haven't been down there in decades. In fact, I don't know if anyone has been in there for centuries."

"That might not matter," said Declan. "Would you mind

taking us there? We might find a few things that could help us against the Ghoules."

With a nod, Rafia led Declan, Tarin, and Jerad into the Library of the Magii, turning left at the entrance, circling all the way around to the rear, before she came to a stop at a large door made of hardened oak wrapped in steel bands. There was no keyhole, which Declan, Tarin, and Jerad didn't find all that surprising considering where they were. Placing her hand on the door, a tiny stream of energy drifted across the surface, hidden runes carved into the wood flashing at the touch of the Talent, before the huge slab opened on silent hinges.

To pierce the darkness, Rafia crafted a ball of light that drifted above them as they walked down worn stone steps covered in a faint layer of dust, the musty smell testifying to Rafia's belief that no one had been down here in quite some time. They then walked down a long hallway that led away from the tower and beneath the island.

"I take it that we'll be coming this way when we try to make our escape?" asked Declan.

"You're almost too smart for your own good, Declan," said Rafia. "I see now where Bryen gets that same quality."

"I'll take that as a compliment, Magus."

"Don't," replied Rafia, though she said it with a warm smile and a wink. "It wasn't meant as such. But you're right. If all goes well, we'll be back down here tomorrow at some point. Until then ..."

Rafia stopped in front of another large door without a keyhole made of hardened oak that was wrapped in steel bands. Placing her hand on the door just as she did on the one that had led down here, a stream of the Talent infused the surface, revealing the concealed runes carved into the wood, the door once again opening on silent hinges.

With a flick of her wrist, the light floating above them drifted through the doorway and into the large chamber. As the three soldiers followed Rafia into what proved to be a very large storeroom, they could only agree with her assessment. Judging by the dust, no one had bothered to come down here for centuries.

The room stretched at least another hundred feet into the darkness, the dim shadows of shelves appearing at the very back, although there was no way to tell what might be on them. Recognizing the problem, Rafia added more of the Talent to the floating orb, which lit up the entire space.

"Do you think you might be able to use any of this in our defense?" asked Rafia, her arm motioning toward what was before them.

Jerad, Tarin, and Declan walked deeper into the room, examining what was lying on the dust-covered tables, walking down a few aisles and picking through what was on the shelves that rose all the way to the ceiling, then rummaging through a few bins set in the corners that held what appeared to be various odds and ends.

"Yes, I believe we can," said Declan, as he picked through a barrel at the far end of the room that held dozens of long pieces of steel that resembled lances, although their ends weren't sharpened. He also found long strands of razor-sharp coiled wire on a hook on the wall just above the steel rods.

Tarin walked over to Declan, showing him a handful of nails that were as long as his forearm.

"Do you think any of your gladiators would be able to turn these into caltrops?"

"I'm sure I could find a few if we can find a few tools," Declan confirmed. "We'll start with Kollea. She used to be a blacksmith."

"This will all prove helpful," Jerad said, who had just finished inspecting the shelves at the very back of the room, pulling free some large springs and pieces of loose steel. "But it's not going to be enough."

"You're right, though it's a start," said Declan. The Sergeant of the Blood Company turned his attention toward Rafia. "Bryen and Aislinn set some traps for the Ghoules when we left the Breakwater Plateau. I'm assuming that you and Sirius could work with them to do that here on the island?"

"It would be my pleasure," Rafia replied with a nasty grin, several ideas for inflicting the greatest pain and suffering on the Ghoules already coming to mind.

"I thought as much," said Declan, his grin matching hers.

"Since we're too few to defend the entire shoreline, we narrow the battlefield as Declan suggests," said Tarin. "We push the Ghoules where we want them to go and cause them as much harm as we possibly can."

"Right," said Rafia. "And when we judge the time is right, we try to disengage and leave the Ghoules here holding the bag."

"Try?" asked Jerad.

"Nothing is ever certain in life, Sergeant," said Rafia, "and as you know, nothing ever goes to plan. The only guarantee that I can offer you is that if we don't make it off this island, we'll take a good number of Ghoules with us."

"That works for me," replied Jerad.

"Good, then we're in agreement," said Tarin. "Jerad, could you please find Dorlan and the other Corporals? We need to start bringing up the material that we'll be using."

"And while Tarin and Jerad are working their way through the storeroom, I had one other question for you, Magus Rafia?"

"What would that be, Declan?" The Magus' sharp gaze suggested that her mind had turned down an unexpected and certainly not an unpleasant path.

"Is there a small forge or a workroom in the tower?" he asked, ignoring as best as he could the spark that shot between them. "We're in need of some tools if we're going to make the Ghoules pay the price we want to set for them since they're so intent on visiting us."

THE GHOULE OVERLORD had yet to move, still staring intently across the water. The purpose of the shield encircling the tower and its surroundings was to absorb the power thrown against it. A smart approach, the Ghoule Overlord had to admit, though it pained him to do so. It would make it that much more difficult to penetrate. No matter how much power he applied, the protective energy would bend, not break.

He had to give the Magii who had constructed the barrier a great deal of credit. Nevertheless, those Magii probably had never considered what would happen when someone of his strength in Dark Magic attempted to destroy the magical barricade.

After giving it some thought, he knew exactly what to do. Applying pressure evenly across the barrier, the Talent would remain strong and whole. It was like pressing down on a fragile shell held in the palm of his hand. Nothing would happen so long as the pressure was constant across the shell. But, if he picked one spot on the shell and applied an increasing amount of pressure there, eventually it would shatter.

The Ghoule Overlord decided to try that now, drawing forth more of the Curse from his staff until the black cloud above him billowed and fluxed, the turbulent mist beginning to spin in an ever tightening circle. As more of the Curse was added to the mix, the wispy streams gained greater solidity and soon resembled a massive tornado that soared hundreds of feet into the sky, the swirling black still connected by a thin stream to the black diamond set in the top of the Ghoule Overlord's staff.

With each rotation of the Dark Magic, the power of the storm intensified, forcing many of the Ghoules and Elders standing on the beach to crouch down. Several reached desperately for the large rocks and fallen tree trunks that littered the shore to avoid getting swept up into the maelstrom.

Once he was satisfied that he had called forth enough of the Curse for the task that he had in mind, the Ghoule Overlord pointed his staff toward Haven. The swirling storm of Dark Magic cut loose from the black diamond and drifted out over the lake, picking up speed as it went, churning the surface into what resembled a boiling kettle of water before lifting higher into the sky and settling right over what the Ghoule Overlord judged to be the center of the island.

He then tilted his staff toward the Magii's tower, the massive tornado moving closer to the ground until its spiky tip bit right into the top of the shield. At the first touch between the two competing energies, a blinding flash of light and a thunderous boom rattled through the hidden valley, the Talent and the Curse warring with one another, black and white streams of power flaring hundreds of feet into the sky.

Firmly in place despite the initial resistance, the tornado spun with greater intensity. The flashes of white and black sped up as the shield attempted to subsume the Dark Magic, the Ghoule Overlord's creation repelling the effort and beginning to do its work. Functioning much like a drill, the sharp tip of the storm plunged into the barrier, seeking to dig through and burst the protective dome.

At the start, the magical barrier held, resisting the Curse. But as the tornado of tainted power pressed harder upon the shield, the point pushing deeper and deeper, creating a bulge at the very top that extended down toward the roof of the Library of the Magii, cracks began to appear where the tip of the Dark Magic bore down on the gleaming white barrier, those cracks rapidly spreading across the sides of the pulsing dome.

As the tip of the storm continued to press down, more fissures spiderwebbed across the surface, splitting off the ones that already marred the dome, spreading rapidly across the shield. When the pressure became too much, with a sound that resembled glass shattering and was so deafening that it started a small avalanche on one of the mountains to the west of the lake, the magical barrier imploded, the pressure from the storm of Dark Magic too much for the Magii's creation.

The Ghoule Overlord grinned in pleasure as he watched the magical barrier fragment and then break apart. That grin quickly turned into an irritated grimace when he realized that destroying the shield had created a massive backlash, plumes of the Talent streaking up into the air and curling back down toward the beach upon which he stood.

Working quickly, he released his hold on the tornado, the Dark Magic over Haven dissipating. He then called forth the Curse once more, striving to raise a shield above his Ghoules and Elders to protect against the flares whistling down toward them at a breathtaking speed.

In a flash, the streaks of the Talent slammed down against his hastily constructed barrier, which absorbed most of the deadly energy contained within the flares. However, the lack of time to prepare still cost him dearly, the barrier too small to cover the entire beach, leaving those Ghoules on the periphery of the attack vulnerable.

In all, more than a dozen Ghoules and Elders simply disappeared when the streaks of energy slammed against the rocky shore, the incredible power that struck the beasts leaving nothing but swirling ash and the melted metal of their spears or charred staffs to offer any evidence that anything might have been living in that space just a moment before.

The Ghoule Overlord kept the shield in place for a few seconds more. Once he was satisfied that no other threats would be coming from the island, he released his hold on the Curse, staring once more at the gleaming tower that even with night falling in the valley sparkled at the touch of the moon just now rising above the surrounding peaks.

He growled in anger at what had just occurred. He had fought against the Magii for more than a millennium. He should have known better. He should have been better prepared. He should have assumed that those practitioners of the Talent had lain a trap within the shield. A trap that he had stumbled into like a novice Elder.

But there was nothing for it now. And though he had lost a good number of warriors and Elders, destroying the shield, which really was an impressive piece of work on the part of the Magii, though not impressive enough, outweighed the cost of his mistake.

He had eliminated the primary magical defense protecting the island. Now there was nothing to stop his Ghoules from moving forward with their attack. Now he needed to shift his focus to the next obstacle.

Breaking through the Talent shielding the tower directly would be a challenge. Still, it was nothing that he couldn't manage. He would simply need to assume that as with the dome, there would be at least one snare set within the magic protecting the Library of the Magii.

When he took on that task, he would be ready for when that trap was sprung. And he would spring that trap, because it was the only way to ensure that he took the Seventh Stone. It would just require a slightly more delicate touch compared to what he had just done.

BRYEN STEPPED CAREFULLY AROUND and over the large boulders and many fallen trees that cluttered the shore of Haven.

The gladiators had followed Tarin and Jerad's instructions to the letter. They placed these natural obstacles in such a way as to increase the level of difficulty for the Ghoules when they finally waded ashore by using them to guide the beasts in the desired direction. The fallen trunks piled onto one another and the boulders bunched together were aligned in such a way so as to create a manmade wall that appeared to be natural while leaving other sections of the beach free of stumbling blocks.

As Bryen moved away from the water gently lapping at the shore, he walked backward up the moderate slope, a stream of the Talent pouring out of his hands and settling onto the rocky earth. The energy flashed when it touched the ground, then faded away into the landscape. It would only activate if a creature touched by the Curse wandered by within a few feet.

Some of the traps that Bryen lay were the same ones that he had used to slow the pursuing Ghoules when the Blood Company left the Breakwater Plateau and made for the Shattered Peaks, knowing just how effective that they had been. A few were new creations, as he wanted to test a few ideas that had come to mind after setting his first series of lures. All of the snares would offer the attacking Ghoules some very nasty surprises that he hoped would complement the ones positioned by Jerad and the gladiators.

Farther along the shore Aislinn was doing the same as he was, Rafia and Sirius already having taken care of the other side of the island. Declan had given the same instructions to the Magii as he had to the Company of Blood. Follow the pattern that he had shown them and leave a trail between the traps for the Ghoules to follow once they reached the beach.

The beasts weren't going to like what they found at the end of those paths, which was just fine with the Master of the Gladiators. They were only getting what they deserved.

Working his way slowly toward the tree line, Bryen felt a touch of guilt once again, something that had been bothering him off and on since he had set foot on Haven. He had placed the Company of Blood in this position. The deadly threat that they would face come morning was because of him.

He knew that he needed to keep that guilt to himself, Asaia

and several other gladiators already having taken him to task for not respecting their choice. He had already had the larger conversation about this, and there was no point in rehashing it.

The gladiators had full knowledge of what was coming for them. They had known before they left for the Sanctuary. They understood the dangers that they faced. Yet despite all that they came here with him. The men and women of the Blood Company all had chosen to be here. They had chosen to follow him.

No matter how guilty Bryen might feel about the gladiators' decision to join him on this quest, about how he was the cause of the lethal threat facing them in the morning, the last morning they all might ever experience, it was their choice to be here. That was the most important thing for them. For him.

Having the ability to make that choice.

He understood that. Needing to have a choice is what had driven him after he was taken from the Pit.

He couldn't take that away from them. He just didn't like it. So he promised himself that he would do all that he could to ensure that his friends and peers survived the coming battle with the Ghoules.

Having worked his way through the trees and then back up to the long grass that grew around the Library of the Magii, Bryen released his hold on the Talent. It was just past midnight. All was quiet. All the work preparing for the fight to come was complete.

There was nothing more to do but think about the morrow, and that didn't appeal to him in the least.

He was about to head into the tower when he saw two figures standing on the very end of the broken dock, glimmers of white shining brightly above their heads. It didn't take him long to understand why as he sensed the dozens of spheres of Dark Magic, all larger than a man's head, all darker than the night, streaking across the water toward the Library of the Magii.

Sirius and Rafia didn't appear worried by the nighttime assault. In fact, it looked like they had expected just such an attack. Even before the orbs began their downward plunge toward the island, the two Magii calmly crafted a shield from the Talent that winked into existence halfway across the lake, each pitch-black sphere sparking like a lightning bolt when it smashed into the barricade, the blows coming so fast that it sounded like a single, long rumble of thunder echoing throughout the dale. None of the Dark Magic broke through the defense and hit the island.

The barricade remained in place for a few more seconds, Rafia and Sirius wanting to make sure that a second strike wouldn't follow the first. When they were certain, the two Magii allowed the barrier to dissipate so that they could offer something in return to the Ghoules.

Several dozen spears of flaring light streaked from their palms and arced high over the lake so that the lances of power crashed down on the far shore. For almost a full minute, a series of explosions rocked the hidden valley as the blazing spears crashed into the Elders' hastily constructed defenses.

The quiet of the night finally returned after that, the only evidence of the skirmish between the Talent and the Curse the several large fires that could be seen raging along the lakeshore.

"The Ghoule Overlord?" asked Declan, who emerged out of the darkness to stand next to Bryen, both of the gladiators admiring the fires that grew a bit larger and wilder thanks to the gusts of wind that rushed down the steep mountain slopes toward the lakeshore.

"My guess would be his Elders," replied Bryen. "He wouldn't waste his time and energy on that. Too mundane for his tastes."

"Rafia and Sirius must have hit some of the rafts the beasts are building."

"Probably. That's really a shame," said Bryen drily.

"Isn't it, though," agreed Declan. "I wouldn't be surprised if the Elders try again."

"Trying to make it harder for us to sleep?"

"That would be my guess. That and their desire to keep us in place. Now that they've got us on this island, they don't want to let us go. Although how they expect us to escape with two small skiffs and Ghoules hidden around the lake, I don't know."

Bryen grunted his agreement, then took hold of the Talent, extending his senses for more than a dozen leagues around the valley.

"What did you find?" asked Declan, recognizing from Bryen's posture what he was doing.

"The additional Ghoule packs coming from the north will be here by morning. The Ghoule Overlord is consolidating the forces that he has in this part of the Kingdom. He likely believes that tomorrow will be our last fight."

"We'll do our best to dissuade him of that notion."

"Of that I have no doubt," replied Bryen. "Still, the Ghoule Overlord doesn't seem all that concerned that we're here. That we gained this temporary refuge."

"Maybe he's not too worried because he destroyed the shield that defended the island. He knows that he's stronger than we are. Even if we hunkered down in the Library of the Magii, in time he'd still be able to pry us loose."

"Maybe," said Bryen, his skepticism clear in the tone of his voice.

"You think he's got a trick up his sleeve?" asked Declan.

"That would be my guess," Bryen said with a shrug. "Although I doubt that he'll think that he'll need to do anything other than send his Elders and Ghoules across the water and overrun us. When those other Ghoule packs arrive, they'll be a match for our current numbers. More than a match, in fact, which doesn't bode well for us. Also, he knows that none of us here on the island have the capacity to effectively defend against the Dark Magic that he controls if he decides to use it against us."

"So he's confident," said Declan. The Master of the Gladiators grumbled humorlessly. "He's just playing with us now, which isn't necessarily a bad thing for us. Maybe he's even overconfident. If so, that's a good thing. We can use that against him."

"We can. If we do it the right way."

"So no rafts, especially now that it appears that the beasts have lost a few thanks to Rafia and Sirius."

"No rafts," agreed Bryen. "Not tonight anyway."

"But definitely tomorrow."

"Definitely tomorrow," Bryen repeated. "Still, I get the feeling that the Ghoule Overlord knows something that we don't. That the rafts might not be his only strategy for invading the island."

"What could it be?"

"I don't know," said Bryen, shaking his head in frustration. "All we can do is be ready for it and hope that it's something that we can defend against."

Declan was about to ask another question when he saw Aislinn approaching through the thin screen of woods that surrounded the tower. He got the distinct feeling that she had something on her mind and that it had to do with Bryen.

"I'll leave you be, lad," said Declan. Bryen had just turned his head to catch Aislinn's approach, a smile breaking out when she smiled at him. "Can I give you just one piece of advice before I go?"

"Anything I can say to stop you?"

"No, but you already knew that," said Declan with a quiet laugh. "Life is short. Enjoy what you can of it when you can."

"Gurzen!"

"Yes, Master," replied the scout, who had just returned to the beach with several of his Ghoules.

His packs had just cut down several dozen trees, stripped them of their branches, and begun dragging them down toward the lakeshore so that they could be lashed together into rafts. The beasts had needed to start over. The Magii's attack had been much too accurate, destroying the rafts they had already completed and that waited for them along the lakeshore.

"How many rafts will we have by dawn?" asked the Ghoule Overlord in the guttural language of the beasts.

"More than a dozen, Master."

The Ghoule Overlord considered that for a moment. That would be enough for the Ghoules with him now, though not for the several other packs that would be joining him in just a few hours. He wanted all his Ghoules heading across the water at the same time, because he wanted to make sure that the humans had no chance of defending against what he believed would be the last attack. This had gone on long enough.

"I'll give you two more packs," said the Ghoule Overlord. "I want twice as many rafts before the break of day."

"Yes, Master."

"With the remainder of the packs, set up a perimeter around the lake so that none of the humans can slip away if they dare to risk it during the night."

"Right away, Master."

Without another word, Gurzen strode toward the Ghoules waiting on the beach and issued a series of orders, two dozen Ghoules running up the slope and into the woods toward where Gurzen's other Ghoules were working on the rafts, the remainder sprinting off in both directions around the lake to put in place the cordon demanded by their Master.

The Ghoule Overlord turned his gaze once more to the island that was less than a mile away, now no more than an imprecise shape in the water with darkness having blanketed the valley.

The humans would be safe for a few hours more. That didn't bother him. They had the Talent and the stone walls of the tower to protect them, but they had nowhere to go now. There was no escape.

And with their primary defense against the Curse destroyed, it was only a matter of time before they died. Whatever sense of safety they might feel was false.

He would send his Ghoules across the water at first light, and then, finally, after weeks of hunting, he would have his prey. He would take the Protector and gut him himself, in the process reclaiming the Seventh Stone for his own.

So he hoped the humans who had escaped to the island enjoyed the night. Because it would be their last one. Once his Ghoules captured the Magii stronghold, his beasts would feast on the humans, their last moments filled with pain and suffering.

~

"Are you nervous?" Bryen asked.

He and Aislinn walked along the lakeside, nodding to the soldiers of the Blood Company concealed along the periphery of the island as they passed them. Several of the gladiators brought their spears to their forehead in a sign of respect.

"Just a little bit," Aislinn replied. "It feels like right before I dueled Marden in the Pit, probably just like it did for you before a combat on the white sand."

"The anticipation," Bryen said, nodding in understanding. "That's often the hardest part."

"Yes, I don't like waiting," she replied with a grin and a

nudge of her shoulder against his, the playfulness helping to cut the tension that they were both feeling.

"Most of the warriors here would agree with you, except maybe for Dorlan. Nothing seems to bother him. The actual combat is nothing to them. They're trained for that. They know what to expect. They know what to do. They just don't like the waiting that precedes the fight. It's too easy during that time to let your fears get the better of you. To allow your mind to wander off track when you need to be completely focused on the task at hand."

"And you?" asked Aislinn in a lighthearted tone. "The imperturbable, always composed Volkun, perhaps the greatest gladiator in a generation. Does the waiting bother you?"

"I think you already know the answer."

"You don't like waiting either," Aislinn confirmed with a smile.

"I don't. I get nervous just like everyone else."

"But unlike everyone else you hide it exceedingly well."

"I've had a lot of practice and training," he replied. "Declan was quite demanding, and I'm glad that he was."

She nodded, then reached across and took his hand in her own, squeezing their fingers together.

"Always so sure of yourself?" she asked.

"Not always," he replied, looking at their hands.

"No?" she laughed. "So the dangerous Volkun is nervous walking alone with me in the dark of night?"

"Well, that depends. Are you planning on taking advantage of me?" Bryen's voice sounded almost hopeful.

"I haven't decided yet," Aislinn replied.

"One can always hope."

"One always can," said Aislinn, giving him another gentle nudge with her shoulder.

"No, I am not nervous being alone with you," said Bryen,

giving her a gentle nudge with his shoulder in return. "I thought that was fairly obvious by now."

"Not always," she said with a knowing smile. "You're very good at hiding your feelings."

"Something else that I give Declan credit for."

"Maybe," Aislinn said, giving him an appraising look. "I think that there's more to it than that."

"If I'm so good at hiding my feelings, how do you know there's more to it than that?"

"Because I know you," Aislinn replied.

"I won't argue that with you," said Bryen with a laugh. "Come on. Let me show you something."

They had reached a point along the lakeshore that was at the back of the tower. From there, Bryen carefully led Aislinn through the moonlight across the rocks and down toward the water. Pushing aside the drooping branches of two massive willow trees, he helped Aislinn jump down into a small, grassy nook that was hidden on all sides except for the one that allowed them to look out over the water and view the Shattered Peaks beyond, the snow covering the summits of the mountains gleaming brightly in the moonlight.

"This is beautiful," said Aislinn. "How did you know about this spot?"

"I take all the girls who come with me to Haven here," replied Bryen as he settled down onto the grass next to Aislinn, both of them leaning back against the trunk of one of the willow trees.

"Funny," said Aislinn, not laughing at what he thought had been a good joke.

"I found this place the first time I was here," explained Bryen. "I spent a lot of time in the Library with Rafia and Sirius while they taught me how to use the Talent and, perhaps more importantly, how to do that while also controlling the Curse that resides in the Seventh Stone."

"You needed a place to get away, just as you did when you were in the Colosseum."

"Exactly," nodded Bryen. "I learned a great deal from those two, but they spent just as much time bickering with one another as they did instructing me. When I needed some time to myself, and some space from those two, I came here. It helped me stay sane while I was stuck on the island with them."

"I can only imagine," laughed Aislinn. "Rafia and Sirius certainly do go at it."

"They do," Bryen agreed.

"Do you think they still care for one another?"

"I think they do," Bryen replied after giving Aislinn's question some thought. "Although I don't think in the same way they did before. Neither of them was very open with one another to begin with, and that hasn't changed. I think that's hurt them over the years. I almost get the feeling that they continue to argue with one another because they're comfortable with that. They don't really know how to interact with one another in any other way. If they stopped arguing, they'd have little reason to be with one another."

"Remarkably insightful for someone so good at hiding his feelings."

"I have my moments," said Bryen with a mischievous smile.

They then lapsed into a comfortable silence, watching the moon drift in and out of the clouds, listening to the gentle waves murmur against the shore. Every few minutes the hoot of an owl broke the quiet, just to remind them that they weren't entirely alone.

"You might as well just ask," said Bryen, finally breaking the peace that had settled over them.

"How do you know that I want to ask you something?"

"Because just as you know me, I know you."

"You sound very confident about that."

"I am very confident about that."

"Because of the collar?" asked Aislinn, reaching her fingers up toward Bryen's neck and brushing them against the cool silver.

"That might have been the reason when I first arrived in the Southern Marches," admitted Bryen. "There's more to it than that now. After we spent so much time together, I learned about who you were because I was at your side almost every minute of the day. I saw the very best of you and the very worst."

"And despite all that here we are."

"Here we are," nodded Bryen. "I assume you know me as well. The good and the bad."

"I do," Aislinn replied quietly. "Or at least I'd like to think I do."

"So then why ask the question?" said Bryen. "You probably know the answer before you ask it."

"It's not something I'm sure about, and I want to be certain."

"Then I'll answer whatever the question might be."

Aislinn took a deep breath, trying to settle her nerves. She did want to know the answer to her question, though what the response might be still worried her.

"Why did you come back for me? For my father? After what we did to you? You didn't have to, but you were willing to risk your life for me. You were free, yet you still came back."

"You took me out of the Pit."

"Yes, but my father put a collar on you. You were still a slave. The only thing that changed was where you were. Why did you come back after all that?"

"You," Bryen said in a voice that was barely more than a whisper, Aislinn having to strain to hear the word as it drifted on the wind.

"What?" asked Aislinn, her eyes widening, not sure if she had heard him correctly.

"You," Bryen said more strongly. "I came back to Tintagel to free the gladiators, to free my friends. I also came back for you."

For several seconds, Aislinn was speechless, only able to stare into Bryen's grey eyes. She saw the truth of his words there, as well as the emotions he was so good at locking away.

Not wanting to think any more, only wanting to do, Aislinn reached up with her arm again, this time placing her hand on the back of Bryen's neck and pulling his lips down to hers, everything else around them falling away as their bodies pressed together.

19

WHAT WE DON'T KNOW

"I just want to make one thing perfectly clear," said Aislinn, her hands twisting nervously in the folds of her cloak, one of her habits that she hated yet didn't seem capable of stopping.

"What would that be?"

After having a quick breakfast before the sun touched the sky, Bryen and Aislinn had taken a seat on the dock that jutted out into the lake, avoiding the jagged holes and the splintered and cracked timber. It allowed them to look out across the water to the far shore.

Despite the distance, they had no trouble identifying the Ghoules as they swarmed on the beach, the additional packs that the Ghoule Overlord had been expecting having arrived, bringing his numbers to almost two hundred Ghoules and Elders combined based on Aislinn's latest survey with the Talent. That would be more than enough to eliminate the Company of Blood if they were drawn into a pitched battle in the open, so that was an event that Tarin and Declan were working very hard to avoid.

Aislinn reached for Bryen's hand, grasping it with both of hers. She looked deeply into his eyes. He wanted to make a joke as his discomfort increased, not used to such intimacy, then rightly decided against it, realizing that this was a moment where humor wouldn't be appreciated.

"This doesn't change us," said Aislinn. "This doesn't change who we are."

"I'd like to think that it does."

"All right, yes, in some ways I guess it does," admitted Aislinn. "But in terms of what we're facing today and in the future, when it comes to fighting the Ghoules or dealing with other dangers, this doesn't change us."

"I'm a little lost," said Bryen. "You need to explain what you mean."

"I'm just trying to say that you do what you need to do and I'll do what I need to do during the fight," clarified Aislinn. "We both have our own responsibilities. You don't need to worry about me. You only need to worry about what you need to do."

Bryen looked at Aislinn for a moment with raised eyebrows, then his eyes softened when he smiled. "I always worry about you. That's not going to change."

"You are not my Protector anymore."

"No, I'm not your Protector," replied Bryen, seeing how she had tensed at his comment. "You don't need a Protector. You can protect yourself."

"Then why?"

Bryen chuckled, not understanding why this was so difficult for her. "I just care about you. It's as simple as that. I'll be there for you if you need me."

"Thank you for that," Aislinn replied with a squeeze of his hand. She had been wanting what happened the night before for quite some time, yet now that she had experienced it, she felt a bit out of sorts, trying to come to grips with what had shifted between them.

"I'm just speaking the truth."

"Where did you two disappear to last night?" asked Davin,

his red spiky hair blazing brightly as it caught the first light of the day, the gladiator strolling down the pier as if he didn't have a care in the world, twirling his preferred spear from one hand to the other, then back again, apparently oblivious to the Ghoules preparing to launch their rafts and begin what would likely be the fight of their lives.

"We had some things that we needed to discuss," Bryen replied evenly.

"Is that what we're calling it now?" asked Davin with a roguish grin.

"Calling what now?" asked Aislinn, who pushed herself up from the dock with Bryen's help so that they were both standing, her voice having taken on the commanding tone of the Lady of the Southern Marches.

"Well, I was just ..." started Davin, eyes widening, slightly embarrassed, not sure how to respond since it appeared that his attempt at humor had offended Lady Winborne. Because of his growing anxiety he missed the small smile that played across her lips.

"You were just getting yourself into trouble again," said Declan, who walked to the end of the dock to stand next to Bryen, Rafia and Sirius right behind him. "It's a habit that you can't seem to break."

"Well, I could have a lot worse habits," said Davin.

"True, but those might not be as annoying as this one," replied Declan, his comment completely deflating the gladiator. "Is your squad ready?"

"It is, Declan," Davin replied, trying to recapture his confidence. "The Ghoules will be less than pleased to meet us."

"Good. Now if you could do me a favor, please check with all the other Corporals and make sure that they're ready to go. If they need anything, take care of it. This battle is about to start."

"Right away, Declan," replied Davin, who trotted back down

the dock, pleased to escape with no more than a minor tongue lashing.

Declan then turned his attention to the two Magii. "Rafia, last night you were explaining how Bryen needs to reconstruct the Weir. What it will require."

"Do you really want to talk about this now, Declan?" she asked. "The Ghoules are about to put their rafts into the lake."

"We're ready for them. Besides, better to keep our minds occupied before a fight."

"Agreed," Bryen and Aislinn both said at the same time, neither wanting to return to the topic that Davin had interrupted.

"You have more questions then?" asked Sirius.

"I do," Declan replied. "I understand where we're going and what we need to do. Why the Sanctuary was built in the Trench and how the Seven Stones work together to maintain the Weir, the power of that magical barrier weakening, thereby giving the Ghoules the opportunity to force their way through to Caledonia from the Lost Land."

"Is there a question in there?" asked Sirius, his gaze fixed on the far shore. The Ghoules had dragged the first raft down the beach and into the water. It didn't appear to be a very stable craft. Unfortunately, it stayed afloat.

Sirius grimaced. That's all that the Ghoules required. They had less than a mile to pole their way across what was a very placid lake this morning. Sirius watched a few seconds more, his eyes narrowing with a malicious intent. Perhaps he could do something to remedy that.

"There is," Declan confirmed. "Will the Ghoules be able to enter the Sanctuary when we do?"

"You seem very confident, Declan," said Rafia, "considering that we have a battle to fight this morning. Why are you so certain that we'll make it to the Sanctuary despite the challenges that we face?"

"What's the point of all this if we don't believe we're going to succeed?" responded Declan. "To dare is to do, after all."

"Another of your aphorisms," Rafia murmured with appreciation. "I like that one. Very appropriate."

"To answer your question, Declan, yes, eventually the Ghoules will be able to enter the Sanctuary. The magic of the Weir will weaken to the point where it can no longer prevent the beasts from approaching the Seven Stones. We just don't know when we'll reach that point."

"Fair enough," said Declan. "Just one more question."

"Go ahead," gestured Sirius, getting impatient as the Ghoules dragged more rafts into the water.

"You mentioned something when we were talking last night," said Declan, turning his unyielding gaze toward Rafia. "You were explaining about how the Seventh Stone disrupts the Weir. How Bryen could disrupt the energy flow of the other Stones when he enters the Sanctuary."

"So you were listening," said Sirius, clearly pleased.

"I listen to everything," Declan said. "It's more productive than talking all the time."

"An astute comment," said Rafia.

Sirius remained silent, staring hard at the Master of the Gladiators, not certain if Declan's statement was directed toward him and he should be offended.

"Back to the Seventh Stone," said Declan. "When Bryen enters the Sanctuary -- and he will enter the Sanctuary, of that I have no doubt -- that would upset the balance of the power in play there, which means that the Ghoules and their Master likely could follow right after him. Correct?"

Sirius and Rafia both thought about that possibility for several seconds.

"Yes, I guess that would be true," Rafia replied finally, her voice carrying a hint of irritation at herself for not thinking through to the very end the logical consequence of the Seventh

Stone entering the Sanctuary. "I hadn't considered that. That's a reality that we need to plan for."

"We do indeed," agreed Declan. "And based on our conversation from last night, we're still a bit foggy about several other key points."

"Such as?" asked Sirius, Declan's questions beginning to bother him, in large part because the Ghoules had gotten almost all of their rafts into the water. Even more so because he hadn't thought through these issues himself and, worse in his opinion, he didn't really have any answers, and he liked to have an answer to everything.

"Such as how Bryen is supposed to repair the Weir once we reach the Sanctuary. Do we know how that works? With all the research you did here at the Library, do we know how Bryen is supposed to achieve that objective?"

"We don't know," answered Rafia.

"Do we know how Bryen connects the Seventh Stone to the other Six Stones?"

"We don't know," admitted Sirius reluctantly.

"And assuming that he can make use of the Seventh Stone, that he somehow figures out how to link the power within him to the other Stones, do we know how he can do it without killing himself?"

"We don't know," Sirius grumbled again.

"More than one question, I know," said Declan, "so please bear with me. I have just one more."

"You said that last time," protested Sirius.

"This time it really is the last question."

"What is it? We don't have all morning."

Declan gave everyone standing at the end of the dock a broad grin. "What do you know?"

Declan's last question made Rafia smile, while Sirius' frown deepened. She knew what the Sergeant of the Blood Company had been doing. His questions were not designed entirely to elicit the information that he wanted to acquire. He was also trying to keep their focus on something else before the fun began. Frazzled nerves often led to a frazzled mind, and that happened frequently when you thought about the same thing for too long.

"What we don't know," Rafia replied.

"Finally a voice of wisdom," Declan said in his gravelly voice, giving Rafia a nod and a smile. "Just one problem after another, but those are problems for another day. Let's deal with these Ghoules that are about to come across the lake first, then we can move on to solving these other issues."

20

COMING ACROSS THE WATER

"What do you say we get started," suggested Sirius, his impatience plain.

The old Magus stood at the end of the damaged jetty, itching to begin the fight. He watched with just a touch of justified trepidation as twenty large rafts, constructed from roughly cut tree trunks that had been lashed together, began to make their way across the lake toward Haven, each craft carrying an Elder and a dozen Ghoules. At the pace the beasts were poling themselves across, it wouldn't take them long to reach Haven. So in his opinion, better to begin now.

"Let's give them another few minutes to get a bit farther out onto the lake," suggested Tarin. "There's no need to rush this."

"That might be cutting it a bit too close," protested Sirius.

"I have faith in you, Sirius. Don't worry. Just a little while longer. I'd like the Ghoules about halfway across before you make them question their decision to attack across the water."

Sirius grumbled, his eagerness feeding his anxiety. Still, he waited as Tarin requested.

The Captain of the Battersea Guard kept his gaze fixed firmly on the rafts as they drew nearer, the Elders on each one urging the Ghoules to pole faster, all of the beasts responding with a swifter stroke, eager to sink their claws into their prey.

So far Tarin was happy with how the scene was playing out before him. The haste that radiated from the approaching Ghoules played to the Blood Company's advantage. The beasts tended to focus solely on their prize and always assumed that they were the superior fighters. That was their mistake, because they should have learned after their chase across the Breakwater Plateau and then into the Shattered Peaks that the Blood Company was not easy game.

"It looks like some of the Elders are preparing to use their Dark Magic," said Tarin. "Would you care to begin?"

"With pleasure," Sirius grumbled, tired of waiting, his nervous energy putting him on edge, a malicious grin confirming that the Master of the Magii had taken the stage.

Reaching for the Talent, Sirius pulled in as much of the natural magic of the world as he could without putting himself at risk. Rather than attacking each of the individual rafts with bolts of searing white light, Sirius had decided on a different approach to thwart this attempted invasion, choosing instead to avail himself of the natural resource stretching out before him.

Satisfied that he had enough power to do what he had in mind, Sirius shifted his focus to the water lapping gently against the broken pier, releasing the energy that he controlled slowly into the lake. After just a few seconds, the water along the shore began to bubble and hiss, great gouts of steam billowing into the sky in response to the heat of the Talent. Pleased that it was working as he thought it would, Sirius steadily increased the flow of energy, the water churning wildly, resembling the whitewater of the Eastern River.

Certain that he was ready, Sirius directed his gaze toward the Ghoules and their rafts, the beasts now slightly more than halfway across the loch. He had to admit that Tarin was right to make him wait before beginning his assault.

Now was the perfect time to catch their attackers. The beasts had no chance to escape what he was about to unleash upon them. With a nasty smile, the old Magus clearly was looking forward to what he was about to do next.

Lifting his hands above his shoulders, the boiling and churning water rose into the air in response to his command. In less than a second, Sirius had a wave twenty feet in height that extended along the length of the shore towering above him and obscuring his view of the approaching Ghoules. With a nod of his head, he released the wave, which sped across the surface of the lake toward the far shore.

A good start, the Magus thought, but he wasn't done. If nothing else, Sirius was thorough, incredibly meticulous in fact, when he put his mind toward the task of killing Ghoules and Elders. Another wave quickly rose above him, which he sent after the first, and then a whole series of waves, a dozen in all, one after the other surging toward the Ghoules.

Tarin stepped up next to Sirius, the Captain of the Battersea Guard watching with pleasure as the attack played out exactly as they hoped it would. The hastily built rafts couldn't withstand what the old Magus sent against them, the surface of the usually calm lake resembling for just a few minutes the massive waves of the Silent Sea that crashed regularly against the eastern coast of the Southern Marches.

Desperate screams echoed off the surrounding peaks as the Ghoules and Elders struggled to keep their rafts afloat, the first wave rushing over a half dozen of the poorly made crafts, the rafts unable to rise over the crest and either getting flipped or smashed apart. The waves that followed with terrifying regularity swamped the remaining rafts and forced many of the Ghoules and Elders into the water despite their frantic efforts to keep hold of the logs that ripped free from their bindings.

It was a doomed effort. The incredible force of the waves crashing down upon them pried many of the Ghoules' claws free from the wood and submerged the beasts beneath the surface.

In less than a minute, the usually gentle water of the lake returned, the waves releasing their pent-up energy as they crashed against the far shore and forced the Ghoule Overlord and the beasts standing with him to retreat farther up the slope toward the trees rather than risk getting pulled into the lake by the harsh undertow.

Tarin and Sirius both smiled as they surveyed the scene before them. Splintered pieces of rafts and hundreds of individual logs were visible on the surface with the few dozen Ghoules and Elders who survived the assault holding on with their sharp claws, the bodies of the less fortunate floating atop the surface of the lake.

"Well, that answered a question that I had been wondering about," said Tarin, nodding in appreciation at what he saw before him.

"What was that?" asked Sirius.

"Whether Ghoules could swim."

Based on the number of beasts that had drowned and how the surviving Ghoules were clinging precariously to the debris to keep their heads above the water, the Captain of the Battersea Guard certainly had his answer.

"Not very good in the water, are they?" growled Sirius, the malevolence with which he had begun his day still with him as he relished the success of what he had just accomplished with the Talent. "They probably should have thought about that before trying to come across."

"Such a shame," agreed Tarin, although his tone suggested otherwise.

He had hoped that what Sirius had planned to do would disrupt the Ghoules during their first attack. He had never suspected that the old Magus would prove so successful in his efforts. Nevertheless, Tarin's pleasure at the quick turn of events in their favor proved to be short-lived.

The old Magus kept his gaze on the Ghoule Overlord, who stalked back down to the lakeshore as soon as the devastating waves had played themselves out against the rocky beach. Sirius had a bad feeling about what might happen next. Clearly, the monster was enraged, having just lost more than half of the beasts he had gathered for this fight.

And he wasn't going to wait before attacking again. A dark cloud of wispy black formed above the Ghoule Overlord's head, the strands of evil frothing much like the water of the lake had just minutes before. Out of that swirling mass of evil a sharpened harpoon crafted from the Curse and attached to the Ghoule Overlord's black diamond shot up into the sky and across the lake, arcing down directly toward the old Magus.

"Get back!" shouted Sirius.

Tarin sprang into motion, scrambling down the pier, dodging the many holes and shattered boards that marred the jetty's surface, until he was safely back on land. And just in time, as a resounding boom resonated across the lake, Tarin forced to look away because of the blinding flash that accompanied it.

When he could finally turn back toward the pier, Tarin saw with some amazement that Sirius had caught the harpoon on a shield that he had crafted of the Talent that resembled the scuta preferred by the Blood Company. The harpoon had almost punched through the barrier, the power of the Ghoule Overlord's Dark Magic so great that he had almost pierced Sirius' defenses right from the start, only a thin layer of the Talent now protecting the old Magus from the touch of the Curse.

Sirius couldn't help but recognize the seriousness of his situation. Not having the strength to challenge the Ghoule Overlord for very long, a fast end was the best that he could hope for, although he suspected that with his irate adversary, it would likely be a slow, agonizing death instead.

To combat the Dark Magic that had begun to slither across his shield, reaching for him around the edges, wanting to make him its own, Sirius pulled on more of the Talent, trying to rebuild his shield as fast as he could and push out the tip of the harpoon. Nothing that he tried worked. Even as Sirius directed more of the Talent toward his shield, an even greater amount of the Curse streamed through the pulsing black rope that connected the harpoon to the Ghoule Overlord's staff.

Sirius realized his dilemma immediately, his fear of failing against the Ghoule Overlord, of not being able to assist Bryen, almost becoming too much for him.

He was caught in a losing battle, and he knew it. Sirius had no way to counter the immense power that the Ghoule Overlord had brought to bear on him. That was made more obvious as the Dark Magic continued to worm its way across his shield despite Sirius trying to prevent just that, almost covering his magical scutum entirely, the Curse beginning to cut away at the rim of his defense.

Not knowing what else to do, Sirius again tried to add more of the Talent to his rapidly disintegrating barrier. It had no effect whatsoever other than to prolong a combat that Sirius discerned had only one inevitable, horrifying conclusion.

That realization both angered and sickened him. Sirius was one of the strongest Magii in Caledonia. Still, he was no match for the power of the Ghoule Overlord.

"Sirius, let go of the Talent!" screamed Rafia, who had ignored the danger and run out to the end of the pier. "You can't fight him! He's too strong!"

Rafia wanted to help him, but she didn't know how. If she tried to join her Talent to his, Sirius probably could prolong the combat, though that brief instant of distraction also would give the Curse the split second that it needed to pierce his scutum, and with her and Sirius connected through the Talent, they would both become corrupted by Dark Magic.

So the only thing that she could think of that might work was for Sirius to release his hold on the Talent. If Sirius did it right, his action would take the Ghoule Overlord by surprise and allow him to escape the harpoon and cord of Dark Magic attached to it, the Curse potentially whiplashing back toward its Master.

"I can't," growled Sirius, the strain of the fight starting to wear him down. He was at the limit of how much Talent he could safely manipulate. If he attempted to take in more, he would burn himself out. And if he let go, he knew that without a doubt the Curse would consume him before he could evade its touch. "We're too closely tied together now. I can't break free unless that monster lets go first."

Rafia's eyes widened with fear as she realized the truth of Sirius' words, having examined more closely the interplay between the Curse and the Talent. The Ghoule Overlord's Dark Magic had bit into and wrapped itself around Sirius' Talent to create a bond that only the Master of the Curse could break.

Sirius was right. He couldn't release the Talent. If he did, he would die. And his ability to fight the Curse that constantly sought to find a way through his weakening shield was waning as well, the combat proving too much for him. There was nothing that Rafia could think to do. She had no way to help him.

"Sirius, I'm sorry, I can't …"

A massive explosion rocked the far shore, boulders and toppled timber blasted a hundred feet into the sky. Another explosion followed the first. And then another, until it turned into a constant rhythm, huge rocks, stumps, and trees thrown up into the air as if they were no more than a child's playthings.

The cause stood just a dozen feet behind Rafia and Sirius. Bryen rapidly spun the Spear of the Magii from hand to hand, the twin blades of the weapon glowing so brightly that the two Magii could only stand to look at him for a second before needing to turn away. With the air sizzling around them because of the immense amount of the Talent that Bryen was using, they both guessed that he was harnessing the Seventh Stone as he shot bolt after bolt across the lake toward the Ghoule Overlord.

The combat that had almost cost Sirius his life ended abruptly when the Ghoule Overlord released the Dark Magic that had hooked the old Magus so that he could defend against Bryen's unanticipated and quite effective bombardment. Finally free, Sirius released the Talent and slumped to his knees, exhausted, Rafia grabbing him around the shoulders so that he didn't fall off the pier into the lake.

Bryen sent a few more bolts of energy toward the far shore before he stopped his attack with the Talent, wanting to be certain that he had achieved his objective. Thankfully, it had worked out in his favor. He had saved Sirius. But he knew that there was still more to do as he waited for the huge, billowing cloud of dirt and splinters of wood and rock that obscured the beach to clear so that he could examine the extent of the damage that he had caused.

"Thank you, lad," whispered Sirius. "You saved my life. You didn't have to do that."

"Actually, I did," replied Bryen. He didn't offer any more of an explanation than that.

The Ghoule Overlord may have ended that first attack, but Bryen knew that the beast wasn't done. Far from it, in fact.

Through the Seventh Stone, Bryen sensed the huge amount of Dark Magic the Ghoule Overlord was calling upon now. Even with the Spear of the Magii held tightly in his hands, the massive power of the Curse that the Overlord manipulated reached out to him, the bottomless pool of evil demanding that he connect the Dark Magic locked away within him with that of his nemesis.

For the first time since he had gained possession of the Giant-crafted weapon, Bryen had to fight to control the Dark Magic that responded hungrily to the call of the Ghoule Overlord, the imprisoned Curse surging against the internal barrier that he had crafted to keep himself free from the taint.

The challenge of holding back the Dark Magic intensified, Bryen closing his eyes as he struggled to concentrate, his hands gripping the steel haft of the Spear of the Magii until his fingers turned white. Bryen feared that his resistance wasn't enough. The Curse continued to call to him, unaffected by his efforts, demanding that it be freed, demanding that it be released so that it could join with the Dark Magic of the Ghoule Overlord.

He could give in. He could give the Curse what it wanted. Then it would be over. The constant struggle. The pain. The fear.

No! No, he couldn't.

He needed to fight the call. That's who he was. He couldn't forget that.

But the Curse was too strong. How was he supposed to continue to resist?

Not knowing what else to do, Bryen fell back to the practice that Declan had ingrained within him that he had employed so effectively before stepping out onto the white sand of the Pit.

Taking a deep breath, Bryen sought to clear his mind. To push away everything that was going on around him and within him.

It was a struggle to do so, making him feel as if he were tearing himself apart from the inside out. Yet slowly, ever so slowly, the pull of the Dark Magic lessened, the barrier to hold back the Curse strengthening, the Seventh Stone aiding his efforts as he infused himself with the Talent until the call that had threatened his sanity, that had threatened his life, once again became no more than a faint whisper in the back of his mind.

Opening his eyes, he looked out across the lake to the far shore. The cloud of debris was beginning to clear, showing the Ghoules who had survived Sirius' assault pulling themselves out of the water to flop on the beach, drained by their efforts. And standing exactly where he had been when the fight had begun was the Ghoule Overlord, staring malevolently toward the island, a black mist beginning to spin once again out of the black diamond set atop his staff.

The Company of Blood had survived the first attack. Even so, Bryen knew that this was just the beginning of the larger battle. How that would play out was still to be determined, though he feared that he might already know the answer.

THE GHOULE OVERLORD towered in the middle of the slowly dissipating cloud of detritus, the winds sweeping down from the mountains and swirling the gritty mixture up and over the lake. Unable to contain himself any longer, the massive beast roared in rage, his howl echoing through the mountains, as his fury boiled within him, roiling out of him like the waves that had thrown back his Ghoules from the island.

He had assumed that this was going to be a relatively easy hunt. Only a hundred or so humans. Even with the Magii escorting the group, this chase should have been over by now. His Ghoules should have attained their bone knives, and he should have the Seventh Stone.

Yet this chase had become so much more than that, a challenge that he hadn't expected and certainly didn't want. Every second that he wasted pursuing these humans was time that could be better spent bringing his Legions across the Shattered Peaks after he destroyed the Weir.

"Rise, you cowards!" roared the Ghoule Overlord, infuriated that so many of his warriors continued to struggle toward the rocky coast, grasping a log and kicking with all their strength. Those who had already made it safely ashore were bending over as they spit out water or were caught in the midst of dry heaves after escaping the carnage that had swept through the makeshift flotilla. Those beasts who reached the shore considered themselves lucky, not joining their many brethren whose bodies floated across the surface or slowly sank beneath the waves. "We are Ghoules! We do not suffer defeat! We will attack again, and this time you will have no excuses! You will take the island, or you will die!"

In response to the Ghoule Overlord's overwhelming anger, the misty Curse began to surge out of the black diamond affixed to the top of his staff, spinning discordantly in the sharp gusts coming off the mountains as the Dark Magic rapidly expanded and placed the shore in a shadowy dusk.

The commander of the Ghoule Legions could feel the power of the Seventh Stone. He had sensed the boy drawing on that power to prevent him from corrupting the old Magus.

It had been an impressive display by his prey, but the Protector also had demonstrated that he was a fool and a coward, only having the courage to pull on the Talent. If the boy had been smart, he would have called upon both the Talent and the Curse, and that would have made him virtually unstoppable.

So powerful, in fact, that the Protector could have challenged the Ghoule Overlord directly.

Still not capable of defeating him, not yet, though it would have been a worthy combat, the Ghoule Overlord admitted to himself. Thankfully, the boy was wary of the Curse, and that would be his downfall. Only when his last breath left him would the Protector realize all that he had lost. Just because he was afraid to accept the gift the Curse could give him.

The Ghoule Overlord tilted his massive head back and roared in fury one more time, releasing as much of his anger as he could, the boil within him slowly returning to a simmer. He needed to think more clearly. He needed to focus.

He and his Ghoules had suffered a setback. That was all. What the old Magus had done wasn't enough to keep him from taking the island. No, the old Magus' efforts simply had delayed what could not be stopped.

The Magus had had his fun. He had destroyed the rafts Gurzen and his Ghoules had made.

That still wouldn't be enough to save the humans. These Magii who played with a weaker power had no chance against the evil that he wielded.

Tired of playing games, the Ghoule Overlord pulled on so much of his Dark Magic that it rapidly covered the beach in a heavy black mist that blotted out the sun. Knowing that the Seventh Stone had no way to defend against what he was going to do next, he dipped the black diamond into the light swells of the lake.

Streaks of sable shot across the surface toward the island, solidifying as the jagged lines stretched out across the water into what resembled a shimmering black glass that was harder than stone. In seconds, the Dark Magic touched the shore of Haven, the magical construction expanding and strengthening until an unnatural bridge several hundred yards wide connected the island to the beach.

"Leave the Seventh Stone for me," seethed the Ghoule Overlord, turning his bottomless black eyes to Gurzen. "Now take your packs and kill all the other humans!"

❧

"LET ME HAVE A TRY," suggested Rafia, sensing Sirius' exhaustion and wanting to give him more time to recover.

"Keep an eye on the Ghoules while I'm at it. Something's brewing over there."

Sirius grumbled his assent as he released his weak hold on the Talent, then shifted his gaze to the far shore. He and Rafia stood at the edge of the dock, having tried and failed to destroy the black ice that now served as an easy gateway to Haven. Dark Magic continued to swirl above the beach, but whatever else the Ghoule Overlord and his creatures might be planning, he didn't know.

Despite the tiring struggle with the Ghoule Overlord, Sirius had pulled on as much of the Talent as he could in his attempts to break apart the bridge constructed of the Curse, first sending spikes of searingly hot energy toward the shiny black surface, then trying spheres of condensed energy. Neither effort accomplished much, the natural magic of the world slamming against the pulsing black and having no effect whatsoever, not even scuffing the span.

Next, Sirius tried calling down several bolts of lightning, hoping that Rafia's favorite weapon when destroying Elders would have a similar effect on the bridge. Still nothing. It appeared that the Ghoule Overlord's creation was indestructible.

With all that in mind, Rafia stared down at the hardened Dark Magic, searching for some kind of weakness in the span. A crack. A crevice. Any imperfection that she might be able to use to shatter the Ghoule Overlord's link to Haven.

She identified nothing that might help her in her efforts. The shimmering black glass, gleaming brightly in the early morning sun, appeared to be perfectly smooth. There were no visible flaws. There were no weaknesses that she could locate that would allow her to fracture the surface.

That thought brought to mind one possibility that Sirius hadn't tried that might actually work.

Reaching for the Talent, Rafia blasted the shiny black

surface with a razor-thin flare of energy. If she could pierce the first few layers of the bridge with the concentrated stream, then she could cut through in other places and weaken the span before the Ghoules came charging across.

But no such luck. Even though Rafia drew on as much of the Talent as she could, sparks shooting up into the air because of the intensity of the beam she directed toward the Ghoule Overlord's creation, nothing happened. The power employed by the Ghoule Overlord was too strong.

"Any success?" asked Sirius, his gaze never leaving the far shore, the cloud of Dark Magic thinning.

"No," groaned Rafia, her frustration intensifying with each passing second. "Nothing is working."

"It was worth a shot, but our time's up. The next part of the battle has begun." The black cloud had begun to lift, the Ghoules sprinting out of the mist, their clawed feet digging into the smooth surface of the bridge and helping to speed them along as they raced toward the island. "We need to tell Declan and Tarin to prepare the Company of Blood. The Ghoules are coming."

21

THE BLACK ICE

"Archers, prepare to fire!" shouted Jerad, the Sergeant of the Battersea Guard trying to judge the best time to start the attack as he had to take into account the Ghoules' blinding pace in an open space.

The soldiers of the Blood Company grabbed a handful of arrows, jabbing the barbed steel heads into the rocky ground so that they could grab them quickly, selecting one arrow for their long bows once done, doing their best to ignore the howls and screams that preceded the Ghoules as they raced across the unnatural surface.

"Nock!" commanded Jerad.

The archers affixed their arrows to their strings, watching impassively as the Ghoules streaked toward them in a blur. They knew how hard it would be to take down any of the Ghoules from such a great distance. Still, that was no reason not to try. Even if just one Ghoule died, it was one less Ghoule that they would have to fight on the island.

"Draw!"

They pulled back on their strings. The soldiers attempted to pick out individual targets, but the speed of the beasts made that impossible. The archers had to resign themselves to putting as many arrows in the path of the beasts as they could and hoping that a few found the mark.

"Release!"

A dozen long, steel-tipped shafts flew into the sky. Jerad had no intention of waiting to see what kind of success the archers might achieve before continuing the attack.

"Nock!"

The soldiers pulled their second arrows from the ground, affixing them to their strings, and then pulling back as they targeted the charging Ghoules once again.

"Release!"

Another flight of arrows shot into the air. Still, Jerad wasn't done.

"Nock!"

The archers went through the same process that they had the previous two times, ready to launch their arrows in just a few seconds.

"Release!"

A third flight of arrows shot into the sky just as the first flight of quarrels descended toward the Ghoules. All of those arrows clattered harmlessly on the black ice, the Ghoules already having streaked past the point the archers had been targeting.

The second flight had more of an impact, several arrows slamming into a couple of the beasts. Yet, these had little effect. Almost all of the shafts struck the armored shoulders or thighs of the beasts and bounced off the creatures, except for one arrow that with just a touch of luck pierced a Ghoule's eye, digging into his brain and killing the creature instantly, the force of the blow knocking the beast backward as he collapsed on the ice.

"Archers, fire at will!" shouted Jerad, just as the third flight streaked down toward the fast-approaching Ghoules, several of the arrows punching through the beasts' mottled green flesh now that they were closer, knocking those hit by the barbed quarrels off stride or to the ground to slide across the span. Unfortunately for the archers, none of the injuries were serious enough to stop the creatures, who simply pushed themselves back to their feet, snapped off or pulled free any of the shafts protruding from their bodies, and rejoined the attack.

With the Ghoules so close now, the soldiers had an easier time targeting them. Even so, the remarkable speed of the beasts remained a daunting problem, particularly since several of the creatures struck by arrows no longer ran in a straight line, dodging from side to side, zigzagging across the span, as they sought to evade the long shafts that flew through the air in a ragged rhythm.

"Did you want to try your hand at slowing them down?" asked Jerad. "I doubt we'll do much better than we already have."

"We'll give it a shot," replied Bryen, who stood just to the side of Jerad, Aislinn right next to him.

"I'll focus to my right," said Aislinn. "You take the left."

Bryen simply nodded in response, the two Magii taking hold of the Talent.

Aislinn understood that striking the advancing Ghoules with the Talent would be just as difficult as hitting them with an arrow. She and Bryen had spoken about that challenge the night before and had decided on a strategy that, although not as precise as they might like, could prove more effective against the beasts.

Rather than shoot bolts of energy or throw spears of light, Aislinn motioned toward a spot just a few dozen feet in front of the charging Ghoules, a blazing wall of fire suddenly shooting up from the span, the white-hot energy startling the beasts, all of the Ghoules trying to stop themselves in time so that they didn't run right through the inferno.

Some succeeded, some did not. Those unlucky enough to stumble through the crackling flames emerged blackened and burned, the Talent leaping across their flesh, burrowing down to the bone, the beasts dead, just not knowing it yet.

The archers standing with Jerad recognized the opportunity that Aislinn had presented to them, firing their arrows into the beasts that escaped the flames and were now trying to figure out what to do next, ignoring the Ghoules that writhed in agony on the black ice, their flesh flaking off and turning to ash. More often than not, their arrows found a home in the beasts now that the flames had negated their primary advantage, the Ghoules approaching the island with greater caution, not sure in which direction to move as they feared getting caught in the fire that had sprung up right in front of them without any warning.

Much the same occurred on Bryen's side, the Ghoules' charge fizzling out, the beasts trying to determine how to get past the blazing energy that sparked randomly across the bridge. The beasts were so concerned about stumbling head-long into the flames that they didn't realize that they were being herded together, Aislinn and Bryen placing the brief bursts of fire in a pattern that forced the Ghoules toward the center of the black ice, thereby giving the archers a better chance of finding the range.

Pleased by their success, Bryen and Aislinn continued their efforts for several minutes, demonstrating a dangerous preci-sion, a handful more Ghoules dying as a result of their persis-tence and creativity. That lasted until the Elders trotted across the black ice to join the assault. Black mist began to spin up into the air from their staffs as the servants of the Ghoule Over-lord turned their attention toward Bryen and Aislinn, seeking to put an end to the two Magii who had stalled the Ghoules' charge.

"What say we join the fight," suggested Rafia. Neither she

nor Sirius had succeeded in destroying the bridge, though they certainly could do something about the Elders, having waited impatiently as Bryen and Aislinn brought the Ghoule advance to a stop before the beasts reached the rocky beach.

"With pleasure," Sirius replied, feeling stronger now that he had a few minutes to rest.

As Bryen and Aislinn kept their focus on the Ghoules, limiting the beasts' movement, Sirius and Rafia began calling down bolts of lightning. Although the strikes failed to shatter the bridge, that wasn't their purpose, as the two Magii instead sought to reduce the number of Elders opposing them.

The first few bolts caught the Elders by surprise. Several of the beasts were obliterated by the energy that crashed down upon them, nothing left other than a swirling black ash to suggest that moments before they had posed a threat to the Magii.

Rafia and Sirius relished their early success against their adversaries, knowing full well that it wouldn't last long as they watched the beasts gifted with the Curse coordinate their efforts so that they could offer a real challenge.

Soon, the dozen Elders who still remained on the black ice were keeping not only Rafia and Sirius busy, but also Bryen and Aislinn, who were now expending just as much effort on defending the Blood Company from the Elders' attacks as they were trying to keep the Ghoules from stepping off the span of Dark Magic onto the island.

The Talent and the Curse shot across the span in a mesmerizing display, sparks flying whenever the two energies met, shouts of anger and frustration erupting from the Elders as the beasts failed time and again to destroy their antagonists. Yet even so, it was becoming clear to Declan and Tarin that keeping the Ghoules from reaching Haven was quickly becoming an impossibility. With the four Magii fully engaged with the

Elders, there was nothing to prevent the Ghoules from restarting their charge.

"Pull back!" yelled Declan. "Get to your assigned locations!"

The archers swiftly stepped away from shore and back toward the Library of the Magii. Hearing Declan's call, Rafia and Sirius began moving back from the black ice as well, keeping the Elders busy and leaving Aislinn and Bryen to their final task.

"Ready?" asked Bryen.

"As I'll ever be," Aislinn replied with a forced smile.

Taking on so many Elders at once was a tiring proposition. Yet neither wavered in their commitment to do what was required.

Working together, the Protector and his charge used the Talent to create a blazing wall of flames that stretched across the width of the bridge. Once done, they both called down a dozen lightning bolts, all aimed at the Elders. That forced the creatures to focus solely on their defense for just a moment, removing any thoughts of attacking them or the Blood Company.

The assault and the barrier of fire gave Aislinn, Bryen, and the Blood Company the time they needed to pull back and reach their designated positions, knowing that it wouldn't be long before the beasts stepped onto the rocky coast of the island and the battle against the Elders and the Ghoules would resume once more.

THE GHOULE OVERLORD waited less than an hour before continuing the attack, unconcerned by the flames licking at the black ice and the loss of life, a half dozen more packs reaching the rocky beach to take the place of the Ghoules and Elders who had been lost during the first assault. This time, the beasts knew what to expect, so a good number of the Elders led the way as they raced across the black ice, shields of Dark Magic preceding them, making for their brethren already waiting on the span.

Advancing toward the island with greater caution, the beasts spread out in a long line, a good bit of distance between each Ghoule so that they could cover most of the shore on the eastern side of the island where the damaged dock stuck out into the lake. They hoped that such an approach would reduce the risk of being struck by an arrow or the Talent.

Yet it seemed that their newfound caution was unnecessary. All was quiet, and strangely so. The white fire that had been blocking their approach had vanished.

No arrows streaked through the air. No walls of flame shot up unexpectedly. Not a sound greeted them. Not a movement could be seen. There was nothing but the soft touch of the wind coming down off the mountains that surrounded the lake.

Despite none of the Ghoules sensing any immediate danger, the Elders kept their shields in place, finding the whole situation suspect. It was as if the entire island had been deserted since their first attack, many of the beasts assuming that the humans had locked themselves in the tower and were daring the Ghoules to dig them out.

Gurzen wasn't so sure. He stood on the black ice deep in thought, studying the beach, looking for any hint of what might be waiting for him and his Ghoules.

Nothing caught his attention, and that's what worried him the most.

"Take your pack forward, Ersin," ordered Gurzen. "Find out what we're up against."

Ersin nodded, then stepped off the black ice onto the island.

The atmosphere among the Ghoules was one of expectation rather than resignation. Instead of storming the island as the Ghoules normally would, shrieking and howling, terrifying their adversaries before even encountering them, Ersin and the Ghoules trotted up the rocky beach in silence, long black spears held loosely in their claws, their deep black eyes continually scanning the environment around them, searching for any threat, for anything that would explain why it was so quiet.

The Ghoules took no more than a dozen steps up from the black ice before they came across large boulders, fallen trees, and water-soaked logs strategically scattered about the coast. Because of the press of time, understanding that their Master was anxious to claim the Seventh Stone, the beasts had no choice but to move in the direction the makeshift piles and constructions guided them. Knowing that they were easy targets for the archers or Magii if they climbed to the top of the obstacles, the beasts stayed low, making use of the cover provided for as long as they could.

Gurzen strode onto the island with the rest of the Ghoules when Ersin and his pack walked down a narrow path between the logs and other debris and disappeared from sight.

Just seconds later, Gurzen heard the screams coming from up ahead. Several of the Ghoules with him prepared to rush forward into whatever Ersin and his pack had stumbled. A quick shake of Gurzen's head kept them in place.

Ersin was a seasoned warrior as were the members of his pack. There was no reason to rush into the unknown and put any more Ghoules at risk than necessary. Instead he moved forward slowly, carefully, his Ghoules following, alert, ready for any threat that might be sprung upon them.

As Gurzen and his Ghoules walked down the channel, his irritation increased, as did his concerns. He knew what was happening, yet he had no good way to stop it. Just as they did on the black ice, the humans were herding them together. That didn't bode well.

After just a few more steps they came upon the caltrops, long metal nails that had been twisted and bonded together and then strewn liberally across the rough ground. The spiked metal devices were more an irritation than anything else, Gurzen picking out spots of black blood in the rocks, many of the Ghoules with him hissing in pain and then hopping about as they struggled to pull the sharp metal out of their clawed feet.

The caltrops weren't going to kill any of the Ghoules. Gurzen knew that wasn't their purpose. The caltrops were a distraction. So they wouldn't see the real threat.

Worried, Gurzen called out to Ersin, who couldn't have been more than a few dozen yards in front of him. Silence.

He confirmed his fear just a little farther down the channel.

Ersin and his Ghoules completely missed the barely visible threads strung across the path at shin height. As soon as the first few Ghoules walked through the filaments, the tension was broken, releasing the springs that held in place the long pieces of metal hidden within the logs. The flexible steel, a dozen steel spikes welded along the length of each one, whipped out from the sides of the path, gutting any of the Ghoules unlucky enough to be in the way, the beasts' armored flesh no defense against the terrific force of the blow.

Many of the Ghoules stared in shock as Ersin and his pack bled out, long steel spikes puncturing their chests, the sharpened points sticking out of their backs, the beasts stuck on the barbs, their blood trickling down to the ground as they slowly expired, their brethren unable to do anything, not knowing if something else was waiting for them if they tried to assist the dying Ghoules.

"Single file," whispered Gurzen, who was in the middle of the packs making their way along the path. "Move carefully, be wary, but don't stop. We need to get through this, so pay attention to what's around you. If you see anything that looks out of place, shout a warning. Clear?"

The Ghoules around Gurzen nodded their understanding.

"Then let's get going."

The beasts carefully walked past their dead and dying brethren, spears waving in front of them, fearful that similar traps lay ahead of them and not wanting to meet the same fate as the Ghoules that now sagged lifeless on the steel spikes.

As the Ghoules headed farther down the path, the beasts continued to poke with their spears to their front, scraping their blades along the logs, digging into the dirt, looking for any indication of what might be waiting for them farther down the trail.

Several feet now separated each beast from the other to lessen the likelihood of another trap taking more than one Ghoule at a time.

It was a good decision that Gurzen had made, but also the obvious one. As the Ghoules crept cautiously past their impaled companions and continued farther up the beach, their eyes searching for any new threats, their well-attuned senses hoping to discover any other surprises that may lay in wait for them, a handful of Ghoules just a few paces ahead of Gurzen shrieked in surprise when the ground beneath them gave way.

The Ghoule scout stared down in shock at the carnage just a few feet to his front. Somehow the humans had dug a trench between the logs that was fifty feet long and covered it in a thin layer of dirt and rocks, the trap only giving way after a certain number of his Ghoules had put enough weight on the mechanism to release the latches that had held the hidden top in place.

An ingenious lure, and one that set the scout's blood boiling. Six of his Ghoules had landed on the steel spikes set in the bottom of the hole, their chests and backs punctured by the razor-sharp spikes that pointed to the sky.

For just a moment, the scout was speechless. This was not supposed to happen when he and his Ghoules stormed the island. It was supposed to be a straightforward slaughter, the humans too weak to defend against the overwhelming number of Ghoules charging across the black ice.

Yet in just minutes he had lost almost two packs without even seeing a single human.

Fearful not only of what might lie ahead, but even more so of his Master's reaction when he learned of how many Ghoules had died, Gurzen decided that he needed more information in order to make his next decision.

He could see nothing but what the ragged walls of the channel allowed him to see. That couldn't continue if they were to have any chance of reaching the tower. After telling the Ghoules at the most forward part of the trench to hold their positions, he motioned to the pack of Ghoules trailing behind him.

"Over the top. See what you can see. I want to know how much farther we have to go. But be careful. I wouldn't be surprised if there are archers waiting for a chance at a lucky shot."

The Ghoules nodded, then dug their sharp claws into the logs lining the sides of the path and began pulling themselves toward the top, none of them rushing, as none had any desire to be the next victim of one of the humans' traps.

The first Ghoule poked his head warily above the top. Just a few inches at first, wanting to be certain that all was well. After a quick scan, confident that he had nothing to fear, he pushed himself over the lip of the rampart.

As soon as the Ghoule stood on the logs, streaks of the Talent whipped toward him from the side, slicing through his body at the hip and chest, the three pieces of the Ghoule's body tumbling down the makeshift wall to land at Gurzen's feet.

Two more Ghoules simply disappeared, surges of bright white light that blasted up from the logs turning the beasts to ash in less than a second. And then three more of the beasts fell victim to the same kind of trap. That was followed by another three Ghoules who, when they reached the top of the logs, despite being as careful as possible, discovered that they couldn't move.

Their screams of agony broke the silence when their flesh began to sizzle and then char before flaking off. This trap mimicked what happened when a Ghoule became caught in the Weir, the Talent flashing regularly as the searing energy refused to release the beasts, burning through their flesh first, their organs and muscles next, and then their bones, and doing it slowly so that their brethren could watch and listen in horror.

The last Ghoule charged with climbing up the logs decided to simply poke his head above the top and not actually set foot atop the barrier after having observed so many of his companions die such painful deaths. That cautious decision gave him a chance to glimpse what lay before them without having to worry about getting caught in the traps set by the Magii.

Dropping back down onto the path, the only Ghoule to survive what should have been a simple assignment turned toward Gurzen, trying to ignore the howls of his comrades caught in the traps that gradually burned them alive.

"The trail narrows, but it's less than a hundred feet before we're through. The tower stands at the end of the channel."

"Can you do anything about the traps constructed of the Talent?" Gurzen asked one of the Elders who had pushed his way forward to the edge of the trench cut out of the path so that he could see for himself what had happened to the Ghoules who had fallen through the thin layer of dirt and rock.

"No, there is nothing that we can do to combat those threats. We can't sense the Talent. If we have no way to sense the Talent, we have no way to disable any of those traps."

Gurzen shook his head in frustration. There was only one option that remained to him. He didn't like it, but he didn't have a choice. His Ghoules were hesitant now, and with good reason after having seen so many of their brethren fall with not a human in sight.

Besides, who knew what waited for them farther along the trail. And though he preferred to keep his Ghoules alive, he was more concerned about them losing the edge that they needed to fight effectively. So better to be aggressive regardless of what might stand in their way, and better to risk the dangers of the path than the Talent waiting for them above it.

"We go forward as fast as we can," ordered Gurzen. "Get down the path and don't stop for anything!"

The Ghoules responded immediately, preferring to move rather than delay, and much to their surprise not a single trap awaited them as they sprinted through the last section of the channel.

When the beasts finally emerged, taking just a second to get their bearings, the Ghoules let out a collective roar and sprinted across the long grass toward the soldiers positioned in front of the tower, long steel spikes tilted toward the Ghoules set to both sides of the humans, those fields of steel forcing the beasts to come at their prey from only one direction.

The limitation didn't bother the Ghoules. These humans had proven to be more difficult prey than they should have been, and they were going to pay for their insolence, for the cowardly ways they employed to kill their comrades rather than standing with steel in their hand as they did now.

The humans were going to die, and once the Ghoule Overlord took the Seventh Stone, the Ghoules were going to eat. They would be able to take their time, carving the bone knives that so many of the beasts craved for their own.

22

EVERYONE DIES

"We are the Blood Company!" roared Davin, his voice carrying over the din of the battle. He didn't have the chance to say all that he wanted to say.

The Crimson Giant twisted his body to the left just in time to avoid a blood-covered spear thrust toward him by a Ghoule who had knocked over the shield bearer positioned right to his front. The beast was trying to force his way through the men and women opposing him with brute strength, hoping to crack the shield wall so that he and his brethren could push through the gap and then sweep around them from behind.

The only person who could prevent the beast from achieving his goal was Davin. With his free hand, he grabbed the Ghoule's spear before the beast could draw it back and yanked the weapon toward him. The creature stumbled, pulled off balance.

Davin didn't hesitate when he saw his opportunity, driving his own spear up through the Ghoule's gut until the sharp point appeared through the creature's back. As the beast sagged to the ground, his life bleeding out onto the long grass, Davin released the Ghoule's spear and gave his own a sharp tug, thankful that his spearpoint didn't get stuck in the dying beast's ribs.

"We stand! We fight! We die!" Davin was able to finish shouting now that he had dispatched his most immediate threat, the soldiers around him closing the gap the Ghoule had created. "That's who we are! That's what we do! Do it well!"

He and Lycia stood with their fighters at the end of one of the two obstructed paths Declan and Tarin had created that led up from the shore. So far, their strategy had worked well. The effort expended during the night to limit the Ghoules' movement had funneled the beasts to the two locations where the soldiers of the Blood Company waited for them. The traps crafted by the Magii forced the beasts to stay on the trail and not attempt to climb over the obstructions, while the steel stakes set in the ground on both sides prevented the Ghoules from skirting their flanks.

The beasts had no choice but to come at the soldiers from the front, which was fine with Davin. He and the several squads of gladiators lined up with him and his sister, shields to the front, spears right behind, swords in the gap, had held their own ever since the Ghoules had rushed out onto the long grass that fronted the Library of the Magii, the beasts intent on slaughtering the humans who had already cost them so many lives just to reach this point.

The Ghoules found out immediately and much to their disgust that Davin and his soldiers would not be easy meat. When the Ghoules charged up the gentle slope, slamming into the soldiers' shields, the men and women of the Blood Company stood strong, refusing to give an inch. Even worse, their natural armor offered no effective defense against the glowing steel that cut, lunged, and slashed toward them with a disturbing regularity.

Some of the Ghoules parried the soldiers' spears with their own, knocking them aside or driving the sharp point of their weapons through leather armor and into a chest or shoulder. Yet even when the beasts drew blood, a sword swung down or thrust forward, a soldier in the third rank doing everything within her power to keep the Ghoule in place so that the beast couldn't break through the formation.

More often than not, the Ghoules missed their targets or only gained superficial strikes as the shield bearers prevented the beasts from getting in a good blow, and those Ghoules who proved to be overly aggressive in their efforts to push their way into the soldiers' ranks usually met the same fate as the Ghoule who had just faced Davin, a spear in the gut or the chest, maybe even a sword removing a limb or a claw.

As Davin and Lycia urged their soldiers to stand their ground, they realized that even though they were holding their own against the beasts that towered above them, the hard fight was beginning to turn against them. The Ghoules were extremely difficult beasts to kill, just as many spear thrusts or sword slashes clanging uselessly off the Ghoules' spears and swords as slid into their flesh.

The Ghoules' overwhelming strength and size also were now coming into play. The beasts began to direct their strikes over the heads of the shield bearers, who could offer little protection against these attacks because raising their shields off the ground in an attempt to obstruct the Ghoules' lunges over their heads would leave them vulnerable to a slash across their legs and midsection. So the fight had become one of attrition, and every member of the Blood Company fighting with Davin and Lycia understood what that meant for them in the end.

"Any time, Lycia," urged Davin through gritted teeth as he stabbed with his spear, drawing a painful hiss from a Ghoule to his right when the sharp edge sliced across the beast's neck.

The Ghoule's natural reaction was to bring his claw to the wound to check on how severe it was, forgetting for just a split second the battle raging around him.

That was all the time that Chesin needed. The thin, almost slight gladiator stationed right next to Davin rammed the point of his sword through the creature's claw and into his neck, then pulled back, allowing the beast to collapse to the ground as blood gushed from the wound, the gladiator immediately turning his attention to the Ghoule who had rushed forward to take the fallen beast's place.

"We're losing too many fighters to stand much longer," he continued.

Lycia heard her brother's warning. Still, she waited. With a nimble slash of her blade, she parried a Ghoule's spear aimed for Jenus, the gladiator just to her left, who had stumbled back, losing his grip on his shield when the Ghoule facing him had rushed into him with his shoulder like a charging bull.

Any other gladiator likely would have died, falling on his back to be stabbed through the gut like a turtle. But Jenus wasn't like anyone else. He recovered quickly, pushing himself up, always keeping his scutum in place, the man broader than a doorway and built like a barrel, continuing to absorb the Ghoule's heavy blows in a way that most other gladiators couldn't.

Lycia's quick thinking saved his life, keeping the Ghoule's spear from his flesh, and Jenus' stubbornness and cleverness gave her the chance to kill the beast. Leaping back to his feet with a surprising dexterity, Jenus blocked the Ghoule's spear thrust with his shield, then slammed the bottom of his curved steel scutum down onto the Ghoule's clawed feet, the metal slicing into the Ghoule's flesh, crushing bone and removing several clawed toes.

Howling in anger, distracted by the pain, the Ghoule failed to notice Lycia lunge with her blades. With two quick flicks of her swords, the Crimson Devil sliced across the beast's throat, the creature's black blood streaming down his chest.

"Lycia!" Davin called again, this time his voice a touch more desperate.

She glanced at her brother, observing that one of the gladiators right in front of Davin had been pulled down and lost his shield, opening a gap that the other shield bearers in the front rank struggled fiercely to close. Despite their best efforts, one of the soldiers even sheathing his sword and picking up a fallen spear to try to push back the attacking Ghoules, the gap remained.

Seeing the opportunity, the beasts pushed forward, attempting to take advantage of the breach.

Lycia wanted to make sure that all the Ghoules standing to her front were fully engaged, but she couldn't wait any longer without risking the possibility that the Ghoules were just seconds away from overrunning them now that a gap had appeared in their shield wall.

Her brother was right. Now was the time. Raising both swords above her head, she crossed the blades.

In a flash, a dozen archers appeared on top of the logs and boulders that helped to hem in the Ghoules. Because of the height of the obstructions, the Ghoules wouldn't be able to reach the top easily, and they probably wouldn't even try having learned quite painfully what would happen if the traps made of the Talent that had been placed along the edge caught them. So having little to fear beneath them, the soldiers pulled back on their bows and began shooting arrow after arrow into the Ghoules from the sides and the back.

The initial shock of the surprise attack gave the soldiers a brief advantage, which they needed since the Ghoules were pressing them so hard, several more gladiators falling to Ghoule steel or claws in just the last few minutes. That advantage quickly disappeared when the Ghoules shifted their approach. Some of the beasts, even with as many as a half-dozen arrows puncturing their flesh, took to throwing their spears at the men and women standing above them, forcing the archers to spend just as much time dodging the blackened lances as firing down at the Ghoules.

Davin and Lycia had hoped to gain more time with their surprise, but it wasn't to be. The Ghoules responded too quickly to their new strategy.

The brother and sister also recognized another problem they faced, a problem that had no solution. Unlike the Ghoules, who had more packs coming across the black ice, the Company of Blood had no reserve. They had no other soldiers to call upon.

They had no choice but to fight. To fight until they couldn't fight anymore.

~

"Everyone dies!" shouted Declan. "Not everyone dies with honor!"

"That's a good saying, Declan," said Rafia with what she hoped would be taken as a lighthearted tone. "But perhaps we don't need that reminder right at this moment."

The Magus stood just a few feet away from the Sergeant of the Blood Company, who continued to exhort his soldiers to even greater achievements despite the formidable number of Ghoules seeking to break their shield wall. She and Declan had assumed responsibility for defending the other path that funneled the Ghoules up from the beach, fighting only a few hundred yards away from where Davin and Lycia were making their stand.

So far, the gladiators from the Pit had done well even with the rapidly worsening odds. How long they could continue was anyone's guess. The only certainty was that Declan and his warriors would never stop fighting, not even as the beasts pushed the soldiers harder than they had ever been pushed before, the Ghoules knowing that if they penetrated the Company's defensive formation, the battle would end shortly thereafter.

"You may be right," grumbled Declan, who lunged forward with his sword, slicing across the knee of a Ghoule who had knocked over a shield bearer and tried to gut the gladiator standing in the second rank who at the same time was lunging at a different beast with his spear. Although the wound wasn't deep, Declan's slice affected the Ghoule's movement, allowing Kollea to step in and cut across the back of the beast's other leg with her sword.

As soon as the Ghoule collapsed to the grass, his legs now more hindrance than help, the beast's death was assured. Dorlan, never far from Kollea, screamed viciously as he slammed his spear down into the back of the beast's neck, the creature flopping for a few seconds as its brain caught up to the physical reality of the Ghoule's death. The large gladiator pulled his spearpoint free with a loud sucking sound and was then right back at it, working to close the all too frequent gaps that were appearing in the Company's line.

"But I'm running out of things to say just as we're running out of options," admitted Declan.

Rafia could only nod in agreement, her attention drawn to a trio of Ghoules who were attempting to force their way past the gladiators fighting right next to the steel stakes planted in the ground that kept the beasts from flanking them. Two shield bearers had fallen, one never to rise again, the other trying to push herself back to her feet while still keeping her shield in place, finding that task almost impossible as the Ghoules seeking to rush past her waited impatiently for any opening, no matter how small, that would allow them to cut into her flesh and then slip past her so that they could get into the Company's rear.

It was a surprisingly good plan on the part of the Ghoules.

Only Asaia stood in the beasts' way now, having strapped her preferred barbed whip to her hip and taken up a spear as she tried to keep the beasts in front of her. A losing proposition most likely, even for the skilled gladiator. But the one thing the Ghoules hadn't counted on was an angry Magus in their midst.

Rafia recognized the danger immediately. She had every confidence that Asaia could manage one Ghoule. Maybe two at one time if she had no other choice. Three was asking a bit too much, even of her.

Reaching for the Talent, in a flash two spears of energy shot from Rafia's hands, the searing power blasting through two of the Ghoules and leaving behind the smoking wreckage of what had once been the beasts' chests.

Dead before they tumbled to the grass, the surviving Ghoule sensed that something was wrong behind him, although that wasn't his primary concern right then. The creature had a bigger problem to deal with, as Asaia took to the offensive now that Rafia had eliminated two of her adversaries from the combat.

The gladiator jabbed with her spear quickly and often, keeping the Ghoule thinking about where she might strike and not allowing the beast to shift to the attack. Her movements were so fast that several times her blade sliced across the Ghoule's flesh, leaving bloody streaks across the beast's shoulders and forearms. Despite her success, Asaia knew that she couldn't keep this up forever, so as the Ghoule continued to track her swift jabs, Asaia pulled free the barbed whip and with a quick flick of her wrist, sent the spiked tip into one of the beast's eyes.

The Ghoule cried out in agony, the eyeball ripped free and a deep, bloody gash marring the creature's cheek. Before the Ghoule could react beyond acknowledging the terrible pain of his wound, Asaia struck again, the barbed tip of her whip slashing across the beast's other eye. Although not as clean a hit as the first, it was enough to remove a large portion of the flesh just above the beast's eye socket, black blood streaming down and effectively blinding the Ghoule.

That was all the time that Asaia needed as she stabbed the tip of her spear into the Ghoule's groin, the creature collapsing to the ground with fiery waves of agony sweeping through his body. Before she could finish the Ghoule, two other gladiators were there with their swords, eliminating one more beast from what was becoming an ever more discouraging fight.

Declan watched Asaia earn her victory with pride in his eyes, thankful to have Rafia at his side to help his gladiators. He continued to urge his fighters on, stepping into the thick of the action whenever necessary.

Even so, too many breaks were occurring in the shield wall, and he understood that if the Ghoules continued to reduce the Blood Company's numbers at the current pace, and there was no reason to assume that they wouldn't, it wouldn't be long before no one would be available to step into a breach. When that happened, that would be the beginning of the end of what was proving to be a valiant resistance.

It was inevitable, even with Rafia there, because now three Elders had stepped up behind the Ghoules, requiring the Magus to focus her full attention on them.

Rafia did the best that she could, going on the offensive right from the start because she knew that she had no good way to defend the Company if the Elders turned their attention away from her and onto them. So she attacked the servants of the Ghoule Overlord in a variety of different ways, spears of white light followed by spheres no larger than a marble but capable of blasting through flesh and bone followed by blazing shards of energy.

Much to her chagrin, the Elders opposing her defended each attack competently, and Declan saw that Rafia was beginning to struggle. One of the Elders had stepped back from the other two, allowing his ilk to defend against the Talent while he focused on removing Rafia from the battlefield.

Having no choice but to defend herself, Rafia used the Talent to burn away the black mist that swept toward her. She then formed a shield on her forearm that she used to block the fragments of the Curse that the Elder Ghoule now free of the larger combat shot toward her.

Declan had to give the Magus credit for pushing the beasts hard and doing all that she could to keep them from coming at his soldiers. He knew, however, that the odds favored the Elders. It was simply a numbers game.

No matter what she tried, the Magus had little chance of killing the three Elders without the element of surprise. And it would be unfair of him to assume that Rafia would be able to maintain her efforts for much longer. It was just a question of when the combat came to a close.

That concern drifted into the background when Declan noticed a shield bearer in the center of the Company's line fall, a Ghoule's spear taking the man in the throat. The gladiator fell onto his back, the shield covering his body, the fighter struggling for his last breaths as his throat filled with blood.

The Ghoule who had killed him was anxious to take advantage of his good fortune. The beast sprinted forward and used the shield as a steppingstone to leap over the other two ranks of fighters who stood in his way, becoming the first Ghoule to get behind the Company's shield wall.

Rather than attack the soldiers from behind, the Ghoule had eyes only for Rafia, the beast relishing the opportunity to kill a Magus.

A smart move on the beast's part with Rafia's attention diverted by the Elders. She had little chance of defending herself from the Ghoule who now stalked toward her from behind.

Declan, who had moved to the far side of the formation to

help a gladiator who had found himself facing two Ghoules at the same time, tried to push his way back through his troops as they fought the Ghoules, desperate to reach Rafia before the beast stabbed her in the back. He cursed in frustration. He couldn't do it.

The fighting had intensified, and there was no way that he could make his way to her with so many of his gladiators battling for their lives. Too many Ghoules were now threatening to break through the weakening shield wall.

With a sickening feeling, Declan realized that the Magus was about to die. He could only watch with growing horror as the Ghoule pulled back his spear and then stabbed toward the small of Rafia's back.

Shockingly, the spear never bit into the Magus' flesh. Jerad got there just in time, knocking the Ghoule's spear off course with his sword.

The Ghoule roared in anger, his gratification at killing a Magus momentarily delayed, the enraged beast turning to face this new threat.

Before the Ghoule could attack, Tarin approached from behind and sliced across the back of the Ghoule's leg, cutting through the beast's hamstring. The Ghoule stumbled when he turned to face Tarin, and that's when Jerad pounced, lunging with his sword for the Ghoule's side, sliding the steel between his ribs and slicing through his lungs.

The beast collapsed to one knee, no longer able to breathe. Yet despite the severity of his wound, the Ghoule refused to give up the fight, and now Jerad found himself in a difficult position. His sword had become wedged between the Ghoule's ribs, and he had lost his grip on the hilt.

Jerad tried to pull the dagger free from the sheath on his hip, recognizing that the dying Ghoule only had eyes for him now. Even though he couldn't draw a breath, the beast pulled back his arm so that he could punch the spear he still held in his claw right through Jerad's chest, wanting to take one more victim with him before he himself died.

The Sergeant of the Battersea Guard knew that even with the dagger in his hand he didn't stand a chance. A spear always trumped a dagger in a fight like this.

Right before the dying Ghoule plunged his spear into Jerad's chest, Declan finally arrived. The gladiator sliced down with his sword, taking the Ghoule's arm off at the elbow, and then with a backward slash cut across the beast's throat, the Ghoule finally crumpling to the ground.

Jerad took a moment to catch his breath, his nerves still twitching after having come so close to his own death. Then he turned to Declan, and they both nodded to one another in thanks.

The Magus hadn't even noticed what was going on behind her, so focused on her combat with the three Elder Ghoules, the duel becoming more of a challenge with each passing second. She had even tried calling down the lightning that she so preferred to use when killing Elders.

It didn't work. Each time, the beasts used the Curse to defend against her strikes, and now she was rapidly running out of options.

With few other choices coming to mind, she did the only thing that she could. She continued to fight, just as Declan, Jerad, and Tarin jumped right back into the battle. All four understood that they wouldn't be able to beat the Ghoules if circumstances didn't change drastically. There were too many of the beasts and too few gladiators.

They would hold for as long as they could.

That's who they were.

That's what they did.

Come what may, they would die on their feet.

～

"THE GHOULE OVERLORD isn't coming over to join the fight?" asked Aislinn. "I thought that he was desperate for the Seventh Stone."

"He is," replied Sirius. "But he won't cross the black ice until he's certain the fight is almost over. He sees no need to bother with us just yet. Not until it's time to kill Bryen."

Bryen, Sirius, and Aislinn stood atop the parapet that ran along the circular length of the Library of the Magii, observing intently as the fight against the Ghoules unfolded beneath them on the two battlefields that were separated by only a few hundred yards. The approach recommended by Tarin and Declan to force the Ghoules up the beach and toward the tower along prescribed paths had proven to be an effective strategy. But like any good strategy, it rarely survived for very long, the rapidly changing circumstances during a fight requiring flexibility and creativity.

Although the Company of Blood gave as good as they got against beasts that towered above them, beasts designed for the sole purpose of hunting and killing, the three Magii sensed that now was the time to make some adjustments to their strategy before the Ghoules penetrated the gladiators' defenses.

They saw the pressure that the Ghoules were bringing to bear on both groups of fighters, and that pressure was only going to increase now that the Elder Ghoules were joining the fight. The servants of the Ghoule Overlord had stalked up the paths that led from the beach, three of the Elders already engaged with Rafia who, though she was holding them off, clearly was in the midst of a difficult combat.

"Let's see if we can make him wait a little while longer," suggested Bryen. "If these Ghoules want to take Haven, I want them to earn that privilege in blood."

"Did I ever tell you how much I liked your approach to certain matters," commented Sirius.

"I can't say that you did," replied Bryen, his eyes tracking

Davin and Lycia as they jumped into a breach that had just opened on the right side of their shield wall, eliminating the threat quickly by taking the Ghoule's leg at the knee, unfortunately losing a shield bearer in the process. "And I'm not sure what you mean."

"Your bloodthirstiness, lad. When certain situations must be handled in a certain way, you don't hesitate. If blood must be spilled, then you make sure you do the spilling."

"It's not a matter of being bloodthirsty," countered Bryen, "it's just the way of the world at times, something that I learned time and again on the white sand. Honestly, I don't know if I should take that as a compliment, Sirius."

Bryen's gaze shifted toward Rafia. A Ghoule had vaulted behind the three ranks of soldiers and was about to drive his spear into her back. He breathed easier when Jerad and Tarin got there just in time, Declan helping to finish the job so that the Magus could maintain her focus on the three Elders challenging her.

"Take it as you like, lad," said Sirius. "I'm only speaking the truth." Sirius scanned what was going on beneath the tower, reaching the same conclusions as Bryen and Aislinn. It was time to implement the next part of their strategy. "If we're going to keep the Ghoule Overlord off of Haven for a little while longer, we need to deal with those Elders."

"There's no guarantee that we can beat them," said Aislinn. "Eight of those cursed beasts. We won't be able to take them by surprise, not after what we did to stop the first attack across the black ice. They know what they're up against."

"Agreed," said Sirius. "But I had an idea." The old Magus turned to Bryen once again. "Remember what you did on the pier the first time you were here when the Ghoules snuck across the lake. Do you think that you can do that now?"

Bryen took a moment to consider the request. "Are you sure that you want me to take that risk?"

"I trust you," said Sirius, after the old Magus stared into Bryen's eyes for several seconds, giving him a nod. "I know you can do this without me having to kill you."

"Thanks for your support, Sirius," Bryen replied sarcastically. "That's assuming, of course, that with me continuing to learn more about how to use the Seventh Stone that you can even kill me now."

"True," admitted Sirius, the old Magus not yet ready to consider that possibility. "I'm not so sure about that myself. Still, that's a problem for another day."

Looking back out across the two battlefields just to gauge if the circumstances had improved for the Blood Company, and realizing that they had not, Bryen nodded in acquiescence, willing to take the risk.

"I'll give it a try. You'll need to distract the Elder Ghoules. It's easier if I can take them by surprise."

"That's why Aislinn and I are here, lad," Sirius replied with a malicious grin. "Aislinn, see if you can occupy the Elders coming up the slope toward Davin and Lycia. I'll offer some assistance to Rafia."

"With pleasure," Aislinn growled, the Lady of the Southern Marches immediately taking hold of the Talent and turning her attention to the north.

Five Elder Ghoules had just emerged from the manmade channel that led up the slope toward where the Company of Blood continued their desperate fight against the invaders. Aislinn knew that she couldn't kill five Elders by herself, even with the element of surprise, though she certainly could make their lives more difficult long enough for Bryen to do as Sirius requested. To achieve her objective, she decided to try a variation of several of the traps that she had set atop the logs and boulders to keep the Ghoules from climbing over them.

The Elder leading the group was just about to speak with the Ghoule commanding the assault on Davin and Lycia's position when he jumped back in alarm and pain, a spark of white flashing beneath his clawed feet. The beast's effort to escape led to a quick series of additional flashes.

The beast moved gingerly, hopping from one clawed foot to the other, leaping into the air several times, in a useless attempt to evade the bursts of Talent that Aislinn was sowing into the rocky ground. When the Elder Ghoule finally came to a stop, he howled in anger, the soles of his clawed feet singed and smoking from having stepped on so many snares.

The other Elders were soon reacting in a similar manner, jumping up and down, never leaving a clawed foot in one place for more than a split second, their black eyes fixed on the rocky ground, trying to locate the traps constructed of the Talent so that they could avoid the flashes of light that carried a nasty and excruciating burst of energy.

They had little luck. It wasn't long before all of the Elders shrieked or cursed in pain, scrambling off the path so that they could find a spot that didn't contain a charge that was strong enough to char the hardened flesh on their feet. Finally safe, they began looking for the cause of their discomfort and embarrassment.

Perhaps not the most elegant approach, admitted Aislinn, though certainly effective. Now that she had had her fun, it was time for her to take a more direct approach. To that end, she began crafting a dozen foot-long spikes made of the Talent that she believed would keep the Elder Ghoules busy for a time.

Sirius, on the other hand, took the more direct approach right from the start, going for brute strength rather than a devious gambit. Taking in a huge amount of the Talent, he started throwing sizzling shafts of light toward the Elders who were seeking to corner Rafia and place her entirely on the defensive. The old Magus hoped that he might get lucky with his first strike, the Elder he had targeted turning away from him as the beast sought to attack Rafia from the side.

It was not to be. One of the other Elders called to his comrade just in time, the huge beast leaping out of the way before the blast of energy burned through his body.

Even though Sirius missed, his tactic worked. Two of the Elders shifted their hate-filled eyes toward the old Magus standing atop the tower, the beasts immediately sending streaks of black through the air that Sirius blocked with a shimmering shield of energy.

Sirius grinned as he took on the Elders. He was quite pleased with himself. His involvement helped to lessen the strain on Rafia, who now faced off against just one Elder rather than three. Those were odds that the Keeper of Haven would like.

Bryen watched as Aislinn and Sirius drew the attention of the Elders, chomping at the bit to join the fight, frustrated that he still needed to wait before beginning. But there was nothing that he could do other than give them the time they needed to distract the Elders. Otherwise, what he was about to try would be much more difficult and perhaps place a strain on him that would be almost too much for him to resist.

Thankfully he didn't have much longer to wait. Judging the time right for him to intervene, the blades on the Spear of the Magii glowed brightly as Bryen grasped the Talent and then called forth the power resting within the Seventh Stone, using his weapon to manage the immense flow of energy that surged through him.

He was careful as he began his work, just as he had learned to do through hard experience, to ignore the seductive call of the Curse, keeping the Dark Magic locked away and only releasing the huge reservoir of the Talent contained within the artifact. That still didn't mean that it was easy, a niggling promise from the Curse of what he could become, what he could do, flashing through the back of his mind ceaselessly, forcing him to lock away that dangerous urge as well.

Once he was satisfied that the Dark Magic was under control, Bryen imagined eight thin cords of the Curse snapping free from the Seventh Stone and snaking their way toward the two groups of Elders, the cords encased by the Talent so that Bryen would remain safe from the taint of the Curse.

The Elder Ghoules, so consumed with their combats, never even felt it when the cables latched onto the Dark Magic that the beasts were using in their combats against the Magii.

After testing the connection to make sure that all was as it should be, Bryen started slowly, draining just a trickle of the Dark Magic employed by the Elder Ghoules, wanting to confirm that he had nothing to fear before taking a more aggressive approach. Satisfied, the trickle swiftly became a flood as Bryen focused the full power of the Seventh Stone on bleeding the Elders dry.

No longer constrained, it didn't take long. With its voracious appetite, the artifact gorged on the Curse, the Dark Magic flowing back through the cords and into the space that Bryen had set aside within himself to hold the massive amount of corrupted energy.

As the pull intensified, the Elder Ghoules, finding it more difficult to use the Curse, finally realized that something was wrong. By then, though, it was too late. The beasts had no way to combat the incessant demand of the Seventh Stone. They had no way to defend themselves.

A few of the Elders tried, identifying the source of this new, terrifying attack, their gaze drifting toward Bryen as the blades of the Spear of the Magii shined brightly, pulsing in rhythm to the Dark Magic being stolen from them. Yet the beasts could do no more than that, their strength already fading, their very essences joining the flow of the Curse, until nothing remained of the eight Elder Ghoules except for their withered bodies crumpled on the long grass.

Task complete, the battle around the Library of the Magii

faded into the background as Bryen stared at his handiwork. It had been so simple, and so much easier than he had expected.

He could feel the additional power within him now, within the Seventh Stone. That voice in the back of his mind, always there, usually no more than a whisper, was louder now.

More insistent. More enticing.

If he could do what he had done to so many Elders so rapidly with no problems, what else could he do with the Seventh Stone? He was the Seventh Stone after all. So did he really need to fear the Curse? Did he really need to worry about the corruption of the Curse if he was more than a Magus?

It was an interesting thought, one that the voice playing through his head took up. Pushing him.

Teasing him with two new questions.

Since he was the Seventh Stone, could he not make the Curse his own? Could he not use the power of the Ghoule Overlord without fear?

Before he could explore those intriguing thoughts further, a different voice broke through his thoughts.

"Bryen! Bryen! Are you all right?"

Whose voice was that?

It sounded familiar.

Aislinn. It was Aislinn.

Bryen took a deep breath to steady himself, nodding to Aislinn that he was fine. For just a moment, he had been about to follow a path from which he might never have returned. But Aislinn had pulled him back, and just in time.

Feeling more like himself again, the insistent, tempting voice fading into the background, he used the Spear of the Magii as his focal point, ensuring that the Curse he had drained from the Elders was locked away safely. That done, he waited for a few heartbeats just to make certain that all was well within him.

It was. For now.

Despite that one instance of hesitation, even with the immense amount of the Curse now contained within the Seventh Stone, he felt energized. He felt good.

It was as if there wasn't anything that he could do if he put his mind to it. Anything at all.

He'd need to think about that more, assuming that he and the Blood Company survived the battle of Haven.

Pleased by his success, Bryen returned his focus to the two battlegrounds, preparing to use the Talent to help his friends in their fight against the Ghoules. He discovered immediately that his assistance wasn't needed.

As soon as he had employed the Seventh Stone to lock onto the tainted power of the Elder Ghoules, Rafia, Aislinn, and Sirius had shifted their attacks to the Ghoules. With the Elders removed from the clash, even though the Ghoules fought valiantly, it was still a hopeless effort, the beasts unable to withstand the force brought to bear against them by the three Magii.

With their losses mounting, the Ghoules had no choice but to retreat a second time, streaming back along the paths they had followed to the base of the tower, forced to risk the wrath of the Ghoule Overlord.

The Blood Company's success at holding off the Ghoules brought a smile that cracked Bryen's grim visage. It only lasted for a few seconds. Because Bryen knew that the Ghoule Overlord wouldn't have a choice now. The beast would have to cross the black ice the next time his Ghoules attacked.

The Ghoule Overlord would have sensed what Bryen had done and the immense amount of power that he had used.

Too much was at stake for the Master of the Curse.

So Bryen would take the bloody victory that the gladiators and the Magii had won. But he understood that it was only one small battle in a larger war.

He wasn't certain that he and his friends stood much of a chance once the Ghoule Overlord joined the fight.

He was certain that the Company of Blood needed to escape Haven before the Ghoule Overlord stepped onto the island and brought his terrible power to bear.

~

Keep reading for the first two chapters of Book Six, *The Protector's Resolve.*

BONUS MATERIAL

If you really enjoyed this story, I need you to do me a HUGE favor – please follow me on Amazon and BookBub. And if you have a few minutes, consider writing a review.

Keep reading for the first two chapters of Book Six of *The Tales of Caledonia*, *The Protector's Resolve.*

THE TALES OF CALEDONIA
BOOK SIX

THE
PROTECTOR'S
RESOLVE

PETER WACHT

ISBN: 978-1-950236-28-2
eBook ISBN: 978-1-950236-29-9

PROLOGUE

"He's stronger than I ever imagined possible."

"That's good, Sirius. He needs to be strong if he's to have any chance of rebuilding the Weir."

Sirius and Rafia stood on the parapet of the Library of the Magii, looking out over the glacial lake currently linked to the far shore by a span of the Curse set there by the Ghoule Overlord. It was still dark, the sun the faintest of glows behind the towering peaks encircling the hidden valley.

"Yes, but you felt what happened when he removed those Elders from the fight, didn't you?"

"How could I not, Sirius," Rafia replied with just a hint of exasperation.

The Ghoules had been pressing the Company of Blood hard, threatening to breakthrough to the tower upon which she and Sirius now observed the lake and the surrounding environs. The Elders had joined the fight, seeking to tip the balance, and it was Bryen who stopped them, using the Seventh Stone to drain them of their corrupt power as well as their very essences. With the Elders no longer a threat, the

Magii and the gladiators forced the Ghoules to retreat from the island.

For the time being.

They would be back.

Soon. Very soon.

The Ghoule Overlord did not manage defeat well.

The Ghoule Overlord needed the Seventh Stone, needed the Protector, and Bryen's latest display of power most assuredly had caught his attention, had intensified his craving for the artifact reclaimed from his so long ago.

"He was close to going over the edge, Rafia. You know that just as well as I do. If he does that, he doesn't come back. We lose him, and he loses himself."

Sirius' voice revealed his worry. There was something else there as well.

Fear.

Whether for the lost opportunity to repair the Weir or for Bryen or for what he and Rafia might need to do if Bryen actually touched the Curse ... she wasn't sure. It could be a combination of all three.

"Yes, but he didn't, Sirius. That's what matters." Rafia motioned toward the end of the dock where Bryen stood, the Lady of the Southern Marches right at his side.

"Aislinn was there. She brought him back before it was too late. She helped him even though she probably didn't know she was doing it. She kept him with us."

"And what if she's not there next time, Rafia? What if there is no one there to stop him from going over the edge?"

Rafia understood Sirius' concerns. Much of it was driven by what was required of the Protector. Because the Seventh Stone had joined with him, he was the only Magus with a chance, slim though it may be, to rebuild the Weir and prevent the Ghoule Legions from flooding into the Kingdom.

She sensed, though, that there was a great deal more to

Sirius' concern than just that. His relationship with Bryen was much more complicated than he was willing to let slip, and he was struggling to come to grips with what that actually meant. For Bryen and for himself.

"Sirius, you need to let this go for now. We have enough to deal with as it is. If we don't get off Haven, then everything else will be moot."

"I know you're right, Rafia. It's just that with Bryen I ..."

Sirius' words trailed off, not knowing how to express what he wanted to say, needing to start again.

"Bryen means more to me than ..." The old Magus stopped himself again, at a loss for how to explain what he was feeling.

Rather than making fun of him, which was her initial instinct, because it was such a rare occurrence when his words didn't flow, she gripped his arm strongly.

"I know, Sirius. I understand your fears. That you want to be there in case he needs you. However, the reality is that the Protector is quite competent on his own. If he is to succeed in the task we've set before him, we must trust him. Even when we fear that he might be making a mistake, even when we fear that he might be too close to the edge, we must trust that in the end he will do what is required no matter how much it might cost him."

1. ALL YOU CAN DO

"You did all that you could."

Bryen stood at the end of the pier that jutted out into the lake, staring down at the molded Curse that resembled black ice, the span that would give the Ghoule Overlord and his creatures the opportunity to attack the island once again. He was certain that this time the Master of the Lost Land would be directing the fight, because the beast couldn't afford another failure.

That likely would lead to one result. A result that would doom the Company of Blood.

Aislinn could tell by the spark in his eyes and his grim expression that Bryen was angry, even though as usual he kept his emotions hidden well. She wanted to help him, to ease his burden, understanding the other pressures that he was facing.

She couldn't, however. This wasn't her struggle. It was his. All she could do was try to give him a path that took him away from the dark thoughts and self-recrimination that plagued him.

"I should have done more."

"You healed as many gladiators as you could."

"Yes, but we still lost too many fighters. It seems that even with the Seventh Stone I can't bring my friends back from the dead."

Aislinn reached for Bryen's arm and squeezed warmly, her sympathy flowing through her touch. She understood what Bryen was going through.

The gladiators had pledged their lives to him, and he felt responsible for them. He wanted to help his friends, to keep them from harm.

He was discovering on this quest to reach the Sanctuary, however, that sometimes despite putting forth your best effort, that simply wasn't enough. That you couldn't control all that you wanted to control.

"All you can do is the best that you can do," Aislinn said quietly, leaning her head against his shoulder. "Beating yourself up about your perceived failures doesn't help anyone. You do the best that you can do, and then you move on to what you have to do next. That stricture applies here just as it did in the Pit. Any gladiator of the Blood Company would tell you exactly that."

"I think you've been spending too much time with Declan," grumbled Bryen. "That sounds like something that he would say. In fact, I think he has said it. Many times."

"That might be the case," Aislinn admitted with a small smile. "Still, it's good advice, and I hope that you will listen to it."

Bryen reached across and squeezed Aislinn's arm in silent thanks. She was right. He didn't have to like it. But she was right, and he needed to deal better with the reality that she had just pointed out to him because it wasn't going to change.

More of his friends were going to die before all this was over. He couldn't escape that fact, no matter how much he might try.

"I hate this. I hate that so many people have to die for me. I wish there was another way."

Bryen stared more intently at the black ice linking the island to the mainland. He couldn't save the gladiators who had died defending Haven, though maybe he could help those who still lived, an idea percolating in the back of his brain.

Perhaps there was a way that he could make the Ghoule Overlord's pursuit more difficult and give the Blood Company more time to recuperate from the last battle. It might even improve their odds of escaping.

"I wish there was as well. But you know as well as I that ..."

"Hoping doesn't make it real," finished Bryen.

"You've been spending too much time with Sirius," chastised Aislinn with a gentle smile.

"I agree with you on that," confirmed Bryen. "I really haven't had much of a choice." He motioned down toward the black ice. "You know, I think there is something that I can do. That will help us now."

Bryen had just used the Talent to search around them, having sensed several more Ghoule packs coming their way. The Ghoule Overlord's reinforcements would arrive by dusk. Soon after that, his forces replenished, the Master of the Curse would lead his beasts against them.

Although the gladiators would give everything they had against the beasts, the Blood Company could not defeat the Ghoules who were hunting them. They could only delay them. There were too many. For every Ghoule they eliminated from the fight, another soon appeared to take the place of the fallen beast.

He and his gladiators were on the wrong end of a battle of attrition. Yet Bryen believed that he could at least increase the level of difficulty for their pursuers.

Neither Sirius nor Rafia had enjoyed any success when attempting to break apart the sheet of Dark Magic the Ghoules used to cross the lake, so clearly the Talent wasn't the answer to his dilemma. That being the case, he did have another tool at his disposal that might work.

Just as he did only a few hours before, Bryen reached for the Talent, this time also opening himself to the Seventh Stone. He used the Spear of the Magii as a focal point, the twin blades of the weapon glowing brightly as the energy surged into him.

"Bryen, what are you doing?" asked Aislinn, squeezing his arm with a stronger grip, not knowing if she should be worried or curious or both.

"I want to test a theory," he replied. "There's something that I might be able to do that Sirius and Rafia can't."

Aislinn nodded, her eyes betraying her slight trepidation, already having an idea of what he had in mind. "Just be careful."

Nodding in response to Aislinn's demand that masqueraded as a request, he applied the same approach that had been so effective in draining the Elders of their power to the span that connected Haven to the lakeshore, sending a hollow tube of the Talent down toward the shining surface. The cord latched on when the Dark Magic contained within the Seventh Stone surged out and joined with the hardened Curse.

Bryen was certain that the principles he was applying were sound, the primary difference compared to what he did to the Elders being the scale of his effort since the Ghoule Overlord had used so much of the Curse to construct the bridge. So he took his time, working slowly and cautiously. He checked, and then checked again, making sure that when he connected the cord of Dark Magic to the black ice that there was no way that the Curse could corrupt him.

For several heartbeats nothing happened. Bryen worried that he might have misjudged. Maybe he couldn't manage this much of the Curse at one time.

His eyes brightened just a moment later, his concern fading

away. He had been right. His calculated gamble was about to pay off.

The transformation began slowly, the black ice shimmering, taking on an almost liquid appearance before switching back to a rigid form, that transition between states accelerating as Bryen used the Seventh Stone to pull on the Ghoule Overlord's Dark Magic with greater insistence. The shiny, solid black surface flashed several times, from solid to liquid to a foggy gas, and then back again, faster and faster, before it finally shifted permanently into a hazy mist, Bryen drawing in the Curse, adding it to the Dark Magic the Seventh Stone already contained. After only just a few more heartbeats, it was done, the span dissolving entirely, the Ghoule Overlord's creation destroyed.

Having taken in a huge amount of Dark Magic, Bryen took a moment to regain his bearings. He confirmed again, just to make certain, that he protected himself properly, the Curse never breaking free from the constraints he had set around that corrosive power.

For the first time in days, he smiled broadly. Now the Ghoule Overlord would need to work a little bit harder to attack the island. After what Bryen had just done, his adversary would begin to wonder, perhaps even doubt, which likely would unsettle the beast. It might even affect his thinking, leading to some bad decisions, which was fine with Bryen. If the Ghoule Overlord began to second guess himself that was all to the good.

The soft and subtle voice in the back of his head that was always there and that he wasn't sure was entirely his own was cackling with glee at his success.

He had done it, the voice was saying. He had made the Curse his own.

With those thoughts drifting through his mind, several

questions joined them, and he wasn't certain that these questions belonged to him.

If he was the Seventh Stone, did he really need to fear the Curse? If he could make the Curse his own, was he bound by the strictures of the past? By rules that might not apply to him? Could he not become more than even the Ghoule Overlord?

"Bryen."

He heard a voice just at the edge of his consciousness. He tried to ignore it, wanting to think more on those questions. The answers could be crucial to the larger task set for him. But he couldn't, the voice becoming more insistent.

"Bryen!"

"Sorry," he said sheepishly, struggling to come back to himself.

"Show off," said Aislinn teasingly, giving Bryen a nudge with her shoulder, finally breaking his train of thought, those troublesome questions fading away.

She was clearly pleased by what he had just accomplished. She also seemed worried, though he couldn't tell for sure, as he couldn't understand why she would be.

"Just doing what needed to be done."

"Another of Declan's sayings?" asked Aislinn, that trace of concern in the back of her eyes fading away.

"Either one of his or Sirius'. It's hard to keep track of them all."

"You all right, lad?" asked Sirius.

He and Rafia had rushed down to join them at the end of the dock when they realized what Bryen was doing with the Seventh Stone. The looks on the faces of the two Magii told Bryen that they weren't as impressed or pleased by his action as he thought that they might be. Rather, they were anxious. Maybe even a little afraid.

Because of that, they were both on edge.

"Fine," Bryen replied evenly after several seconds had

passed, deciding to keep his thoughts to himself. Deciding the two Magii didn't need to know everything. "It just took a bit more out of me than I thought it would after today's fight."

"So nothing for us to worry about?"

Bryen studied dispassionately the similar looks that Rafia and Sirius were giving him, both obviously worried that he might have touched the Curse. Bryen's gaze sharpened, his voice coming out as a challenge.

"Would you like to check yourself just to make sure?"

Both Magii were somewhat taken aback by the sharpness of his tone, neither expecting it. Sirius' eyes narrowed, his brow furrowing. He was about to accept Bryen's challenge, to reach for the Talent to confirm that the Protector indeed was free of the Curse, when Rafia placed a hand on his arm to stop him.

"No, no need," she said, her gaze appraising. "We trust you. We just wanted to make sure that you were all right."

Bryen nodded, then watched with a hint of distrust as the two Magii walked back down the pier toward the Library of the Magii, their heads together, deep in conversation. He needed to remember that Sirius and Rafia were there to help him if he required their assistance, but their greater loyalty was to the Kingdom, to protecting against the Ghoule Overlord and the Curse, and not to him.

He hoped that it didn't reach a point where the two Magii would need to make a decision between the two. For their sakes, not his. He hoped that they did, indeed, trust him.

Because he feared that if they tried to kill him, he might try to stop them. Then his training as a gladiator would take over, and even if the two Magii combined their power, even with their greater experience and knowledge, he was still much stronger in the Talent than the both of them. Particularly when he made use of the Seventh Stone. So he had no doubt as to how that combat would end.

~

The Ghoule Overlord growled angrily, furious at his Ghoules' latest setback. He had only a few packs left, and the Protector who had become the Seventh Stone had eliminated all his Elders. He would have to wait until the additional packs coming toward him from the north arrived before trying for a third time to conquer the island.

He believed that he could defeat the Protector in a combat. He just didn't want to have to deal with the distraction of the Magii joining that fight, so better to allow his Elders to deal with them, better to control all the variables that he could before taking that risk.

Gurzen and the Ghoules who had survived the failed incursion had found a spot to wait farther down the beach, unwilling to be too close to him in that moment, unwilling to risk his wrath.

They were right to be afraid, because all he wanted to do in that moment was lash out, to release the fury building up within him.

Struggling to contain his rage, he stared across the lake with death in his eyes.

The Ghoule Overlord had watched what the Protector had done, following what he was doing as he did it, astounded by what the human had achieved. Most frustrating was the fact that he had no good way to stop him.

He could have tried to use his Dark Magic to maintain the bridge at the same time that the Protector drained the Curse from it. He had stopped himself the instant before he did just that, a rare caution coming into play. He worried about what might happen if the Seventh Stone grasped not onto the Curse but onto him.

He held few concerns when it came to fighting the Protector, but the artifact was a variable that he could not control.

Could the artifact empty him of his immense power just as it had emptied his Elders? Just as it drained the span he crafted of the Curse?

He didn't know, and that bothered him, although not as much as the touch of fear that had settled within him as he considered what the result might be if the Protector did, indeed, turn the Seventh Stone directly against him.

That disturbing thought wasn't even the most worrisome that passed through the Ghoule Overlord's mind.

The Protector had become the Seventh Stone. Just a host for the artifact, he believed. However, he was beginning to realize that there was more to it than that.

Because now the Protector was mastering the Seventh Stone.

And if he could master the Seventh Stone, what else could he master?

The Ghoule Overlord growled again as he considered that question.

The Protector needed to die.

Before he became even more powerful than he already was. Before he learned more about what he could really do with the potency that had joined with him.

2. TIME TO MOVE

Bryen and Aislinn strode down the pier, stepping around the large holes scattered around the dock and avoiding the cracked and splintered posts.

"You're certain?"

"Yes," nodded Aislinn. "Just a few hours at most. They're moving fast. Faster than we expected."

"Then we'll need to move faster than they are," replied Bryen. "I just wish that we had more time."

"So do I, but we're not going to get it. The Ghoule Overlord hasn't demonstrated much patience during this hunt."

"That he hasn't," agreed Bryen. He and Aislinn stopped where the pier met the shore, a small group having gathered there to discuss what to do before the Ghoule Overlord attacked again, the conversation pausing when they saw the two young Magii approach. "How many did we lose?"

"Seventeen," Declan replied sadly. "All good men and women."

"Could I have helped them?" Bryen asked, his frustration evident in his tired voice and sad eyes.

"You couldn't have. I can say that they went to the other side quickly, and they went as the gladiators they were. They fought until they couldn't fight anymore."

He sympathized with Bryen, and Declan was glad that despite fighting in the Pit for ten years he hadn't lost his humanity. Nevertheless, this was a reality of war. People died no matter how hard you fought to keep them alive. It was terrible, it was heartbreaking, and it was inevitable.

Declan shook his head grimly. They could mourn the dead later. Now, they needed to focus on the living and ensure that they didn't follow those who had already gone to the other side.

"There's nothing that you could have done to help them," explained Declan. "They were killed before you destroyed the Elders. Lock away the sorrow for now and don't allow the guilt to stay with you. You did all that you could. We need to shift our focus to how we stay ahead of the Ghoule Overlord."

"You're right," nodded Bryen, pushing aside his anger at how many of his friends had to sacrifice themselves so that he could live. He would deal with his grief later, because he didn't want to waste the gift that the fallen gladiators had given him. "We need to get moving again. The Ghoule Overlord is already beginning to recreate the black ice. Once he's done with his latest creation, we won't be able to stop him this time, even if we applied the same strategy that worked so effectively for us during the last attack. He'll be coming across at the head of his packs. Of that, I'm certain."

"Why are you so sure about that?" asked Rafia with a raised eyebrow, her natural curiosity coming to the forefront.

"I can sense the Ghoule Overlord through the Dark Magic of the Seventh Stone. I imagine that my ability to do this is similar to how he can sense the Seventh Stone within me."

"You can do what?" demanded Sirius, his eyes a bit wild at Bryen's declaration, the fears and concerns he had been discussing with Rafia just moments before returning with a vengeance.

"I can sense the Ghoule Overlord and, roughly -- no more than a few pieces here and there -- what he might be thinking through the Dark Magic of the Seventh Stone."

"That shouldn't be possible," protested Sirius, at a complete loss, which surprised everyone around him. The old Magus always seemed to have an answer for every question. "How is that even possible?"

"I don't know."

"You haven't touched the Curse, have you?" Sirius stepped right up to Bryen, his fears getting the better of him, his eyes becoming flintier when he asked the question.

The old Magus' personality shifted in a heartbeat. He was no longer the somewhat befuddled tutor. Instead, he was the powerful Master of the Magii, his intensity as he focused on Bryen almost suffocating. And, in Rafia's opinion, although she hoped desperately that she was wrong, he was a man who appeared to be about to reach for the Talent and strike down Bryen if he gave the answer that Sirius didn't want to hear.

"No, I haven't. You're welcome to check if you like, if you don't believe me."

Bryen's voice came out through gritted teeth in a quiet, emotionless tone, matching the hardheartedness that had settled within his eyes. The same challenge that he had voiced just minutes before. The Volkun stood in front of the Master of the Magii now, and he clearly did not like what Sirius was insinuating.

Even more telling, he wasn't frightened or intimidated. The thought of a combat with the Master of the Magii didn't appear to faze Bryen in the least. Rafia didn't know if she should be impressed or worried by that conclusion.

"Sirius, calm down, please," requested Rafia. "We've been

through this before. Just because Bryen now has certain unexpected and unexplained capabilities because of his close connection to the Seventh Stone does not mean that he's become corrupted by the Curse. If we are going to achieve our larger goal, we must trust one another. There is no reason not to trust Bryen, and there is no reason for Bryen not to trust you, at least when you're thinking clearly." Rafia added that comment at the end hoping that it would grab Sirius' attention.

Declan watched as Rafia's words washed over both Sirius and Bryen, although neither man appeared ready or willing to back down just yet. The behavior of the two resembled the stare downs that frequently occurred in the Colosseum before the start of a combat, one gladiator trying to get the better of the other even before steel met steel. It was impressive and it was dangerous. He prepared himself to push between the two if it proved necessary to separate them.

"We can talk about this later, although I see no need to do so," Aislinn interjected, having adopted the commanding tone reserved for the Lady of the Southern Marches. "We've got other issues to deal with at the moment, and we're losing time. We need to counter what the Ghoules are going to do next."

Even with Aislinn's admonition, Sirius and Bryen continued to glare at one another, neither willing to look away. Sirius' fingers flexed, as if he were itching to reach for the Talent. Bryen stood there calmly, his gaze strong, his body relaxed, his hands gripping the Spear of the Magii comfortably.

Neither had grasped the natural power of the world. Yet. How much longer that would prove to be the case was anyone's guess as the tension between the two intensified.

Bryen had been in circumstances such as this more times than he could count. The only question that passed through his mind in that moment was whether this confrontation would progress to the next step. The drawing of blood.

If so, he was ready. He would do what was necessary to protect himself. But he would allow Sirius to make the decision as to whether there would be a next step.

Just when Bryen thought that the combat was about to begin, the old Magus' eyes narrowed sharply, Sirius letting out a deep breath and nodding. Finally, he turned away from Bryen, apparently agreeing with both Rafia and Aislinn.

"Lady Winborne is correct," said Declan. "The Ghoule Overlord needs more fighters. By winning this battle, we've bought some additional time. Even so, we don't have much of that left. We can't afford to waste what we've earned."

"We can't stay here," said Tarin, the Captain of the Battersea Guard having watched the encounter between Sirius and Bryen with a great deal of interest. The tension increasing with each passing second, he wondered which of the two would win the combat if it came to it. And then he had thought about whether he would observe the combat or try to step in, because although he knew both Sirius and Bryen quite well, only one had earned his allegiance. "Declan is right. We'll be overrun during the next attack when that black ice appears again."

"Rafia and I tried to destroy it with the Talent but we couldn't," said Sirius, almost as if he were apologizing for their failure to do so. "As you saw, only Bryen has the capacity to do anything to hinder the Ghoule Overlord's Dark Magic when applied in such a way."

"It was a difficult thing to do," Bryen admitted, recoiling somewhat at the thought of taking in so much of the Curse into the Seventh Stone so soon after his last effort ... and the growing temptation to actually use that power, a temptation that he feared was becoming more seductive. "If the Ghoule Overlord expands the size of the span he's building to give his Ghoules more avenues for attack -- assuming, of course, that he's going to want to avoid the side that contains our defenses that already have proven to be a difficult nut to crack -- I don't know that I'd be able to handle that much of his Dark Magic or would want to take that risk. Even with the Spear of the Magii, I'd be too worried about losing control." He then gave the old Magus a pointed look. "And I wouldn't want to worry Sirius any more than I already have."

Bryen meant for his last remark to lighten the mood, attempting to ease the strain between them. Based on Sirius' expression, Bryen could tell that it hadn't worked.

Sirius ignored the Protector's comment, lost in thought. If Bryen was learning how to use the Seventh Stone, if he was connecting more profoundly with the artifact within him, which clearly seemed to be the case based on how he destroyed the span of Dark Magic, then Sirius wasn't certain that he could kill Bryen if it became necessary to do so, his rising doubts in that respect becoming more real.

He would try if it came to it, though *try* was now the critical term. The Protector might be too strong an adversary, even with Rafia and Aislinn aiding him, and that was a conclusion that he didn't want to contemplate.

"The Ghoule Overlord will never admit his mistakes," said Sirius, finally pushing to the side his burgeoning concerns, at least for the present. "He will learn from them, however. I expect that Bryen is right. He will work with his Elders to expand the spread of his Dark Magic. Rather than create a span a few hundred yards wide, he will do it in a way so that the Curse encircles the island. The Ghoules can then attack from any direction that they choose. Our fates will be sealed before the beasts even set foot on Haven again."

"That's the bad news," said Aislinn. "I've got even worse news."

"There's worse news than that?" asked Jerad with a grin and raised eyebrow, trying to interject some humor into a somber discussion and not having much luck with his attempt.

"Unfortunately so. I've been using the Talent to search around us. In addition to the half dozen that should be here by late afternoon, there are a dozen more Ghoule packs coming from the northeast. I'm assuming that there is at least one Elder with each pack."

"The Ghoule Overlord summoned them from the Winter Pass," murmured Rafia.

"I expect so," agreed Sirius.

"We're not in a position to handle that many reinforcements," said Declan. "Not now. Not with so many Elders coming this way."

"It's time to take the next step in our plan," said Tarin. "We need to get Bryen off the island. If it proves necessary, the Company of Blood can serve as a rear guard and delay the Ghoules for as long as possible."

"I won't leave the Blood Company here to fight my battles for me," protested Bryen. "And I don't think ..."

"Lad, I don't question your bravery," interrupted Sirius, his voice sharper than he intended, blaming it on his fears, which still colored his perspective. "No one questions your bravery. But as several have said, you are more important than the rest of us. Only you can do what needs to be done with respect to the Weir. No matter the cost, you need to get to the Sanctuary. Not us. So if the only option is to sacrifice ourselves so that you can do that, then so be it. That's the price we have to pay."

"I was going to say," said Bryen with a grin, unsurprised by Sirius' reaction and strangely grateful for it despite the strain existing between them, "that I don't think that we'll have to leave a guard in place, not with what Rafia has in mind."

"I'll start getting the Company in order," said Declan. "It won't take us long to get ready. I just want to go through the storerooms one more time to see if there's anything still there that we might want to take with us that could prove useful."

"We'll help you with that," offered Tarin, who nodded to Jerad, the two soldiers of the Battersea Guard following Declan.

"Wait, what are we talking about here?" asked Sirius. "I feel like I've missed an important conversation."

"You haven't missed anything, Sirius," Rafia stated matter of factly. "It's time to brave the tunnel that leads to the Trench, and if we're fast enough we won't need to leave anyone to guard our backs. It will take the Ghoule Overlord quite some time to break into the tower and find where we've gone. Even better, we can leave a few surprises along the way that should delay him further."

"Wait," said Sirius, holding up his hands. "I thought that tunnel was destroyed centuries ago."

"That was the rumor," said Rafia. "From what I was able to determine through my explorations while serving as Keeper of Haven, most of the tunnel still should be intact."

"Most of the tunnel should be intact? You're not certain? We're going to risk the success of a mission that will determine the fate of Caledonia on an assumption?"

Sirius sounded as if he couldn't quite believe his ears. Rafia just ignored him.

"Well, I wasn't able to get all the way to the Trench," said Rafia. "I didn't have the time. From what I discovered, though, we should be able to make use of the passageway. We'll just need to be cautious. Structurally, there are some parts of the tunnel we'll have to negotiate very carefully, as well as some unanticipated dangers we'll need to avoid if we can. But those worries can wait until after we've gained some distance on the Ghoule Overlord."

"Why didn't you tell me it was passable?" demanded Sirius. "Wait a moment. What do you mean by unanticipated dangers?"

"I assumed that you knew," said Rafia. "You're the Master of the Magii, after all." She shook her head as if she couldn't quite believe that he had never obtained the information from the previous Keeper of Haven. "Some portions of the tunnel may be difficult to traverse, but we should be able to make it through, particularly with Bryen as part of our group. I'm sorry. I thought that you knew. And as I said, let's deal with the more immediate threat first before worrying about what we might find in the tunnel." Rafia's contrition appeared to be genuine, which mollified Sirius to a certain extent, though not completely. "Besides, I didn't want to tell everyone else because I feared that would reduce the incentive to fight as would be required of them."

"That was a mistake and an insult," said Bryen softly. "You saw how my gladiators handled themselves. It doesn't matter if they have an escape route or not. We only know one way to fight, so you had nothing to worry about in that regard."

"I'm sorry," replied Rafia, acknowledging that error. Bryen was right. She had made a mistake. It wasn't her first and it wouldn't be her last. "I know that now. I don't trust easily, and I allowed that to affect my thinking."

Bryen nodded, accepting her apology, because he was much like her just as he had demonstrated in his confrontation with Sirius. Trust remained an issue for him. "Besides, the Blood Company already knew that there was an escape route. We wouldn't have come to Haven otherwise."

"You told them?"

"Of course I did," replied Bryen. "We're a free company, Magus. We don't keep secrets from one another." With that statement, Bryen's gaze brushed over both Rafia and Sirius, hoping that they understood the point that he was trying to make. "My gladiators fought as they did because that's what they do. They only know one way to fight."

"So everyone knew about the tunnel's functionality but me," cut in Sirius, still perturbed that he had no idea that the proposed escape route was passable, not yet willing to let the perceived slight go.

"Sirius, I told you that I thought you already knew about the tunnel and that it could still be used. I wasn't trying to keep it from you. As I said, you're the Master of the Magii, so I assumed that you of all people would be aware of this option for leaving Haven."

"Apparently being the Master of the Magii doesn't guarantee that I know everything I need to know," grumbled Sirius, still miffed at not being privy to this essential information.

"I couldn't agree with you more, Sirius."

"You're not helping, Bryen," chastised Aislinn, her expression suggesting that she wasn't amused by his quick wit.

"Sorry, I couldn't resist."

"Can we move on to more pressing issues, please?" requested Rafia, fearing that they were about to slide off onto a tangent that would waste even more time that they didn't have.

"I still don't understand how I didn't know," complained Sirius.

"Sirius, would you just let this go," pleaded Rafia with a touch of pique. "No one was withholding information from you intentionally. I simply had assumed that you were aware that the tunnel was passable, at least the section that I negotiated myself."

"All right," replied Sirius, shaking his head angrily. "But we're going to talk more about this later."

"I can't wait," replied Rafia, her sarcasm plain. "Now even though we can use the tunnel, we will still need a head start. Perhaps instead of being angry because you didn't know about the burrow that you could have found yourself if you had used the Talent, you could think up some ways to prevent the Ghoules from immediately following after us."

"I can probably do that," replied Sirius, his devious mind already turning toward this new task.

"Good, then start thinking," said Rafia. "Because we need to leave Haven before the sun sets and the Ghoule Overlord gets here."

I hope you enjoyed the first two chapters. To keep reading *The Protector's Resolve*, Book Six of *The Tales of Caledonia*, order your copy today.